The Opal Blade

By Kristy Nicolle

Queens of Fantasy Saga
The Ashen Touch- Book 4

First published by Kristy Nicolle, United Kingdom, October 2017

QUEENS OF FANTASY EDITION (1st EDITION)

Published October 2017 by Kristy Nicolle

Edited By- Jaimie Cordall

Adult Paranormal/Fantasy Romance

ISBN: 978-1-911395-09-6

www.kristynicolle.com

For Amelia Shaw,

The very first voice that made itself known above the din.
You got me through high school and were the start of a long line of
voices that brought me to where I am today.

This story rose from the ashes of yours,
Thank you.

PROLOGUE

HAEDES' DESCENT

WE ALL KNOW THE story of Haedes, God of the Underworld. Though less of us know the true story of how he came to be there and what his reign cost him. It began with two souls, one feminine and one masculine, alone in the great expanses of time, in The Higher Plains of Othrys. These two souls were known as Cronus and Rhea, and their love was so mighty that it could not be contained to merely themselves.

Rhea bore Cronus three sons. The first named Haedes, the second Poseidon, and the third Zeus. As she birthed each of her sons in turn, Rhea could not imagine loving any single being more than she did her children, and with each one's coming, her love did not diminish but multiplied. The mother's love was split from its once single target between four, quartered and showered upon them as they grew. This, however, was not the only thing that grew, as Cronus' anger at the division of her affection raged within his soul, making him jealous and cruel. If this were not bad enough, his sons were powerful and outnumbered him. He feared being supplanted by his children, and he let his fear consume him.

One day, Cronus decided he'd had enough of his wife's distractions. He'd lived with the fear of being outgrown and spat out for long enough. He pondered this a moment before determining that there was no other way to regain the sole attention of his wife other than to do away with his children altogether.

As they slept under the glow of the Crucible of Gaia, he approached, taking each one in turn and consuming them, power and all, until he could no longer stand.

The power was just enough to satiate his needy soul.

Satisfied, Cronus went to bed his wife Rhea, who coaxed him forth with a cup of wine. He drank deep and wretched, poisoned by the protective mother. Rhea watched as her children were spewed, reborn, one by one, from last to

1

first. Haedes, who had been brought into creation first, became the youngest, and Zeus, the eldest.

Years passed, and Cronus, unable to rid Othrys of his three prodigies, became a tyrant, terrified of his rule coming to an end. His sons were not oblivious to this fact.

Once they were grown, the three young Gods decided they had surpassed the need for their father and were better candidates to rule over the Othrys and The Lower Plains it governed.

They launched an attack, uniting to dethrone him.

After many days and nights of bloodshed, the three brothers triumphed, banishing their father to a far-off dimension, called The Island of the Blessed, where an elder power, Tartarus, would watch over him. Here, all souls rested equal, and the brothers knew their father would be stripped of his envy and power-lust, trapped and never able to return.

Triumphant, Zeus, Poseidon, and Haedes renamed The Higher Plains and set about building a council house before dividing the realms amongst themselves. Zeus became ruler over The Higher Plains and those realms devoted to its protection, Poseidon became ruler of The Seas, and Haedes was assigned ruler of The Underworld. After this decision had been made, they set about making a new order.

Zeus decided that to avoid the problems of the past, each of his brothers would assemble a council of the divine, familiar with their realm, to advise them, helping them to see clearly and preventing them from following in Cronus' footsteps.

Zeus brought together divine entities from the other Kingdoms within The Higher Plains, outside of the newly renamed Olympus, and asked that they begin a more democratic way of life with the three brothers. Zeus recruited those who'd been closest to Rhea to form The Aetherial Court. Poseidon closely followed him, naming his council The Circle of Eight as they joined him and his wife to rule over the waves below.

However, not all of the brothers were happy with this arrangement. Haedes didn't agree with Zeus' decree that he should be ruling The Underworld with the aid of others. "After all," he thought, "What kind of God needs help ruling over their own domain? Surely not a good one." He wanted to rule his kingdom as he saw fit and didn't feel, as the true eldest son of Rhea, that he needed aid or Zeus' advice. Zeus looked upon Haedes, seeing his father's rage resting behind the fire in his brother's eyes.

Frowning, he thought for a moment before his eyes widened and an idea struck him.

"Alright Haedes," he said, "If you can answer me this, then I'll know you need not foster a council, for you truly understand your domain. If you fail, you will, as I ask, set up the council and undertake more research, facilitated by me, into your domain. Yes?" As he spoke, Haedes narrowed his eyes, sensing his brother's aptitude for bargaining, but reluctantly agreed.

Zeus recalled the riddle of the Sphinx, which he had heard on the winds of The Higher Plains along with rumours of Oedipus. He smiled down at Haedes and recited the riddle.

"It walks on four legs in the morning, two legs at noon, and three legs in the evening. What is it?" Haedes thought for a moment but came up empty. Frustrated, he launched himself at his brother, who merely laughed, being the strongest of the three, swatting him away as though he were no more than a fly bothering a rotting corpse.

"How dare you make a fool out of me!" Haedes hissed.

"I need not make you anything brother, for you do not even know the premise over which you are God. The answer to my riddle was man, for you know as mortals travel through your antithesis, life, they move from crawling on all fours, to walking, to needing the aid of a cane. You, of all Gods, should know this. How can you rule over death if you do not understand death? You say you do not need a council to assist you, but perhaps you need not only the council, but as I suggest, a little first-hand experience with that which you rule."

Haedes, at this, cocked his head.

"What do you mean brother?" he asked, fear taking hold of him.

"I am ruler of the heavens— am I not?" Zeus asked him.

"You are," Haedes replied, bitter.

"Then I can expel you from this place. You will be placed in a mortal coil, to live out your life and be reborn a God once you have learned this most important lesson. I will not be subject to another tyranny. You must learn the preciousness of life if you are to rule the dead." Haedes opened his mouth to protest, outraged, but Zeus' mind had already been made up.

Zeus, nodding once, expelled Haedes, banishing him from the heavens and sentencing him to exile in The Underworld. When he awoke, with a throbbing temple, he found his godly essence funnelled into that which he despised most.

A mortal body.

1

JUST A LITTLE LOVIN'

SEPHY

THE SOUND OF RAPPING knuckles on heavy wood startles me into consciousness.

Head pounding, I reach under my pillow, wrapping my fingers around the hilt of my pocket knife before rolling over, nude and draped only in sheets, to hurl the blade without looking. It embeds itself firmly in the fine mahogany door, which opens at the thud, leaving only the vibrations of the blade to echo throughout the room.

A hungover moan escapes my lips.

I instantly regret the noise as the mere utterance of it causes yet more thudding on the inside of my skull.

What the hell did I do last night? Or more importantly, who did I do?

I contemplate my blended memories of the last sixteen hours, licking my raw bottom lip. Reaching across the mattress behind me, my long limbs assure me that I am alone.

Phew. I breathe out, relieved, sitting up and blinking a few times, frail and tender in the early morning.

Jules, my butler, stands on the other side of the gaping doorframe, collecting my breakfast tray from the portable stand where it's propped outside the door before walking into my room.

I groan.

"Good morning, ma'am," I hear him say. I bring my hands up to cradle my head.

"For the love of Christ, Jules, small voices," I complain as he places the tray stand bedside, putting my breakfast selection atop it with expert grace.

I wrap the sheets around me, knowing that Jules has seen far more of me than I ever want to admit, but, as ever, not really caring.

I'm hot, so why should he complain?

"Brad left his number, ma'am," he announces, and then it hits me.

"Brad. That's right!" I exclaim, remembering the name of the man I'd mounted last night.

He was fun, but I've had better.

"Yes ma'am. His number."

Jules pulls a card with a number scrawled on the back from the inside pocket of his three-piece suit. His green eyes remain nonchalant as I snatch it from between his gloved fingertips. I crumple it within two seconds before throwing it behind me and onto the floor. He rolls his eyes, so I cock an eyebrow at him.

"Something you want to say, Jules?" I demand, reaching forward to take my bloody Mary.

Jules beats me to it, picking up the cocktail with distaste and handing it to me. It's served in a fine china teacup with red flowers around the rim and sits upon a frail-looking saucer, a celery stick beside it. I hate all this fine china crap, but Jules insists I should drink my beverage like a lady, even if it is alcoholic and I'm already hungover. He hates that I drink anything that isn't tea, and so I sip the tomato juice and vodka concoction slowly, looking up at him, expectant.

His mouth twists into a grimace.

"Persephone Sinclair, I've known you since you were no bigger than a loaf of bread. I know that you have heard it all before and that you may think you know better than an old codger like me, but I'm going to tell you what I think your father would want you to hear if he was still alive." He clears his throat, preparing for the same speech he always gives me in the mornings. "You're far too beautiful, and far too smart, to be playing with men into the early hours and then discarding them like they're no more than a joy ride. What about love?" he implores.

I give him a deadpan stare.

"One, you know I hate it when you call me Persephone. Seeing as how you've known me since before I could tell you that, I'd think you'd remember. Two, I am smart and beautiful, and I'll flaunt those qualities and utilise them however I choose, whether that be riding men all night or not. You know I don't want love. Love is bullshit." I stick up my nose, and he gives me a look of utter superiority, walking around the frame of my king-sized bed that's carved from some sort of pale wood. It's expensive, just like everything I sit on, wear, drive, or sleep in. In fact, the cheapest thing around here is the fleet of men

I bring back for fun before discarding them as utterly replaceable the next morning.

"Bath, Ma'am?" he enquires.

I sigh.

"For the love of all that is holy, Jules. SEPHY! My name is fucking Sephy! Enough with the ma'am crap!" I yell, instantly regretting it as my eyelids flutter, the pain in my head amping up a notch. I've only been back here for a month after graduating from Oxford with my doctorate in classical studies but you'd think he'd never met me.

Being stuck here with my Uncle Peter has clearly done more damage than I thought.

"Sorry, Sephy," he corrects himself as he walks across the plush lilac carpet and up two rose quartz stairs into my open-plan bathroom.

The bath is sunken into the vein-mapped pink stone and around it four rose-gold Grecian pillars rise. They trace its lazy white curve as they meet with the high domed ceiling, lacquered in a luxurious cream paint that swirls.

I gaze around the room as I hear the tinkle of running water hit the air.

It's been this way since I was six, before I'd been shipped off to boarding school in England by my Uncle Peter, and it hasn't changed since. Lilac carpet meets with cream and pastel pink wallpaper covered in shimmering silver roses. My bedframe is ivory, and the sheets are crumpled silk. A cream armoire stands in the far corner of the room with my prized record player atop it, an essential I simply can't live without.

Next to the door, a lilac sofa with gold armrests sits on gilded feet beside a large doggy bed pillow on the floor. As I look around at each of the pieces of furniture, I realise I've fornicated on nearly every single one of them (excluding the dog bed) and smirk.

I inhale as I take in the space, waking fully, the scent of fresh flowers wafting from several of the surfaces. Not that I put them there. It's Jules' feminine touch that has kept this place modern. I really need to redecorate though, because the pink, white, and purple theme is just so over.

Rising from the bed, I place my feet on the floor and my teacup and saucer on the tray. The motion causes my stomach to turn from the obscene amount of whisky I consumed last night, an immediate queasiness hitting me like a bus. I stretch, letting my arms extend, the sheets falling around my ankles as I reach my full height of five foot eight, spine unfurling like a whip.

Walking around the frame of the bed, I don't even blink as I step up into the bathroom before sitting straight down in the water.

Jules coughs, averting his gaze from my slender form as the hot water caresses my skin with tenderness.

It's just what I need because Brad had been anything but.

"How you sit in scalding water without so much as blinking I'll never know," Jules sighs, and I laugh as he adds bubbles. They begin to froth and foam, the scent of cinnamon rising with the steam and filling my head with a comforting spicy heat.

"We can't all be weaklings," I remind him and he smiles as I let the water continue to rise around me, bubbles pluming as I examine the flawless alabaster sheen of my skin.

"How very observant of you," he quips.

I smirk as I raise a long and muscular leg out of the water, taking my time as I check myself out.

"You'll get it down eventually, Jules. After all, you learned to wait until after I throw Ol' Faithful at the door before entering. So at least I'm not having to call an ambulance like I did that first morning." I remind him of the horrible surprise he'd received after walking into my room, tray in hand, only to be in the direct line of my daily projectile. It had only nicked him, which I'd found amusing as he'd cried like a baby. Nonetheless, it taught him to knock and wait quickly enough.

There is nothing like throwing a knife and hitting my target when I'm half asleep and hungover. It really raises my expectation for the rest of the day as I get my first adrenaline hit of the morning before I've even opened my eyes.

"You know some people would say that you take advantage of me being at your beck and bloody call," Jules complains, halting the flow of steaming water as he turns the rose gold faucets back to their original positions. I feign innocence, relaxing at the fast pace of our usual morning repertoire.

"Well, some people don't pay your salary. I do," I remind him and his eyes narrow, a smirk appearing reluctantly on his lips.

"Actually, you don't. Not yet. You're not officially an heiress until you get around to signing those documents your Uncle keeps reminding me to remind you about." He glares at me sideways and I sigh, crossing my arms over my breasts.

"Why would I want to sign a load of paperwork meaning I get more money on top of the already extortionate allowance I receive, with an added shit ton of responsibility over the empire my father built?" I demand. "Who the hell wants to be a businessperson when you can just swipe a platinum card and avoid all the boring paperwork?" I ask him with a serious expression.

He snorts.

"Apparently, not you."

"Ahh, Jules, you're a bright one." I click my tongue against the back of my teeth, running my hands through my long red tresses.

Jules rises from his knees to his feet, spine remaining abnormally straight as he does so. He's certainly one graceful man, that's for sure.

"Anything else I can do for you this morning, Ma'am?" he enquires.

I scowl.

"I don't know. Does letting me hit you for calling me shitting ma'am count?" I scold him yet again, not allowing my expression to soften.

"I am so glad your Uncle paid out all that money to send you to England so you could come back with such a colourful array of multicultural profanities at your disposal. Truly." His sarcasm seeps into the muggy air of the bathroom before he nods his head, dismissing himself. Striding silently from the bathroom, he leaves the breakfast tray, my meal still untouched under a silver cloche beside the bed.

Craning my neck to ensure he's shut the door behind him, I return to my bath, gazing down at the milky flesh that covers my tight muscles.

I have a personal training session booked with Jacque later in the downstairs conference room, which is good as I'm feeling anxious for some boxing despite my night's rigorous array of activities. New energy is already bubbling up beneath the surface of my skin as the vodka of my morning pick-me-up rushes to my brain in the heat of the bath. My veins dilate, blood rushing through my body like hot river rapids. Reaching over to the bath controls I turn on the jets, sinking deeper into the hold of the tub and closing my eyes as I let my mind empty ready for another day of fun, followed by a night of finding yet another man to conquer.

After I'm decadently relaxed, I move across the plush carpet wrapped in a white monogrammed robe. Sitting on the edge of my bed, I remove the cloche from my breakfast plate and tuck into poached eggs and thin sliced Parma ham. Jules is an amazing chef; my

Mother hired him specifically for that purpose because she hated to cook so much. I've always been grateful for his culinary skills because food is second only in my life to sex.

I eat with vigour, and as the last yolk bursts in my mouth, making my tongue slick, I push thoughts of her away and instead walk over to the armoire.

Chewing the last slice of ham and washing it down with a zing-filled sip from my alcohol-tainted teacup, I put the stylus onto the slick vinyl of one of my favourite records, pausing to enjoy Dusty Springfield's angelic tones seeping out into the room.

This definitely puts the cherry on the cake of my morning relaxation ritual.

The lyrics continue to soothe me as I open the doors to my walk-in closet, a space large enough to warrant its own postcode. Revealing the interior, I sigh, knowing it's an unfortunate juxtaposition of my young and old selves colliding in a mess of pastel pink walls and un-apologetically gothic black clothes. Stiletto boots are scattered across the floor, threatening to impale unwanted guests.

Selecting a pair of riding trousers, a low-cut black vest, and a long-backed riding jacket to match, I turn on my heel to find that the door to my bedroom is trembling on its hinges. Shaking my head, a small smile quirks my lips as I exhale at what I know is a too-persistent animal.

Stupid dog.

Throwing my clothes on the sex-stained bedsheets I pad the length of the room and let loose the Leonberger. He's so enormous that he comes up to my upper thigh when he's on all fours. Stood on his hind legs, we can practically tango.

"Morning, Cerb, how's it hanging?" I ask, raising my hand for a high five as the furry beast of a dog lurches across the threshold, bowling right into me as I bend to greet him. His wide chestnut eyes look down at me, non-judgemental, and I laugh as he licks the side of my face. "Ew!" I yell out, shoving him off me and watching as he paces the length of the room, sniffing his surroundings with far too much energy before finding some leftover morsels on my breakfast tray.

Swatting him back from Jules' fine china, I roll onto my feet from the floor where I've fallen, deciding that he needs a walk. He settles, curling up by my bed, and I try to remember a time when he hasn't been in my life.

Cerb was my main reason for coming home during the summers when I was out of University or home from boarding school. I love this damn dog more than most humans, but he's got to be getting on in age now, which saddens me. You wouldn't know it with the way he bounds all over the place like a puppy, though.

As he rolls onto his back, presenting his enormous fluffy belly for a rub, I think about how he did the same thing for my mother and father before their deaths. I think about how he had made them smile and laugh, how they'd watched as he'd become my best childhood friend. I'd even ridden him like a pony when he was a pup; he was, and still is, the mightiest of steeds.

The chasm of their never-ending absence opens a tad, and I feel myself becoming vulnerable.

Putting my feelings away and replacing them, as ever, with forward motion, I throw myself into the day.

My first priority is to muck out the stall of my onyx Percheron, Nightshade, before taking her riding and getting in some shooting practice. Then, I have training with Jacque to sweat out last night's toxins so I can replace them with brand-new ones tonight.

I stand in front of the gilded, floor-length mirror mounted on the back of the closet door, staring at my long, fiery, red hair and cognac eyes. They burn the colour of whisky, my pale skin making them sheen even brighter as I'm still almost translucent with the early hour. The tight-fitting riding pants and vest show off what my mama gave me, hugging my crotch, tits, and ass, and I pick out a pair of flat riding boots, wishing they came in stiletto style but knowing that, unfortunately, it'd hurt my horse.

Leaving my suite in haste, I turn off the music, eying my vanity but deciding not to bother with any makeup. It'll just run off once I start mucking out Nightshade's stall anyway.

In the corridor outside my room, I'm surrounded with inescapable nostalgia in the form of the high ceilings and deeply hued walls of my early childhood. They give a luxurious, high-class feel that spreads throughout the entire mansion, and yet I find no joy in the decadence, no warmth in the finery. My bedroom is, in fact, the room with the softest colour scheme; something I'll be changing should I decide to remain here indefinitely.

I'm pondering having the entire place redecorated to remove the memories of those I've lost as I reach the top of the grand staircase.

This central lobby bridges the east and west wings and truly is cavernous.

Turning to make my way downstairs into the lobby, I find an aged, familiar, and entirely unwanted face below, waiting for me on the bottom step with a disapproving stare.

"Good morning— or should I say, afternoon." My Uncle Peter gives a disappointed smirk, immediately succeeding at pissing me off.

This guy deserves a medal.

"I was out late. Besides, it's not like I have a job to go to," I remind him, shrugging my shoulders as I button my double-breasted riding jacket and descend the bottle green velvet runner with as much speed as I can manage.

Peter's eaglesque, citrus-gold eyes flick the length of my body as he runs a hand through his grey hair, visibly frustrated.

"Well, that's not strictly true. You're the heiress to an enormous fortune, but also an enormous business. I need you to sign this paperwork, Sephy. I'm not kidding around. You have a responsibility to your father's legacy, and I've let this avoidance go on long enough. It's been over a month."

As I brush past him, his final sentiments reach me, infuriating me more than I'd ever want to admit.

I turn on the spot, eyes narrowing.

"I'll get to it when I'm damn well good and ready," I bite out, temper flaring at his attempt to use the loss of my parents to get me to do what he wants. He doesn't care about what I want at all.

"I know you will— right now." Peter puts his hand into the inner pocket of the mossy tweed jacket he's wearing, pulling out a thick wedge of folded paper and an ornate black crystal pen.

As he's rummaging around with this and trying to corner me, I turn and walk away. Striding the length of the gargantuan lobby, the heels of my riding boots ring out against the chequered black and white marble, echoing even still as I enter the east wing. I pass one of our libraries, several sitting rooms, my old ballet studio, and a formal dining room before proceeding out of the east-facing French doors that lead to the stables.

I hear Peter call after me several times, but I don't stop, nor do I care for his crap at this time of day, or any other. He might have been my legal guardian and the treasurer for the Sinclair Fortune, but I'm twenty-five now, and a PhD no less. He's no longer the boss of me.

Walking across the sprawling and carefully maintained turf, I take in the fresh air and enjoy the smell of moist grass, still wet from last night's rain. I don't look back to see if Peter is following me, and as I enter the stables, the smell of hay and manure is oddly comforting, diminishing the flames of my temper to mere embers.

Nightshade stands in her stall, treading over to me immediately as our eyes meet, her hoofs clipping the cement. I close the space between us and exhale, the irritation at my Uncle's lack of respect dissipating at the touch of the horse's soft muzzle against my fingertips.

I hear Cerb enter the stable through the door I've left wide open, having followed me like a lost child from inside the house, and close my eyes, surrounded by two of the only beings on the planet I assume actually care about my feelings, and I about theirs.

I love Jules, and in a lot of ways he could be my father with the amount he worries, but I don't have a lot of friends. Those I attended school and University with are half a world away, and I've never really spent enough time in Chicago to meet many people, even though I was born here.

Besides, once they find out about my lineage, I can never tell whether they like me or my money.

Picking up a brush, I begin to groom Nightshade before refreshing her feed trough, hoping it'll help clear my head and return me to my usual state of reckless abandon.

That is most definitely how I operate best.

I've been carved into who I am, not formed organically. Etched out against my will from hard stone, blood, sweat, tears and made into something jagged.

Elite gymnastics, figure skating, athletics, martial arts, shooting, flying, and racing were the things that filled my summers for the last eighteen years, and I am in no short supply of discipline, motivation, or skill. I've always worked hard, but after getting my doctorate, after working my ass off for four years, I just want to stop for a while and have fun.

I want to live.

To breathe.

My education has been elite and fastidiously strict, and I am not ready to step into the world to slave away for forty years in a company purely because my father created it. Nor is my only ambition to marry, pop out two babies, and have a husband whose biggest challenge in life is to get our picket fence the purest shade of white he can.

I want more.

I don't even know what that is. But I know it doesn't lie in some boardroom with a bunch of shareholders and advisers, or in marriage to some aristocrat with a failing family fortune.

Continuing in my fast-paced attempt at tackling the day and maintaining inner peace, I step over to the tack room of the stable that smells of the raw pine from which it's crafted. Opening the fridge beneath a pin board of first-place ribbons and old horseshoes I find that Jules has prepared fresh carrots as a treat for my equine bestie.

Moving back to stand before her enormous height and gait, I stare into her dark glistening eyes and feed her as I croon in horsey whispers.

As I speak absentmindedly with the Percheron mare, I let myself float back to last night, to the man I'd slept with, to how free I'd felt as I'd climaxed atop him before collapsing and falling into a blissfully untroubled sleep.

It wasn't even about him; he was just there. It was about me, taking control of my own pleasure, my own life.

That's what I want.

I don't want to be tied down.

In fact, I'd much rather be the one doing the tying up.

Craving that same freedom as an addict craves heroin, I know that riding will be half a fix. I dress Nightshade quickly, relishing her black shining coat beneath my fingertips and inhaling the scent of her as I put on reins, a bridle, and a saddle. I pat her attentively as I work, and she shuffles anxiously from foot to foot.

After about ten minutes, I unbolt the door and lead her into the slate-paved courtyard outside. Climbing atop her with the aid of a mounting block, my heart races in my chest as Cerb takes flight in front of us and the wind whips my hair from my face.

The grounds are sprawling, my Mother's pride and joy, and have been maintained fastidiously by my Uncle since her passing. Large expanses of lush green grass surround the house, transitioning gradually into a thick forest lining the borders of the property.

As the mare lurches forward into a trot, I stiffen my spine, compensating for her motion as we begin at a tame speed across the grounds. Nightshade is one of those animals that needs to be worked and ridden hard, she needs her heart racing in her chest and her pulse thumping in her ears on a regular basis to stay sane, so I suppose she and I have that in common.

Running my fingers through her thick glossy mane, I pat her neck as we rise over the slight incline of the estate's seemingly endless grounds. Crossing the colossally long driveway, her hooves click against the ivory as I bide my time, trying not to hurt her feet by pushing her too hard.

When we hit grass, I urge her into a gallop instantly, squeezing my heels into the side of her body.

I focus on Cerb as he leads us forward, and before I know what's happening, I realise that we're heading toward the part of the property I try to avoid.

The mausoleum where my parents are buried.

I turn the horse, letting the reins fall slack on one side and twisting her enormous black head left as Cerb changes direction and contin- ues to bound around Nightshade's hooves, her breathing becoming laboured and anxious.

Cantering in a semi-circle, I come face to face, yet again, with memories of the event that destroyed my life all those years ago. The upper west wing of the house, the place where my parents' master bedroom had been the night that the fire had broken out and taken them from me at only six years old. My heart breaks in my chest at the sight of the refurbished windows, wondering why Peter kept the same design, the same rooms, the same décor, even after the event.

I can't go past the door to my bedroom, can't walk up the corridor or visit their old room even though the fire damage is fixed, simply because it causes me too much pain knowing they'll never be just behind that door again.

I've learned to avoid the memories at all costs because at least this way, I can function without being heartbroken every damn day.

Pulling hard on the reins and once more squeezing the underbelly of my steed, we ride faster. I urge her onward, swallowing hard, as we gallop away from the past as fast as her hooves will carry me.

The training session with Jacque was intense, and I'm sweating profusely, my white tank now see-through and my workout shorts clinging to my legs, damp with perspiration. His dark hair falls across his forehead and his navy-blue eyes are beginning to look weary as we continue to spar until the song playing over the studio's built-in surround sound finishes.

Then, he lets out an exhausted breath.

"Damn girl, you're giving me a run for my money. Whatever you're taking to get this kind of energy, I want some!" He winks at me, and

I smile at him, wondering momentarily why I haven't slept with him yet.

Then I remember, Peter forbade me to sleep with the staff in case of sexual harassment lawsuits, reminding me of yet another reason why being a billionaire isn't all it's cracked up to be. It's true what they say, once you have money, everyone wants a piece of it, regardless of whether they gotta screw you over to get it or not.

Jacque and I part ways as he packs up his bag and exits through the double doors, a crisp one-hundred-dollar bill clutched in his hand for the hour. I hear his car pull away seconds later.

Heading up the stairs, my heart rate lowers within minutes.

I slip off my sneakers and close the door behind me as I re-enter my room, restless even still, despite riding, knife throwing, shooting practice, and boxing, which I've managed in only an afternoon.

Jules is unintentionally hiding inside, and I jump at the unexpected sight of him hanging up clothes in my closet as I move to undress.

"Jeez, you almost gave me a heart attack," I complain, and he shakes his head with an unimpressed face.

"I could say the same. Those shorts are—" he begins, but I stop him.

"Called shorts for a reason," I finish his sentence for him, and his mouth contorts into a disapproving smile as I strip off my shirt so I'm stood in only a black sports bra and the forbidden workout shorts, abs glistening.

"Your Uncle finally hired someone for the security position," he informs me as he moves toward the bathroom, abandoning the laundry to run me a shower.

"Security? What on earth do we need that for?" I ask him, and he cocks an eyebrow with a half grimace.

"Oh, haven't you seen today's paper?" He reverses a few paces to the breakfast tray I left unattended upon heading out for riding this morning, picking up the paper, folded and untouched beside my empty breakfast plate. He opens it and hands it to me as I look at him, mystified.

"Page five," he orders.

I flick through the flimsy paper, my fingers leaving sweat marks and smudging the ink at the edges of columns of supposedly breaking news.

When I reach page five, I see an unwelcome and familiar face with slurring lips and alcohol-glazed eyes. Mine.

"Oh, crap," I cuss, seeing the article about my late-night activities and cringing.

"Yes, you made quite the impression on the Daily Herald." Jules condemns me with his tone, but I shrug it off.

"It's just a crappy article," I sigh and he cocks his head as he turns on the shower.

The wet room is built into the corner of the bathroom next to the tub, and the entire ceiling is equipped with twelve separate faucets, making the experience inside not unlike standing under boiling hot rain.

"Look, I'm just your butler. But I'm sure you'll hear it far clearer coming from me than your Uncle when I tell you that your shareholders don't like to think that their money is in the hands of a drunken teenager with no self-control." He reminds me of the fact I'm tied to the stupid Sinclair name and I roll my eyes, exhaling heavily.

"Yes, but that still doesn't explain why we need a security guard." I change the subject.

"If you'd have had a security guard around, maybe he could have tackled that photographer. I'm sure you'd agree it's not your most flattering appearance," Jules explains, going back to putting away my laundry as he walks past me with continuously perfect posture.

"I don't care what other people think of me. Least of all shareholders. I'll party if I want to. It's just another great reason for me not to sign the paperwork Peter keeps trying to ambush me with." I make the excuse automatically, moving up the two small steps and into my bathroom before stripping off completely and getting into the shower. I sit down on the quartz ledge of the wet room, relaxing back into the cool pearlescent tiling and letting the hard, fake, rainfall of the shower cleanse me. My sweat is washed away and in the heat my tense muscles reluctantly relax before I take them out for round two— or is it round three?

"You shouldn't be so careless." I hear Jules call in warning as he clears away the breakfast tray and leaves the room, shutting the door behind him with a bang. He's probably pissed off at me, and for a moment as my fiery red hair becomes sodden through, I almost feel bad for him.

Almost but not quite.

After all, he's getting paid a pretty penny to put up with my crap, and it's not like he's even responsible for me in any way, shape, or form.

I take deep breaths in the thick, moist, steam of the shower as the smell of cinnamon fills my nostrils, and lather up, ready to party, ready to let go and ready to get the hell out of this house and back to where I belong.

Roaming the streets of Chicago looking for my next easy thrill.

Thick bloody lips, black-rimmed eyes, and high-set cheekbones are applied to my pale face as I put on the last of my makeup. I'm dressed in leather pants with partially transparent lace panelling in the sides and a black backless halter top. Silver chains hang from the ruched material down over my bare midriff, reaching just below my pierced navel, tickling my skin with their coolness.

I sling my leather jacket over my shoulders and take a look down at my knee-high platform stiletto boots. This is me, the real me.

Not Persephone.

Sephy.

My red hair tumbles down over my shoulders, fading from its natural, rich auburn to strawberry blonde right at the tips. Everyone is always convinced I dye my hair, but the truth is I'm just a natural firecracker. Or that's what my mom used to call me anyway.

Pushing the nickname away and into the recesses of memory, trying to forget it exists, I leave my suite, Cerb at my heels.

I don't carry a bag, only my ID and my credit card stowed safely in my cleavage, as well as my phone and a set of car keys that press into the flesh of my ass through the back pocket of my skin-tight pants.

"Persephone!" My legal name is called, and I jump mid-step. Not realising I'm really making a break for it; I suddenly feel like a criminal for trying to get out of my own ridiculously luxurious home.

Raising my gaze from the sexy black of my boots, I see Peter approaching me from across the landing, and he's not alone.

Well, hello there— I purr internally as I take in the tall drink of water on his heels.

"Who's this?" I demand, suddenly curious and semi-interested in what my Uncle has to say.

"This is Xion; he's your new security guard," Peter informs me and I scowl.

"You know you can't hire someone who looks like this dude and then tell me not to sleep with the staff," I complain.

Peter looks over his shoulder at the new security guard with an awkward expression.

As he's making this face, I take the chance to linger too.

This guy is seriously hot, with a stubble-lined jaw that looks like it was carved by Michelangelo himself. I catch his gaze, liquid gold and warm bronze alloyed eyes staring into mine with an intensity not unlike that of something actually molten. He's got olive skin, much more tanned than mine, and an enormously wide chest that's smattered with hair and clad in a long black beater vest with a knee-length leather coat over the top. His hair is thick and glossy, coifed somewhat effortlessly to make him look both handsome and intimidating at the same time. His eyes are enormous and his nose looks like it's been broken a few times because it doesn't quite line up with the rest of his face, and yet this does nothing but enhance his gorgeousness. Rock-hard biceps bulge against the leather of his jacket, and he's even taller than me, which is saying something because I'm five feet eight inches and wearing enormous freaking heels.

As the air around us stills, he raises a thick, dark, and perfectly arched eyebrow, the side of his mouth rising into a smirk.

"Hello to you too, Persephone." I almost don't get mad that he doesn't use my preferred name, but then remember that I'm not one of those women who will lose her inner bitch over a guy with a hot-as-hell face and nice ass to boot by the looks of things—

"It's Sephy," I reply with a scowl and nonchalant gaze. He smirks.

"Whatever you say, princess." I look between the two of them and go to leave, but Xion stands in my way, stopping me with his broadness as he crosses his arms and spreads his legs. A stubborn ass human barricade in all senses of the word.

He really is enormous, but I can't help but start calculating how messed up it would make my hair if I tried to take him on.

I do love a challenge.

"Don't you have some paperwork to sign?" he asks me, raising that pesky eyebrow again and making me narrow my eyes, unimpressed.

"Does a restraining order count? Get out of my way," I retort, temper flaring again. I don't like being told what to do, least of all by handsome strangers.

Peter speaks up, coughing to get my attention in the most cowardly way possible.

"You're not leaving here until you sign these contracts, Persephone. I tried doing this the painless way, but you've refused. So, it's come down to this. You only have yourself to blame." My Uncle brings out the papers and the same black crystal pen, like he's been carrying them around just so he can ambush me whenever I leave my suite.

I look at Xion with a semi-plea in my stare, but his expression deadens to one of emotionlessness. I feel my heart sink.

I don't want to do this.

I don't want to sign these stupid contracts.

I take a moment to calm myself, anger turning my thought processes ever so incrementally slow as we stand on the landing, none of us moving. Peter continues holding out the black crystal pen to me with a hard-ass look on his stupid pretentious face that he really can't pull off.

If I sign them, then I'm free. I guess that's one thing I can take comfort from. Peter will stop bothering me, and maybe I can even sell the company to someone else. My father always said that you can have anything if you have enough money, and I have nothing but, so maybe I can buy my way out of this ridiculous shackle around my ankle.

"Fine!" I snap, making the decision hastily and without care for the real consequences. I just want to go out, get drunk, and find a guy to grind with. Even if I have to sign these stupid papers to do it.

I stride over to my Uncle, swinging my hips, fully aware that Xion is watching me from behind. My stilettos perk up the curve of my ass, and as I grab the pen and sign on three separate dotted lines in swirly and well-practised motion, I cock my hip and look back over one shoulder. Scowling at the security guard, I hope that he gauges the smoulder behind the hatred in my gaze.

"Aren't you going to read it?" Peter asks, and I look up at him with an incredulous stare.

"If I do, will it change the fact you're forcing me to sign them?"

He sighs at my query, so I take this as a no, and give him a pissed-off stare, puckering my lips as the issue falls moot.

Once I hand back the fistfuls of papers listing all the responsibilities I've never wanted, I turn on the ball of my foot and storm up to Xion.

"Can I go now, sir?" I ask, cocking one eyebrow and looking up from beneath my lashes with wide fiery eyes, pretending to be furious but unable to deny the fact that I find him practically delectable.

"Be my guest— I'll be close behind," he informs me as I take off down the stairs, balancing expertly in my heels and making sure I flip my long hair over one shoulder as I go.

"You know if you want to stare at my ass some more, all you have to do is ask—" I call back over my shoulder, cocky and carefree as I shrug off the resentment of both men forcing my hand so I can enjoy my night.

Without turning to look back at them, I pull the Aston Martin keys out of my back pocket and head out into the chill air of the Chicago night, strutting all the way.

2

NIGHT FEVER

XION

"WELL— THAT WASN'T WHAT I expected," I grumble, my deep voice reverberating around the airy landing of the Sinclair mansion. I haven't been here in years, but to be honest, it hasn't changed at all.

"I told you she was a handful," Peter reminds me, taking off his glasses and wiping them on the white crumpled shirt beneath the tweed of his jacket. This man is seriously style impaired.

"She's not like I thought she'd be—" I don't know what to say. I don't want to insult the girl, but I'd kind of expected her to be doe-eyed and young. Instead, she's— well, she's certainly not doe-eyed.

"The last time you saw her she was six years old. A lot has changed. She's lost more than you can imagine," Peter comments, though there is a lack of sympathy in his tone and he states this more as fact than disappointment.

I peer at the bottle green runner beneath my feet, then at the deep midnight blue of the walls, the highly polished rich wood of the balustrade and surrounding bannisters. Persephone may be, in fact, the only thing about this place that has changed. It's almost haunting in its timelessness.

"Well, I'll be needing those contracts to take back with me for the courts." I hold out a hand, and he exhales heavily again, reaching into his pocket before halting and looking up at me.

"I should probably make copies of these actually, just in case. Though that may take a while, these are pretty hefty and my copier is ancient." He moves his hand from within his jacket, patting the fabric protectively, as if this could stop me taking them if I wanted to.

I frown. I'm on a deadline, though the fact his copier is ancient doesn't surprise me; this guy could give Rupert Giles a run for his money.

"What am I supposed to do? Go play fake security guard?" I demand, irritated as the obsidian pendant around my neck cools against my skin in warning. Peter's gaze burns into me, bored and unimpressed.

"Why not? It's not like you have anything better to do, she needs looking after right now. She's developed the least healthy coping mechanisms I've ever seen. Speaking of which— how is he?" His eyes widen a little at the mention of my boss, and I shrug.

"I don't know. It's not like we're friends. I'm just the muscle. You know that." I don't give anything away; I'm not supposed to talk about Mortarian affairs with mortals, let alone one who needs to be manhandled into getting a young woman to sign a couple of damn papers.

"Well, as the muscle, I'm sure you're more than up to the job of making sure my charge doesn't get herself intoxicated beyond what's sensible. Take my car, it's out front. The Beetle." Peter reaches into his trouser pocket and pulls out a pair of keys, which he throws carelessly to me as he begins to stalk back towards his office.

"Look, I don't have time to be chasing after her—" I begin to protest, running my fingers through my thick, dark hair nervously. "I don't even know where she's going," I remind him, my voice getting deeper still with my growing reluctance. Peter pivots to face me, smiling a satisfied smile.

"Oh, she's headed to a club called Retropolis. You'll find it on North State Street on the outskirts of Chicago. Tell Barry I sent you." He waves me away with a flutter of his pale hand, and I nod, not knowing where the location is but too bored of this conversation to want it to continue any further. Maybe I'll just go and drive around for a while, I haven't been in a car for ages.

"How do you know she'll be there?" I call back, beginning my descent down the steps toward the chequered marble floor of the open-plan lobby.

"Because that's where she goes every night." Peter relinquishes this information, looking down at me over the bannister, and my eyebrows rise in surprise. Not at the news, but at the melancholy note which it strikes with me.

"Oh— right." I shrug, turning on my heel and feeling the leather of my coat move with my momentum, brushing against the harsh denim of my jeans. My boots thud on the remaining stairs, then pound heavier against the stone as I make my way out of the mansion, annoyed that I don't yet have the contracts in hand.

Like I need more delays; these papers are already late as it is. I curse internally, my face falling back to its regular stoic expression.

Outside, I hurry down the wide front steps, surrounded on either side by two high Grecian pillars carved from mocha-coloured stone. My heart thuds slowly as my feet hit the gravel of the drive, muscles relaxing at the smell of pine from the surrounding forest.

I remember this place so vividly. The deep woods. The wet, pristine grass. The gargantuan high ceilings that had been perhaps my only saving grace as smoke had filled the upper west wing.

I still remember her terrified screams, the way her enormous co-gnac eyes brimmed with tears and her ribs shuddered as soot filled her lungs. I still remember knowing beyond all else that I had to save her. That she had to remain alive.

It is just a shame I could not have done the same for her parents.

Guilt overcomes me in an unexpected wave. I'm drenched in the emotion I so often try to flee from, that which I try to push down back into the depths of my darkness where it belongs. But being here again, seeing her, however different she may be, is making me wish I could have saved her from the pain of losing her family altogether.

I spot the car parked at the edge of the gravel semi-circle that narrows into a long winding driveway, distancing the estate from the busy road beyond.

Slipping the keys into the old-fashioned lock, which I'm grateful for as I have absolutely no patience with technology, I duck under the hideous mouldy green of the car's metal frame while wondering exactly how much torque it would take to twist it beyond recognition. Cars these days fascinate me, mainly because I can't believe people drive around like psychopaths in them. They're weapons on wheels, and I have to wonder what kind of person has the balls to speed in one of these things, let alone pull crazy stunts.

I mean, if you ask me, that's just a death wish in disguise.

SEPHY

"Ma'am, do you know you were doing a hundred miles per hour in a fifty-mile-an-hour zone?" the officer asks me, his teeth far too white and his face far too young for me to take seriously.

Though, I think, *this may be usable to my advantage.*

"Was I? That's fast," I comment with cool reserve as I relax my posture and unfurl my fingers from the steering wheel. Shrugging, I watch as he rolls his eyes.

I flutter my eyelashes.

"License and registration please?" he demands as I lean back into the heated leather of Spectre, my pride and joy. My father has passed his love of Aston Martins down to me, and I haven't been able to help but follow in his footsteps by naming mine after Bond villains either.

I reach into the glove compartment on the passenger side of the car and brush aside a pile of grocery store gift cards, pulling out my registration as I extract my license from my cleavage and hand it to him with a flourish of my long dark fingernails.

"Sinclair? As in Sinclair Diamonds?" he enquires, and I smile.

Gotcha.

"The very same. I own the company actually," I reveal, and he gapes at me, eyes giving an unmistakable twinkle of impress.

"I'm saving up for an engagement ring for my high school sweetheart—" He looks hopefully at me, and I smile at him, even though he's making me nauseous with his besotted puppy-dog eyes.

"Well, if you call our main office and tell them that I sent you, I'm sure we can arrange some sort of discount— if you'd be willing to let me be on my way of course. I have places to be, running a company and all," I sigh, watching him eye up my outfit with those very same besotted puppy eyes. I catch a stir of something like desire behind the glassy surface of his irises as he hands back my documentation.

"Well, there's no point giving you a ticket. It's not going to teach you anything; you have more money than most people see in a lifetime." He

25

looks at my car enviously now, backing up a few paces and examining the sleek outline of the Quantum Grey DB9.

Placing my license back into my bra, I throw the registration papers onto the passenger seat.

"Well, give the head office a call and tell them I sent you, okay?" I remind him.

"Drive carefully," he warns with a stern stare.

I turn away from him, face falling slack as my sociable mask falls away, pressing the button to start the engine again.

The car roars to life and I waste no time in pressing my foot down on the gas pedal, returning without a second thought to my prior high speed and racing down I-94, hoping to make it to Retropolis in under my record time of only twenty minutes.

Approaching the city as I swerve between slow-ass drivers, the Chicago skyline rises and shimmers against the star-spattered and comforting black of the late hour. The moon is gloomy and crescent, the traffic slowly becoming sparse as most people are back at home with their normal boring spouses and children, living their normal boring lives.

I, however, am not, and the anticipation of dancing my ass off and filling my veins with fire water builds as I crank the stereo up, *Night Fever* flooding full force around the interior of the car.

I leave the window rolled down and enjoy as the leather of my heated seat vibrates with the bass, my face becoming chill with the wind of the cold Chicago evening.

It's times like this when I never want to sleep. Never want to slow down. I just want to keep driving, keep dancing, keep running, keep partying. It's times like this when I feel most alive.

Downtown, I park outside the sculpture centre and shove a bunch of gift cards in my pocket. I hate leaving my car close to the club, worried it'll be the target of vandalism or worse, so I always park here. I'm often too drunk to drive home anyway and end up taking a cab back to Forest Glen. Jules will come to collect my car tomorrow morning as per our non-verbal agreement, long before I'm awake and usually on his way to show out my latest male companion.

My heels click against the sidewalk as I make my way down South LaSalle Street and then turn onto West Monroe. The tall buildings of the urban jungle rise cruelly, casting shadows across the world below and giving nothing less than an utterly oppressive feel. There is nowhere more resonant of corporate oppression than American cities, with skyscrapers that shed darkness upon those of us below and CEOs who watch over us like gods. I should probably be less anti-corporate, especially considering how I'm now the CEO of one of the biggest in America, but something about how calculated it all is, about how the rich only work to benefit the rich, makes me want to throw up in my mouth a little bit.

"Hey, Sephy." I hear the familiar tone of Jono, one of the many homeless individuals I often see on my way to party. He's sat among a pile of dirty blankets and his dog, Snapper, is at his feet looking cold and tired.

"Hey, how's the city treating you these days?" I ask, rummaging in my back pocket.

"Nights are drawing in, so I'm enjoying the last of the light as much as I can," he explains, looking up at me from the ground. His ragged clothes and dishevelled hair blow around his skeletal form in the light yet chill breeze. Passing him a gift card, I bend to pet Snapper. Jono's face lights up momentarily before his eyes glaze over with guilt.

"You know you don't have to—" he begins, but I stare at him with a pissy expression, causing him to fall silent.

"Once a week — we talked about this. I have more money than I will ever need, especially now, and you need looking after. Besides, it's for services rendered. You and your family keep my pride and joy safe," I remind him that he and the other homeless, who I frequently help with grocery store gift cards and the occasional night in a hotel on particularly cold nights, keep an eye on my car while I'm otherwise occupied.

My father was always wary of the homeless, telling me never to give them my change as they would only spend it on drugs. So now I give them gift cards instead, ensuring they have the means to stay fed and warm.

Giving Snapper one last pat on the head, I rise, balancing expertly on my heels and smiling at Jono as he waves at me.

"Have a good night. I'll go and check on Spectre for you in a few," he calls as I walk away.

I smile, glad to have been able to help him out tonight. Usually, I pass more homeless, stop at least three or four more times, but tonight the city streets are empty.

Taking strides down the sidewalk to my own rhythm, I pump myself up for dancing. By the time I arrive outside Retropolis, the anticipation for the night ahead is about ready to burst in my chest like a balloon full of sparkly confetti. I'm determined to make signing those stupid papers worth it if I have to screw every guy in Chicago to do it.

"Name?" A bald African American bouncer in a black suit with a Rubik's cube style tie demands with a grin as I cock my hip.

"Come on, Barry, it's me." I give him my most dazzling smile and hold out my arms in exasperation. He laughs.

"I'm only kidding with y'all." He winks, flashing a gold tooth as he smiles before pulling aside the bright blue velvet rope. I step smugly through, much to the disgruntled cries of those waiting in line.

Barry and I go way back, almost a whole month now, but it doesn't hurt my case that on our first meeting I'd pulled out a wodge of cash from my bra and handed it over without another word.

Inside the electric violet glow of the lobby, I check my jacket before climbing the winding stairs around the edge of the building's boxy interior. I reach the club upstairs and am greeted by a familiar *Saturday Night Fever* style dance floor. It's crowded with people crushed together and the air is filled with the scent of booze and cheap cologne.

I inhale fondly.

The squares of the dancefloor alternate in neon, illuminating the place intermittently as I walk over to the bar.

My first task, as always, is to get my drink on.

"Whiskey, neat. You know how I like it." I raise my voice over the sound of yet more Bee Gees tunes as the bartender, Simon, who I slept with my second night here, turns smartly. He's wearing a black shirt with a Rubik's cube patterned bow tie, and he's totally hot. He was, of course, a great time, but we're just friends now.

Besides, he has a girlfriend.

"Unfortunately for me, that's true. Evening, Seph. How's shit down in rich town?" Simon asks, referring to Forest Glen with a faux posh accent as he sticks up his pinkie finger.

I remember the night we'd tumbled through the gargantuan double doors of the estate, how he'd been too wrapped up in my kiss to notice the size of the place until he reached my bedroom. As we got into the bathtub he'd suddenly noticed where he was, gaping at the luxuriousness of the bubbles pouring from the jets in the floor sunken tub. He quickly became distracted again though, obviously.

The next morning, as he left with a guilty look on his face, I watched him gazing at the house around him in surprise. I know he didn't expect that of me, mainly because I don't like to discuss my inheritance, and I certainly don't dress like I've got money either, despite the car I drive.

As my drink arrives, I shrug.

"I'm officially an heiress." I raise my glass to him with a grimace.

He looks hopelessly confused at my reaction.

"You seem thrilled," he chuckles, shaking his head as though I'm crazy.

"Oh, I am," I say, sarcasm dripping from my words.

Then, I begin to chug the searing dark liquid like it's the last glass of whisky I'll ever lay my hands on.

Hanging my head back, I down the dregs of it in one gulp, the long waterfall of my fiery hair tickling the base of my spine as I lean back on the glowing lime barstool.

"You know I'd give my left testicle to be an heiress—" he sighs at me, exasperated.

I gesture for him to pour me another drink.

"You'd have to— and the right one, not to mention your joystick," I remind him, making him snort as he raises the whisky bottle again and expertly delivers more burning nectar.

"For your fortune, I'd throw in a kidney too," he jokes.

I sip, slower this time, my mind unravelling under the familiar smoky haze that comes from the woody, chocolatey notes.

Yeah well, the grass is always greener on the other side— especially if your neighbour is a dealer. I think, smirking and turning away from the bar, swivelling on my stool to face the room.

It's time to eye up tonight's potential candidates.

The music switches to *Easy Lover* by Philip Bailey and I shake my head slightly, letting my hair fall over my shoulders before flipping my head back and fluttering my eyelashes at the first man my eyes find in the crowd. He's blond with glistening sea-green eyes and a slim but well-muscled body. He's also dancing with someone else, but as my attentions fall on him, he abandons her, moving toward me and gesturing with one finger for me to join him.

I smirk, knowing I won't be won over so easily.

He'll at least have to come over and offer to refill my glass first.

He gets the message, strutting over like a male peacock in heat.

"Hey there." He shakes his head, brushing a few rogue blonde strands from his damp forehead. It reflects the retro lighting, muted, back at me.

"Hi." I take a sip of my whiskey and swallow deliberately, leaning slightly forward to make sure he can see down my cleavage.

"Are you—" he begins in a raised voice as the song's chorus reaches fever pitch.

"Am I?" I demand, staring at him over the rim of my glass.

"An *Easy Lover*?" He smirks, and I cringe at the tacky line on par only with the *'someone call 911- this girl fell from heaven!'* ploy.

Oh Jesus, this was a misfire. Abort! Abort!

"Not with that line." I swivel once more on the stool as my interest dwindles quicker than a single candle in a hurricane.

I wait a few moments before I hear the blond exhale, "What a bitch!" in a voice barely audible above the music and smile to myself.

What can I say? I'm proud that I'm not one of those doe-eyed women who would fall for a man's face and nothing else. After all, if he's uninventive when trying to pick you up, he's probably uninventive everywhere else.

I take another sip of whisky, heart pounding to the rhythm of the song.

I love it here, particularly because I like to think I have *really good* taste in music. My mother and father brought me up on the classics; Michael Jackson, The Bee Gees, Dusty Springfield, AC/DC, The Conchords, Guns N' Roses, White Snake, and Foreigner to name a few, and this club is the only one in the city where retro music is the only thing on the audible menu. I mean, the music probably doesn't draw in this most attractive crowd of men, but I'd rather dance to *Night Fever* than *Wrecking Ball* any night of the week.

As I cross my legs again and Simon pours me another glass of whisky, I catch the eye of a dark-haired man standing at the other end of the bar. He's leaning upon the illuminated counter, face changing through a multitude of glowing hues as the bar changes colour in time with the dance floor. He smiles at me, revealing a collection of pristine white teeth. He's gorgeous, almost celebrity-level gorgeous, and I immediately feel saliva flood my mouth as I give him a small wave and timidly take another sip of my drink. We gaze into one another's eyes, assessing the goods like predator and prey as the music fades into a purely distracting din.

I feel myself locking onto him like a man-seeking missile.

His expression, however, becomes suddenly anxious and his eyes shift to look over my shoulder. He turns, walking away in a sudden and unexpected darting motion, disappearing into the crowd.

I almost get to my feet to go after him, but then realise his gaze wasn't on me right before he left. I spin the stool fast, coming face to face with Xion.

"Hello." He smiles, cocky, as he slides onto the electric blue stool next to me.

"Oh, my god. What did you do? That guy was hot!" I complain as he gestures for Simon to serve him.

"I'll take a water," he requests, and I snort at his softcore order. "Oh, and I didn't do anything. Just a little stare down. Pretty standard. You should be grateful; any man worth your heart would have stayed." He locks his fingers together, staring straight forward into his reflection in the artsy mosaic mirror behind the bar, stoic.

Simon's gaze shifts between us rapidly like he's watching a tennis match.

"Just a stare down? I thought your eyes were going to cause him to burst into flames!" he interrupts, unable to help himself.

My mouth falls open.

Simon becomes the object of Xion's next incendiary glare as he quickly delivers his drink before scurrying away to the other end of the bar.

"My heart? What the hell has that got to do with anything? I just wanted to screw him!" I explain, eyebrows rising high on my forehead as my skin becomes clammy with unexpected fury. This guy is getting under my skin far too easily.

"Either way, he's not worth your time," he states, taking a pointed sip of water and not meeting my gaze.

"Oh, and you are? You just basically forced me into accepting over a billion dollars! You bastard!" I slam my fist down on the counter, making my whisky jump in its glass. Xion smirks.

"Oh, excuse me while I go and find my tiny violin to play for you." He shakes his head. "Don't flatter yourself either. I prefer my women with a little more—" he begins, but trails off as I stare at him incredulously.

This guy is cheeky as hell.

"More what? Tits, ass?" I demand an answer as he leans back and stares me dead in the face.

"Class," he retorts, smirking.

I roll my eyes.

"Nothing wrong with my outfit." I push up my breasts inside my shirt, trying to make a point, and he coughs.

"Nope, not a thing, but I wasn't talking about the outfit. Clothes do not a classy lady make." He delivers his infinite wisdom, and I finish my drink off, head becoming seriously fuzzy. I've had a lot to drink, having downed several glasses faster than I normally would because, for *some* reason, my relaxing evening has become unexpectedly stressful.

"Well, you would know I suppose. You're certainly one classy lady." I look sideways at him as I gesture for another refill. Simon comes over after serving a few customers at the other end of the bar near the bathrooms.

"That guy over there wants your number—" Simon whispers in my ear, trying to be discreet.

Xion immediately squares his shoulders, staring down the length of the glowing surface scattered with dirty, clean, and half-filled glasses.

How the hell did he hear that?

I sigh, knowing that with Mrs Beefcake sitting beside me that there's no way any modern man in this club will even bother trying to approach me.

"It's cool, Simon. Thanks though. My Dad is here, as you can see, so I best behave myself." I gesture to Xion, hoping he can hear me and hoping that he gets the message.

Why the hell is he even here?

"Your Dad?" he whispers to me, "Really? After what you said about sleeping with me earlier?" I feel the hairs on the back of my neck stand up on end as his breath tickles my ear. He smirks.

"You're hot. A blind man could see that. I'm not apologising for having eyes. I just call it like I see it. Unfortunately for me though, I wasn't carrying my asshole detector when we first met. My mistake." I inhale more whisky like it's air, trying to ignore the sensations creeping over my arms at his proximity.

"You couldn't handle me anyway. I assure you," he murmurs under his breath, leaning back so he's bolt upright on his stool as my head snaps toward him in surprise.

"Is that a challenge?" I narrow my eyes, puckering my lips.

"No. Not at all. It's just the truth. I, too, call it as I see it."

He cocks his stupidly beautiful eyebrow and finishes the glass of water he's holding with a smirk still plastered on his face. "Anyway, let me know when you're finished and I'll get you home."

He slips down off the barstool and, navigating the space with far too much swagger for a man of his size, takes up residence in a booth behind the dancefloor. His molten irises glow in the dark, making me only too aware of his relentless presence.

I can feel his gaze burning into the back of my neck as I sit at a loss for what to do, and so scowl at my broken reflection.

I suppose I won't be picking up a guy tonight after all— not with him watching my every move.

Oh well.

I'll just have to settle for drinking myself stupid instead.

XION

I sit in the multicoloured booth with checked upholstery, a table topped with a giant vinyl record in front of me as I continue to watch her.

She's got her back to me and is talking to the barman, who I'm most certain has seen more of her than I want to picture mentally, but she knows I'm here. I can tell by the way she's purposefully not looking over her shoulder in defiance, which amuses me a great deal.

I slide my jacket off. The humidity of the air around me, full of tainted sweat and pheromones, causing me to overheat.

When that happens, nothing good ever follows.

I fiddle with the obsidian pendant hanging on a thick steel chain around my neck, feeling it cool as my irritation grows.

For some reason, whether it's some kind of ridiculous possessiveness from seeing those same cognac eyes wide and child-like in the past, or because bantering with her gives me some sick sexual thrill, every time a man so much as approaches her I feel myself having to pull back the darkness that makes up half of who I am.

I feel my true self stirring beneath the layers of leather and skin, wanting to rip out the throat of any rival who so much as assumes she is his.

This needs to stop.

She's not mine to protect. She's not even any of the things I would expect to find attractive, like sweet or kind. She's feisty as all hell and every single time she looks at me I feel a part of my soul scorched black by her stubborn, single-minded, mean streak.

Sighing, bored, I lean back into the too-bright faux leather of the seat, looking around the flashing multi-hued space. Things have certainly changed since I was a child. Back then, it was all swing and jive. Not this mashing together of skin and fluids that I find oddly repulsive.

I watch a couple slamming their faces into one another and cringe. It takes me back to my first, to the way I'd been so careless, or at least from what I remember. The only woman I've ever truly loved, the woman I decimated beyond what I'd known was even possible.

The flashes come in a torrent, unavoidable, reminding me once again why I never drink. I remember her face, contorted and terrified of me. Petrified of the one person she was supposed to be able to trust more than anyone else in a situation more intimate than any other. I don't allow her name to come to me, too ashamed to even speak it. I am not worthy.

As I'm dwelling on this, I notice that Sephy is now standing, finally having turned to face the rear of the room where I'm sitting. She's unsteady on her feet and her expression is aggravated as the disco lighting illuminates her too stark features. My senses prickle at her uncomfortable posture so I turn my attention to the man who's standing in front of her, looking half desperate, half aggressive.

Grabbing my jacket and throwing it over my shoulders, I lurch to my feet, taking the length of the club in only a few quick steps and spinning on a knife edge so I'm stood between Little Miss Sunshine and the guy seemingly harassing her.

"Excuse me," the guy with dark hair and limpid green eyes grumbles as I tower over him.

"Yes, excuse you. Get lost," I order him.

His expression turns heated with arrogance.

"I'm just talking to this pretty lady. We spent last night together, so it's not like I don't know she's easy. A real sparkplug— aren't you honey?"

Before I know what's happening, my fist is balled and flying toward his face. My knuckles connect directly with his nose, causing a spattering of blood to spray in spectacular slow motion as his head flies sideways, unable to stop the momentum of my enhanced strength.

"Woah! What the fuck?!" he yells, looking around to see if anyone else has noticed the altercation between us. I feel Sephy push herself around my broad width as my heart pounds in my chest and I try to get my spontaneous bout of rage under control.

"What the hell?!" Sephy exclaims, moving forward to comfort the guy who I've just hit defending her apparently non-existent honour.

My rage spikes at the entire situation, particularly her blatant disregard for her safety, and realise I need to get out of the club. I need to get into the cold night air and cool off, but there's no way in hell I'm leaving her here to do so.

Launching forward, I hook one arm around her curvy waist and heave her up over my shoulder. She's heavier than she looks, no doubt packed with muscle beneath her taut silky skin. She protests, kicking my abs and screaming, but this is lost on me as I focus only on getting out of the building with her in tow.

I pass the bartender who looks between us and smirks as I shoot him an unamused and tired glare, hearing him begin to laugh under his breath.

Regardless, I descend the stairs and people moving up into the loft of the club stare at us as we pass.

I don't care.

Sephy continues to kick and scream but I don't care about that either. She's going home, right now. Whether she likes it or not.

Stirring, I'm taken back to when I was a small child, a very small child, before the death and loss, to my birthdays. I always loved waking up on the morning of the anniversary of my birth because I knew the day was going to be full of good surprises.

My life now, though, is kind of like this but with a Russian roulette twist, partly because I could either wake up in bed alone after an amazing night or naked and chained to a lamppost. I can honestly never tell which it will be, but I guess that's part of the fun.

I open my eyes to find myself at home, surrounded by nothing but darkness. My shoes have been removed but my clothes from last night are still clinging to me as tight as they ever were. I look over at the clock on my nightstand— it's four in the morning.

Why the hell am I awake?

It takes me a few moments to begin to understand why I've stirred from my drunken stupor, realising quickly I'm feverish, my heart racing in my chest and my pulse thrumming in my veins like a rapper's beat. My head is pounding with the force of my blood rushing in a tidal wave of delayed intoxication, no doubt from the whiskey I put away like it was nothing more than the water Xion had so ridiculously ordered.

I try to remember how I got home, how I have ended up back here so early and alone, but my mind is blank, filled only with fire and red mist.

Getting to my feet, I can hear my heart still beating against the alabaster of my ribs like an angry prisoner against cell bars too loud in my ears. I start to panic, the gargantuan space I'm standing in suddenly shrinking.

The walls press in as the air becomes stifling and my breath comes only in shallow wisps, alluding me like a cheap and cruel magic trick.

Not knowing what to do or how to stop the feeling that my chest is being shrink-wrapped, I run from the room, bare feet slamming into the hardwood of the landing floor as I descend the stairs in a flurry of panic and anxiety that has come from nowhere.

I almost trip over my own legs as I reach the bottom stair and my foot catches the edge of the velvet runner. Stumbling forward and flying across the hall, my arms flail at my sides in an ungraceful leap as the dark corners of the mansion's lobby creep in closer.

I reach the front door, blood so close to the surface of my skin that I fear I might start bleeding from all open orifices. Slamming into the wood, I pray that they've been left unlocked.

As they buckle beneath my weight, I let out a shallow sigh and fall out into the cold rain.

The droplets fall like heavy bullets, merciless, and yet exactly what I need as they cool my rabid, blood-flushed skin. I'm panting like a wild animal being hunted, mind racing, muscles aching, body shuddering as I stand in the driveway and adrenaline refuses to cease its hold on me.

I fall forward, hands smashing into the gravel but not feeling any pain, trying to catch my breath but failing with every single inhale.

After a few moments, I realise that the cold night air isn't doing anything for my racing heart, so stumble to my feet once more, pushing up off the ground like a slow-motion sprinter and putting one foot in front of the other with unbearable effort.

I don't know where I'm going, what I'm doing, but I know that the gravel is hurting the bare skin of my feet, even if I can barely feel it. I hit the grass, the slick glaze of rain cooling my soles, and continue to run with sodden hair trailing in my wake.

Dashing across the grounds I have no idea where I'm running to, but I do know I'm terrified of stopping. Even worse, I'm terrified of the simple fact that in this moment I'm operating under no logic, only instinct.

So, I push onward.

I meet the line of the small forest which leads toward the road, trees rising on either side of me as the grass turns sparse, morphing instead to wet soil that reeks of wintergreen and pine. My feet bury in the dirt, cooling as I run on and on, further and further into the dark, over roots and through thickets, past tremoring spiderwebs and around fallen logs.

I run until I finally reach a clearing I didn't even know existed.

The tree is enormous, charred like it's been hit by lightning and terrifying in its twisted darkness. It is silhouetted against the dim light of the sinking crescent moon, and the base of it appears to be made up of two twisted trunks that bend into what could be a doorway. Instead, though, the doorway is filled in by whorls of solid wood. The roots of the tree sprawl, like snakes, through the dirt, and I trip over one, falling to the ground as it catches me unexpectedly by the ankle.

"Sephy?" My name echoes from the dark, a familiar and entirely unwelcome voice emitting from the dense shadow of the surrounding trees.

Xion, still dressed in the same long leather coat, jeans, and beater vest as earlier, reveals himself.

"You know—" I pant, "—this is starting to get creepy." I breathe heavily, heaving on all fours as his voice brings me back to myself.

My lungs expand, finally, taking in a substantial amount of air.

I sputter with relief.

"What are you doing out here?" he demands, a suspicious look on his masculine face.

"What are you doing here? And how did I get here?" I shoot questions back at him, standing up on bare feet and trying to calm my tattered nerves. The pounding in my head doesn't stop; instead, it gets slightly worse as I narrow my eyes, even the dim light painful to me now.

"You got drunk. A guy — he said his name was Brad — tried to take you home with him. I stopped him. Brought you back here," Xion explains, and I exhale heavily.

He clenches his fists as he takes another step forward, stilling as leaves crunch beneath his feet like he might scare me away.

I notice his central knuckle is bruised.

Suddenly, I find myself wondering if Brad is still breathing.

"Oh yeah, he's a friend— well, sort of. I met him last night," I explain, chest rising and falling in an irregular and painful rhythm.

"I'm sure you did. Well, I don't think you'll see him around much anymore." Xion smiles at me, though the sentiment doesn't reach his eyes.

"Is he— is he dead?" I ask, serious in my expression but unable to hide the absurd amusement in my tone.

"No. Of course not." He doesn't act like this is an unreasonable question, startling me.

"Look, I appreciate that you were hired and all, but really— I don't want a security guard. I'm happy to pay you for your time, but I'd just be appreciative if you could— you know, piss off." I use the most British slang I can think of as I feel a second wave of alcohol begins to take effect.

"I'm not the type of person you just dismiss. I'll go when I feel it is time." He's intimidating as he takes a few steps closer and grabs me by the elbow, trying to perp walk me back through the forest.

"Stop manhandling me! Jesus! You're an employee! You work for me! If I say you're fired, you're fired! Got it?" I yell this time, not feeling the cold of the surrounding air as I had before.

My temperature is rising again.

"Sephy, you're drunk and soaked. Let's go inside before you catch your death. Come on." He grabs me by the elbow again, and I shove him away this time, beyond pissed.

I stumble, not expecting him to be quite as heavy as he is, and scowl.

"How about you just get the hell out of my face and let me take care of myself? I was doing it long before you came along, and I'll be doing it long after you're gone," I spit, not even thinking about how my words might affect him.

He pats the inside pocket of his coat, feeling around for something and then seems satisfied as he lays his hand on a noticeable bulk beneath the leather just over his pectoral.

He doesn't say another word to me. He doesn't look angry or upset. He just turns and walks away into the shadows of the forest, leaving me standing under a stormy sky, hot, bothered, and jaded.

3

COLD AS ICE

PANDORA

RETURNING FROM THE OBSIDIAN shores of the Sea of Shadows, I take my final few steps from the portal. The intimidating silhouette of The Fallen Kingdom's only remaining building, The Halls of Antiqua, a sprawling, cathedral-esque structure, towers high against the bloody red sky of mid-morning. It's nestled in the shadow of the ominous volcano, Mount Mallum, that rises at a steep incline, shrouding the dark colosseum on the opposite side from view.

In the distance, beyond rotting gardens of native Mortarian flora, I can see the ruins of what had once been the beginning of a great and dark empire.

Unfortunately for the residents, that empire has long since turned to ash.

As soon as my feet hit the cracked stones of the ground, being transported in only seconds from the dunes of black crystal sand on which I have been standing for the last few hours, I continue to ponder the way the waves these days are becoming nothing if not choppy. They now shift at what can only be described as an ever-increasing and spontaneously furious rate.

It's almost as if Leviathan is stirring, and Kraken, his servant in this place, is gearing up for something big; though what, I couldn't tell you. I'm sure I'm not privy to the thoughts of such an old being, and even if I was, I don't do meetings with anything sporting tentacles, sort of a rule of mine.

Climbing the charred jasper of the crumbling steps rising from the edge of the building and ascending toward two enormous black doors, I hear Banshee screeching in the distance. I roll my eyes. The way they complain, you'd think they were nothing more than toddlers. As it is, they're powerful, primal beasts and really should know how to deal with hunger in a much quieter manner if you ask me.

Behind the enormous African blackwood doors, which swing open with the minimal effort of two Abraxian foot soldiers in human guise, I hear the clicking of my heels ring out with an unending echo around the cavernous and dimly lit hall. It's vast, with broken stained-glass windows that had once depicted mortal suffering. Chandeliers hang from the ceiling, holding candles burned down to the quick. They haven't been lit for years, leaving a chill, dank, darkness over the entirety of the building. Spider webs hang like grim party streamers between them, a thin veil of glistening white overhead.

At the end of the corridor, the hexagonal room where the Demon Lords meet, or should anyway, resides. That was the idea when they were created, but as with most creatures wielding great power, teamwork is far from a priority. Perhaps, this is yet another reason why today they are barely living.

Yet again, I exhale at this problematic fact, knowing that if I am to ever truly seize my revenge, I need to unify them under one cause.

However, it's been over a century, and I'm being used as nothing more than meals on wheels. Patience has certainly become a virtue of mine, and I often wonder if I wouldn't be better off taking my box and touring this widely interesting universe alone in search of better company.

I have done it before, seen all there is to see some might say, but as many different skies as I have lain under, as many different suns as I have watched rise over various horizons, I cannot get rid of the burning within my soul. I cannot flee from the desire to destroy him.

Striding the length of the ridiculously long hallway in quick time, I catch my reflection in the puddles of blood on the cracked and broken floor, left over from some Succubi lurking, I'm sure. It's twisted and vermillion, but my beauty is unmistakable. Long black flowing hair, dark violet eyes, and a stunning figure made only more beauteous by my wide Victorian hemline and tiny corseted waist. I am a Goddess among mortals cursed bold, banished from where I truly belong by the most misogynistic meathead you've ever seen with lightning bolts instead of brains.

The Higher Plains deserve better, truly.

Reaching the central meeting room, from where the wings that each Demon Lord occupies sprawl out in multiple directions, I find myself surrounded by— well, myself. Every wall of the hexagonal space is covered in mirrors with gaps only for doors, as though the Demon Lords had known they'd need to watch their backs during meetings from the very moment they'd been blessed by dark ancient gods.

They're a strange group, barely holding themselves together as a unit with the power-lust and bloodthirst between them, but somehow managing to anger one another at every opportunity, especially now that hunger is the main enemy some are trying and failing to overcome.

"Hello, Pandora." Lilliana's voice falls from the shadows encapsulating the far end of the room, and I spot her alabaster irises glowing dull in the dark against what should be the stark whites of her eyes.

The centre of the room is occupied by a round stone table, cracked in half with spider-webbing and bloodstains all over it, demonstrating more savagery than democracy.

"Lilliana," I greet her, nodding my head and trying not to blink. I know I'm superior to her. I know I had more power once, but as it is that power is gone, and all I'm left with is a lot of rage, a box, and my mighty wit.

"How was the beach?" Katerina's voice comes from the doorway behind Lilliana, as though they've both been waiting to pounce on me the second I arrive.

"Brisk." I recall the wind blowing my hair back from my face as I scrutinised each breaking wave and surface ripple.

"We were hoping you were going to kill something for us—" Lilliana gets to her feet, neck wrapped in dark fur, her hair backcombed and wild. Her face is almost skeletal, the skin stretches too thin over her skull, and tiny animal bones hang from her earlobes and around her wrists, sick adornments of death.

Katerina saunters forward next into the dimmest light, her low-cut burgundy corset pushing into her ribcage so hard that it looks as though her collarbone might burst from beneath her tumbling locks of glistening raven hair and turn weapon instead. Scarlet pupils illuminate her face in a bloody hue, only exaggerating her pallor and deepening the shadows cast by her cheekbones and chasmic eye sockets, made abyssal by the onyx surrounding her bright irises. Her deep crimson lips pull back in an unimpressed grimace, revealing two jagged incisors as an instant threat.

"Our Kindred are hungry," Lilliana snaps, bearing forward on the cracked stone of the table, shoulder blades rising in steep dual peaks.

"And what, exactly, do you propose I do about that? You know I've suggested taking back your hunting grounds a hundred times. But Abraxis, Gorgon, and Barbas don't agree. They don't think we have the— resources required." I remind them of my stance on taking back what is rightfully theirs, and their expressions both settle back into mild irritation.

"Yes well, they do not know the hunger. The desperation— the cannibalism among our Kindred— it is— harrowing to behold." Katerina swallows deeply, as though the thought of the Sanguine Forest alone is enough to send her over the table and her teeth inch deep into my carotid in one swift motion.

"I have tried to persuade them. You know I have tried. They are— resistant." I choose the final word of this sentiment carefully, never quite sure who is listening in this unending labyrinth of chilling echoes and screams.

"That's all very well, but what are we supposed to do? Our children— they cry. The torment— it is unbearable to a mother." Lilliana narrows her eyes, trying to implore my sympathy.

I know what they are implying. What they want from me. But I am unsure whether I am willing to give it.

Every time I let them feed upon mortals, it is a risk. I am risking exposure to those from whom I have made such effort to hide, and this isn't the first time I've been close to being discovered either.

I think back to when that half-breed had been discovered— what's his name again?

Xion. That's it.

I had been a fool, thinking Abraxis would lend me his forces for merely allowing him to go among the mortals and seduce their women, and it had nearly gotten me exposed and targeted as a result.

I look between the two women as their dark hair casts further shadow upon them, turning them even more formidably demonic as they mull it over.

While it is a risk, every day the Banshee and Succubi go hungry is another day that the forces I already have on my side weaken, fight among themselves, and die for fresh meat, even if their method of attaining it is cannibalistic.

"It will have to be discreet. Only a few can go. Your weakest," I concede, reaching into the deep pocket of my skirt and pulling out the dark wooden box with a tree burned into the side facing me. I hold it in my hands, my limited power exposed before them as they visibly relax and exhale.

It is with this that I know I've made the right decision.

"Gather them," I order, my evident power over them and their kindred making me bold.

They smile wicked smiles and leave the room to collect their weakest, hungriest children, and I take a seat at the cracked table, skirt billowing around me as I wait patiently for feeding time.

SEPHY

Jules knocks his familiar rhythm on the door and my head pounds. I would normally throw Ol' Faithful, but this morning I'm just not in the mood.

"You can come in, Jules," I sigh, instantly regretting it as the thudding in my temples worsens. You'd think I'd be used to it by now, but apparently not.

Jules pokes his head around the side of the door, tentative in his motion as though I may be waiting to throw my pocketknife directly at him. He's surprised to find me sitting up in bed, fully awake with Cerb at my feet. I still haven't been able to find sleep again after my little jaunt into the woods last night.

"You're awake early," he observes in surprise, dark brows rising suddenly on his large forehead.

"I'm awake still," I admit, looking down at my muddy feet. I'm surrounded by my duvet, freezing, and I'm beginning to wonder if I should've dried off before climbing back into bed in rain-soaked clothes.

Maybe Xion was right after all.

I feel something I'm not used to for a fraction of a second; guilt.

The night is coming back to me in fragments, and as I recall how persistent Brad had been getting, I'm reluctantly grateful for Xion's intervention. I'm also feeling guilty for yelling at him.

"You might want to think about catching up on your rest and cancelling with Jacque this morning if that's the case. Your uncle just informed me that he's called a meeting to introduce you to the board of directors."

He sets down the tray with my usual breakfast on it, but I feel oddly uninterested in eating anything. I wrap the duvet around myself tighter, goosebumps prickling my skin.

"Seriously? I signed the damn papers, and now I have to make nice with a bunch of suits? Why can't I just sell the damn company?!" I exclaim, wondering if I might throw up as the room begins to spin on an invisible axis.

"Your father came from nothing, Persephone. He'd be turning in his grave at the thought of you handing off his hard work to someone else," his reply stings like an ice bath, and I feel his judgemental gaze burn into me, especially as he uses my legal name which he full well knows I hate.

"I don't feel well anyway. Can't we reschedule or something?" I ask, pulling my legs up under my chin tighter, trying to keep in the fleeting heat.

"You think your uncle will reschedule this after the problems he had getting you to sign those contracts? For a hangover? I'm going to be calling up Oxford and getting a refund. We paid them good money to make sure you didn't turn out stupid." He's sassy this morning and I wonder why. He's my employee. Why the hell does he care so much?

"This isn't just a hangover; you know those don't stop me. Honestly, I feel horrendous. I think I might be getting the flu or something," I whine, and he looks at me with a deadpan expression.

"Pulling a sickie isn't going to work this time. Peter will have Xion in here dragging you down the stairs by your hair if you're not careful. He's frustrated because you refuse to cooperate." He's giving me a lecture now, and so I snap, body shuddering with an unwanted chill as it plays slalom down my spine.

"Look, just run me a bath. I don't need advice from you." I scowl and turn from him, closing my eyes and giving my mind sweet relief from the overload of light and sound. He doesn't reply or complain. He just walks up the shallow steps into my bathroom and begins to fill the tub with boiling water in tense silence.

After a few minutes filled only by the sound of running water, he leaves the room without so much as another word. I know I've upset him. The problem is, he wants to be my father; he loves me. But he's not my father; he's my butler and I pay him to make my life easier, not lecture me.

Scrambling out of bed, I keep the duvet wrapped around me, letting it trail on the floor until I reach the bathtub. Examining the scene before me, I let my eyes settle on the grounds beyond my bathroom window for a moment as a team of gardeners cut the grass and prune the rose bushes surrounding the building. I gaze beyond them to the forest, to where I'd run last night and where I found the most gothic-looking tree I've ever seen.

Maybe I hallucinated it or concocted it in a dream, but from the dry mud stuck to the bottom of my unwashed feet, I'd say not.

Bracing myself, I shed my cocoon, letting it fall to the marble of the floor as I strip off my still-damp clothes. Hurrying as quickly as I can, I ready myself to step into the hot water.

I plunge into the depths of the tub, not even faltering as the burning liquid touches my skin. I sigh out, warm finally, but only for a few minutes before the chill returns with an unexplainable edge despite the steam curling in the air, fogging the windowpanes.

I sit back, exhausted, as though someone is physically dragging the energy from my bones. I mean, I know I haven't slept, but I've done more on less before.

Why the hell do I feel so drained?

Is it this business? Knowing now I've got a long hard road littered with responsibility and a million decisions to make, or is it something more? Do I feel that badly about having yelled at Xion last night?

No.

The answer rings in my ears and I know it's true. I'm a little guilty sure, but not enough to warrant feeling physically ill.

I run my long fingernails across my skin, feeling the goosebumps rising over every inch of my body. I'm flushed red, a sign that usually means I'm warm at least, but today I just sit here and shiver, trying not to throw up.

Attempting to relax, I lean back so I'm neck-deep in the still-steaming water before closing my eyes and attempting to let everything that's changing around me go. Trying to forget about Xion's feral gaze as he moved in to protect me last night, trying to forget Peter's smug grin as I'd signed the contracts binding me forever to my father's financial legacy, and trying most of all to forget how my skin is crawling right here this very moment.

As my mind empties far too slowly, I feel a sudden pull at something within my gut.

An urge.

I sit up in the bathtub, water sloshing over the edge, and stand, unable to sit still any longer.

Cerb perks up at my meercat-esque motion, rising onto all fours and watching me anxiously.

It's like a trance, a frenzy in my blood, the one I felt for the first time last night. The chill disappears, and in moments I'm warming like a small candle has flickered to life in my gut.

Stepping out of the bath, I don't know where I'm going, I just know I want more. More heat, more warmth, more fire.

Placing a pair of black silk pyjamas over my still sodden body and not even stopping to dry myself, I proceed out into the hallway, dripping on the wooden floor as Cerb trots behind me.

With every step I take, I become less in tune with the outside world, the only audible sound my blood pounding inside my skull. I trail across the landing to the upper east wing, feet moving of their own accord, one in front of the other. My hair leaves a trail of droplets behind me on the runner, turning it intermittently dark.

I turn down a corridor I never frequent, mainly because Peter's office and suite lie at the end of the hall, and as I step around the corner, the heat beneath my skin grows. My pulse heightens, my strength returning fractionally, giving me incentive enough to keep moving forward.

The corridor holds very little, other than a few doors to the old library, collections of antiques in storage, and a few spare rooms filled with my parents' things that I cannot bring myself to sort through. Cerb licks my hand, but I shrug him away, uninterested in anything other than following the call haunting me.

There is, however, something out of place in all this, something I've never noticed as being obviously misplaced. Now I'm walking toward it though, it's sticking out like a virgin in a strip club.

I turn to face the bookcase, looking at the titles stacked on its shelves and cocking my head.

There's a library right next door with plenty of space, so why is this here?

I read the spines, one by one, but only one truly pulls my interest.

Placing a finger on the top of Dante's *'Paradise Lost'*, I pull. The heat grows more intense within my veins.

As I remove the book from the shelf, the entire thing moves backwards, and Cerb barks, revealing a room I haven't known existed until this very second.

I'm not surprised— I mean, I mainly use this place as a hotel and leisure centre between drinking binges, but still, a hidden door is kind of cool for a stuffy old mansion like this.

Stepping inside, I seek a source of light. It seems there are no windows and no doors other than the entrance where I'm standing. I find a light switch on the wall near the doorframe as my hand instinctively reaches out and traces the wall.

Flicking it, the interior is revealed in showroom intensity lighting.

It's a tiny space, a secret space, and the focal point of the room is unmistakable. In the centre of it all, enveloped by a glass case and erected on a pedestal, a blade made entirely of fire opal is displayed, glistening rainbow-coloured in the too-white light. The walls are deep black, and the carpet is a similar jade green to the corridor outside, putting all focus on the knife.

What the hell is this? I wonder, unable to tear my gaze from the weapon. Taking a few steps forward, I lean down to gaze into the case and examine the blade.

As I let its razor-sharp opalescent edge ingrain itself into my mind, I have the undeniable instinct to seize it. It *needs* to be in my palm. It's beyond beautiful, and it should be wielded by me and me alone.

I reach out to remove the glass, but before I can so much as lay a finger on it, a voice rings out behind me, breaking the trance it has over me and causing me to jump.

"Persephone. Don't touch that." Xion's voice comes rough and deep as his shadow appears in the corridor beyond the door frame. I look back at him, my hair dripping cool water down my breasts, making me even more desperate to fuel the fire within my veins by continuing to obey.

"Why? What is this?" I demand, curious. I'm relieved by his presence, and I realise I must have been more anxious than I thought.

"You don't know what it is. You shouldn't touch what doesn't belong to you, especially if it's in a case like that. It's hidden for a reason I'd assume," he warns, but I only shrug.

Not breaking his gaze, I ball up my fist and slam it, knuckles first, through the glass.

I reach out as he continues to stand in the doorway, not trying to stop me as I refuse to diminish the intensity of my stare. Hopefully, this is because by now he's realised standing between me and what I want is futile. Then, I wonder if he told me not to take the blade knowing I'd do the opposite and pause with my fingers only inches away from the solid gold handle as blood runs up my forearm and down my wrist.

Cerb looks between both of us with wide and curious eyes.

"I can protect you from a lot you know— but I can't protect you from yourself." Xion's voice wields an edge of brokenness, but his expression remains stoic and cool. It causes a wave of sudden anger to come over me, my hand lurching forward inside the case, bloodied fingers claiming the hilt of the blade without second thought.

Heat shoots up my arm, radiating throughout me and chasing the chill I'd been fighting from every inch of my skin. My muscles tighten and my heart races as something I cannot explain takes hold of my body, removing the pain I've felt all morning and energising me entirely within seconds. I don't know what's happening to me, or why, but I know beyond a shadow of a doubt this blade is *mine*.

"I don't need your protection. I never asked for it, and I don't want it either," I inform him, one eyebrow cocked.

He turns from the doorway but looks back over one shoulder, shaking his head.

"Good for you."

4

FIRESTARTER

SEPHY

I STILL FEEL CRAPPY, though I'm no longer shivering, but instead playing the part of a menopausal woman. I flash hot like someone's put gasoline in my veins and is using my nervous system to spark a blaze. Lying flat on my bed, hair strewn bloody amongst pale pillows, I close my eyes and try to relax.

I never get sick. Ever. And it's not as if it's even a good time as today I have a director's meeting. The appointment encroaches faster and faster with each chime of the grandfather clock down the hallway, irritating me immensely.

Cerb is lying at my feet, chest rising and falling dramatically as he watches me with an anxious gaze. Even he can tell I'm not feeling right, and he's a dog for Christ's sake.

A knock at my door startles us both, and the Leonberger launches himself off the bed, claws scratching hard against the wooden door only moments later. He rises on his hind legs, overly excited as a puppy, and barks so deeply I can feel the air around me vibrate.

"Come in," I call, making sure the opal blade is stashed under my pillow beside my pocket knife.

I sit up, flushed and sweating.

"I just wanted to make you aware that the directors will be here in one-hour, Ma'am," Jules says with a brisk, snappy tone before spinning and exiting the room again without so much as a pause to wait for my usual sarcastic reply.

I sigh, I must have really hurt his feelings earlier.

Why do I keep doing that lately?

"Well, Cerb, at least you still love me," I mutter.

Cerb gives me an odd look before bounding out the door and after Jules, who whistles for him, no doubt to feed him his evening meal.

I roll my eyes.

Get a dog they said. They're so loyal they said. Loyal my ass.

Getting up from the bed, still wearing my black silk pyjamas from earlier, I walk over to the open door and close it softly. My hair is un-styled and ratty after drip drying naturally, and I cringe as I walk past my reflection in the floor-length mirror attached to the door of my walk-in closet.

Slumping down on a plush pink loveseat positioned at the back of the closet, I look over my selection of clothes, wondering what is appropriate to wear when being forced to attend a meeting with the directors of your own billion-dollar company. It's a wonder, in fact, that Chanel or Gucci don't have a line specifically for this kind of occasion named *'for formal shit you don't want to do'*. I suppose they're the kind of people who love getting dressed up and making nice with a bunch of stuck-up strangers in too-tight suits.

Then it occurs to me. I have the suit I graduated in.

I can wear that.

Standing, I pick the garment bag out of the mass of black hanging from the railing against the opposing wall, remembering the long walk across the stage to collect my doctorate. I had worked hard for that piece of paper— not that I needed it, but I'd wanted it. It was a challenge, and I love the ancient myths, stories about times when sass, personality, and hard graft were enough to get you a place in the hall of fame without needing a bunch of paper with some old guy's face on it.

Throwing the garment bag over the back of the loveseat, I grab a hairbrush from the vanity next to the door and ponder on how I should present myself.

Do I even care about this meeting?

I think back to Jules' words about my dad turning in his grave. It had stung me, cut into me, but maybe that's because I know he is right. My mother and father hadn't been happily married. I remember that at least, because my father had rarely been home, and my mother felt neglected. Nonetheless, he'd sacrificed the family life she desired to give us all financial security, to give me the childhood and future he never had. He wanted me to be taken care of, to have all the advantages I could because he knew only too well that the world can be a cruel place. He also knew too well, while I may loathe it, that money keeps you safe.

It keeps you *free* in the loosest sense of the word.

Maybe I need to do this, then. If not for me, for my parents. They brought the company this far, so maybe I can bring something of my own to it. I'm a smart woman, and I usually achieve whatever I set my mind to, so why not this? Maybe I can turn the corporate world on its head from the inside. Make a difference. Do some good. Maybe I can make my parents proud, even though they're gone.

Giving myself a determined look in the mirror, I begin to brush out my hair, sweeping it from my face and attempting to look semi-professional. This isn't what I wanted, but I need to make the best of it regardless, and that starts with looking the part.

I gloss my lips with a neutral shade that I barely ever touch, finding it too subtle for my usual style. I pull my fiery hair up in a high ponytail and button a black silk blouse over a matching bra and panties before pulling on wide-legged suit pants and a tight-fitting jacket which exaggerates my cleavage. I finish the look with a black lace choker because I can't totally lose myself in all this sophistication, and apply light mascara and foundation, bringing my face back to faux life despite the pallor and dark circles beneath my eyes.

Slipping on a pair of black stilettos I take a deep breath, knowing I need to be an adult for at least an hour, for the sake of my family name. With this boring truth clear to me now, I turn to leave my suite.

Outside the door, Xion stands, arms crossed over his chest, in a wide stance, ready to come in and pull me out by my hair as Jules had suggested earlier. He's been staring so intensely into the wood of the door I'm surprised he's not burned a hole right through it, and as it pulls back, revealing me, his eyes widen.

"You're ready, and on time— This is— shocking to say the least." He cocks his head, as though I am the world's most complex entity.

"Thanks for your confidence in me," I grumble, stalking through the doorway and out into the hall.

He follows, tread heavier than an elephant's. Clearly, stealth is not his forte. "You know for a security guard, you're the least covert person I've ever met?" I round on him, almost crashing into his chest. He doesn't see the move coming and is tailing me so close I can practically feel his breath on the back of my neck.

"Yeah, well, for an heiress, you're the most miserable," he retorts. I shake my head.

"I'm not miserable, I'm frustrated that I have some six-foot-four mountain troll following me around like freaking big foot. It's annoying as hell, and I'm trying to focus on what to say at this stupid meeting that I'm being perp-walked to." I scowl and his mouth twists as if he wants to laugh but doesn't want to let me know I've amused him. His eyes sparkle bronze through gold and back again as he stares at me.

Turning away, I'm determined not to let him know just how attractive I find him.

Reaching the end of the hallway in silence, I notice that he's fallen back.

Well, at least he knows how to follow instructions. Maybe I should speak my orders to him in hilarious metaphors alone. Maybe sarcasm is his native language. I muse.

"You look nice by the way. I'm pleasantly surprised," I hear him say under his breath, like he's too nervous or afraid to speak up, but my ears catch it, and I spin.

"A compliment? From you? I must be on par with freaking Angelina Jolie. Oh, and remind me never to wear this suit again."

I storm off, using the quip as a sort of repellent force and hoping it leaves him with whiplash.

As I reach the top of the staircase and fall back onto my kitten heel.

Below in the lobby, the suits have assembled in full boring-ass force. I can tell already that they're going to be the most effective sleeping aid in the world and wonder momentarily if my company should start employing them as voiceovers for those sleep-by-hypnosis tapes.

I bet we'd make a killing.

Descending, and all eyes rise to me, but no one looks more surprised than Peter. He doesn't smile, looking oddly upset about the entire demeanour that has fallen over me in an icy cold and entirely uncomfortable shower of badass propriety and decorum.

"Please welcome Dr Sephy Sinclair," I hear Jules announce from my left. Beside the newel, I find him serving ice water on a silver tray and catch a look in his eyes which tells me that everything between us is forgiven.

He looks proud.

"Please, call me Miss. Doctor makes me feel old," I plead and the crowd bursts into forced laughter. I smile politely, but inside I'm dying, mainly because what I've said isn't even funny; it's just the truth.

Let the race to crawl up my ass begin.

I let out a discreet sigh, looking to Peter for instruction as he moves to usher the crowd into the conference room in the east wing. It all happens very quickly, partly because I'm sure he thinks I'm going to flee the premises at any given opportunity.

We turn into the spacious room, my ballet studio from when I was a child, which has been transformed into where the meeting will be held. The entire space is a mix of pale polished wood, white walls lined with mirrors, and large floor-to-ceiling glass windows which look out over the grounds of the estate.

The sun is falling through the sky, and twilight approaches in an orangey-red glow muted by black swirling clouds. The bloody shadow refracted from every mirror casts the lengthy mahogany conference table, surrounded by leatherback chairs, in a hellish light. This is entirely fitting when you think about it.

"Let's be seated," Peter instructs, ushering me forward and towards the seat at the head of the table. I note with irritation that it's furthest away from the door.

As the suits file in behind us, Cerb makes an appearance, blundering through the door and coming to sit in the corner of the room. He watches over the meeting with a suspicious gaze.

Maybe he isn't so disloyal after all.

Peter exits, but Xion positions himself just inside the doors as they close, blocking me inside with the directors of my own company.

I swallow hard, watching as they ruffle pages, pull pens from the inside of their finely tailored jackets, and sip water which has been provided in tall, pristine glasses.

They look at me expectantly, and I realise I suddenly have no idea what the hell this meeting is even about.

"Hi," I introduce myself again, giving a small wave and wondering exactly what it is they expect. "I'll be totally honest. I have no idea why we're all here. Anyone want to enlighten me?" I try to pull back the cocky in my tone, but it's difficult, especially when they all have vacant glazed expressions like they've been zombified.

"Um, hi— Miss Sinclair. I'm Glen. We're here to let you know where your company investments lie. What industries we're currently growing in or pulling out of. That kind of thing." The fresh-faced suit smiles at me, the youngest of the group by far. I'm grateful for his assistance, but my annoyance that I'm in this situation in the first place is beginning to heighten again to boiling point.

"Right, so tell me. Where do my investments lie?" I ask, sitting back in the chair and propping my feet up on the table as the group jumps, alarmed by my heels on the wood.

I put my hands behind my head, leaning back and eyeing them casually.

"Well— we have the diamond market of course. We are still dominant, though coloured diamonds are coming into fashion in quite a big way, so we're looking to expand there—" says a balding man with a thin face and grey eyes in the most boring yet pointed tone I can imagine. The man next to him picks up right after him, not giving me a chance to draw breath before moving on.

"We're also buying several more vineyards in southern California and checking out numerous other sites in Italy at the moment," a man with thick grey hair, pulled back into a low ponytail, adds.

"Wine— Diamonds— what else?" I demand, wondering exactly how far the Sinclair fortune has spread.

How many markets will I be operating in?

I haven't ever asked about what's going on with the business, mainly because I'm not interested. It's true that even in the UK, I've seen my family name spattered across a wide variety of products, but I've mainly tried to stay out of it all, happy with my allowance and freedom.

The group of suits shuffle in their seats as I stare between them.

Glen takes the initiative and coughs before speaking the truth I don't want to hear.

"This, Miss Sinclair, could take a while."

"So, you're telling me— I own what? *Everything?*" I ask them after several hours, cocking my eyebrow and sighing as I look over the millions of pieces of paper strewn across the conference table.

"Not everything, but a lot," Glen corrects me, looking nervous as I sigh for what feels like the thousandth time.

"So— what does that mean for me?" I demand, wanting an honest answer but severely doubting I'll get it.

"Well, it can mean whatever you want it to. The company has been running without you for quite some time. We have things in place and people who are excellent at their jobs. If you want to be involved, you can be as involved as you wish, or you can just let us handle things and keep watching cash fall into your various accounts and trusts every month. Of course, if you want control over how your family name is used, I suggest you be as involved as possible."

The man with the long grey ponytail, who I now know is called Jefferson, replies this time. He's the head of the wine branch of the sprawling business, and I wonder momentarily what to do. On the one hand, I like my freedom, but on the other hand, my family name is attached to this, and I have never truly known how far my father's influence has spread. I don't want the responsibility here, it's true, but I also don't want his legacy dragged through the mud; the thought is too painful to bear.

"Well, I—" I begin, but Cerb lets out a loud, deep, bark followed by a feral sounding growl. It's not like him at all.

I turn as Xion shifts, for the first time in hours I might add, from his statue-esque position in front of the doors.

Cerb is sat upright in the corner, ears pricked forward and teeth bared. I look around the room for anything he could be growling at, but quickly realise it's probably a stray cat or the scent of one of the director's dogs that is making him agitated.

I stare him down for several long moments, asserting my dominance, and he doesn't bark again. Looking at me with wide brown eyes, he seems to have calmed.

I turn back to the group, trying to remember what it was I was going to say, but as I open my mouth to speak the dog barks again, this time in an urgent and unmistakable warning.

I turn to silence him, embarrassed by his lack of obedience after he's been so good all afternoon, when the sound of smashing glass pierces the air and my breath catches in my throat.

I wrench around in my seat as Cerb launches forward from behind me, flying through the air as though he weighs nothing. I follow his course with wide eyes, watching as he meets some kind of enormous, dirty, white wolf, head-on.

As the two beasts collide, smashing together in a frenzy of teeth and jaws, the entire conference room falls into terrified chaos.

Glass showers down around us like rain, moonlight refracting at all angles from its broken edges. I stand, not sure of what to do as Xion becomes a blur before my eyes, pulling the conference table back off its legs and shoving the directors behind it, using it as a barricade.

Unable to move in my terror, I gape as the wolf and Leonberger continue to scrap. I hear the screams of men, the pounding of my heartbeat rapid in my ears. However, all this is eclipsed as Cerb smashes one of his enormous paws into the wolf's stark alabaster eye, and it emits a scream so deafening I'm instantly certain my eardrums are imploding.

The mirrors fixed to the walls explode inward, reflective glass splintering and ricocheting from wall to wall and ceiling to floor as the sound hits in a merciless tsunami of pain.

I see Cerb, cowering as the beast nears him, but before I can react Xion dashes toward it, a black twisted dagger in his palm. His expression is pained, angry, as though he's trying to restrain himself for some reason, and I find myself transfixed as his chest rises and falls in forced, slow time.

How is he so calm?!

My dog is cowering close to the ground, whining, seeking my comfort as I stand paralysed, a sudden and unexpected rage blooming like a mushroom cloud in my gut. The adrenaline in my veins ignites like gasoline with the rapid firing of synapses.

It comes from my palms, but I don't know how. I don't know why.

Flames crawl out like vines, creeping forward and slashing through the air, extending intuitively towards the flesh of the beast who's intruded on my home.

Cerb runs back to me, tail between his legs as I try to focus, keeping my palms raised instinctively, my brain shutting off as I act without thought, afraid that logic will make me vulnerable.

Not sure what I'm doing, I kick off my heels, watching as the trails of fire wrap themselves around the wolf's shaggy limbs, causing it to scream out again.

I need to stop the noise, to end it. I can hear the men behind me cowering, fearing for their lives, as the pale monstrosity rears.

With a group effort, they pull the table closer to them as the beast takes a few steps forward, six-inch-long claws leaving gashes in the wooden floor splintering beneath its tread. As it approaches, I realise that I must protect the directors. If anything happens to them, I really will have no hope of understanding how to run this company on my own or have the option to palm it off on strangers.

Xion is no longer looking at the monster, preparing to strike as he twizzles the blade between his fingers, but has turned to face me as I power forward.

His expression turns stunned as he stills, motionless amid the chaos.

My bare feet are cut to ribbons by shattered glass and mirrors as I claw my way up onto the haunches of the wolf in one agile leap, wrapping my legs around the girth of its enormous neck as it bucks like a pissed-off stallion, trying to throw me to the floor. I inhale the scent of rot and decay from its matted fur and fight the desire to wretch, wishing only for the luxury of a bucket to vomit in.

It's not all that different from mounting Nightshade when she's in a strop, and so I find my rhythm atop the bucking beast, closing my eyes and nostrils, imploring myself to find focus.

Xion isn't moving, isn't intervening as I look to him for aid. Instead, he's simply staring, too stunned at my unexpected bravery to spring into any kind of action.

I bring my arms around the creature's neck and pull its head sharply to the left without thought or even a real awareness of the brutality of what I'm doing, bringing my focus back onto the immediacy of the threat. I hear a sharp crack, and relief falls like hot rain, my skin scorching as adrenaline continues to shoot through me like I've injected it right into the vein.

I try to master the too-red flames as they fill the room with black billowing smoke and the smell of burning hair. They cut into the legs of the fatally wounded monstrosity beneath me, the scent bringing back the wisp of a memory long forgotten. A sense of panic I've never quite forgotten threatens to overtake me at the proximity of the fire.

The wolf falls to the floor and the flames devour it within seconds, leaving only ash behind. As my fear grows larger than my gall, the flames extinguish in a blink, as though they were never there at all.

Xion looks at me with wide eyes, mouth agape as moonlight and silence falls over everything.

Feeling a little giddy, not to mention like I need a stiff drink, I get to my feet, having fallen amongst the piles of glass and ash as the beast beneath me disintegrated as though it was a bad dream.

Perhaps it had been. Perhaps I'm so bored of all this money talk that I invented a monster wolf attack for my own entertainment.

I mean, that does sound like something I would do—

I scan the terrified eyes of men in glass-peppered suits, staring at me like I'm the real monster, and then turn to Xion who is still standing, watching me in silence. His knuckles remain white around the hilt of the dark blade.

Walking past him, I pat his shoulder and exit the room, still in utter shock and complete disbelief as I call back,

"Thanks for the help. I couldn't have done it without you, really."

XION

The tinkling of glass reaches my ears as several of the directors stand up, looking between me, the pile of ash on the floor, and then the broken window. Through it, a cool breeze is now whistling.

"What— what was that?" the youngest one, Glen, asks with a shaking voice and trembling hands as he brushes down his expensive jacket.

"A wolf. A hybrid species no doubt," I reply, looking at them all with a serious gaze. "I suggest you all head home now. We need to get this cleaned up. The meeting will have to continue another time." It takes all my effort to remain calm enough to explain. My blood is roaring in my ears, and I can feel the demon part of me straining against the confines of my skin, clawing at my insides in an attempt to break free. To fight. To kill.

Yet, I'm standing here, holding the blade I usually fight with so hard that my knuckles are white. I'm clutching a single shard of obsidian, twisted cruelly into a cutting edge, yet I've done nothing.

She doesn't need defending. She doesn't need me, or anyone. Her palms did something I've only seen one other person attempt, and there's no way in hell that she can be related to him—

Is there?

When I saw her earlier, hand outstretched, reaching for the opal knife that glowed with a power only my demon half could see, I wondered why she looked so dazed, so dreamy in her expression. Could it be that what she had found in that secret room wasn't something new, but something old? Something taken from her?

I hear the door behind me open as the men leave in shocked silence with tentative treads. Cerb, the enormous dog that leapt to Sephy's defence quicker than I could, follows them out, clearly fearful of staying in the room.

I look at the ashes, at the glass, at the mirrors which are no more, and know that I've just witnessed a Banshee attack. There's no doubt about it. No creature from this world could produce a scream like that, regardless of genetic tampering.

Staring out through the now glassless window, I squint out into the moonlit grounds as I step over the sill, climbing through and jumping down onto the damp lawn.

Treading cautiously out into the dark, I check for more Banshee, aware they usually hunt in packs. Then it occurs to me that they might have gotten in through The Hollow, however ridiculous that sounds. I mean, we have The Hollow guarded around the clock, but somehow my father had found his way into this dimension to make me, so they're obviously finding ways to use it somehow. I mean, there's no other way to travel between Mortaria and the mortal world— or at least none that I know of.

Reaching the front line of trees, I think back to that night again, the night I saved her from the fire that killed her family. It was an accident. Sparks catching on the antique rug from the upstairs fireplace, wasn't it?

I sigh, wishing I'd been there when the fire started. I could have done more, saved them all, but as it was, I was only there as a debt collector to scare her father.

As I reach The Hollow, I catch Banshee tracks in the damp earth and more than one set by the looks of things. I walk around the perimeter of the woods, mind cast back further to the deals Adam Sinclair made before his daughter was born. About how he traded the thing my master wanted most for money and material objects, which if you ask me matter little. Could it be that perhaps Persephone Sinclair's lineage is more colourful than I've previously known? Than anyone has previously known?

Frowning, the night sky above bears down on me, making me feel small. The Banshee tracks stop as I follow them back to the front of the forest where the trees begin to thin, claw marks unmistakable in the earth.

The light shining from the destroyed ballet studio acts as a beacon as I stalk the edge of the shadowy copse, but here is where only one set of tracks continue. The others probably turned and disappeared shortly afterwards.

But how? I wonder, heartbeat heavy in my chest.

Everything is becoming shrouded in mystery far too quickly, and where I can't get answers on how a pack of Banshee seem to have disappeared into thin air, I think I can get answers about the Sinclairs, about why they still haven't appeared in Golgotha after all this time.

Peter Smith had been appointed to the Sinclair family as next of kin to watch their only remaining heir and had promised, all those years ago, to make sure the debt they owe to Mortaria will be repaid. It has been his responsibility to ensure that, as their remaining heir, Sephy will inherit their riches and their penance. It is vital to avoid tilting the balance of our universe unfavourably if their unexplainable lack of appearance in the underworld continues.

Perhaps though, he hasn't played as big of a role in Sephy's life as I'd thought, or maybe he knows more than he's letting on and is keeping things from The Nexus on purpose.

Either way, it's time to find out.

5

GIVE IT UP

SEPHY

SITTING ON THE QUARTZ steps that lead up to my bathroom, I stare down at my shaking hands. My long dark fingernails become blurred by my inability to calm myself.

What the hell just happened?

I take a few moments to ponder this as Cerb appears around my door, which I've left wide open, not even thinking to shut it. He gives me a terrified stare, and I beckon him, ignoring the fact that my feet are bleeding out onto the cool rose stone and my entire body is on fire.

The Leonberger bounds across the lilac carpet, his weight making deep thuds on impact as he whines. He sits before me and licks his lips so I can place my hands around his neck, burying my face in his thick fur and letting out a deep breath. His presence brings a feeling of slight relief for the first time since before the attack.

It was the biggest wolf I've ever seen, wrong in colour and expression, unnatural almost, and that scream, if you can even call it that—Well, it was enough to wake the dead.

The mere memory of the noise is torment.

Nuzzling Cerb, the silence covers me like a blanket, folding over me in soft layers and comforting me as reality seems so suddenly brittle, so fragile; like a mere whisper can shatter it all.

After a few minutes of cuddling Cerb, who is shaking slightly, I realise that I'm probably overreacting. The wolf was strange looking, sure, but with the amount of evidence to support off-the-record genetic experimentation in this country, I'm not surprised that something like this has happened.

It was a freak accident. Nothing more. Nothing less.

Maybe I imagined the fire; maybe I was too terrified and too caught in the moment to know what I was seeing or doing. Like one of those women who finds herself able to lift the weight of a car when her child's life depends on it— yeah, that's probably it.

Pulling my hair down from its high ponytail, I glance down at my bloody feet. I probably need to get them bandaged, but in examining them closer and pulling out several shards of glass, I see the shallow cuts have already clotted and are feeling much better thanks to the cool of the stone steps. I stand, a wince overtaking my face, and shake out my hair, letting it tumble in fiery waves over my shoulders.

I need a drink.

A *big* one.

I call out, "Jules!" several times, before realising that turning him down when he offered me one of those little silver service bells was probably a dumb idea.

Sighing, I make my way out of the room, frustrated that my personal stash of whisky has mysteriously disappeared. Well, I say mysteriously, but I honestly can't recall if I finished the last of it late one night and was too drunk to remember, or if my overprotective butler has confiscated it while I've been out dancing.

I step gently along the corridor, soles still painful but not as bad as I expect, until I reach the landing. Here though, I don't find Jules, but Peter and Xion screaming at each other.

Standing a few paces short of the open landing behind the archway leading to the upper west wing, I listen in on what they're saying, still eclipsed from view.

"Peter, do you realise what this means? How could she keep this secret? How could you?!" How could she not think there would be repercussions? This is madness! Did you think he wouldn't find out?" Xion's deep voice is bouncing from the walls like he's just made a home run with a beehive.

"We hoped he would never find out. Do you realise what kind of life that girl stands to lead with that kind of blood tie? With that kind of power? She'll be hunted down like a dog and killed!" Peter is feral-looking, hawk-like eyes burning into Xion. Even from this angle, I can tell he's beyond angry, but Xion doesn't just take it, effortlessly earning my respect.

In a few seconds, he's ascended the stairs, closing the distance between himself and my Uncle and grabbing him by the collar. He lifts him off the ground, fists balling tightly in the tweed of Peter's jacket as his feet dangle inches above the runner.

"Do you realise what kind of havoc you could have caused, leaving a demi unchecked? Do you realise what you could have done? The damage you might have inflicted on the balance of the universe? Do you?" he bellows, and suddenly I can't take it anymore. I wonder if he might kill Peter right in front of me, and though the guy is a pain in my ass, he doesn't deserve to die for it.

"Stop! What the hell do you think you're doing?!" I yell, striding forward with fury and reaching out to touch Xion's shoulder to pull him back.

As I near him, he backs away, placing Peter back down on the floor and flinching almost. "You're a security guard! You work for me! Got it?" I exclaim, putting my hands on my hips and giving Peter a sideways glance. "Are you alright?" I ask him, but before he can reply, Xion is laughing.

"Oh, come on, give it up. You can't honestly believe I'm just a security guard? After what you've just seen? Don't you think any normal security guard would have messed himself at the mere sight of that thing? I also don't know why you're defending *him*. He's the reason you were almost just killed." He looks at me with wide pupils and simmering irises. I snort.

"Almost *killed*? Were you and I watching the same fight?" I demand, cocking an eyebrow as he rolls his eyes.

"Peter. Tell her. Tell her the truth, right now. She needs to know. She's in danger." Xion corners Peter, who takes his glasses off his face and moves them down to his shirt to clean them, mouth contorting in a grimace.

"I swore to her mother I'd protect her. I swore it. I don't owe you anything," he retorts, and suddenly my anger flares in the opposite direction as I turn to face him head-on.

"What the fuck is going on? Seriously, get your head out of your ass, Peter. I'm not a child. Whatever you know, I need to. Or you can get out of this house. You're not the treasurer of the estate anymore; you're not even my legal guardian. If you're keeping secrets then you don't belong here. You wanted me to sign the papers, to take responsibility, well I am. So, fess up, or get out."

He looks shocked as I talk to him in the most authoritative way I can muster.

It's true; he might be my Uncle, but I don't owe him shit. He hasn't protected me at all. He just shipped me off to boarding school as soon as the funeral was over and left me to fend for myself.

He opens his mouth to speak, but no sound comes out.

I tap my foot on the corner of the stair. "I'm waiting." I give him a stare that could shrivel fresh fruit and he sighs.

"Fine, let's go and sit in my office," he concedes, and I look to Xion as he makes his way up the stairs.

"Come on then. You're clearly not who you say you are either," I say it without feeling or care, but then it occurs to me that I'm hurt. I can look after myself. I'm an adult. So why is everyone around me suddenly being exposed as lying assholes?

"Sephy I—" he begins, and I wonder if he's trying for an apology, but before he can finish, I whirl on the ball of my foot, eyes blazing with a rage I so often tame. I don't want to hear anything he has to say. I don't trust him. Even if I had before the lies, that's shot to hell now.

"No. You don't get to say shit to me," I growl at him through clenched teeth. The sheen of his metallic eyes diminishes as a mask of cool reserve slides across his far too attractive features.

He doesn't reply, the only sound the fall of his heavy soles against the runner as we move across the landing and then turn toward the upper east wing. I'm wishing now that I'd managed to find Jules and some whisky. I'm guessing whatever Peter has been keeping from me can't be good.

Walking past the bookcase leading into the room where I'd found the opal blade, I try to ignore the dull ebb in the soles of my feet, mind racing with a feeling of grim foreboding I can't shake.

I enter Peter's office, a room I very rarely frequent. To tell you the truth, I'd forgotten it was even in this part of the house, which is a shame. He has some of the most beautiful works of art, books, and artefacts in this room, which is wallpapered in an antique burgundy peppered with fleur de lis. The lighting is warm, with a gilded crystal chandelier which refracts the light and throws rainbows onto the walls and shelves, giving an intimate feel.

Taking a seat casually in a chocolate leather armchair that cups my spine, I prop a tattered foot atop my knee and frown at Peter as he sits in the high-backed chair behind his mahogany desk. He frowns back at me and folds his fingers in front of him, straightening his nameplate, which if you ask me is redundant.

Xion enters the room behind us and continues to stand, an odd masculine pillar of muscle and brood amongst the fine décor.

"Sephy, before I tell you this— I just want you to know that—" Peter begins, but I cut him off.

"Cut the crap. Just tell me, for Christ's sake!" I exclaim, bored and not in the mood for stalling or pleasantries. I've had one hell of an evening.

"Alright. Your mother and father— they made a deal, or several, with Haedes— it was how your father amassed the business empire he did." Peter looks at me with a stony expression, and the side of my mouth quirks against my will.

Well, shit. Where are the cameras? I'm being punked, right?

"Haedes? Like— God of The Underworld?" I smirk, unable to keep the amusement out of my tone. I look at Xion, trying to find a hint of humour in his gaze, anything to tell me that they're playing me.

"That is correct." Xion nods, collaborating with Peter.

And I thought he was at least semi-sensible—

"Don't you ever wonder where the diamonds come from Sephy? Don't you ever wonder where your father got his big break?" Peter asks, but I only shrug.

"I don't know, some mine somewhere?" I roll my eyes, completely done with this conversation.

"Not exactly." Xion smirks now, as though I'm too stupid to know what's really going on, aggravating me more than I make apparent.

"Your father made many deals with Haedes, but the most significant was the capture of a young Merman. The Mer cry diamonds. We'd been bartering with them for years, but eventually, we ran out of things to give. So, your father— he traded your mother, temporarily, to gain limitless resources. To obtain one of the Mer for himself." Peter says this with unwavering seriousness, and I start to giggle. I mean, I'm sorry, but how am I supposed to keep a straight face when he's talking about freaking *Mermen?*

"This isn't funny, Persephone," Peter scolds, leaning back into his chair and frowning.

"Oh, my god! Are you kidding me? Not funny? You're telling me my dad made a deal with the God of the Underworld and traded my mom for a Merman who cries diamonds?" I'm leaning forward now, ranting in disbelief as hysterical laughs wrack my body and my eyes begin to water. "God, I know I drink, but my brain's not that badly impaired. I went to Oxford, remember?" I sputter.

"You don't understand, Sephy. Your father has an outstanding debt to Haedes. A debt he's somehow managed to avoid. That debt now falls to you—" Xion explains. I blink a few times.

"Ha. Ha. Ha. Oh, no. I'm so worried about the debt collectors of the underworld— Ooooh they're going to come and repossess my soul!" I drape myself over the arm of the chair and throw my arms outward in a dramatic plea.

Xion rolls his eyes at me.

"This is serious," he grumbles, and I feel the giggles starting to build again.

"Oh, I'm sure it is. Totally serious. So serious, in fact, that I'm out for a drink to dull the obvious seriousness of it all." I get to my feet and feel oddly energised. I guess a good laugh was all I needed to get me over my bizarre afternoon.

"Sephy, how can you overlook what just happened? You just killed a demon with fire which came from your hands—" Xion stutters, trying to stop me but failing as I practically bound towards the door.

"I don't know. Ask Peter. He'll tell you if there's one thing I'm great at, it's denial," I reply, convincing myself all too easily that it's all just some big misunderstanding. Besides, it's not like any of this could be real. I'm probably hallucinating after having my drink spiked last night. I mean, who knows— maybe I really am losing it.

Either way, it doesn't matter. I don't have time for this crap.

"I'm going out," I call over my shoulder, walking off down the hallway to get changed for another night on the town, leaving Xion and Peter staring down the corridor after me.

XION

"She's unbelievable," I comment, exasperated, watching as she leaves down the corridor. Her ass swings and the scent of cinnamon fades to nothing in her wake, making me realise I've been inhaling deeper than I thought.

"If I was her, I wouldn't believe what I just told her either," Peter sighs, taking off his glasses for the millionth time since I've met him and cleaning them on his shirt. I doubt they're even dirty.

"Well, that would be because she's been lied to her entire life. You must have known Adam Sinclair wasn't her father. You don't just birth a child who can master The Eternal Flame from nowhere. You and her mother both knew that she is most likely Haedes' daughter—" I want to yell some more, possibly bang his head into that fine mahogany desk in an attempt to knock some sense into him, but Peter scowls.

"Demi was going to leave Adam. She was going to return to The Underworld to be with Haedes, but then she found out she was pregnant. You know the rules of the Mortarian sun; you know that raising a child anywhere near a place like that is just plain wrong. What was she supposed to do? We were trying to protect Persephone," Peter snaps, placing his glasses back onto the bridge of his too-pointed nose.

"Protect her?! A Banshee just came through the downstairs window!" I yell, banging my fists down on the desk. He startles.

"Look, I did a ritual, one which nearly killed me as a mortal, stripping her of any powers she might have had after what happened with my sister and her husband. She shouldn't be a target. She shouldn't be anything more than mortal," he explains.

I sigh.

"You didn't happen to store those powers in an opal dagger, did you? Because she found it. It called to her. You should know better than to separate anyone from their inherent magic for so long, Peter. Don't you realise what you've done? She's now totally unaware of how much danger she's in, too stubborn to listen to anyone, and in complete denial about everything. How the hell is she supposed to learn to defend herself? Because once people find out who she's potentially related to, you know that they'll hunt her down like a damn dog." I'm breathless, the obsidian pendant around my neck growing cool against my skin as my rage blooms.

"She found the knife?" Peter asks, eyebrows rising on his forehead. I nod with an unamused expression.

"Yeah. Though I'm surprised it took her this long with your totally secure fake bookcase." I roll my eyes, aware of the fact that magic, when separated from the host, will call out. It's only a matter of time before the power is reunited with its point of origin. Or in this case, person of origin.

68

"Look, there's no solid proof she's his daughter. For all we know, Demi was pregnant before she went into The Underworld and it screwed up her pregnancy, giving Persephone powers. We just don't know. The truth of all of this has never been clear to me. I've been doing the best that I can in an extremely trying situation. As you can tell, she's far from an easy person to deal with." He is getting more put out, a thin layer of sweat forming on his forehead beneath the receding line of his hair.

"Look, I'll take care of this. Clearly, everyone has overestimated your ability to handle this kind of situation. You're only human." I shrug, no longer angry at him, realising that no amount of fury will solve this. No amount of rage can give me answers. Peter doesn't have as many as I'd hoped, and it's increasingly obvious that everyone surrounding the Sinclair family has been operating under the façade that everything is totally normal and that the family debt can be simply forgotten.

I, however, know this is far from the case.

Spinning on the heel of my boot, I stalk out of the overly decadent office and down the corridor. I take the broad landing in but a few quick steps, meeting Jules who is making his way up the stairs, no doubt to bring Sephy the whisky jostling atop the silver tray in his hands. Rushing down the corridor towards her room, I knock heavily on the door. I wonder if she'll call out or ignore me altogether, but after mere moments the door swings open, revealing her in lingerie and nothing else.

My eyes widen as the curves of her muscular hourglass figure are exaggerated in a black velvet corset with transparent side panels. She's only wearing a black garter belt and thong below the waist and scrutinises me as I stare at her, a partially victorious sparkle dancing behind her irises.

"Let me guess, the tooth fairy is after me for some kind of tip because I've not got an overbite?" She tilts her head to the left with an unamused glare, fiery hair falling over one shoulder.

"Not exactly, though I'm sure the attitude fairy is expecting a return any day now," I retort, a fire igniting within my chest. What is it about this back-and-forth with her that stimulates me like this?

Jules stops short behind me, finally catching up, and Sephy pushes me out of the way, stronger than she looks. Grabbing the whisky off the tray, she takes a deep gulp. Her eyes rise above the rounded rim of the glass, lashes fluttering as her irises reflect the fiery chocolate hue of the whisky up at me.

Jules looks between us and scurries away as quickly as he'd come, clearly realising he's not wanted as a spectator in this game of catch and chase.

"Look, I'm going out. I don't know what Peter's been smoking, and honestly, I don't care. I just want to forget about whatever the hell it was that came through that window and move on with my life. I've had enough drama for one lifetime. I just want to be happy, whatever that means."

As though the whisky has prized opened the cast iron, flaming gates that she erects to protect herself, her eyes become wide and vulnerable for a moment, the sass and anger in her expression gone. She's innocent again, a child who doesn't know what she's doing or where she's headed. She's an orphan.

"Okay. Be safe. I'll be back later. I need to go and get some answers," I inform her in a gentler tone than usual, the glare I've been giving her softening as my eyes trace her body.

"Answers? Aren't you going to berate me about going out and being wild?" she taunts, taking another sip of her drink and relaxing a little more as she leans against the doorframe.

"You can clearly look after yourself. Besides, I have more pressing matters to attend to than making sure you don't drink yourself stupid," I mutter. She only smiles at that.

"Oh, I'm already stupid, so there's no risk of that. Or at least, that's clearly what Peter thinks— I mean, how stupid do you have to be to believe your father made a deal with Haedes to get a Merman in captivity?" she chuckles, almost choking on her latest sip of whisky.

Closing the door in my face, she goes back to getting ready.

I smirk. She's certainly not stupid, but as she'll soon discover, neither are the Demon Lords.

6

CARELESS WHISPER

LUCE

IT OCCURS TO ME as I sit, looking across at Haedes as Annie serves us firecracker shrimp presented in fine crystal cocktail glasses, that he might have sucked me into his melancholia.

Every week it's the same. Thane goes out on surveillance, and we meet for dinner at exactly seven o'clock, despite the fact there's hardly a clock to be found in the entire Exilia Multum, before dancing the night away together.

Annie's demure face looks down at me, wide eyes innocent. I know she's anything but, almost having walked in on Haedes mounting her like a rodeo bull several times. Regardless, I smile in return and nod, dismissing her as she tops up my white wine. I watch the bubbles rise within my glass as the fizz sizzles into silence.

Haedes leans back into the leather of his ebony armchair, the smoky quartz floors and ceilings capturing the flickering wicks of many candles lit with the scarlet and orange ombre blaze of The Eternal Flame. The air is filled with white sparks, emitting the voices of those Haedes has made famous via the mortal music industry. They float above us, singing a mellow melody as we tuck into our food, just the same as every week.

"You look beautiful tonight, Luce," he expresses, cobalt blue hair vibrant against the slate grey of his gothic tailored suit. He's wearing a black shirt and contrasting electric blue tie which only brings out the colour of his hair further. His grey eyes appreciate my off-the-shoulder burgundy gown, the tulle skirt flowing down to the floor in a deeply hued and weightless waterfall.

"Thank you. How was Yama last night?" I ask, referring to their weekly chess match. We all take turns keeping Haedes occupied, mainly because we're all worried he's going to attempt to fornicate or drink himself to death.

"Predictable." He smirks, taking a fork in hand after placing his whisky glass down onto the fine black linen beneath our solid silver plates. He places a firecracker shrimp into his mouth and chews a few times, watching me as I tuck into my food too.

"And your nephew? After watching him in that council meeting, which you insist we put on like cabaret every time anyone from The Higher Plains visits, I think he was rather aggravated. Especially at the attire." I smirk, knowing full well that Haedes has a special resentment in his heart for Hercules, if for no other reason than the fact he's related to Zeus.

"You know I think my brother is finally getting to him, but you also know I can't let go of the enjoyment I get from watching him struggling to get his giant arms into our slim-fit ceremonial robes—not that we ever actually wear them. Still, appearances are important, especially where my brother is concerned." He takes another sip of his drink, a smirk on his lips as the image of Hercules struggling to fit into the floor-length black overcoat with skeletal adornments amuses us both considerably.

"How is Thane? Have you two decided to let me join you yet?" he asks, picking up the flow of the conversation with ease. I give him a look that could shrivel a mummy.

"You're a dirty old man. You know that?" I bite, picking up my crystal glass and sipping my wine. I roll my eyes over the rim at him before setting it down on the table and continuing to devour my appetiser. I know Haedes is only joking about me and Thane. He asks me every single week just to annoy me. He's like the ridiculously perverted older brother I never wanted.

"Old? Why would you say that?" He actually looks worried for a moment, and I feel my lips upturn in the corners, finding it nothing but amusing that this is the part of the insult that bothers him. He stares down into the silver of his plate, checking himself.

"Alright, Cinderella. Calm your tits. You look beautiful too."

"You know I hate it when you speak like them." He raises his eyes to me, abandoning his pursuit of fleetingly perfect vanity in his warped reflection. This is why I had all the mirrors removed in the main hall, but I'd forgotten about the silver.

Damn.

I scowl to myself. I'm not his mother. He's a God, for heaven's sake, and way older than me to boot.

"You're a complete hypocrite. You swear and cuss and roll out the sarcasm more than anyone I know," I remind him of his usual demeanour, especially when he's drunk.

"Well, yes, but I do it with godly magnificence, not like some mortal street walker." He makes the excuse, something he's profoundly adept at.

"Well maybe if you actually went and talked with the mortals, you'd discover that they and their languages are much more fun now. Less formal. More sassy," I retort, biting down hard on another shrimp without mercy.

"Why would I spend my precious years talking to mortals? I've had my share of that, and you know the problem with mortals is—"

"That they die?" I interrupt him, pointed in expression as I cross my ankles. He blinks multiple times in quick succession, processing what I've said several times over before his eyes narrow.

"That they never have anything interesting to say—" he finishes, hair turning orange at the tips. Even if his hair didn't morph into a spectacular tangerine when I made him angry, I'd still be able to tell. However, the fact I can make him look like a well-dressed torch always has amused me. I'm sure it will continue to do so for many years to come.

Just as I'm moving to pick up the argument again, I hear the doors behind us open. Not those which lead to the servant's quarters, but the ones which open out into the staircase above the cavernous domed crystal of the entrance hall.

We both turn in our seats, leaning sideways to peer over the winged backs of our armchairs, trying to get a better look at who dares disturb us. I mean, everyone knows Haedes and I have dinner on a Thursday, even the sinners.

"Haedes, just who I wanted to find. I thought I'd missed you." Xion's deep voice rolls out like a blade against flint, blunt and displeasing to my ears. I prefer a more feminine tone.

"I wish you had. I prefer my dinner without a side of pointless interruption," Haedes complains, his wide brow and chiselled jaw hardening. His expression continues to reflect the unmistakable ir-ritation flickering orange in his irises as he leans back in his seat.

"Well alright— if you think the fact that you might have a daughter is pointless, then I'll just be on my way." Xion, now only halfway between the doors and the centre of the ridiculously large room where we're sat, a single table set for just us two, spins quickly on the heel of his boot. Then, without pause, he begins to walk the other way.

My eyes widen.

"Wait!" I call out, pushing my chair back from the table and getting to my feet. My fine stilettos click against the crystal of the floor as I spin and Xion stills, smirking at my outburst.

"I don't want to interrupt though—" Xion begins, and I place my hands on my hips.

"Xion, I'm the closest thing you have to a goddamn mother, so you will listen to me. Come here right now. We have things to discuss, clearly," I order him, my eyes narrowing and gaze intensifying as he shrugs, pleased to see he's caught my attention. He travels the rest of the distance between us faster than a normal mortal could ever manage, and I turn around to see what Haedes is doing. I'm disappointed to find that he's merely examining another shrimp before placing it into his mouth.

"Did you just say Haedes has a daughter?" I ask, and Xion's face becomes intense. The burning metallic pools of his enormous irises always alarm me, probably a side effect from his half-Demon lineage, which is much like my own only more diluted.

"Yes. I think so. Though I'd need confirmation of that from Haedes. She used The Eternal Flame on a Banshee and killed it by herself. I've never seen anything like it. Surely, she can't be mortal." Xion drops this information like a bomb, and I turn once more to Haedes, waiting for the explosion which never comes.

"Haedes? What do you think about this?" I prompt him, and he looks between me and Xion, picking up his whisky in one hand before downing the entire contents. He speaks, wiping his plump bottom lip on the back of his sleeve with a sneer.

"I think that this half-breed has come to me with nothing more than guesswork. Not facts, not evidence, not even a decent story. I don't have time to deal with his crazy delusions. As I just mentioned, mortals never have anything interesting to say. He's just proved my point." Haedes' hair remains cobalt as he returns to his appetizer.

"You don't want to even check this out? You didn't seem to think Demi Sinclair was uninteresting—" I begin, and his eyes blaze, an orange glow emitting around his dark pupils as he rises to his feet in a sudden jerking motion. His chair flies back a small way with a grinding sound against the floor.

"Don't you say her name to me," he spits, hair turning scarlet with his untameable, grief-fuelled rage.

"It is her daughter. Demi Sinclair. It's her daughter—" Xion looks between us, and I notice something in the back of his eyes. A kind of desperation that wasn't there before.

What's he worried about?

"What exactly do you want me to do about that? Throw a party? A parade? Dance a showstopper in celebration that you've made an enormous fucking assumption?" Haedes snaps, sitting back down as his hair dulls back to blue again, though the tips remain orange, hinting his anger has not entirely diminished.

"This girl, whether she's your daughter or not, she's in danger. This Banshee attack—" Xion continues, but Haedes raises a hand.

"Demons are not my concern. Mortals who are still breathing are not my concern, either. Why don't you go and inform Anubis of this little altercation? It's much more her area of expertise." He waves a hand, dismissing Xion completely. I watch him, stunned, as he finishes off his prawns and rings the tiny silver bell on the table, summoning Annie back to clear our plates before I've even half finished.

"Wait— but—" Xion is stuttering, something I've never seen him do before. He's reserved, always has been, having to remain cool and collected to fight his inherent Demonic persuasions. I frown at him, turning to Haedes and staring him down with a serious gaze.

"Haedes! Don't you care? This girl could be your daughter." I remind him of the fact that when it comes to parenting and how not to do it, he has plenty of opinions, what with his own father, not to mention his hatred for mine. Despite this though, he simply shakes his head, smoothing his lapels beneath long suave fingers.

"Not. My. Problem." The words fall from his lips as Annie comes bustling, frantic and anxious, from the kitchens below us with a silver trolley. Atop it, our entrees steam, making me unwillingly salivate. Haedes knows I love a good steak.

The God of the Underworld continues to gaze past me to Xion, giving him a dead, hateful expression.

"Get out." These are his only words, but the look he gives could set fire to the Arctic as he settles back into his chair stiffly and turns next to stare at me, expectant.

"Shall we eat?" he asks.

After we finish a main course of chargrilled steak, sweet potatoes, and greens, I watch Haedes set a baked Alaska with pomegranate glaze alight tableside before he serves me a plate.

As I tuck into the dessert, the flavours coating my tongue in a creamy, tangy mix which he knows I can't resist, I think of my father. A God of Ancient, Moloch, who raped my mother Hecate during his rule over the Higher Plains.

I am the unhappy result of that assault, and I have always known it. I think back to the day I had been cast out of The Higher Plains by my mother and by Zeus, for my inability to resist the call to the darker arts such as alchemy.

It had been she who had cut off my horns at birth, ashamed of half of who I was, who I still am. I can't escape it; I'm half him, half dark, but unlike him I choose to leave that part of my power untapped, fearing as ever, that it'll take my soul with it and corrupt me beyond recognition. I don't fast like I used to. I don't cut out the call to ancient dark magic, using my abilities to help Haedes whenever I'm able, or when it's vital, but I also don't practice like I should, have never studied like I could have. I'm too afraid. Too afraid to become what everyone already thinks I am.

Recalling what I know of my father, of how he had violated my mother, I look at Haedes over the candles in the middle of the table and take him in a moment.

His features have hardened in recent years, and his jagged, sexually blatant, and androgynous body looks worn and tired beneath his fine suit as he slumps in his seat. He barely uses his powers anymore, barely rules anymore. He just sits— rotting in a living body upon a throne, in a palace-shaped coffin, too afraid to die.

He had loved Demi Sinclair, more than he'd ever thought possible, and her death had not come easy on him. Still, he waits, asking me over and over to check the registers at Golgotha, but she never rises, and he never ceases in his self-destruction when she fails to appear.

I think he'd be a good father, if he can let go of the fact that she's not coming back. If he can learn to love again. But then, what do I know about being a good father? The only thing I know about them is how they can ruin your life without even being in it.

"You're quiet," he breaks the silence between us finally, and I look up at him from the dessert I'm still gratefully spooning into my mouth, savouring each bite.

Mortal bodies experience food in such a different way than I have been used to growing up, and I love it.

"You're evasive and stubborn. Kind of like an old woman." I tease about his age again, knowing it bothers him, and watch the corner of his sculpted mouth twitch as he cocks one eyebrow.

"Care to dance with an old dear?" he suggests.

Waving a hand, he executes one of the few exertions on his magic he makes these days. Borrowed voices begin to croon about careless whispers at his command, and the sound of a saxophone vibrates out from the swirling musical mist overhead. The eerie glow grows denser as more instruments join the melody and I feel the beat, infectious, stir my dark soul.

"Well, I can't let you dance by yourself now, can I? You have absolutely no rhythm."

I'm teasing of course; Haedes has the best rhythm of anyone I've ever met. He's a fantastic dancer, a sexual dynamite when it comes to rock, roll, rhythm, and blues. The way that he sings as well as his ability to master any instrument by only picking it up is undeniably attractive. It also never fails to ease his pain and suffering, at least on the surface.

He adores music, and I'm pretty sure if it wasn't for that, he'd have gone utterly mad years ago. It's not often I don't wake up to the sound of him on the piano, or the saxophone, or the electric guitar— at *all* hours of the night.

Still, better that than screams I suppose.

Getting to his feet, his angular frame makes smooth work of the transition from sitting to standing. He's not what you'd expect from a God, not when you look at his brothers. He's not broad or muscular. He's tall, slim, and handsome with a dark, sunken ruggedness that's bordering on androgyny, especially when you watch him move. He's one of the most graceful entities I've ever seen, and that's saying something because I grew up among some of the most beautiful Goddesses you can imagine.

"Shall we?" He offers a manicured hand as I get to my feet, red dress pinching my waist as the amount of food I've consumed causes my curves to push against the silk. The dress is dark in hue, contrasting starkly with my white-blonde hair and pallor bordering on translucency. The tulle of the skirt trails behind me, weightless like bloody smoke.

We tread away from the table and out across the sweeping quartz floors sprawling in billowing and smoky greys, blacks, and whites. He wraps an arm around my waist, and I place a light hand on his shoulder before the other finds its usual spot just above his elbow. The love song about broken promises and secrets spilt continues to play, and we dance, covering distances in ethereal motion together as though we're no more than spirits ourselves.

"I love our Thursday nights," Haedes admits, looking down into my eyes and making me blush. He's charming, sweet, and kind, with a wicked mean streak and temper that would make any sensible person run in the opposite direction. He is a juxtaposition of all things, making him utterly irresistible to all women— well, except me of course. I've got absolutely no interest in delving into the tangled web of pain spun thick within his chest. Not a single ounce.

"Me too. I just wish—" I begin, whispering against him as we turn again and our feet move in synchronised time, as though we were crafted from two halves of the same whole.

"You wish what? What could you possibly wish? You shall have it. You know— I love you, Luce. You're like a sister to me. A sibling I actually want." Haedes' hair shimmers beneath the warm lighting of the eternal flames, certain strands of his cobalt hair morphing lilac. My eyes widen, wanting to seem innocent, knowing that what I'm about to suggest might well get me thrown from the room altogether.

"I wish that you'd at least find out if this Sinclair girl is your daughter."

He opens his mouth to speak, but I bring my hand from his shoulder to his lips, hushing his retort as I continue to spin in his arms. "If I'd had someone like you as a father, I'd have wanted to know him. She'd be lucky to have you. Even if you don't see it, I do," I express.

He cocks his head, raising one blue eyebrow with a look of half-amused disdain on his lips and malice in his eyes.

"You think I'd make a better father than a rapist reptilian Demon God? Gee— thanks. I forgot how high your standards are when it comes to parenting." His tone sings victory, as though this is the end of the matter, but I narrow my gaze, tilting my chin upward in defiance.

"Well— if you won't do anything about it, I will," I whisper the threat, pushing back out of his embrace and turning from him on the ball of my foot. The skirt of my bloody gown swirls around me, hypnotic as I stalk away from him.

As I'm about to reach the high-arched double doors that lead to the entrance hall, hoping to catch Xion before he leaves, my pupils contract instinctually.

I raise a hand in front of my face as flames rise from the floor, revealing a pissed-off God.

Haedes stands stony before me, blocking my path.

"Don't do this, Luce. I don't want her. I don't want anything to do with her. I can't. I just can't," he pleads with me, weak and unlike himself.

I push him aside, not caring for his personal shortcomings, and take off through the doors, rushing down the sweeping crystal steps which are peppered with blacks and greys.

My breathing relaxes as I spot him, a mass of leather and muscle, waiting by the edge of the small gondola dock that'll allow him to board transport on the River Styx.

The river runs directly through the centre of the open-plan lobby of the Exilia Multum, surrounded only by wide arches interspersed with the supporting crystal columns holding up the enormous, faceted shard. The light in the lobby is pouring in, vermillion, from the sky outside, and the horizon looks smoky. I expect a spark shower any minute now.

"Xion! Wait!" I call out, pulling my skirt up so it's fluttering around the middle of my calves as I hurry toward the rushing river waters.

It's running high today, a sure sign that there'll be plenty of paperwork waiting for me tomorrow with a bunch of new arrivals in tow.

"Luce? I thought I was delusional." He looks unimpressed as he turns to me.

"Hey, don't blame me. It's not my fault he's the Goddess of Denial," I quip. Xion laughs.

"Yet another thing he and Sephy have in common," Xion enlightens me, and I pucker my lips as I scrutinise him. Every time he talks about this girl he gets a heated look behind his eyes, making me curious about his intent.

"Do you really think she's his daughter, Xion? I mean, we can't just bring her here unless you're certain. Are you?" I ask him with an earnest expression. He shifts on his feet, serious as he widens his stance.

"If I was going to put a bet on it, I'd say yes. She even looks like him. She has control over the Eternal Flame— besides, she's *Demi Sinclair's* daughter. What are the odds of that happening and her being entirely mortal after everything that happened? Something's not right. I just need proof."

I sigh, seeing the undeniable certainty on his face as his eyes crease in the corners and his lips press into a hard line. The dark skies and dim lighting cause shadows to paint his edgy features, revealing his anxiety.

"Right. Well then, there's nothing else to be done—" I begin, but suddenly he looks uncomfortable.

"Wait a minute— did you say you want me to bring her *here*?" he asks, circling back to my previous statement.

"Well, of course. She needs to head on over to The Indicatus Courts. Only The Fates can reveal what has passed. Only they can give us the proof we need to convince Haedes of her legitimacy." I feel as though this is an obvious next step, but Xion looks less than convinced.

"It's not going to be easy— I mean, I tried to tell her about her father's debt and she looked at me like I was insane. She isn't exactly going to willingly take a journey with me across dimensions just because I say please—" He frowns and I laugh.

"She had trouble believing you? I thought you said there was a Banshee attack? That you'd seen her use The Eternal Flame?" I query him, suspicious.

How could any mortal deny the existence of this place after seeing the horrors that come from within its blackened rotten heart?

"You know how I said she and Haedes have that whole denial thing in common? Yeah, well, she's *really* good at it," Xion explains.

I sigh, shaking my head.

"Didn't you present her with your true self? I would have assumed you'd have shifted when the Banshee attacked?" I ask him, knowing that the level of threat when confronting Demons is one of the most likely things to cause his Abraxian self to present.

"I uh— I didn't have to. She took care of it. I just stood there and watched." He looks hideously embarrassed and blushes, something I've never seen him do in all the years I've known him. Not ever.

"Wait— this girl, she killed a Banshee, and you just *watched*?" I want to laugh, but for his sake, I pull back the urge and settle for a smirk instead. He looks a little pissed at my amusement, quickly changing the subject.

"If you think that scaring her into coming here is going to work, then you need something a little more drastic than my face. Trust me. She's pretty hard to rattle." As he explains her further, or at least attempts to as she seems to have him utterly perplexed, a gondola moves beneath the external columns of the Exilia Multum, approaching us at constant ebbing speed with the cloudy current.

"Look, just get her to the courts. Besides, it's for her safety. If she's been the victim of one attack already, who knows what'll happen when the Demon Lords work out who she is— If they don't already know by now that is. She'll be dead within a week without proper protection." I grimace, not sure why I care so much about Haedes being a father, but unable to resist the urge to meddle in his personal affairs. Maybe it's because I've been bored lately, or because I feel that being woken up by the sounds of his electric blue Gibson Les Paul at three a.m. gives me the right to dish out a little payback.

Either way, we need to know the truth, if not because the girl is in danger then because I'm nosey, curious, and I want my questions answered like a spoiled child wants a pony.

"Okay, I'll try," he sighs, stepping into a gondola guided by a female ferrywoman with white hair and cornflower blue eyes.

The gondola shakes, dipping as he steps in, and I hear the wooden bones that make up its structure, carved from the black charred trees of the sanguine forest, creak beneath his weight.

"Good luck." I wish him on his way, the gondola not stopping to allow a long goodbye. Instead, it just keeps on moving with the current of the ghostly river.

I turn, not one for sentimentalism, and decide to return to my room, too excited by the prospect of fresh blood around these musty old halls to sleep.

Besides, I'll be able to watch the spark shower that is most definitely brewing from my balcony.

I ascend the spiral staircase at the back of the lobby that rises into the tallest tower of the Exilia Multum, bar one; the Solar Observatory belonging to Haedes.

I climb into the shadows of the tower holding my alchemy chamber and the sprawling suite where Thane and I spend most of our time. It's beautiful, but the truth is the room wasn't chosen for any other reason than that it's at the furthest point away from Haedes' room. From here, the sounds of orgasm and expertly played instruments are at least dulled by the distance.

I reach the heavy wood of the door and fall into it with my full weight, treading quickly into the only place I've ever really felt at home.

It's onyx, alabaster, and scarlet in colour scheme, with crystal fixings and crushed velvet upholstery stuffed into every nook and cranny. The large chandeliers tinkle as I close the door behind me, the deep red of the eternal flame within each of the candelabra flickering with the disturbance in the air.

I tread through the room, looking for any sign that she might have returned, and that's when I hear it.

Mangled cries, all too familiar, coming from our enormous balcony. I hurry through the suite, grabbing a black velvet throw from the edge of the settee and make haste towards the ceiling-height, faceted glass doors. I see her silhouette, transforming as she cries out in pain, and throw the doors wide open. Behind them, the shaking and angularly broken form of my lover, as she shifts from raven to mortal once more, is revealed.

"Thaney! You're home!" A grin spreads across my face, the kind that only her presence brings on, as she looks up from her crouched position on the floor. Her skin is flawlessly rough again and only a few black feathers remain, scattered around her on the floor where she's changed from bird to woman.

I sweep forward, wrapping her in the blanket and pulling her lips against mine, desperate to feel her ragged breathing hot against my wanton flesh.

Ushering her inside, I forget for a moment the events of the evening and take in her androgyny, her stunning stormy eyes and messed black hair cropped wild against her bony face.

She is beautiful. Just like the day I'd first laid eyes on her in the Othrysian Orchard. A memory which I relive every chance I get and a rare highlight from my painful childhood.

"Yes, I thought I best come back early. Looked like a spark shower," she breathes, clearly glad to be home.

I know the transformation takes its toll on her, a curse from her mother Nemesis for choosing me over her place among the purest Gods in The Higher Plains. Of course, it was masked by the guise of duty to Zeus after his spat with Prometheus, but I digress—

I run my fingernails along her bare arms as I wrap the throw around her tighter, but she pulls away, shedding the material and stretching up high, presenting her breasts to me in their full glory. Her spindled form is an artist's dream, and I wonder if she'll let me paint her again—

I realise I'm getting distracted, letting my gaze rise to her face as I try to cool the wanderlust of my eyes which trek, adventurous, across her skin.

"Something's happened," I announce and she raises one eyebrow. I love it when she does that—

"And what might that be?" she asks, taking a few paces forward and dangling her long arms around my neck. "You look beautiful by the way— far too beautiful to be wasted on Haedes." Her eyes sparkle with mischievous intent, and I almost fall into silence, moving to kiss her again with no intention of stopping.

Instead, though, I check myself, blinking slowly and realising that my curiosity might, on this rare occasion, be greater than the want to bed my woman.

"Haedes might have a daughter." I drop the bombshell and Thane falls from her tiptoes, which she's using to leverage her body against me, wrapping her limbs around my form like vines. Her expression turns confused.

"Excuse me?" She looks rattled, so I move to explain.

"Demi Sinclair's daughter— Xion just came from their estate. Apparently, she's got the ability to produce The Eternal Flame. She single-handedly took down a Banshee. Rendered our boy useless in the process—" I smile, remembering Xion's embarrassment.

"Well, I would've paid to see that." Her eyes light up, and I feel my connection to her strengthen as we share the same thought.

"Me too. Anyway, I told him to bring her to The Indicatus Courts. The Fates will know what to do," I explain my plan, waving a hand as I move to begin kissing her again.

"Wait— what are you still doing here? You need to be there, Luce." Thane's greyish-sapphire eyes are serious now as she steps back from me, causing my heart to deflate in my chest as the excitement in my gut dissipates like cooling mist.

"But— you just got home—" I complain, and she smiles.

"There'll be time for that later, baby. You need to be there. You know Haedes will believe anything more readily if he hears it coming from you. He thinks The Fates are decrepit enough as it is. I'd love to hear them trying to convince him he's a father."

She's right. Of course, she is. She's the smartest person I know.

"I better get changed then. Can you call down for a carriage?" I ask, and she nods, crossing her arms across her bare chest. "Oh, have you seen my headdress?" I ask, stalling her attempt to get dressed with a cheeky glint in my eye. Etching her nakedness into my memories, I walk over to the dresser.

"Oh, Luce. You're not going to scare this poor girl, are you?" Thane asks me, running her fingers through her dark hair and ruffling its edgy style in that way I adore.

"Well— I do love to make an entrance," I retort, smiling back at her with wicked intent.

She stares at me, more love in her eyes than I deserve, her perfect face adoring both my smooth and jagged edges as she whispers,

"Oh— don't I know it."

7

WELCOME TO THE JUNGLE

PANDORA

THE SCARLET HEAVENS OPEN and clouds of smoke from the lilac Mortarian sun start to dissipate as a spark shower begins overhead. There is no mystery as to why everything here is scorched black, nor as to why the Nexus were wise enough to build their city from crystal. The showers can be brutal, not that I mind. I've never been afraid of a little fire, especially not when it comes from Haedes.

The box inside my skirt pocket shakes slightly with the unmistakable rhythm of Banshee tread as Lilliana and I sit opposite from one another across the cracked table. Luckily for me, demons can sense weaknesses in dimensional walls where portals have opened before, or I'd be babysitting all the time.

Lilliana's eyes widen at the sound of her Kindred's call, which I'm sure she can hear as though it's nothing more than whispers in the wind. The demon pack reaches out to her from the mortal plain, her brow furrowing and her pupils dilating, casting her face into greater darkness as the whiteness of her irises shrinks.

"No!" she cries out, only seconds before I grasp the box in my palm and throw it high into the air above the broken ceiling.

The pack launches themselves from the innards of the tiny wooden contraption, falling through the roof of the building and the disrepair of the ceiling, morphing to full size as they land atop the table between us.

I lean back, the smell of wet dog too much to bear, as I realise that it's no wonder the place is in ruin. The way they treat it, I'm surprised it's not worse.

Claws scrape along the stone of the table and unbearable whines emit from the matted fur muzzles of the three approaching Banshees, shoulders sharp as they bend before their master with ghostly white eyes.

"What is it?" I ask, placing my hand over the pocket in my gown where I store the box, returning it to its rightful place as it falls back to the table. I do this often, feeling its weight when I need to be reminded of the power I still possess, even though it's not physically held within my bones.

The two scars on my back tingle and I sigh out, anger boiling within my blood.

"Alpharia— he's dead." Lilliana gets a look on her face like she might cry, her eyes becoming round and childlike like an orphan lost in the forest.

"Dead? How on earth? Demons can't just die!" I exclaim, knowing full well that even starvation cannot destroy the darkness within such a beast. It might be painful, torturous even, and the demon may become weak as a newborn kitten, but still, they'll return, reborn from the Mortarian soil. It is their curse for wielding such a primal power. The only way to destroy them at soul level is with The Eternal Flame.

"They say it was a girl." She moves her head from left to right, as though she's hearing a song audible to no one else. The small animal bones around her emaciated neck clatter against one another, the only sound apparent in the silence.

"A girl? Killed a Banshee?" I voice the absurdity of this claim, wondering how intelligent the beasts before me actually are. They can pack a good punch vocally that's for sure, but when it comes to logic, I'm not sure exactly how many brain cells are swimming around inside their massive skulls, if you know what I mean.

"They say she wielded the fire of eternal damnation," Lilliana speaks for them, trancelike in her utter detachment. She reaches up, placing her long, dark, claw-like fingernails onto the side of one of the Banshee's faces. She looks into his eyes and I watch as something passes between them.

"We smelled her power— the magic in her bones. We hungered for it— Then, when we saw Alpharia fall, we ran," she breathes, eyes half closed now as though she's not speaking of her own volition but channelling the Banshee as a collective.

"A Kindred soul perhaps?" I ask, wondering if the Circle of Eight or Aetherial Court have been up to something.

"No. We could smell no blessing," Lilliana's voice rings out, and she lowers a hand, pupils contracting as she moves to look directly

86

at me now, her brow furrowed with grief. "It is lucky that the Succubi have already returned," she sighs, peering anxiously over her shoulder and down into the red lighting of the crumbling corridor leading to Katerina's quarters.

"Indeed. Where exactly was this girl?" I ask.

Lilliana turns to the Banshee who is closest to her, looking it deeply in the eyes as she cocks her head again, as though something is being pushed into her ears against her consent.

"— Chicago," she announces as the lighting in the room morphs intermittently bright with falling sparks that disintegrate to ash just before they reach the top of the building. The pale grey flakes fall around us like scorching hot snow.

"We must go. We must see for ourselves. I will not let my children be slaughtered this way. Alpharia will be avenged." Lilliana's face blazes in a terrifying hue of blood and fire from the downpour of sparks overhead.

I nod, concerned about this new threat, if that is in fact what it is. The last thing I need right now is some new kid on the scene with the power to destroy demonic souls.

"Yes. Come, Lilliana. We will investigate. Do you want to inform Katerina of where we are going?" I ask her, and she shakes her head.

"No. He was my child. I will go, and you will accompany me. Bring the box," she orders me like I'm no more than one of her mongrels. I narrow my eyes slightly, displeased.

I tame my fury, knowing that perhaps if I do this, I will win further favour, show that I am not in this for purely selfish reasons, but to benefit their collective.

Taking the box from my pocket, I turn to the side with a tree burned into the dark wood, staring at it and watching as the edge slides away at my will.

As the portal to the mortal world re-opens, we step silently inside, and the hunt for deadly magic begins.

SEPHY

I awaken as the dawn breaks over the horizon, dappled sunlight falling over the room. My eyes crack open as the glare hits my eyelids, and my heart begins to race as my eyes shoot open fully only seconds later.

There's an enormous shadowy mass at the end of the bed.

"What the fuck?" I cry out, reaching beneath my pillow for the opal dagger or Ol' Faithful, whichever one is closest. I grab the hilt of one of the knives but pause with the blade mid-air as I realise who the stoic face staring down at me belongs to.

"Good morning." Xion smiles, and my mouth falls open, fury following shortly after.

"Oh, my God! You freaking psychopath! You can't just stand over a woman while she's sleeping!" I get up onto my knees, grabbing a pillow and hitting him over the head with it as I yell in a staccato of fury.

"Do. You. Know. How. Freaking. *Stalkerish*. That. Is?!"

He doesn't move, just takes the blows with an oblivious smile as I feel the night before coming back to me.

Too much whisky— far too much.

My head becomes tender too fast as the blood slows around my system and my heart rate returns to normal. I'm naked, obviously, and take a minute to stare around the room.

"Hey, where's— uh—that guy?" I ask, seeing the dent in the pillow next to mine. Don't get me wrong, I'm relieved he's gone, but with Xion nearby I wonder if he's still breathing.

"Oh, he's gone." Xion smiles to himself, and I scrutinise him.

"Again, crazy I know, but I find myself having to ask, is he *alive*?" Xion laughs, being very careful not to look at me anywhere but directly in the eyes.

"Some might say barely, but yes, he's breathing if that's what you mean."

With this, I exhale an overly-dramatic sigh and fall back among the sheets, not caring for modesty as I gaze up at him through my lashes. The look is provocative as my fiery red hair falls out around me in a flaming halo, but he only laughs.

"What's so funny?" I ask.

He raises an architecturally flawless eyebrow.

"You think you're so hot," he retorts.

I snort.

"I *know* I'm hot, thank you very much," I retort, stretching my arms up above my head as he continues to chuckle.

"And you're *so* easy to bait." His laugh becomes louder now, reverberating off the walls as I get up.

"Well, you're—" I begin my next quip, but the thudding in my head suddenly becomes unbearable as the night's whisky intake comes back to me in full force, and I lose my train of thought.

Where is Jules with my morning pick-me-up?

What time is it anyway?

"Did I just beat the infamous Sephy Sinclair in a shit-slinging match?" Xion asks, the sentiment one I recognise from England. You don't hear it around here much.

Getting to my feet, I find myself wondering where he's from, how old he is, or if he has a family.

Actually, it's pretty obvious from my lack of explanation for his persistent behaviour that I don't know anything about him other than that he's a pain in my ass.

Striding across the room, bare for him to admire, I open my closet doors and step inside to dress. As I do, I hear him cough.

"So, do I need to ask you why you're here, towering over me in my sleep like some mass-murdering freak, or are you going to let me in on that fact?" I call through the doors, placing on a fresh set of panties and a bra. Over the top of this, I pull on some skin-tight leather pants, my favourite pair, and a low-cut black vest top with metal studs along the spaghetti straps. Last night's makeup is smudged but deemed acceptable as I stare into my pale, tired, and hungover reflection in the vanity.

Xion's tread grows closer, his voice louder.

"You've been summoned to the Indicatus Courts." His explanation isn't very informative, and I frown as I open the double doors again in one sweeping motion before stepping out.

I find him leaning against the wall on my right, casual and cocky.

"What's that? Like a gameshow or something?" I ask, moving over to sit on the edge of the bed as I put on some shoes.

"No. It's the courthouse in The Underworld. They want to see you, to review your case." His voice is slow, certain, as though he thinks I'm stupid or something. I scowl.

"You know this really isn't funny anymore. I'm all one for fun and games, the odd prank, but you've got to know when to let it go— you know?" I cock my head, getting to my feet and deciding to go and see

Nightshade. It's too early for anything seriously taxing. In fact, from the looks of things, it's only a little past six am.

Why am I awake?

Oh, right. Psycho bodyguard watching me sleep.

I might as well enjoy the peace before Peter rises and this whole business thing starts infringing on my time again.

Walking away from Xion without another word, I hear him exhale in frustration.

As I pull open the door to make my exit, I nearly walk into Peter who is standing behind it, hand raised. It's weird; he never ventures this far into the upper west wing, which is just the way I like it.

"Persephone," he addresses me, surprised I'm awake, as though I live in a permanent zombified state or something.

"Peter— I was just going to—" I begin but he frowns.

"I've called the directors back this morning, early, so you can get a head start on things after yesterday."

My mouth falls open, but then quickly downturns into an annoyed expression.

What the hell?

He managed to get them back here so soon after they'd almost been eaten by a rabid genetic experiment gone wrong? I mean, I hate him for that, but he must be one hell of a persuasive entity on the phone.

"Well, uh, actually— I have plans. Xion is taking me to the Indicatus Courts." I pull the excuse out of thin air, too lazy to think of something inventive in my fatigue.

"The Indicatus Courts— Oh. Well, I suppose that's more important. I'll reschedule. You uh— talked everything out then? You know all about Mortaria?" he enquires, expression nervous.

"Oh yes, Xion's been very helpful. He explained everything." I nod enthusiastically, the motion making my head pound harder.

I push past him and move into the hall before taking off toward the landing. My tread quickens, but soon I realise I'm not alone as I hear an unmistakably loud and non-covert footfall in my wake.

I quicken my pace, grabbing my car keys from the table beside the double doors, where I usually leave them for Jules when I stagger in.

Running outside, I feel my hair trailing behind me like fraying ribbon in messy un-brushed curls. I hear his call but ignore it, determined to get some space.

Taking a right, I venture around the front of the west wing, taking long quick strides and kicking up gravel as I head toward the garage.

Once inside the open front structure, I realise that my car hasn't been brought back—

Of course it hasn't, the keys were still on the table.

Lucky for me, I'm a billionaire. I have about twenty cars at my disposal.

I select Goldfinger as my ride and am fishing out the spare keys from the safe just as Xion rounds the corner.

"Hey! Wait! Where are you going?!" he demands, breaking out into a jog as I scurry over to the golden Vanquish which I haven't driven since I've been home. I click the button on the keypad, making sure that the doors are open and ready so I can make my escape. "Wait!" Xion yells out.

He's about ten feet away from me one moment, and the next I'm being spun on the balls of my fast-moving feet as his enormous hand falls onto my shoulder from directly behind me.

Huh. He must have been closer than I thought, I muse, turning to look into his smouldering bronze eyes.

"What?!" I yell into his face, angry at the fact I'm being hunted down like a freaking dog for no reason by not only him but Peter as well. It's like I'm a prisoner in my own home, for Christ's sake.

"Where are you going?!" he growls, grabbing me by the arm.

I pull away and slip from his grasp, stronger than I realise.

Thank you, Jacque.

Turning, I dash forward and slip into the interior of the gold Vanquish, starting up the engine as quickly as I'm able to with just the touch of a button.

The engine roars to life and my heart pounds with the excitement. It's sad really, the fact that I'm, yet again, making a prison break from my own home, but it is what it is. I wouldn't spend one more minute with stuck-up or crazy pants if you paid me.

I pull out of the garage, car crawling along under the periwinkle blue of the early morning sky. I'm no longer able to see Xion anywhere, that is until I'm out on the white gravel of the driveway.

Turning right and away from the house, so I'm facing straight down the long exit road cutting through the forest toward the gates, I catch him in my sights.

He's standing directly in front of the car, only a few metres away, expression pissed beyond what I've seen from him so far. His brows are pinched together and his facial architecture is carved into nothing short of what can only be described as feral abandon.

I rev the engine, trying to get him to move, but he widens his stance, almost like he's challenging me. Driving forward a few inches, revving all the way, beeping my horn, trying anything to get him to move, my temper is only stoked hotter by his stubbornness. My fingers tighten on the wheel and my foot twitches over the gas pedal, impatience growing as I get closer and closer to his tall intimidating silhouette.

Finally, when I'm only centimetres away from his kneecaps, something happens that I have no idea how to explain.

Through the broad windshield, I watch as his eyes blaze a hot orange, the hue igniting from the molten gold and bronze of his irises. His skin ripples, becoming charred, and his body expands within his clothes, causing them to tear at the seams. Lines of glowing, burning colours etch themselves through his body, glowing through the material of his shirt, and his entire stature transforms within seconds to something terrifying, something dark.

Bringing his hands down on the hood of Goldfinger with a bang, the entire car shakes under the force of his palms as the metal crumples beneath his palms, the rear wheels lifting off the ground.

My eyes widen, and my heart begins to race as I take my foot off the accelerator. I blink once, then again, rubbing my eyes.

Did I really drink that much last night?

I don't know what comes over me, but I'm unable to stop myself as I open the driver's side door and step out onto the gravel. It crunches beneath my feet as I rise from the driver's seat, turning to stare at him.

The early morning sun is rising to the east, casting his now dark skin in orange and highlighting the red-hot glaze of his swirling tattoos. They run like rivers of fire across his charred skin, cutting through the definition of his muscle as though it were rock and every pulse from his veins is yet another seismic vibration. As he balls his fists on the bonnet, his biceps and pectorals shudder and strain like tectonic plates, immovable, yet volatile beneath his clothes.

He's an organic oxymoron in every sense of the word.

"Xion—" I stutter, taking a few steps forward, unsure of what to do next. He straightens, removing his hands from the bonnet of the car, leaving two handprints in the previously spotless metal.

"Do you believe me now?" His voice has changed; it's deeper, more terrifying than anything I've ever heard, kind of like a cross between Darth Vader and Alan Rickman. It might even be sexy if he didn't sound so furious.

I look him fully in the face, the heat from his body radiating toward me. Reaching out, I go to place my fingers gingerly on his cheek, trying to make sure he's real, but he pulls away.

"No. Don't," he warns. I drop my wrist to my side, curious beyond anything I've ever felt in my life.

What is he?

"So, this is all real? The fire, that thing from last night?" I ask him, frowning, as though the fact that he could be telling the truth about what has been going on has never even occurred to me.

"Yes. This universe is more complicated than you can possibly imagine. There is power, and there are those who wield it. How they do so dictates the fate of this plain and every other. It's serious, Sephy. You need to come with me. You could be in danger." He's pleading with his alien gaze, but behind the new fire in his irises, I can tell it's still him.

"Seriously?" I demand, blinking again, and wondering if I'm going crazy, or dreaming. This time though it's harder to deny, harder to shake off the feeling that this might be real. Mainly because I can't believe that my intoxicated brain could come up with a monster who is not only terrifying but also this smouldering hot— literally.

"Seriously. You might be a pain in the ass, but I don't want you dead," he admits.

I sigh.

"Well, in that case, I better let you take me to this courts place then— if it exists," I add, not ready to be fully compliant just yet.

"Well then, come with me. We have a long journey ahead of us. Char will meet us on the river just beyond The Hollow, but it's a bit of a trek," he warns me. My brows rise on my forehead, excitement seeping through my uncertainty.

"You mean Charon? The Ferryman? And river as in the River Styx? Really?" I challenge him, pulling up knowledge from my degree.

"Yes. Really. And just so you know, if she hears you call her a ferryman, she'll smack you upside the head with her oar. So just leave the talking to me, okay?" he chuckles. I roll my eyes.

"So, you're taking me to hell. Like, really?" I catechize him, trying to gauge exactly how far this charade can go before I have to put my hands up and go along with it.

"Yes, so if you're going to tell me to go there again you might want to think about the fact I have an apartment with a spa tub." He raises an eyebrow at me, the black of his skin fading to flesh as he begins to laugh. Soon he's back to his old self, no different except for a few ruffled seams on the outside of his leather jacket.

"I'll bear that in mind," I mumble, still in disbelief.

With this, he grabs my hand, and I let him take me, willingly, to hell.

PANDORA

"So, they know—" is Lilliana's first reaction.

I've commanded the box to take us to the place it last opened a portal in this dimension, so here we stand, shrouded in the shadow of trees as the sun rises over the horizon, adjacent to some kind of manor house with sprawling grounds. We peer around broad trunks of trees as a chill wind whips around my ankles and lifts my dark hair from my shoulders.

"That monstrosity of Abraxis' loins does, that's for certain," I reply, glancing back over my shoulder and into the gaunt chasms of her eye sockets.

"The other Nexus members must know too. They implied visiting the Indicatus courts, that means they're involved," Lilliana recalls the information correctly in a rasping whisper. Watching, I realise that the couple are starting to walk toward us.

We need to get out of here.

I might be able to easily hide from a mortal with an affinity for fire, but I'm less likely to be able to evade the heightened senses of Xion.

"Come, we must go— I will return with you to the Fallen Kingdom and then go and infiltrate the Courts. We must know what it is they're hiding," I whisper back to her as we slide around the tree trunk, disappearing.

Picking up a long branch from the surrounding bracken, Lilliana begins to sweep the ground, erasing our footsteps. She's smarter than her children had been, that is for sure.

"Do you really think that girl killed Alpharia? I mean, look at her. She's so— childish," she asks me, looking up into my eyes as rage kindles behind the glassy surfaces of her own.

Grasping the box within my fingers and sliding open the side with a septagram etched into the wood panel, the symbol of The Nexus, I toss it into the air, where a screaming portal of red and black shadows opens. I hate travelling back this way because it's always way rougher going back to Mortaria than it is getting out.

"Things are rarely what they seem, Lilliana. I believe that we must learn more about her before we write her off as benign. She might look weak, but who knows what lies underneath that milky white skin and those feisty red curls?" I taunt, taking her hand and pulling her, once more, back into my box.

8

JUNGLE BOOGIE

<u>SEPHY</u>

"THIS IS THE HOLLOW."

Xion stares up at the enormous, gnarled tree, which looks as though it's made from two intertwining trunks hugging each other like charred lovers.

"It doesn't look very hollow to me," I observe, staring hard at the place that seems like it could be an oversized fairy door, the kind my mother had made for me when I was a child.

"That's because we haven't paid the toll yet. When Haedes bargained for your mother, he planted this tree and watered it with his own blood. It links this world and The Underworld so that she could be taken from here to there. There are only a few linkways like this one in the world," he informs me, eyes deadly serious and unwavering as I nod. No longer just content with argument and denial, I decide to humour him and listen for a change.

"Okay, so what's the toll?" I ask.

My words fall into silence as he pulls out the black twisted shard of Obsidian, which forms the blade I'd seen him wielding earlier, from the inside of his leather jacket. He holds out a large, calloused palm as we stand upon the damp earth, leaves rustling around us ominously, before slashing his skin without so much as flinching. Blood runs from the cut, thick and rich in colour. His pale-again skin is littered with similar cuts, suggesting he is no novice to this kind of payment.

Watching him, I hold my breath unintentionally as I wonder if I'm about to have my life changed forever or be shown that this is a seriously elaborate prank. I hope in a way it's the first because at least then I won't look like a complete moron.

He presses his palm to the tree trunk, where the flat piece of wood bridges the two intertwining trunks. Here, they begin to separate at the base of the tree before sprawling into tentacular roots.

"Now you," he instructs, passing me the knife. I stare at him and cock my eyebrow as a rampant chill runs unexpectedly down my spine.

"Are you kidding me? Blood?" I practically giggle as the words leave my lips, finding this all utterly ridiculous. Annoyingly, anxiety still pools in my stomach.

"If you're not a fan of bodily fluids, then Mortaria isn't the place for you." Xion smirks as I sigh and take the edge of the crystal blade to my own palm, hissing through my teeth as my soft skin breaks open and blood pours forth with the easy flow of red wine.

"Who the hell is a fan of bodily fluids? What is there some bodily fluids fetish club I'm not aware of? Because you know if you're into that shit, then we might have a problem— that's just—" My voice is bordering on hysterical as he sighs, cutting me off and reaching out, one hand still pressed to the wood, to grab my wrist and pull me forward toward him.

He slams my palm into the wood of the tree with haste, and I feel the unusual texture of the grain take in my blood like a sponge.

In an instant, where there was once solid wood, nothingness takes its place, leaving me without anything to lean on.

I stumble forward and hear Xion snigger under his breath, clearly amused by my lack of experience with walking through trippy tree portals. Kind of like all the cool kids are doing it, and I'm that one loser who hasn't had the guts or something equally as immature.

Darkness swirls in dense clouds, puffing and buzzing with red lightning sparking in all directions. I take one step forward as I right myself on a floor that doesn't appear to exist, then another with caution. Putting my hands out in front of me, I reach as though there may be some invisible wall waiting to smack me in the face, paranoid despite Xion's claims being proved impossibly true.

"Come on." Xion's impatient now, moving forward into the blackness and grabbing my wrist again, pulling me forward and leading me like I am no more than a small child or a baby lamb, innocent, clueless, and lost in the mist.

As we continue to pace quickly through the dark, the seconds pass, and the only light for a long time seems to be intermittent scarlet slashes until, in a flash, a distinguished line of red appears.

Freudian in connotation, like the opening of a flower or something, it widens. We get closer and closer to the growing vertical slit, before suddenly, I'm standing with my back against a tree identical to the one which I've just walked through. This time though, the height of the tree is surrounded by a gilded metal cage, gothic in design as it towers, cylindrical, up the length of the trunk. The dark metal, which twists like something organic, casts intermittent shadows over my awed expression as I find myself completely out of place.

I take a few moments, blinking as I realise that the setting is far from identical, and lower my gaze to find my feet upon spongey moist soil.

The smell that fills my nostrils is strong, rusty in fact, and overhead a vermillion hue settles over me as I gaze up and tread forwards beyond the cage.

An unsettling bloody sky floods my vision. Free from stars, the only light cast by an enormous violet sun burning brightly as pluming flares of lilac through indigo reach out from it in searing tendrils. I inhale.

It's a terrible beauty, but a beauty nonetheless.

I'm standing in a forest, but everything seems too red, too bright. The tree trunks are distinguishable as charred silhouettes, but the ground is encased in bloody leaves, which cling to the trees, creating a macrocosm of scarlet. There's no breeze and the air is sticky, as though time is standing still here, even in the most natural of ways.

"What the hell is this place?" I ask, smelling the air and feeling my eyes widen. My sass has disappeared, too stunned to find anything witty or sarcastic to say.

I thought I knew everything about the world. I thought I knew how it worked, how to manipulate it. But with this, I momentarily realise that perhaps I'm but a speck.

"Welcome to the Sanguine Forest. Don't be alarmed by the smell; it's a little overwhelming at first, but you'll get used to the blood," Xion explains, stepping forward and looking back at my expression with a smug grin. "Do you believe me now?" he asks, and I nod, unable to speak, or move, only able to gape at the heavy black clouds that barely distinguish themselves in a thin line against a horizon bordering on invisibility.

"Blood?" I ask, my stomach turning.

Why is it always blood with him?

"Yes, the trees, they feed off it. This was Succubi hunting ground once, but not any longer. Not since The Nexus colonised it." He is shooting off information like a maniac gunman with a passion for pulling the trigger just to scare the crap out of his hostage, AKA me.

"Succubi? The Nexus?" I repeat the terms, taking a small step forward and continuing to look down at my feet as I feel the soil beneath me give slightly. Before Xion answers, I find my favourite boots sinking into the dirt, blood squelching out under my weight.

Ew.

I want to run, I want to go back, to forget this place exists, but as I spin to do so, I find the portal is closed, and The Hollow is no longer— well, hollow.

I note that the empty archway within the surrounding cave sports a simple plaque, reading only '*In loving memory*' in swirly calligraphic font.

"Succubi are demons; they feed on blood. Demons come in different species. The Banshee are another type; that's the one you killed the other day. The Nexus are the council that organises the rehabilitation of mortal souls— so to speak," he explains too fast, moving to turn, to walk away, leaving me confused even still. My heart rate rockets, suddenly needy as I stand in this new world, not sure of any of the rules.

"What kind of demon are you?" I ask the question that's the most pressing in my mind, the most dangerous, perhaps, but the one which is burning away at me with the highest intensity.

He looks over his shoulder slowly, not meeting my gaze, almost as though he's alarmed at my continuing gall despite everything.

"I'm an Abraxian— well, half of one. I'm half human too, just like you," he says, and I cock my head, looking at him with an odd expression.

"Oh. Do you feed on blood?" I'm direct once again, not having time for pleasantries, as I so rarely do.

"No. I eat food, just like you," he practically growls this time, looking slightly angry at my implication. I bow my head, not having a witty comeback for this either.

All in all, I'm stunned silent, and that is no small feat to achieve for anyone.

"I know you have questions, but we need to keep moving. Ask on the way, and I'll fill in the blanks for you," he vows. I frown.

"Well, it's all a blank right now. I don't even know why I'm here. Something about my debt?" I take a few steps forward now, rediscovering my footing and confidence as I stare into his familiar face, and we begin our journey through the forest.

"Okay, well I'll explain as best as I can, and then you can ask me anything you like, okay?" he suggests, and I nod, struggling to make words again as I stare at the overwhelmingly alien nature of everything around me.

The oddly coloured sky, the too-dark clouds, the ruddy earth— it's all surreal, and yet, somehow, I feel like I've been here before.

Maybe it's because my mother had supposedly been tied to this place, or because I've read so much about The Underworld in my studies, but even though I feel out of place, the mechanics of the setting don't shock me, don't cause me to pass out or hyperventilate. They just— are.

"Okay, so in a nutshell, The Nexus have reason to believe you might not be entirely human," he announces, and I suddenly feel sick. He doesn't make any sense, and it's becoming increasingly terrifying to me every time he opens his mouth.

He looks around at the trees and then at my confused expression, as though he's worried someone may be listening in. "It is suspected that you might be Haedes daughter," he whispers, voice deep, and my heart stops in my chest for a moment.

Is he serious?

"My father is Adam Sinclair" I retort, irritated as the image of my father's face floating through my mind, clear as crystal, obscuring even the overwhelming nature of the surroundings in which I'm immersed.

"Your mother, when she came down to The Underworld, she fell in love with Haedes. She wanted to leave your father for him, but then she found out upon her return that she was pregnant with you," he continues, but I feel my rage becoming uncontrollable at the inkling my happy family was anything but.

"So why didn't she just bring me here, if he's my dad?" I demand, folding my arms in suspicion. He sighs, rubbing the back of his neck with his palm nervously.

"The sun here— it stops mortal ageing. It's made up of a combination of the Eternal and Resurrection flame. One is red and one is blue, that's why it's purple in colour. It keeps the deceased mortals here alive for as long as we need them. If she'd have brought you here as a child, well, you'd still be one right now. Haedes created it to stop his body ageing. That kind of power would make him age far quicker than a normal mortal," he explains, and my eyes widen again.

"What do you mean? The dead mortals?" I focus in on this particular sentence and my heart expands a little.

Could it be my parents are here?

"This place, it's used to purify mortal souls. To return the darkness that corrupts them during their lifespan back to where it came from, The Well of Eternal Torment. Once the darkness is returned, they can move on to the Crucible of Gaia and be reborn again." The explanation seems complex and doesn't match anything I've studied for the past seven or so years. I mean, there are names I recognise, but everything seems all twisted up.

"Huh—" is the only reply I can come up with, wanting him simply to continue as we hurry past charred trees. The purple sun blisters overhead, eerie and beautiful all at once, especially now I know its function.

"Souls of the deceased rise into permanent bodies which are constructed from the Mortarian soil itself in Golgotha, called Doppelgangers or Doppels for short. Golgotha is the graveyard that lies between the Sanguine forest and the Plains of Ichor. After they rise there, they're taken to The Indicatus Courts, where we're going now, for sentencing," he concludes. My brow furrows.

"Sentencing, for what?" I query as we reach the edge of the forest. The trees here are thinning, and my heart pounds as a light white glow appears from nowhere.

As we close the gap between us and the source of the light, I realise that the glow is coming from the river.

The River Styx.

I gape as we approach the sloping, ruddy bank. Xion watches my face.

It's real. It's really real.

"Their sins. Every sinner has a different role here, and each role helps purify their souls so they can move on." He pauses for breath, and I take it all in. The surroundings, his gaze, the inclination that I might in be caught up with the very Gods I've studied in so much depth for so many years.

Is it fate?

Coincidence?

It doesn't seem very likely that I'd be so fascinated without some kind of divine intervention, or twist, which it is now growing clear to me is entirely possible.

"So, what roles are there?" I ask, my skin turning translucent as the light from the water, which looks like liquid moonlight, casts me in an alabaster hue.

"There is quite a wide variety, but by far the worst is for those sinners whose main crime is wrath or pride. They're sent to the Ashen Waste to protect the city from the demon armies." He looks at my curious expression, smiling, I'm sure at my compliance in listening to what would usually seem like insanity. "The Demon Lords want to take back the city and their hunting grounds, and it's the job of the sinners in the Souldier Forces to stop them," he clarifies, and I blink, following surprisingly well despite the complexity of the issue.

"So, The Nexus, they organise all this?" I ask, and he nods his head, eyes flitting between me and the water.

"Yes, that is their sole purpose here. They are perhaps the most important council of The Higher Plains, because without the constant control over the movement of souls, things can go very badly wrong for the universe," he warns, and my eyes widen.

"I'll get to meet them? The Gods?" I can't keep the intrigue from my voice.

"They're not technically all Gods, some are Titans. I'm pretty sure you're part Goddess yourself, though. You certainly have the attitude of one." He gets in this small dig, but I'm still too stunned to throw back any kind of retort. I watch as his face becomes disappointed before morphing back to his default expression of stoic and serious.

We reach a small jutting dock, made of black crystal, which leads out to an enormous, charred gondola that bobs atop the river. The wood it's made from is carved into the shape of bones, as though the entire thing is supported by the ribcage of an enormous dead whale.

Stepping inside, a tall thin woman turns to me and looks out from beneath the deep dark hood of her floor-length black cloak. Her hair is white as ash and her eyes pale duck-egg blue as she watches me struggle to keep balance atop the bobbing surface.

I smile at her, but she merely turns from me as Xion steps into the boat behind me, and we begin to move forward before either of us has even taken a seat. I perch myself on the edge of the damp, unforgiving, wooden benches, which are cracked in places, looking up at the ferrywoman who I assume to be Char.

"Hello," I call to her, wondering why she's being so rude.

Xion twists to face me with an amused glint in his eye.

"It's alright, Char doesn't talk much. Do you Char?" he prompts her, and she doesn't reply, doesn't even shake her head.

We're left, sitting in silence for a few moments before I feel my curiosity get the better of me.

"So, what's the difference between a Titan and a God? I thought— well I don't know what I thought. It seems like a lot of how mortals perceived this in stories is wrong. If I am actually awake and not insane." I feel my disbelief fading as the wood beneath me remains solid despite the rocking of the boat. There's no wind, only clammy heat, and I begin to regret wearing leather as I start to perspire despite the cool spray of the river at my back.

Xion turns to me, no longer gazing straight out to the river ahead. We pass increasingly sparse forest, which I examine with curiosity from afar as he licks his bottom lip before starting to speak again.

"A God or Goddess, they're descended from one of the original four forces in the universe. Gaia, Eros, Nyx, or Erebus as he is known in male form, and Tartarus." I recognise these names. In Greek mythology, they're the original four powers that came from Chaos, which existed as the sole form of energy at the beginning of the universe. I smile to myself; glad I'm not entirely lost.

"And a Titan?" I push him to continue as he opens his mouth to speak again. I'm impatient, but I can't help it. This is all freaking fascinating.

"A Titan is a mortal soul that ascended to live in The Higher Plains. You have to earn it. Most of the Titans were Kindred souls of one God or another. Some were Martyrs. It all depends on how strong the soul is." He exhales, like imparting all this knowledge is more exhausting for him than it is for me having to take it in. "The problem is, as many Titans will tell you, there's not equality between Titans and Gods like there should be. It's an extremely touchy issue." He sighs heavily again, and I nod, glad he's mentioned this. I mean I'd hate to make a faux pas and end up burned to a cinder under some random God's wrath or something.

"Kindred soul— I don't get it— what is that?" I ask, a frown marring my face. I've never even heard the term in anything I've studied, hence why it stands out to me now. You'd think someone would have written this all down somewhere. Like even on a post-it note.

Xion takes off his coat, revealing a simple black t-shirt about one size too large underneath. I wonder if it's that big to accommodate his demon form.

"The Kindred are mortals blessed by the Gods or Goddesses and put in their service. They keep the demons in check, stop them from causing havoc and breaching the walls between the dimensions." I lean forward, resting my elbows on my knees and looking up at him around a falling curtain of hair as I push it behind one ear.

"I see," I reply, feeling less and less significant by the minute.

I don't fully understand; there's too much information, but as I look out and keep my eyes trained straight ahead on the way the river is taking me, I wonder if I'm supposed to.

"This is just— it's too complicated," I admit and he nods.

"It is. We're talking about the entire history of our universe here. I could tell you a lot more, but for now, I suggest you just go with it. You'd need a diagram to explain everything that contributes to the way the different dimensions interconnect and affect one another. Only the oldest entities truly understand it. I don't even know half of what there is to it." He looks at me and there's a hint of pity in his eyes.

"So, what's the most important thing for me to know?" I ask him, wanting to make sure I'm armed with at least some knowledge.

"Honestly, demons and Demon Lords are bad. The Nexus is trying to do good. That's about it." He smiles, proud of himself for creating the equivalent of *Hell for Dummies*.

"But you're a demon—" I can't help it, I've been quiet and meek for too long, dwarfed by this new information, and I need to get a dig in somewhere. I can't let him have total power after all.

"Oh, I know. There's no need to remind me. I'm no hero. You'd do best to stay clear. That's my other bit of crucial advice." He smirks at me but his eyes are sad. I don't see the reply coming and so fall silent. I expect him to defend his honour or make a case for nobility, but instead, he simply admits he's rotten inside.

Why does that make him more attractive, I wonder?

"You really think I could be half God or something?" I ask, feeling my entire world tilting on its axis like it's had far too much to drink. I've always known deep down that my mother and father had a troubled marriage, but could my mother really have fallen in love with *the* Haedes? It doesn't seem likely, but then the fact I'm floating atop the real River Styx is completely insane too, and apparently that's happening.

"I do. You wielded The Eternal Flame. That doesn't just happen. Not to mortals," he tells me and I shrug, not knowing how to feel.

Adam Sinclair is my father, he raised me, he loved me, and he took care of me. Regardless of what deals he made with anyone else, I'm still his daughter, and he's still my dad.

"Look— I just— Even if I *am* Haedes daughter, he's not my dad. Okay?" I reiterate.

Xion looks surprised.

"I understand. Blood doesn't make you family," he agrees and I smile at him, gazing into his eyes as I realise that he really does understand.

"I guess one of your parents must be a Demon?" I ask, knowing it's a personal thing to ask, but also knowing that we're way past pleasantries at this point.

"My father. He's a Demon Lord. Abraxis," he spits out the name, voice full of hatred.

"I see." The atmosphere between us becomes awkward, so I decide to turn my curiosity onto someone else.

"So, what's Char's sin?" I ask him as the ferrywoman turns to me with a glare.

"You know it's rude to ask— but seeing as how you're new here, I guess Char can let you off." Xion gives her a return glare before continuing, "Any of the transport workers, ferrymen or women, carriage drivers, that kind of thing, usually fall into the sloth category of sin. They're not allowed to step off the river or dismount their vehicle for more than a few minutes. They are sentenced to a life of constant motion, never stopping, if that makes sense."

When he explains it this way, it does make sense; it makes perfect sense.

We turn a bend in the river and Xion and I tilt slightly in our seats. Silence falls between us as I take in the surroundings.

In the distance, a rising jagged shard ascends, cutting into the red sky. It's surrounded by other tall buildings, that wind like some kind of spinal cord, double helix hybrids. The architecture casts unique silhouettes, making me want to explore more, but as we near the outskirts of this urban settlement we turn yet again and begin heading in the opposite direction.

Xion watches my face, and even though I don't turn to acknowledge him, or ask any more questions, his gaze is unwavering. He offers me a hand at one point, draping it across my knee in a subtle act of comfort but I turn from him, not wanting comfort at all. I just want to get this over with.

I think about what he's said about The Courts — that it's where people go for sentencing — and swallow hard.

What happens to me if I am Haedes' daughter? Will they keep me here? Will I be allowed to leave? I know that my lineage makes little difference to me, but what will it mean to them? Will I be a prisoner here, without my expensive cars and manor house to protect me?

"There, you can see The Courts coming up just over the horizon." Xion points ahead, and I lean over the side of the boat, trying carefully not to think about the fact that the water I'm close to is filled with mortal souls. Or so I've been led to believe, based on the myths anyhow, not that this seems to count for much of anything down here.

The building is enormous and looks like the most morbid court-house you can imagine. The entire exterior is constructed from stark, monochrome stone, with white columns that look like a giant's bones forming the skeleton of the building, and black stone filling the spaces in between. Like the boat, the roof looks like some kind of sick ribcage, and I wonder who the hell has been doing the design for this place. It's grim to say the least.

We approach faster than I'd like, making me realise that I'm growing nervous. I haven't felt this way since my first day at boarding school after the death of my parents. It's a feeling I try to stay clear of, so used to deciding on the spot and just going with it, the knowledge that I can easily buy myself out of any trouble always in the back of my mind.

Here though, money probably doesn't mean anything, and I'm suddenly left feeling bare and exposed.

We pull up to The Courts, the height of the building dwarfing me. As we reach a jutting dock and step out onto the ruddy earth once more, Char leaves without so much as a goodbye.

I turn away from the river, casting my back on its eerie flow and looking up at the silhouette of the courthouse. It takes me a few minutes of staring, but eventually, Xion manages to get my feet moving, one in front of the other.

As we turn the corner to the front entrance of the building, adjacent to a road which looks to be paved with bones or something equally as morbid, I see it.

A snake-like line, unending, of people dressed identically in black jumpsuits. They all look tired and drained, *dead* even. Then it clicks.

They *are* dead. They're waiting to be sentenced. To serve their penance.

"I hate this place. The queues are always absolutely awful," Xion curses under his breath, and I sigh.

"And I thought I'd never see lines worse than at the DMV. I guess this place really is hell after all."

9

TRUE COLOURS

SEPHY

I DON'T KNOW HOW long we've been waiting, mainly because the sun doesn't seem to fall or rise in the sky, giving no indication of time lost, but I know it's longer than I can take.

"This is getting ridiculous. We've barely moved an inch, and it's been—" I wish I had a watch, anything to help me measure the time.

"It's only been about twenty minutes, Sephy. You're just anxious." He lets me in on the horrific truth of our standby experience and I gape at him.

"Are you kidding me? Twenty freaking minutes?" I cross my arms over my breasts, beyond irritated.

I hear horse hooves and groan, hoping beyond anything that it's not more people to add to the line. There are enough bodies squished into this small muggy courtyard as it is.

Heads turn as a large, black, gothic carriage approaches, pulled by two Percherons that look almost identical to Nightshade.

"Who's that?" I ask, turning from the scene unfolding on the road and looking back to Xion, who is smiling.

"I think our wait is over." He steps out of the line, and I follow him hesitantly, mainly because I'm going to be beyond pissed if I have to start again from the back.

The carriage driver, who sits with a whip in one hand, is dressed in a worn-looking black jacket and loose slacks with shiny black shoes. He doesn't turn to look at us as we approach.

The carriage door opens as the gilded black handle turns, pushing out from the antiquated vehicle. A small flight of steps descends, unfolding in smooth time, and an elegant woman's foot, surrounded by yards of black lace, protrudes into the timeless humidity of the outside world.

"Lucifer!" Xion exclaims, and I feel myself do a double take.

Did he just say Lucifer?

As in— *the devil* Lucifer?

From within the shadow of the plush-looking carriage, a woman at least six feet tall steps onto the ground. She's even taller than that though because as she straightens, elongated silhouettes make themselves known upon her head. I stare, watching her neaten her skirt as I realise that nestled among white locks are two enormous horns like that of an impala.

I watch her with interest, wondering exactly how powerful she is. I mean, if she really is the devil, that's one hell of a reputation to live up to.

Her gaze immediately finds mine, and our eyes lock as she steps forward, her body towering over me. Her heels and horns add extra height to her already intimidating silhouette as she comes closer, causing me to raise my gaze further.

I straighten my spine, not willing to be underestimated.

"You must be Sephy," she assumes, her gown of black lace swaying around her as she moves, elegant as a ballet dancer.

"And you are?" I try to act cockier than I feel, staring up into her flawless white skin. She's definitely not mortal, nobody human has pores that immaculate.

"Lucifer. You can call me Luce." She holds out her long fingers, nails lacquered in a bloody hue, and I take her hand in mine, shaking it firmly. I hate a limp handshake. Limp handshake, limp everything else if you ask me.

"Lucifer— as in?" I want to be sure I'm not just meeting some woman with the same name. Now I think about it though, it makes sense that the devil would be a chick.

"The Devil, Satan, Beelzebub— yep, that's me." She looks down her nose at me, and I shudder slightly from the chill of her pale stare. "Why are you two waiting in line with these losers?" she asks as I turn to look back at the crowd.

They're watching her with sunken, anxious eyes, and I wonder if she's as nice as she seems. They all appear terrified by her presence alone.

"Come along. I'll get Yama and Muerta to bring your case to the front of the queue. We haven't got all damned day," she tuts, taking long strides past the line as Xion and I follow.

The eyes of the dead follow us, envy filling their souls, which I'm sure will be one more thing they'll be paying for down here, and I shudder, not wishing to be in their shoes. Then I remember that my father should be here, my mother too, and pity fills me in an unexpected rush for their suffering.

Luce steps up exactly three black steps, slamming her fists into the high double doors, one black and one white, pushing them back from her as two sinners, guarding the entrance, step aside like she's dangerous.

"Are Yama and Muerta— are they Gods too?" I ask Xion, nervous as we walk past black jumpsuit after black jumpsuit, sullen face after sullen face.

"Yes, they deal with justice and sentencing. Muerta can see sins, kind of like auras, and Yama is the judge— they used to be married, but not any longer," he adds this little bit of underworld gossip in, as though we're no more than two co-workers chatting over a water cooler.

"Oh— right," I reply, scowling and feeling claustrophobic despite the size of the place. I'm hot and flustered from the humidity outside, and I can't help but wonder why nowhere here seems to have air conditioning. I mean, the stone walls and floors are certainly sapping the heat, constructed of what I assume to be marble in monochromatic hues, but I can still feel sweat rolling down the back of my knees beneath the leather of my pants. The walls are lined with torches that glow blue, not electric lights, so I'm also sure that's not helping, even if they do emit a cold glow.

We reach the end of the long entrance hall, and Luce wastes no time in getting yet more sinners, standing guard, to step aside. Xion looks back over his shoulder to where I'm lagging behind, lacking my usual speed as I try to take everything in.

"You alright?" he enquires, and I nod, not having the words to articulate what I'm feeling, perhaps because I don't even know how that is.

Following in the wake of Luce's black lace train, which trails along the chequered black and white floor with a certain dark grandeur that causes her presence yet more influence, we move into a small waiting room with chairs made from charred twigs.

They look uncomfortable, though I'm sure that's the point, and Xion directs me to take a seat as Luce disappears with him down a long hallway to my left.

I sit in the waiting room, the only thing absent the insanely irritating ticking of a clock. I look around for a magazine to read, but I guess they must be all out of *Sinner's Style Weekly*, and so settle for trying not to focus on what's about to happen.

After ten minutes, Luce and Xion return, triumphant with joint expressions of contentment.

"Come with us," Luce demands, holding out a hand. I don't want to move, so just sit, staring at them both blankly.

"I— I don't know if I want to." I'm more unsure than I have been in my entire life, and that's not something I'm used to at all. Luce looks down at me, but then lowers herself, kneeling in her dress so she's on eye level with me like I'm a toddler. Her expression morphs into one of kindness and almost child-like innocence, something I wouldn't expect from someone with her reputation, comes over her.

"It'll be alright. It's just a meeting. Don't worry. I'm sure Xion won't let anything happen to you." She looks between me and him, eyes glistening as though she's in on some big secret we aren't. It pisses me off, so I get to my feet, swallowing my fear and narrowing my eyes.

"Let's go."

I enter the courtroom through a single door, which seems a little underwhelming compared to the architecture I've seen so far. It's made of wood, and as it swings forward, I'm greeted by the sight of more monochrome. In fact, the room almost looks like a giant chessboard gone wrong.

The benches, raised atop balconies on either side of the room are black on my left and white on my right, sunken into the walls between skeletal pillars.

As I walk down towards the head of the courtroom with more confidence than I feel, I'm greeted by three figures. They watch my every move from the juror's bench on my right, though upon further inspection I see that only two of them have eyes that follow my motion.

The three old women sit together, one of them blind.

They appear to be triplets and are collectively knitting with insanely long needles. The one with bloodshot eyes holds a ball of dark wool in her too-pale fingers which bend at each joint like spiders' legs. They are, as a group, diverse in appearance given the circumstances, with identical grey suits but varied levels of neatness.

The woman with red eyes has bedraggled hair and a skewed bun, while the middle woman with white eyes is neat as a pin, her hands moving with speed as it's she who controls the knitting needles. The final elderly woman, the one closest to me who is holding a pair of mean-looking scissors, appears by far the most aggravated of the three and merely stares at me with her crazed, unkempt hair, freaking me out as her half-moon glasses drop down her crooked nose.

"Is that woman angry at me or something?" I ask Xion, who is walking beside me, his boots unsurprisingly heavy on the floor.

"She can hear you ya know! It's her who can't speak!" The blind woman with bloodshot eyes yells at me, pointing to the scissor-wielding woman I'm referring to, and I flinch, surprised that her hearing is so good. She looks only a few years off being fossilised.

"Oh— Uh— Sorry," I mutter, averting my gaze as silence falls and the only audible noise is the clicking of knitting needles.

"Try not to anger The Fates." Xion sighs, winking at me as the woman who can't see nudges the woman beside her.

She points to Xion and the knitting needles cease.

"Hey, Xion is here! Come here for a kiss, handsome boy!" she calls out like some insane version of someone's grandma. I chuckle to myself under my breath as Xion goes flush in the cheeks, relaxing incrementally. We're all just people, not gods, not fates, or demons. All just people.

I try to hold on to this fact as I see where I'll be sitting.

Through the partition separating the back of the room from the Judge's bench, I'm seated in another chair made of charred branches, central to the room. I cannot escape focus here and wonder if a bright light might suddenly be shone upon me, my wrists strapped to the armrests.

However, as a few moments pass, the only activity is that of others being seated and the unnerving continuation of knit one, purl one.

The sound of doors opening signals that the trial is about to begin, and I'm alarmed as I see two of the most unusual-looking figures proceed out into the courtroom.

A man and a woman, or so they appear, stride out and nod to the three fates, and then Luce, before moving to begin.

The woman, with long flowing raven hair and enormous brown chocolate eyes, purses her full lips at the sight of me. Though, her princess-esque features are not what is alarming, but rather the fact that her skin is decorated so it appears to be not flesh, but skeleton. Her eye-sockets are decorated in the traditional sugar skull designs of Mexico, her lips lined with fake stitching, elongating her grimace. She's wearing a brown corset over the top of a white shirt and a long crimson skirt. A cloak of similar red material hangs from her shoulders and falls in a torrent to the floor before pooling at her ankles.

I watch as her male counterpart, or ex-husband as I assume him to be, takes a few steps up to be seated as the judge before me. This must be Yama, meaning the woman is Muerta. The judge's skin is azalea blue, his hair pressed against his narrow skull in golden cornrows that look like rows of actual corn due to the colour. His robes are a matching gold and so are his eyes, which shine out across the room.

He too gets a look of concern, brow furrowing as his focus moves onto my face, and I wonder why it is that, all of a sudden, I'm the cause of such anxiety.

I stare right back at him, trying to appear braver than I truly feel.

Yama is beautiful, there is no denying it even though he looks nothing short of strange and otherworldly.

Pulling his chair close to the desk, he folds his blue hands in front of him and stares down at me, a mere mortal in the face of a God.

"You are the girl in question?" he asks.

I move my head up and down, transfixed by him.

"I prefer woman, but yes, I am she." He opens a black folder in front of him on the desk and flips through the pages.

"Miss Persephone Sinclair?" He reads my name aloud, and I feel myself getting angry as my nails bite into the armrests of the chair.

"It's Sephy, actually," I reply, letting the usual irritation I feel at the use of my legal name continue to irk me, despite the fact my name is being spoken by a god.

"And your father was— Adam Sinclair?" he asks me, and I nod again, placing my chin in my palm and looking up at him, bored.

"He and your mother, Demi Sinclair, I see as it is here, owe quite the debt— and yet, we have found no trace of them here in Mortaria." He speaks this apparent truth, and I feel my heart deflate in my chest.

So, my parents aren't here.

"But— I thought everyone came here after they die— I mean there can't be many people who haven't got anything to atone for? Can there?" I ask, not caring that I may be out of order, or that I don't know any of the rules here. I just want answers.

Muerta watches me with curiosity from the sidelines where she stands beside the three fates.

"There are only two ways in which a soul evades this place— immortality through blessing at the discretion of the Gods, or through destruction," Yama explains, eyes inexpressive of how he feels, if he does at all.

"And how exactly do you destroy a soul?" I ask, cocking my eyebrow and trying to let the fact he is even more intimidating than Luce wash over me. I need to stand my ground with these people, show them that even though I am mortal, I won't be pushed around.

"The Eternal Flame." The voice comes from Muerta this time, her tongue twisting around the syllables in a gorgeous and unmistakable Spanish accent.

"Hmmm—" Yama looks at the file, then at Xion.

"And you claim that this girl has the power over such a flame?" he asks, expression deadly serious.

What is he implying exactly?

Xion stands from the bench where he's sat, watching the trial with a still stoic expression.

"Yes, that is correct. She killed a Banshee. I saw it."

"And what do you make of all this, Fates?" Yama turns now to the three old women who sit on the Juror's bench, still knitting, as though they're not even paying attention.

For a moment, they still in their motion, touching palms to one another before the red-eyed woman speaks.

"There— is more to this than meets the eye. I have seen," she announces. The woman next to her smiles.

"I have heard," she says, even though I know she is deaf. "And our sister has spoken— spoken with the voices of the past. There is more here than meets the eye," they explain as a twosome, and I wonder what their names are individually.

"Layla, Moira, Anya— please do indulge an old judge and let us in on whatever it is you're sitting on. I don't have all day." Yama looks irritated, and I wonder if the three old biddies try this kind of melodrama with every person who comes in here, or if I'm just special. From Yama's reaction, I'd guess the former.

"The girl— she is indeed Haedes' daughter. She destroyed the souls of her caregivers."

At this inclination, I'm on my feet.

"How dare you?! My parents died in a—" I begin to leap to my own defence before I realise something.

My parents *had* died in a fire.

What if— what if I was the one who lit it?

But no. That can't be. It was an accident. I was only six years old. I don't even know how to use whatever my powers are now. How on earth would I be able to use them as a child?

"Bring us the eye," the bedraggled woman with the ball of wool demands, reaching out a blind hand.

Muerta is handed what looks to be a sphere of quartz by Yama and passes it to the Blind Fate without breaking my gaze.

"This will show you— you will see, child," she promises, dropping the ball of wool carelessly so it falls and rolls across the room, taking up the orb in both hands like it's a baby bird.

After a few seconds, what appears to be a mythical projector powers up, showing me what I think is a memory.

I'm there, small and wide-eyed, with chubby arms and legs. My hair is the only thing that distinguishes me from any other child as it stands out, wavering auburn as the misty projection shimmers in the air. I'm in my mother and father's suite, the place I no longer venture, playing by the fireplace.

My mother calls out to me, her face a stab in the gut as I'm taken back to what I've lost. Her voice comes crashing down over me like the saddest lament you'll ever hear.

"Come on, little Firecracker. Time to say goodnight to Daddy. He'll be gone by the time you wake up." She looks sad as deep chocolate locks fall across her face and the green eyes I miss so much sparkle with tears. She looks miserable, which is amazing to me because that's not how I remember this at all.

"Come here, Firecracker." My father spreads out his arms to me, but I move away.

"No!" I scream, cognac eyes burning with naïve rage. I don't understand he has to leave for business. I just know I don't want him to go.

I back up toward the fireplace, trying to put off the hug for as long as possible, thinking it'll stop the inevitable.

As I reach the raised marble ledge of the grate, I scream out again, tears in my too-innocent eyes.

"No!"

In a flash, the fire within the marble hearth explodes forward, burning from scarlet to orange in an ombre I've seen only once before.

I watch on in horror, but I'm powerless to stop it. I feel my terror at what I've done rise and attack, destroying the walls I've built so carefully over so many years.

I fall to my knees, eyes wide now as they had been then, and flame explodes from my palms. This time though it's from my adult palms, and not from that of a child, causing gasps to emit from onlookers.

Muerta's voice can be heard screaming, "That's enough!"

I close my eyes and wish that everything would just stop, that I could just go back to ignorance.

The sound emitted from the orb ceases and the room goes silent.

I begin to cry, harrowing sobs wrenching my body as my heart is ripped so open that I cannot fathom even trying to appear cocky or brave.

I killed my parents.

I killed them.

It takes but a single touch of Xion's hand on my shoulder to turn my anguish to rage. I don't look at him, leaning forward on my knees as I let my hair fall around me. The curtain of fiery red shields me from his concerned stare, making my fury all the more unmanageable.

"Don't touch me," I spit, furious. Why did he bring me here? Why did he have to expose this and turn my loss into unmanageable guilt? If it weren't for him, I would be back at Retropolis, finding someone to lose myself in. Having fun. Being Sephy again.

I just want to go home.

This desire surprises me, especially when for the last month I've hated being so cooped up in the estate and tried to leave every single chance I got.

Wiping my eyes, I know I cannot dwell on my guilt now. I need to finish up here and get out of this place, and I can't do that sobbing on the floor.

I need to appear strong.

I stand up tall, throwing my hair back over one shoulder and glancing at Xion's expression as it turns surprised.

I take a deep breath, calm myself, and I look Yama straight in the eye. I'm not the kind of person you fuck with. Especially not now.

"So, what now?" I demand, placing a hand on my hip and ignoring the fact that my heart is still racing in my chest. I'm in shock, I know I am. But as usual, I'm excellent at compartmentalising, and so I put my emotions away in a tiny box, knowing I'll have to deal with them when I'm alone and in the company of fine whisky.

"Judging on what I've just seen, I can say with confidence that your parent's souls were destroyed. This is why their debt has fallen to you," Yama concludes.

I nod.

"However, as it is, you're not actually the descendant of Adam Sinclair, perhaps legally in the mortal world, you are his heir, but biologically speaking, you have no connection with him at all it would seem." He presses his fingers together again and looks to Muerta who is watching us both with interest.

"What do you see in her?" he asks, and Muerta squares her shoulders, taking purposeful strides and getting closer to me than I'd like. She seems to have no gauge for personal space, so much so that I can feel her breathing on my face as her warm breath dries the salty trails left by my tears.

She looks into my eyes with her enormous chocolate brown irises and I feel vulnerable like she's giving me an x-ray.

I turn away from her, trying not to feel awkward, and spot Luce up in the gallery above, watching me with interest. She smiles and is beautiful in this expression no doubt, but rather than finding her grin comforting, I'm unsettled. She looks like an angel on the outside, but for some reason — call it listening to too many bible verses on Sundays — I seriously doubt she is one.

"She is proud, her heart is filled with lust for certain— and— there is vanity, a dash of wrath—" Muerta lists off my sins, frowning for a moment.

"But— she is a demi-god no doubt. Her mortal half may be riddled with the start of sins the likes of which we have never seen, and yet her Godly half is pure. She cannot carry the debt of her namesake. She is not a viable candidate." The words spill from her lips, and suddenly the blind Fate gasps as I smirk at the list of my sins, or as I like to call them, best qualities.

"Layla, what is it?" Muerta demands, moving back from me and over to the three women as the clicking of knitting needles ceases and they grab one another's hands.

"The Phoenix— A Chimera of all Souls. Will rise from her ashes—" Layla speaks, hands shaking as the scissor-wielding fate points to me with her shears. I shake my head in automatic protest, not under-

117

standing, worrying that I'm going to be thrown into some kind of torture chamber or something.

"What does that mean?" I ask, looking up at Luce and calling out to her. She frowns a second.

"I don't know," she calls back from above, shrugging. I sigh.

At least if it's rising from my ashes, then I won't have to worry about it; I'll be long gone by then.

"Well, I think it's pretty clear that we can't let you leave here Miss Sinclair. You've been attacked once already, and you're clearly untrained with your powers, understandably so," Yama decrees.

I scowl.

"I'm not staying here. I don't care if you're the god of the entire universe. You can't make me stay here." I'm speaking as though I think it can make an inch of difference. I know I'm no match for him, for anyone in this room, maybe not even The Fates. Well, I'm probably a match for Xion, but that's not much good when he suddenly seems to be the only person on my side.

He clears his throat, stepping forward so he's stood beside me.

"Yama. She cannot just disappear. She is well known in the mortal world. It will cause a stir. I will teach her how to use her powers. I will take her home." He looks at me, and my heart skips a beat. He might not be punching the crap out of someone, but this is definitely the most heroic thing he's ever done.

"You? You cannot teach her how to wield the Immortal Flame— only Haedes can do such a thing. You are completely unqualified!" Yama exclaims, upset that someone has questioned his rule.

"Haedes does not even wish to acknowledge he has a daughter. I believe that as long as Xion is protecting her, she should be allowed to go and live her life as normal." This comes from Luce now, and Yama continues to frown.

Muerta and Luce share a look, and I wonder what it is they're thinking.

"If anything should happen, it is on your head, Xion," Yama sighs, warning him through gritted teeth as he raises his arm toward the black mallet on his left. He lifts it before bringing it down upon the black wood of the bench, striking a sound that signals the trial is over.

I'm so exhausted I want to just collapse, and as Xion comes toward me, my anger for him, which had raged earlier, quells. Fatigue takes hold of my body, and my muscles unclench; my legs feel like jelly, and my heartbeat continues to pulse rapid in my ears.

"Let's get you home," Xion whispers to me, guiding me out of the room.

This entire thing has left me raw. Left me exposed and vulnerable.

As we leave the courtroom, I realise it's the first time since I lost my parents that I feel like what I really am.

An orphan.

PANDORA

I shrink back behind the alabaster pillar of the upstairs gallery. I knew I'd chosen my spot well because everyone was too busy watching The Fates, those ridiculous old crones, to notice me above in the shadow cast by the black walls.

I am startled by the news, to say the least.

Haedes— has a daughter?

Another Demi-God?

How could he have been so careless?

These are the questions which flurry around my mind, making my unending rage for his entire family stir. Reckless, mindless, lust-filled manwhores, and yet *I'm* not worthy?

Oh no. Oh no, no.

I mean, now I think about him and his brother Zeus, I'm surprised he hasn't got a litter of little mongrel pyromancers running around, because according to rumour, he's quite the philanderer, just like his older sibling.

I take a few moments, waiting for the court to empty as I ponder on the implications of what Sephy Sinclair's existence means. She lost her parents in a fire started by her own childish hand. She has potentially a new parent who seemingly wants nothing to do with her—

The cogs within my mind turn, whirring and grating against one another with timeless friction, as I think about how exactly I can use her to further my own goals.

When the final member of the courtroom leaves and the last door slams shut, I step out from the shadows, smiling.

This is good. I determine. *I can use this. I can use her.*

It is with my new path clear ahead and my intentions crystalline in my mind that I reach for the box.

Throwing it into the air, I step into the darkness of yet another whirring portal, heading back to the place I call home, intending fully to finally help the Demon Lords take back theirs.

FREE FALLING

XION

SHE IS CHANGED; SLOUCHING as she shuffles from the courthouse and into the gondola. Hunched silently in her seat, she looks out over the Mortarian landscape which passes us in a morose and stagnant blur. The earth turns from blackened to ruddy once more as we move through the land, the river never slowing in its constant ebb, the gnarled outlines of charred trees becoming more and more consistent in their placement. Slowly, a canopy of red leaves forms overhead, crowding the sky from view and indicating our return to the depths of the Sanguine Forest.

When we reach The Hollow, she doesn't even hiss as I take the obsidian blade to her palm, drawing blood and paying the toll quickly so that we may return to the grounds of The Sinclair Estate.

I don't know how I'm going to teach her how to use her powers; I don't even know the first thing about controlling The Eternal Flame. The only thing I really know is that it's one of the only things in all the dimensions that can destroy me for good. So that's comforting.

We arrive outside the door of her suite, and she moves to enter it, no doubt with the intention of slamming it behind her and locking herself away.

"Sephy, are you alright? I can— I could stay. You shouldn't be by yourself," I offer as my brow furrows, wanting to show her kindness, comfort her, but not used to having to comfort any kind of person, let alone a headstrong young woman.

"No. Thank you for bringing me home, but no. I need to sleep on all of this. To try and process it all." The lustrous fire in her voice has diminished considerably from what I'm used to, and her gaze is cloudy with emotion as she looks deeply into my eyes, brushing her hair behind one ear.

I want to reach out, to tell her that I understand what she's going through because I *do* understand what she's going through, but I can't find the words.

Instead, I let her turn and shut the door in my face without so much as a goodbye, continuing to stand outside for a few moments in the hallway like a miserable spare part. She's sassy and feisty up front, sometimes even mean, but it's like she's been stripped of that part of who she is and has returned to the state of the once naïve child I rescued from the billowing flames all those years ago. She's vulnerable, like a deer in the forest whose mother has just been shot, and it's harrowing to behold, frightening even, to see such a regular powerhouse made visibly weak like this.

Realising I'm standing with no real purpose in front of a door that I don't have the courage to open, I turn on the ball of my foot and take leisurely slow steps down the hallway. I'm half hoping she'll change her mind, let me in so I can make sure she's okay, but it doesn't seem likely.

I reach the landing and find Jules making his way up the stairs with a silver tray atop one palm; it holds a bottle of whisky and a glass with a single ice cube in its depths.

"Did she ask you for that?" I ask him, and he shakes his head.

"No, but I'm used to her needs by now. After going to that place, I'm sure it's necessary." Jules looks me up and down, slight disapproval in his stare.

"She just found out that she was responsible for the death of her parents. I really don't think adding alcohol to the situation is going to help," I insist, and his eyes widen.

"Wait— she was the cause of the fire?" He looks shocked and his expression crumples as I confirm his fear, lips sagging and eyes losing their prim and proper focus. He shuffles in the confines of his suit, clearly not sure what to say.

"Oh Jesus— okay, where is she?" He looks desperate now, like a father in his affections for her, and I jerk my head in the direction of her bedroom.

"She said she wants to sleep it off— to process everything. I wanted to respect her wishes. It's not easy to deal with that kind of information, let alone the fact she's just discovered she's a demi-god." Jules' expression turns partly surprised by this information, but I'm getting the impression that it isn't as big of a shock to him as the fact Sephy had started the fire all those years ago.

"You knew," I say under my breath with a deep exhale.

"Of course, I knew. Look at her. There's not an ounce of Adam Sinclair anywhere in that girl—" he pauses. "Wait, did you say she told you she was going to sleep? To process all this?" His expression becomes suddenly and ferociously panicked.

"Yes, why?" I ask him as he drops the tray he's holding with a clatter. Abandoning all sense of duty, the tray slams into the floor, filling the chasmic hall with the echoes of rattling silver. The whisky bottle smashes at the impact as does the glass beside it, causing the green of the runner to darken, spirit exploding all over the floor.

"She's going to run." He's turning as his words reach me, and I wonder how he knows this as he begins to take off down the stairs.

Then I realise. *I* should have known this.

Sephy Sinclair doesn't process anything. She doesn't sleep on things. She acts. She runs. She denies.

I take off after Jules, catching up to the butler in mere seconds as his light footfall makes quick work of the stairs.

Across the lobby we dash, side by side, before slamming our full weight into the thick front doors and bursting out into the night. Jules spins on the ball of his foot, skidding across the gravel artfully, and I'm instantly intrigued whether he's ever been in the armed forces. I don't know many men who can move that well in a suit without training.

We sprint along the length of the west wing, passing by many windows which reflect only moonlight back as no light exudes from within. Turning the corner so we're adjacent to the back of the estate, I see her outline, halfway down the wall from her bathroom window; she's using her bed sheets as a makeshift rope.

I roll my eyes as Jules and I slow together, waiting beneath her descending derriere for her feet to hit the ground.

When they finally do, she exerts a grunt and turns, only to find me smiling and towering over her, looking down into her determined yet distraught face.

"Aww crap," she exclaims, running her fingers through her hair and looking left then right. Dark circles have appeared beneath her eyes, and her skin is paler than usual, pasted in a light sweat that clings to her red hairline, tinting it dark.

"If you think you can outrun me then I'll just save you the energy. I have demonic speed. I'd catch you before you were even to the trees," I threaten her, though I don't growl as I usually would.

"Well, I was sort of hoping I would make it to the car before you noticed— or maybe even the airport." She looks awkward now, twisting her fingers in front of her and licking her bottom lip, nervous for some reason.

Am I that terrifying?

She's never seemed intimidated like this before.

"Look, that won't help. Trust me. I tried it," I whisper, bending my head and coming in close, just in case she attempts to make a belated break for it. Jules coughs uncomfortably and makes his exit in the most discreet way he can manage.

"What, you mean you killed your parents too?" She cocks an eyebrow at me in disbelief, and my expression drops into one of serious pain.

"No. I killed the first and only girl I've ever loved." I state the truth, even though it hurts me, even though after all this time the guilt won't diminish and never will. I speak it only for her, so she can see she isn't alone.

She doesn't reply; she just gets a pained look on her face as we stare at one another, neither one's gaze diminishing in intensity and neither one of us able to move from a seemingly invisible emotional gravity that's caught us within its clutch.

"You— you did?" Her lack of sass, witty retort, or sarcasm is painful, even though I thought I'd never miss those things about her.

"Yes. The first time we— made love—" I begin, and she snorts. I glare at her, and she cannot help but give a small smile.

"I'm sorry— it's just, that's such an old person thing to say." She blushes and then blinks a few times, dissipating her own amusement.

"Well, regardless, I lost my virginity to her. Then the next morning, I woke up and I couldn't remember the event. She was dead beside me. My demon form presented itself for the first in the heat of the moment, so to speak, and— well, you can guess the rest," I recall the terror, the trauma, and the guilt. Something I've tried to avoid for decades.

"How— how do you live with it?" she asks, deadly serious now as her eyes well with tears.

She looks down to the ground, fidgeting on the damp grass and becoming once more that tiny girl who lost it all in a blaze of flames.

"You just do. The guilt may never leave you, but what happened was an accident, and no amount of money, time, or punishing yourself is going to bring your parents back. They're gone. It's over. They wouldn't want you to punish yourself over it. They weren't like that." I remember the couple vividly, how driven Adam Sinclair had been, even to the point of neglect for his family, and how loving Demi never ceased to appear, to the point where she sacrificed everything to give her daughter a normal life.

Unfortunately, that's been blown to hell. Or so it would seem.

"You knew them?"

She looks surprised, and I nod.

"I did, and I was there that day. The day of the fire. How do you think you got out?" I ask her, and she looks deeply into my face, as though by staring hard enough she'll be able to recall the memory.

"I thought you looked familiar," she mutters under her breath.

"Well, I remember you. I always have. You were so innocent back then," I recall, and she tilts her chin, defiant.

"How can you say that? I killed my parents. I'm a murderer." The word falls like ice from her lips, chilling me deep. I've had the same thoughts, but now I'm looking at her situation, I realise that perhaps an accident really is nobody's fault.

"You're not a murderer. You didn't do it on purpose. It doesn't even count as a real sin. Nothing you do does until you're over the age of sixteen. That's why there are no children in Mortaria. You can't be held accountable for your actions." I try to make her feel better, and I think it works a little because her eyes become curious.

"Is that— is that why you're there? Are you atoning?" she asks me, and I sigh.

"No. I'm damned regardless of what I do. Demon souls— or even half-demon souls, have no place anywhere but Mortaria. Even if I die, no amount of servitude could ever redeem me." I speak this truth, another which I try not to think about, and her eyes widen, pity filling them in place of despair.

It's the most honest conversation we've ever had, and I wonder if it'll help her or if she'll just disregard each word as if it means nothing, just as she always does.

"Do you think— do you think I'm a bad person?" she asks, eyes brimming now.

"No. I think you're a brave person." I respond automatically with a truth I cannot deny. She is brave. Braver than she knows, and behind her usual cockiness and swagger, there is a person who has been alone for a long time. Someone who has had to look after themselves, even when they didn't know how to.

Her eyes begin to overflow with tears and she does something which shocks me to my very core. She steps forward and leans into me for a hug. I put my arms around her, the feel of human contact foreign and terrifying as she sobs in my arms.

I bring a palm up and stroke her fiery hair, hushing her under the silent blinking of many dimming stars. Looking up to the sky, I enjoy the feel of another so close and exhale, knowing that this is wrong. I can't get involved with her, no matter how much I want to, or how much she might make everything inside of me burn in a way it hasn't for decades. I'm destructive, and unpredictable, meaning I'm also cursed to live life alone.

As I cradle her in my arms, which have been empty too long, I know we are the same. Two lone meteorites, free falling from the stars and burning everything we collide with to ash.

LUCE

It's an uncertain but late hour as I once again fall through the door to my suite, only to be greeted by the two loves of my life. Beelz, who is back from her late-night hunt around The Ashen Waste, and Thane, who is wearing a large white t-shirt, men's boxer shorts, and nothing else. She's sprawled, long legs immaculately spindled, along the couch, with Beelzebub, my pet panther, lounging on the rug in front of the enormous dark hearth burning a cool blue flame.

"How did it go?" I hear her ask as I turn toward the coat stand by the door. Throwing my long black cloak over one of the twisted iron hooks, I turn back to face her.

"It was— well, distressing." I bite my bottom lip, not knowing how to describe what I've just witnessed.

That poor girl.

It had been my intention to scare her, but upon seeing her boldness despite everything that was so radically changing around her, she had

126

held her ground. She fought. Despite guilt, and loss, and what I can imagine is an unimaginable sense of shaken identity, she remained fierce.

For that, she has earned my respect.

"Is she— I mean, is she really his daughter?" Thane demands tentatively, moving to sit with her legs crossed in front of her, spine acutely straight as her attention zeroes in on me. Her stormy gaze burns into my own, making me feel like the world around me is simply falling away. How does her magnetic personality always manage to pull me into its distracting grasp?

"Yes. She's his daughter." I exhale heavily, pressing down my hair with long fingers and trying to entertain myself, ignoring the sudden urge to strip naked.

I bend at the knee, knowing Beelzebub will provide apt distraction, and bury my nails into her thick onyx fur. She purrs slightly, but scowls despite my affections.

For some reason, this damn panther has always liked Thane more than me. Haedes captured her from the mortal plain and brought her here to keep me company in those days before Thane joined me, but it's clear, despite our early connection, who she prefers.

A deep purr erupts from within her chest as she stands up, stretching out her long spine and thrusting her ass in the air as her tail curls like heavy smoke. Enormous paws spread and claws protrude, mouth opening in a yawn, exposing her enormous teeth, before she pads around in a small circle and sits down again, facing away from me.

Gee thanks, Beelz, I love you too.

I roll my eyes, and Thane gives her a stroke between the ears. The sassy cat purrs this time but remains exactly where she is, making her preference perfectly evident.

"Are you going to tell him?" she demands, as I take a few steps past her and glide through the misted glass of the Japanese sliding doors which lead into our bedroom.

"I don't think so. Not tonight. I don't even know what to make of it myself. She doesn't want to stay here. He doesn't want anything to do with her either. And he may be the only one who can teach her to protect herself." I begin to undress, pulling the top layer of my black lace dress over my head so I'm standing in only lingerie and dark petticoats. "I mean, you know about Banshee. They can smell power— so what if— what if the Demon Lords don't know about her? What if it was just a mistake?" I muse, hopeful.

Thane snorts and I hear her metronomic tread pacing across the stone of the floor before the sliding doors move apart, revealing her.

"You think that one of Lilliana's children died and no one noticed? Come on, Luce, I know we look like spring chickens, but you can't be that naïve." Her thin lips contort around the words I don't want to hear as she paces over to our bed, taking a seat and watching me undress with a leisurely, feline smile.

I hear snoring from the other room, signalling that my kitty is asleep, hardly surprising as that's what she spends around fifty percent of her time doing.

"I know— I just, I can't help but feel for this girl. I wouldn't wish being a demi-god on anyone. It's only just marginally better than being—" I stop, swallowing hard. Thane gets to her feet.

"Now, that's enough of that. You're beautiful and perfect. With horns or without. I'll love you forever. Even after I'm just smoke on the wind, Luce. You know you need to stop with this self-loathing. You're more powerful than you know. You shouldn't be so ashamed," Thane condemns me, placing her hands on my shoulders as I step out of my underskirts so I'm standing in only my underwear. Her eyes caress me in that way they do, and I shudder, a delicious temptation curling around my heart and constricting in a serpentine vice.

"I can't help it. I'm not pure like you," I whisper as she places a hand on my cheek and crushes her lips to mine. She tastes like blackberries and pine, and her skin is rough against the softness of my own.

"You're the purest person I know, baby," Thane whispers back, bringing her long arms around me and pulling me close to her jagged frame. I melt into her, hard on soft, my shadows cast against her light.

I need to speak to Haedes. There's so much to do. So many things that need to be said.

For now, though, I abandon all language except that of touch and fire. I'll let her show me I'm perfect in her eyes, even if in my own I can never be.

11

TRAIN IN VAIN

PANDORA

I AM GREETED BY the all too familiar sound of mortal screams as I walk into the shadowy broken corridor of Barbas' wing in The Halls of Antiqua. Spiders flee at the sound of my tread, and I feel my hair catch on dangling webs that fall from the cracks in almost every stone of the ceiling. I hear the scurry of the arachnids, their desperation to return to their master and tell him of my approach, but fortunately for me I can move far quicker than a stupid bug, so I doubt he'll know I'm coming.

As I reach the end of the long stretch of corridor, I see smoke, dark and unnatural, pluming around the entrance room.

The screams get louder and an enormous shadow, one I know is a mere illusion cast by the mind of the mortal no doubt hung in chains against the far wall, sprawls forth toward me.

Barbas is lucky; sinners make for just a decadent meal as living mortals, and so his suffering in the loss of Mortarian ground has not come close to that of Katerina or Lilliana. He doesn't need that which can only be procured from living mortals or Mortarian feeding grounds; fresh blood, ichor. He needs only fear. Which, luckily for him, is in no short supply whether the soul is encased in a doppel body or not.

"Barbas?" I call out into the dark, this part of the building the most intact by far.

The screams end at my call and the smoke dissipates unnaturally fast, revealing the stick-thin man belonging to the false perspective shadow which attaches at his feet.

"Pandora. What brings you to my little dungeon of terror?" he asks, voice sharp as a serrated knife. He steps toward me in precise motion, brushing one hand back through his too-white hair which falls in razor-sharp curtains around his face, stopping abruptly just above his waist. His skin is wrinkled, saggy even, and his pale blue eyes are sunken so deep into his face that it's hard to believe *The Scream* by Edvard Munch was not his self-portrait gone wrong.

"I have a little favour to ask of you, actually." I put my cards on the table. No doubt he already knows why I am here. Barbas is by far the hardest Demon Lord to fool or lie to, except of course for Abraxis. Once someone knows your fears, they can discern more about you than I'd thought possible. Fear makes up so much of who we are as Mortals, then Kindred, and then as Titans — it is as though in seeing my fears, he has a map of my heart and soul.

"You're afraid I'll say no. It must be important. Ask." He gestures for me to move across the floor of the chamber and into his personal quarters as the naked body hung up against the far wall whimpers.

Barbas whistles a slow tune, and I hear the scuttle of the Phobias' legs closing in, readying to feed now their master has had his fill.

Stepping under the pointed archway and into an even darker, danker space than the one I've come from, Barbas sits beside a lone candle that flickers, illuminating his face as though he's about to tell me some kind of ghost story.

He doesn't though, instead he merely waits for me to speak.

Taking a seat on a rugged chaise longue of black leather and smoothing my skirts, I begin.

"Haedes, he has a daughter. I've just come from The Indicatus Courts. She's just made some rather unsavoury discoveries, least of all that she's related to *him*." I purse my lips.

"And what, my darling, could be more unsavoury than that?" Barbas cocks an eyebrow expectantly and looks down at his immaculate fingernails. As he does so, his favourite arachnid, a large Black Widow called Mrs Skinny Legs, appears from behind the candle next to him, scurrying across the table before climbing atop his hand and beginning to weave webs between his fingers.

"She killed her parents. It was an accident. Or so everyone will tell her, but I doubt she will believe it." I smile, and he mimics my expression, his mouth becoming a gaping orifice of joy which swallows the candlelight so utterly it's hard to believe his internals are not pure abyss.

"Well, that does sound simply delectable. And what, might I ask, is the reason for you handing me such a weak, innocent, and terrified young morsel on a plate?" he questions my intent, always suspicious. He's probably the most intelligent of the Demon Lords by far, even when you compare him to Abraxis, the master of riddles and lies. Barbas is less flare and more action, which I most definitely prefer.

"I want her in my grasp. I think I can use her against Haedes. To get Mortaria back," I explain.

Barbas' smile grows beyond what should be possible, continually eerie in its gaping width.

"Well, I wouldn't say that losing a child is high up on Haedes' list of deepest fears now. Would you?" He looks at me with a careful gaze, waiting with curiosity as to what I'll say next.

"And what if I told you— that his daughter was also the daughter of one Mrs Demi Sinclair?" I ask him and he throws his head back in a laugh.

"Oh, well isn't that just perfect? You're sharp; I like that." He clips his consonants concise, teeth continually snapping shut too fast like the jaws of an alligator.

"So, you'll do it?" I ask, surprised at the ease with which I've been able to convince him.

"Well, I can hardly deny my Kindred a solid meal of that magnitude— after all, there is no fear in The Underworld like that on the mortal plain. The uncertainty, the fear of death, the weight of memento mori; it gives the fear this taste— a kick unlike any other," he speaks like he's a gourmet chef reading off the specials list and I smile, content.

"She's guilty. Make sure to play on that." I wink at him and he rises to his feet.

"It would be my pleasure," he purrs, the long bony fingers of his hand grasping mine, skeletal and cold, as he pulls me after him and out of the room.

Sephy Sinclair will not evade death at the hands of demon Kindred again. She will perish, and then I will snatch her like the bargaining chip she can become. I'm fearless, and this only becomes more evident as a shudder runs through Barbas when confidence grows.

He calls back to me, leaving me full of delicious anticipation for the night ahead as his words reach me. I catch the excitement in his dead gaze, an odd combination to say the least.

"Come, let's select which of my Kindred will feast tonight."

SEPHY

It's the longest, deepest sleep I can remember having since before my parents died that hasn't been brought on by alcohol.

I stir, waking from my slumber to the familiar knock on the door. I want to reach beneath my pillow for a knife to throw, but after a few seconds, I realise what's passed, and my heart begins to pound frantically, causing me to freeze where I'm strewn amongst the pillows. I let the moment wash over me, the rediscovery of grief and guilt crippling.

"Come in," I call, voice cracking as my arid tongue unsticks itself from the roof of my mouth.

As the door opens and Jules enters, I hear someone let out a slight groan before the rustling of leather sounds and two thuds emit from the bathroom. From around the corner, Xion emerges.

"What— what are you doing here?" I demand, sitting bolt upright in bed now. Then, it all comes flooding back.

Last night had been a huge mistake, a giant mistake. I'd let him see me weak. I'd *hugged* him for Christ's sake. Like one of those needy girls who thinks her problems are so enormous and need to be held like some damsel.

I feel physically nauseous at this thought.

"I— uh — slept in the tub." He rubs the back of his neck, as though it's sore. I scowl at him.

"You know we have over twenty-five spare bedrooms in this house? You seriously chose to sleep in my bath?" I berate him and he sighs.

"I wanted to be close. You— you asked me not to leave you alone," he confesses, and my eyes widen.

That's right. I did ask him to stay—Well, shit.

"You didn't think I was serious, did you? I mean, come on, I don't even know half of what I said last night. I was exhausted and practically delusional after everything I'd seen." I make the excuse only too easily as Jules shoots a confused look between us both, bringing in a larger tray than usual and sitting it bedside.

"I brought you both breakfast," he informs me as he continues to look between Xion and me.

"Thank you. We're going to need it." Xion expresses, and I narrow my eyes again.

"Why?"

"Because I'm going to start training you today. I'm not wasting any time." Xion lifts the silver cloche of the breakfast tray and inhales heavily as the smell of poached eggs and fresh coffee rises into the room. He picks up a plate and some cutlery and begins to eat as I pull a face of disgust.

"That sounds like fun—" I sigh out, knowing that I shouldn't fight him on this. I've already seen what my powers are capable of, and I don't want that to happen again.

"I know. Yet another thing you don't want to do." Xion reads my mind as he places a poached egg into his mouth whole.

"Yep." I twist so I'm sitting on the edge of the bed, still wrapped in sheets, and pick up a fork, ravenous.

"Well, dealing with demons is no small task, Sephy. You need to be prepared, or you'll end up dead." He shoves a small piece of ham into his mouth and chews without pause or etiquette. I begin to wonder if he was raised by wolves as the sound of his lips smacking starts to irk me.

"I didn't seem to have any trouble with that last one— what was it, a Banshee, you said?" I ask and he nods, mouth still full, as I continue, "I'm not exactly your average woman. Not even counting the fact I'm a demi-god, I trained as an elite gymnast for years. I competed in figure skating. I've got medals in dressage, fencing, horse jumping, kickboxing, mixed martial arts—" I continue to recite my long list of achievements, accumulated over summers with nothing but time and a whole lot of money.

I want Xion to look impressed, but he merely lets out a deep throaty laugh, making me scowl as I take an angry sip of coffee which burns my tongue.

"This isn't some kind of underworld warrior princess pageant. I'm sure you're very talented, but training to fight when it's life or death— it's different." He finishes off his breakfast, and I follow him with an annoyed stare as my eyes rise over the rim of my teacup.

"Do I look like Miss Underworld Warrior Princess to you? I mean, what about a redhead with a fetish for leather pants screams *ooh crown me!*" I give him a scowl, and he laughs again.

"It's nice to see you've recovered your sense of humour." He takes a sip of his coffee and winces, obviously hating the taste or the temperature, though which one I can't tell.

"I'll get dressed. What should I wear?" I ask, looking him up and down. He's not exactly in the kind of attire I'd associate with mortal combat. In fact, I'm pretty sure he's been wearing the same outfit since we first met. I wonder if his closet is like something out of a cartoon with like twenty of the same pairs of jeans, followed by twenty of the same leather jackets, and so on. I smirk; this definitely seems likely.

"Wear whatever you like. I always wear tough fabrics because of shifting. You might want to consider that you're also going to be dealing with fire." He places the cup back on the trolley, unimpressed as he stares at it with momentary disgust and leaves the room.

"I'll see you in the main entrance hall in five minutes," he calls over his shoulder as I get out of bed to get dressed.

"It's a date," I call back, and I know after I do that, he's smiling as he goes.

Several questionable outfits later, I descend the staircase, only to find Xion and Jules waiting for me. I'm wearing a leather jacket, a black corset, and leather pants, topped off with knee-high flat leather boots. I look to Jules, eyes widening as I see he's holding a silver tray with a fire extinguisher atop it.

"Your confidence in me is touching, really." I glower at him and he smiles.

"Better safe than sorry. I like my beard intact thanks," Xion adds, and I cock an eyebrow.

"If I was you, it wouldn't be my beard I'd be worried about," I retort, irritated already and sure I'd much rather be training with Jacque, or drinking— or— well, anything.

"You have the only thing that can kill me in the palm of your hand, Sephy. We need to be careful," Xion warns me on a more serious note, and I roll my eyes.

"Is it bad that makes me feel all tingly inside?" I feel my lips curve upward on one side as his broad width turns, leather jacket flaring out around him, pretending like he hasn't heard me. I do an internal cheer.

Sephy, one.

Demon of sarcasm, zero.

With a smirk on my face, I follow the two men out of the front doors of the estate and into the cool Illinois air. It's ever so slightly windy, and I wonder if that will affect the fire I'm able to produce from seemingly nowhere.

Adjourning out onto the lawn, moist with a light glaze of last night's rain, I latch onto an unfamiliar sight at the edge of the forest. Or to be more accurate, hanging from multiple trees at the edge of the copse.

"What the hell is that?" I point toward the crude dangling monstrosities.

"Those would be Banshee piñatas, for target practice," Jules coughs, and I give him a look of utter confusion.

"Are you serious? Where the hell did you get them?" I ask him with an incredulous tone as we near the dangling targets.

"Well, I made them of course. What do you think I went to *demoni cplaydummies.com*?" Jules retorts with equal incredulity in his voice. I turn to him with a smirk.

"You made these? Should I be flattered? And also concerned because— well, you tied them to trees— wooden trees," I ask him, placing my hand over my heart in mock besotted plight. He rolls his eyes but doesn't reply, and as I near the hanging dummies a ridiculous giggle escapes my lips. "Oh my god, you drew little angry faces on them!" I burst out laughing, and Xion lets out a small snigger beside me.

Jules scowls at us both, and Xion looks down at his feet but is unable to remove the smirk from his lips.

"He said to make them realistic!" Jules defends the angry faces attached to bags filled with something I'm hoping is flame retardant. The piñatas have four fake legs made from what appears to be women's hosiery stuffed with rocks. Their heads have crudely stitched ears and drawn features, which in all honesty are the least offensive things I've ever seen.

From behind me, I hear the tread of paws and turn to see Cerb approaching.

"What do you think, Cerb? Threatening?" I ask him, and his ears perk up at the sound of my voice. He pads forward, looking up at the targets. He doesn't bark, or growl, but simply lies down and then proceeds to roll over, displaying his belly as his tongue lolls from one side of his jaw.

"Well, that settles it. You should have trusted the professionals at *demonicplaydummies.com*," I tease, and Jules looks to the fire extinguisher on his still-erected silver tray and then back at me.

"I will remember this conversation when one of you needs putting out." His posh British accent drips with disdain, but I know he's only joking. Or at least, I hope he is.

"Okay, enough joking around. As crude and uh—" Jules looks like he might hit Xion over the head with the tray he's holding as he moves to defend his handy work once again. Xion continues carefully, "—well-made as these might be, they're supposed to bring back the state of mind you had when I first saw you controlling The Eternal Flame." His explanation makes me raise an eyebrow, and I try so hard not to laugh, but it is oh-so difficult.

"These are supposed to terrify me— to make me fear for my life?" I ask him, choking on my words as I stifle a blatant giggle. Jules sighs audibly behind me, and I press my lips together in a hard line, taking a deep breath through my nose and trying to keep my cool.

"Yes, we're going to try and have you destroy them," Xion explains, and I nod.

"Okay— let's get this over with," I express, feeling my heart sink a little.

I won't deny I'm afraid. Who wouldn't be? I've lost first-hand at the consequences that come with powers I didn't even know I possessed, and willingly using them makes me hesitant, to say the least.

"Let's try the first one from close up, then as you get more adept, we'll try from greater distances," Xion suggests, and I nod.

I widen my stance, looking at the demon-pig-sack hybrid and debate momentarily on nicknaming Jules Dr Frankenstein for his troubles.

I hold out my hands, squeeze my eyes shut, and try to focus.

"Hey, no! Don't shut your eyes! Jesus, you need to be able to see what you're doing. This isn't like in some fantasy novel where you're trying to be all zen and shit!" Xion barks, and I jump, humiliated as I spin around on the spot.

"Hey, I don't know what the hell I'm doing here! Why don't you tell me?" I yell at him, and he blinks once, then twice, before looking annoyed.

"Look, I'm not the best person to teach you how to do this. I'm not exactly qualified." The wind stirs the locks of his dark, coiffed hair, and I look at him with an expression of pure confusion.

"So why the hell are you teaching me, then?"

"Because someone needs to, you need to know how to protect yourself, and it was either me or—" he falls into silence, and I place my hands on my hips.

"You or who?" I demand and he sighs.

"Me or your father. Haedes— he'd have you convecting already." He looks sad, pitying me, and it makes me angry.

"Haedes isn't my father. He's just a sperm donor. Alright?" I growl, partially wanting to ask what the hell convecting is, but not having the resolve to calm down enough. Haedes hasn't been a father to me. He hasn't raised me or loved me. He isn't anyone to me. He's just someone who screwed my mother and then messed up her life.

"Alright. Let's try again." Xion doesn't argue back; he merely shifts atop the grass and folds his arms across his chest. I sigh, trying to focus, to recall what I did during the Banshee attack, but honestly, it's an adrenaline-fuelled blur.

"Alright. Here goes nothing."

I hadn't known I was speaking a self-fulfilling prophecy, but exactly five hours later, as rain begins to pour from the grey skies overhead, I return to the house having accomplished exactly what I predicted.

Nothing.

"At least we didn't have to use the fire extinguisher," Jules comments, trying to perk me up. I shake my head.

"Normally, I'd say yes that's great, but I didn't even manage to produce enough fire to light a freaking tea light," I complain.

Xion looks stoic.

"I'm sorry. It's probably my fault. Like I said before—" he begins, but I cut him off.

"Yes, you're not qualified yada, yada, yada, I know— I don't blame you. It's probably just me. I'm not exactly up for using the powers that led to my parent's death." I'm candid and Jules flinches. My words echo out around us in the high ceilings of the entrance hall and silence falls shortly after. Nobody knows what to say next, least of all me.

"Look, I'm tired. I'm going to go try and relax. We can try again tomorrow." I pivot so I'm facing away from them, walking towards the double staircase with aching feet and the beginnings of a headache.

"Do I need to go and hang out underneath your bathroom window again?" I hear Xion call after me, so I turn back and look at him, plastering a cocky grin on my face to cover up the inner turmoil I can't seem to shrug.

"Only if you're interested in catching me getting out of the tub." I feel a little more like myself as the quip leaves my lips, like things are settling as I see him smile up at me, as though he knows to use my level of humour as an indicator of how I'm feeling.

I finish my ascent of the stairs, but rather than turning left towards my suite, I instead turn right, feeling my curiosity overpower my sense of fatigue. I walk the length of the landing and then turn the corner into the deep hues of the upper east wing corridor, venturing left into the library.

The stacks are covered in sheets to protect them from the years of dust that have accumulated. It seems like nobody has used this room in at least twenty or so years, which surprises me because I would have thought Peter or maybe even Jules would have been starved of something to read at some point. I know I've never been in this library because of its proximity to Peter's study, but what's their excuse?

I pull down the sheets, not even truly certain of what it is I'm looking for as my eyes scan the worn leather spines, which are too neat upon the sturdy oak shelves from lack of reading. Standing, I wrap my thin leather jacket around myself as I feel a draft move around the room even though the windows are shut tight. Raindrops on glass are the only audible sound as I spot something that spikes my interest.

The Myths of Ancient Greece.

I grip it with my fingertips and pull, the weight of it coming loose from the shelf as it falls back into my palm. Pacing across the rich wooden floor, I'm drawn to an armchair which is also covered in a dustsheet. Stripping it back and lounging across the arms like I used to sit when I was a small child, I settle into its hold and exhale. Then, reaching back to the table beside me, I pull a heavy spherical lid off a crystal bottle of bourbon and take a swig straight from its depths.

I open the book to the index as the alcohol heats my throat and then my blood, looking down the long list until I find the required letter.

Scanning it quickly, I find him.

Haedes.

Flipping to the first suggested page, I inhale deep and begin to read.

In a swilling together of bourbon, my name, and his, I stir from sleep. I don't know what wakes me, nor when I fell asleep, but something does. The light, which I had turned on shortly before giving in to slumber, flickers, the lightbulb having come loose or being faulty from lack of use no doubt.

The hairs on the back of my neck stand on end as I adjust my position in the armchair, a shiver running through me whilst my stiff spine loosens slowly. I gaze down at the story I'd been reading before falling asleep, eyes still foggy with it.

The tale of how Persephone had been stolen away by her Uncle, Haedes, and forced to remain with him six months of the year.

It makes me wonder, had my mother called me Persephone as some kind of sick joke? Or had she intended for me to follow in her footsteps and live out my adult life in The Underworld?

With the amount of debt my father seemingly accumulated with the Indicatus Courts, it seems unlikely that they wouldn't have told me about it as I grew.

Then again, after seeing the vision presented to me by The Fates, I'm beginning to wonder how well I knew them. I was only six years old when they died. So maybe I didn't know them at all.

The thought depresses me, and as I slump back into the arm of the chair, the scent of alcohol is still heavy on my breath. The light flickers again, the wind outside howling with a ferocity I haven't heard in a long time.

The hairs on my arms stand up this time, and I reach for my jacket, which I've slung over the back of the chair.

As I twist to pull the leather around myself, something catches my attention out of the corner of my eye. A flit of shadow, an abruption of the light cast by the struggling bulb.

I shudder against my own volition, looking around to find nothing before turning my attention back to the book I've been reading, shrugging it off as paranoia.

I look in detail at a depiction of Haedes, wondering how accurate it is, wondering if I look like him. I place my hands on my face, tracing my features, my slim jawline and wide eyes, my straight nose. Now I think about it, I look nothing like the man who raised me.

As I'm pondering my lineage, the light beside me gives up entirely leaving me in the dark.

I sigh, twisting to stand and turn on the main chandelier.

As I do so, I see it again. Several long protrusions, silhouetted against the dim light falling through the window.

Lightning strikes, causing a flash of stark white light, and then the silhouette is gone. I spin, becoming quickly angry, sure that someone must be screwing with me.

"Hello?" I call out, balling my fists at my side, ready to defend myself should I need to.

Instantaneously, white smoke begins to seep out around my ankles from beneath the floorboards, causing chills to run rampant across my flesh.

Murderesssssssss—

The word comes to me in a whisper that curdles my blood as I slam my palms into the side of my skull, trying to block the sound.

Murderesssssss—

It continues despite the fact I've got my ears covered.

It's inside my head.

Smoke begins to rise into the room too fast, and as long-legged arachnid shadows close in, it narrows into trails that move unnaturally toward me like ropes, binding me.

Climbing up my nostrils and into my skull, I feel myself doing the only thing I know how to as I fall to the floor, powerless.

The last thing I hear before the nightmare takes me into its grasp is my own harrowing scream.

12

SWEET DREAMS

SEPHY

IT'S THE SAME SCENE as before, but this time I can't look away. It's like a waking dream, overtaking my consciousness so I can't escape.

Stuck in this prison of memory, I watch on.

I'm standing, six years old, stance wide this time. I've not fallen; I've not moved towards the fireplace. Instead, I'm furious. My wide, innocent eyes transformed by fury and hate. My hands are shaking by my sides, as though my tiny body can't hold my feelings inside. My parents cower, voices barrelling towards me like bullets.

"Please, Sephy! No. Don't. Come on now." They're begging with me, pleading, and I find myself wanting to scream for it all to stop.

"No!" my younger self screams, stretching out her palms and shooting two hot streams of liquid flame directly upon them. They perish before my eyes, their screams torturing me as they rip through my soul, tearing it to shreds.

Is this real?

Did I do this?

"Sephy! Sephy, Snap out of it!" The side of my face is met, full force, with a fleshy foreign object as I open my eyes. My entire body jerks. I'm on the floor, holding my knees and rocking.

Xion is on his haunches, looking down at me as moonlight casts deep hollows in his features and exaggerates the dark grain of his facial hair. He looks over his shoulder at a twitching body, at something not human.

I stir, curiosity overwhelming my pounding heart and the roaring of my blood.

"What is that?" I ask. It looks like an enormous alabaster tarantula, but one that's been genetically modified in some horror flick. It has bright red eyes, eight of them, and a gaping mouth with needle-esque black teeth weeping dark saliva. The body has been ripped asunder from its legs, no doubt by Xion who looks only slightly out of breath.

"That, Sephy, is a Phobia. Barbas' Kindred. The Demon Lords— they must know where you are, and worse than that, who you are." He looks at me deep in the eyes, fear flickering behind his dark pupils.

"What did it show you? Whatever it is, forget it. They prey on our worst fears and show us what we're most afraid of. They lie to us," he whispers to me, placing a rough finger on my cheek and lifting my eyes so they meet his.

"I—" I am lost for words, physically shaking as I get to my feet. Xion offers me a hand, but I use the arm of the chair to steady myself instead, unable to take my eyes off the dead Phobia's body. "Is it— dead?" I ask, brow furrowing with concern as I take a few steps forward.

"This form is dead. But its soul will return to Mortaria and resurrect in another body of the same breed if Barbas so desires. I do not have The Eternal Flame— so any demon I kill is only ended in a temporary capacity," he explains, and I nod, still hearing only his voice and the sound of my blood rushing in my ears.

A bolt of lightning causes the light in the room to flicker, and I take a few steps around the corpse, wondering if it'll turn to ash like the Banshee had. Thunder sounds, finally bringing me back to my surroundings as I tear my gaze away from the body.

A single tear is let loose from my eye and falls down my cheek.

"Sephy, don't think on it. Not for one second. It was a lie. An illusion preying on your worst fears. Please. Don't let it make you believe you're anything less than innocent in all this." Xion's words make me turn back to him for a second, surprised he knows the nature of what I've just seen. "What were you even doing in here?" He picks up the book, still laid open on the armchair, and snorts, rolling his eyes.

"If you want answers about Haedes, these books are nothing but propaganda, a slander campaign run by the muses. I'll see if Peter has any books that are accurate. It's time we give you access to any information you need." He gives a small smile, trying to be kind, and as I turn to move through the doorway, Jules appears, dressed in black pyjamas with a shotgun in one hand.

"Where are they?!" Jules loads the gun in his hands, all business.

"Woah, it's okay, Jules. Xion killed it." I step aside, showing him the body, which is leaking black fluid all over the wood of the floor.

He looks horrified.

"I know, it's terrifying," I state, almost sounding bored, but internally scared at the thought of what that creature could have done to me while I was trapped in my own false memories.

"Actually, I was just thinking that getting that out of the floor is going to be a nightmare," he admits, and I smirk.

"I'll clear this up. You take Sephy and get her a drink," Xion points, directing us to exit the room. Jules grabs my elbow, yanking me away from the demonic murder scene like I'm a little kid.

"Hey, stop manhandling me! I can walk," I complain, and he rounds on me, placing a hand on my shoulder.

"You can't see yourself. You look completely out of it. What happened?" Jules demands, acting more like a parent now than ever.

"They showed me— they made it look like I killed them on purpose." I swallow hard, wiping beneath my eyes as they begin to tear in the corners again.

"Persephone Sinclair, you may not be full of sweetness and light, but you're not a killer. Not in any sense of the word." He looks down at me and I feel tears threatening to spill, this time in greater force.

He puts his arms around me, and I stand stone still, letting him hold me but not falling into the embrace. "Let's go sit in the record room; you'll feel better with some music on," he suggests, and I nod, pulling away and wiping a few stray tears that have escaped my lashes and fallen in salty globules down my cheeks.

"Okay. That sounds nice. I haven't been in there since I came home," I admit, moving quicker down the corridor now as I have a destination in mind.

"I'll go and get you a drink— whisky?" Jules asks, but I frown. I've had enough alcohol for one night.

"Actually— you think you could make me some cocoa? Like you used to?" I ask him and watch as his mouth cannot help but spread into an unmistakably joyful smile.

"Of course! Coming right up!" He turns on his heel promptly, as we reach the top of the staircase, and descends to the kitchens while I carry on, striding straight past the door of my suite and pivoting left.

I stand in front of the door where I'd spent so many hours of my childhood they've all blurred together. Hours spent dancing with my parents, listening to music and being told the history behind each song, each band. My parents loved the music of the '60s, '70s and '80s, and this room reflects them more than any other in the entire house.

My heart's pounding again, suddenly anxious at the thought of stepping inside. I know it's silly and push through, bringing my hand to the door handle and bearing down, letting myself inside.

More dust sheets. More evidence that not a soul has entered here in far too long.

I put the overhead lights on, filling the room with slight warmth as rain continues to slash against the windows from outside. The thunder rolls, but I ignore it as I pull down more dust sheets. The black shelves pop against the cherry red walls, onyx-coloured carpet caressing my feet as I stare up at the records in their thousands.

I've never touched these. I've wanted to, so many times, but never found the strength to disturb the meticulously organised system my father had arranged them with.

I don't know it; I was too young for him to teach me when he died. Moving them has always felt like it could mean washing away the last remnants of their presence here at the estate.

Taking a deep breath, I know it's time. Everything is different now. I know that my happy childhood was anything but. I know that my mother's deep dark secret was what got them both killed. They wanted me to have these records, these words that had meant so much to them.

In this second, I realise something important.

Whether or not I'd killed them, whether it had been an accident, they loved me regardless. They're gone now, but that doesn't diminish how much they loved me when they were here.

Smiling to myself at this fact, the chill place where fear has taken root within my stomach warms as a flickering flame of hope re-ignites within my chest, heating me all the way through.

I look up at the towering shelves filled with cardboard cases, at the collection of vintage phonographs, turntables stationary and sad.

I hear someone coming down the corridor, so quickly select the first record I remember listening to with my father.

The Bee Gees — Saturday Night Fever

"Sephy? Are you in here?" Xion's voice grows closer and I move to turn my back to him, busying my hands with pulling the record from its cardboard slip and blowing on its black grooved surface, making sure there are no scratches or residual dust. I don't want him to see I've been crying.

"Mhmm," I call back, acknowledging that I've heard him.

I hear him round the doorway, a little breathless.

"Look, I know you don't want to hear this, but you can't stay here. This is the second attack in as many days. It's not safe here— we need— you need—" He can't bring up the words, so I turn, flipping my hair over one shoulder and glancing back at him.

"To go and live in Mortaria for a while. I know." I speak the truth I've already surrendered to. I can't stay here. I never want those Phobias in my head again.

"Right. Well, I'm going to head back and set things up for your arrival. Pack a few things, not too much— alright?" he instructs, and I nod, not able to come up with the words to reply. He leaves, hesitantly, but he does leave, so I'm alone with the sound of a needle crackling against vinyl.

The Bee Gees fill the room with their familiar comforting tones, and Jules makes his appearance only moments after Xion's heavy footfall fades to nothing.

"I brought you a blanket, it's pretty chilly around here— I haven't been lighting any of the fires just in case— well, you know." He shrugs, nervous as he hands me a thick plaid blanket.

"Thanks. I appreciate it," I reply, moving to uncover a loveseat near the far wall so I can sit. I wrap the blanket around me, letting the music and warmth envelop me in its embrace.

Jules hands me a cup of cocoa, exactly seven marshmallows bobbing atop the chocolate froth, and then holds out my cell phone.

"What's this for?" I ask, blowing on the hot drink warming my palms.

"You need to call Peter, tell him what happened. He's away on business right now, but coming back here, well, it might put him in danger," he explains, and I realise he's right.

"Alright." I take the phone off him and turn it on.

In all honesty, I hardly ever use my phone. I tried social media once, and it was a disaster, mainly because I became a huge target for people looking for a quick buck.

Hundreds of sob stories flooded my inbox, so after that, I deleted my accounts and kept things simple. I'm surprised, when the phone powers up, to find a string of missed calls, maybe thirty, from an unknown number. I delete the notifications, brushing it off as a keen cold caller.

Dialling Peter's number, I put the phone to my ear as I take a sip of my cocoa. The marshmallows have melted into the chocolate, and the thick creaminess of the beverage coats the back of my throat. I hum, the taste filling me with warm and momentary satisfaction.

Peter answers on the third ring.

"Sephy, what is it?" He sounds surprised to see me calling, which I'm sure he is. I mean, I never call him. Not ever. If I ever need anything I just call Jules.

Jules moves to turn the volume down on the record player as I clear my throat.

"Look, I'll keep this simple. I've become a huge target, the Demon Lords, they know where I am. I'm going into hiding until they've stopped hunting me— Xion's taking me to Mortaria. I'll have Jules lock up the estate, but you should stay clear for a while. Maybe take a long vacation. It's just not safe to be associated with me or this place at the moment." I hear him inhale, coughing a few times on the end of the line, like he's choked on a drink or something before his sullen tone reaches me once more.

"What about the business? The directors?" Now it's my turn to be surprised. He's seriously concerned about the stupid business after all this?

"Gee, thanks for your concern!" I hang up, angry, not wanting to deal with him a moment longer. Then I pause as I lower the phone from my ear and turn it off.

Does he know I killed his sister?

Does he blame me?

I exhale hard.

Jules looks at me, cocking an eyebrow.

"He asked me about the goddamn business. Like that matters right now! I'm more concerned about what I'm going to do with— oh I don't know, the fact I'm being hunted by demons— that I'm having to relocate to— oh, I dunno, *hell*. And what am I gonna do with the dog?" I stare at Jules for help, suddenly overwhelmed by the idea of running and hiding. Most people would think of that as the easier option, but for me, someone who is used to dealing with most stuff head-on, I'm not relishing wasting a whole bunch of time being a target and hiding out in caves or something.

"Well, you can take Cerb with you. He's not exactly from here," Jules makes this comment and I stare at him with wide eyes. "He was Haedes'. He gave him to your mother in case she ever became a target. He's got quite the nose for demons," he announces, and I think back.

He barked before the Banshee attack. Now I think about it, he should probably be dead by now with how old he is.

"Is my dog— *immortal*?" I ask, stunned, and he nods.

"Yeah, I think everyone was kind of hoping you'd just ignore the fact he's getting on in years." He shrugs and I laugh, glad, finally, at some of the news he has to impart.

"Well, I guess that's something. How does that even work?" I enquire, and he laughs.

"Something to do with the effect of the Mortarian sun on animals— they take a lot less exposure to keep alive indefinitely. Besides, Xion used to tend to him, walk him in The Underworld while you were away at school. He probably should have had him taken back to Mortaria indefinitely— but I guess Haedes couldn't stand the sight of him after how much that dog loved your mother. I imagine he probably reminded him of her a great deal," Jules says, thoughtful.

I feel my whole past unravelling before my eyes. Have I been blind, or has everyone been that good at hiding things and lying to me for all these years?

"I see. I'm just— I'm afraid," I admit, changing the subject.

"You'd be insane if you weren't. You are one the most fearless people I've ever met, but with this, you need to be scared. Fear will keep you safe." He puts down the tray that he's holding in front of his thighs, still clad in his black pyjamas, and sits beside me.

"This cocoa is really good," I compliment him as he places an arm around my shoulders. He looks deeply into my eyes, reflecting my fear back at me. I expect him to cry, to become sentimental, but he doesn't. Showing he knows me perhaps better than anyone else, he puts a hand on my knee and simply says,

"I'll make it for you anytime. You need only ask, and I'll be there."

LUCE

Thane's lips rise, shining and wet, spreading in a grin from the apex of my thighs. Her hollow cheekbones cast formidable shadows, making her ghostliness only more apparent in the flickering candlelight of our room.

Crawling over my body like a predator, her nipples trace the silhouette of my hourglass figure, caressing the expanse of silken, milk-white skin covering my skeleton like a masquerade mask. It's beautiful; hiding the bloody reality of muscle and bone beneath, masking the hammering of my heart, which pounds against alabaster bars, reminding me I am mortal, reminding me I am supposedly trapped in a prison, which I love, covet, and worship as though it were the Goddess and not I.

Thane's stormy grey eyes feast upon my flesh, hungry and insatiable as she licks her bottom lip, relishing the taste of us and climbing my body like a vine.

Twisting her limbs around me, she pins me to the bed as my legs fall apart and limpness follows. I swallow hard and narrow my eyes, challenging her as she reaches over to the smoky quartz nightstand and grabs a red delicious apple from the curve of a faceted garnet fruit bowl. Pulling it up to her lips, her dark hair comes to surround her face, and her eyes turn wicked. She draws them back, moving to bite, but stops inches away from the glistening flesh of the fruit.

"No. You," she whispers, caressing the side of my cheek with her long dark fingernails. "Bite," she commands, stern this time, laying her entire weight atop me as her edgy, androgynous frame grinds against my smoothness. Her long fingers curve around the sphere of the apple as she tightens her grip and lowers it to me, letting me raise my head and take a large, cool bite.

Juice runs from the Mortarian-grown produce, dripping down my chin in a sugary, tart stream as Thane buries her fingers in my blonde hair and pulls my head back against the black velvet of the pillows beneath. She exposes my neck, moving to lick my sensitive skin; starting at the hollow of my collarbone before rising to just beneath my ear.

"Ready to go again?"

She promises so much with these words and I feel the lust starting to grow between us once more. As I move to try and kiss her fully, a knock at the door disturbs our fun.

"Damn." Thane smirks, rising in a cat-like and agile leap from my body, relinquishing her touch and taking the fruit with her.

I pout, unsatisfied despite our hours together.

"This better be important," I growl under my breath, picking up a floor-length black velvet robe embroidered with vines and searching for my headdress. Thane moves silently, watching me as she enters from the other room quickly, now dressed in leather pants and a baggy white dress shirt. Her hair is spikey and her thick lashes make me weep internally. She's so beautiful. Too beautiful.

Whoever is disturbing us better be about to expire.

"Have you seen my headdress?" I ask, rummaging around the bedside table as she cocks an eyebrow.

"What, getting horny for our visitor?" she demands. I smirk, finding my horns discarded next to the garnet fruit bowl.

"Always, darling." I wink at her, puckering my lips and letting my eyes rise suggestively, sweeping over her jutting angles and deliciously butch stature. Taking the horns in my hands, I place the headband between my long locks of hair and then turn to face her straight on as she spreads out, sitting sideways across a black velvet armchair in the corner of our bedchamber.

"You know you don't have to wear those— that whole horned image concocted by the muses was a long time ago. You could just let it go." Thane suggests, taking a bite out of the apple and remaining, as ever, utterly relaxed.

"Why should I? They tried to make me an object of fear, to slander my good name. Besides, I look damn good with horns—" I wink at her again, reluctant to let go of the playfulness between us.

"Remind me to get you a little pitchfork for Halloween," Thane laughs between bites of the apple. Her shockingly white teeth make my heart falter, a reminder of my mortal coil.

"Don't tempt me, baby. You might find yourself pleasurably impaled." I promise her darkly. She smiles at me, turning so her shirt falls open and I can see her breasts, perfectly pert, tempting me.

Walking from the room with this delicious threat still rife in the air between us, I stride over to the door of the suite, straightening my horns as I go and owning the regality of the robe covering my naked body as it sweeps behind me.

Reaching the door, I open it, revealing him.

"Xion?" I say his name with surprise. I haven't been expecting to see him for a while, let alone less than forty-eight hours after Sephy had returned to the estate.

"Barbas. He knows where she is. They all do. He sent the Phobias." He brushes past me, stalking across the threshold in a flurry of angst and emotion.

"Woah, hold on. How is that possible? More demon activity in the mortal world? How are they getting through?" I feel myself becoming anxious as I watch him pacing across the rug in front of the hearth. Beelz watches him with an unimpressed and lazy eye.

"I don't know— I don't know!" He throws his hands up in the air and continues to pace. Slowly, I close the door.

"Xion, stop!" I exclaim, stalking toward him and grabbing his wrists mid-gesture. I stare into his crazed expression, into the worry in his eyes.

Woah.

"Calm down," I plead, stroking the back of his hand with my long fingernails and trying to soothe him. Beelz stirs at my heels, sensing the tension as I walk Xion over to the couch and sit him down.

"I'm sorry— I just got worked up on the trip over here. You should have seen her, Luce. Barbas— he went right for where he knew she was hurting." His mouth forms a grim line, and I wince slightly.

"Her parents," I finish the sentiment for him, and he nods.

"Yes. She was so pale, screaming, rocking back and forth— it was— I couldn't stand it." He's visibly shaking with rage now, and I worry momentarily he's going to go full-on demonic right here on my newly upholstered furniture.

"I might have something for that. One second." I dart across the room, over to my drafts cabinet, a gift from Haedes made from an old coffin. Opening it, I run my long nails along the line of neatly labelled bottles inside.

Within the vials swirl everything you can imagine, from a fiery blaze for infatuation to sleepily swirling brews for calm. I select the one I'm looking for, moving back over to Xion gracefully and passing him the bottle with a delicate wave of my hand.

"Have her drink this; it'll settle her nerves. Now, take a deep breath. She's fine now, yes?" I demand, trying to focus on the positive. I hear the partition between this room and the next slide sideways before Thane steps into the room to join us.

"What's going on?" she demands.

Xion turns, resting a balled fist atop the back of the couch.

"Sephy, she's been attacked. I want to bring her here. She can't stay at that estate. She's already been attacked there twice now." I hear his words and know at last why it is he's come to me.

"You want me to talk to Haedes." I sigh.

"You saw him before; he won't listen to me. I need her to have a suite here. It's the most well-protected place in Mortaria. You know that." His gaze is desperate, and I cock my head slightly. It's an odd look on him, one I've never seen.

I frown a little, concern rising in my gut surrounding the entire situation, but know I must act quickly before I too have blood on my hands.

"Go back to her— prepare her. Let her know that what happened to her parents isn't her fault. I'll deal with Haedes," I vow, and he slouches, relieved.

"Thank you, Luce. Really, thank you. I know you don't owe her anything." He runs his fingers through his hair, the stress evident as he cannot be stopped in motion as he rises to his feet.

"I didn't owe you anything either, but I still took you in and taught you to control your demon half, didn't I? It's not about owing Xion; you should know that by now. We take care of our own. She's one of us now." I look to Thane and then back to Xion again, remembering the terrified teenager that Haedes had brought to me, intending to use him as bait against Abraxis.

He's certainly changed, not the scrawny, twitchy, guilt-ridden boy he had been back then. But still, something in recent days has evolved him on a deeper level.

I watch him, rushing toward the door and smile, realising finally what it is I'm seeing.

"Look after her, Xion," I call after him as he turns, hand on the door handle, eyes blazing.

"I never stopped, and I don't intend to now," he retorts, storming out of the suite and slamming the door behind him.

I grin wickedly to myself, licking my bottom lip and turning to my lover.

That much, child, is more evident than you know.

13

HERE I GO AGAIN

LUCE

I APPROACH HIS CHAMBERS with a reserved coolness of attitude. I don't know how I'll find him. I never know, but I know that when I leave, I'll most likely be frustrated as hell.

The sound of Whitesnake leaks down the hallway, *Here I Go Again* thudding in the air around me.

I purse my lips, preferring a much softer melody, but continue onward anyway, knowing that I must keep moving forward. After all, this issue is nothing if not pressing.

The corridor is wide, with sconces set into the slick black walls at close intervals. They burn a blue flame, transforming the entire atmosphere chill and melancholy despite casting a light brighter than what would be produced by The Eternal Flame. The Resurrection Flame is never far from him, hardly surprising considering his vanity.

I remember how he faired when I had first arrived here, finding that Zeus' punishment was far more devious than he had originally intended. Putting the soul of a god in a mortal body is dangerous for one, but also, it causes the mortal body to break down at an increased rate, even with a tether. If it weren't for Haedes' ability over The Resurrection Flame, we'd all be dead and floating around in the Nether by now, which I'm entirely sure was Zeus' intention. All in all, Mortaria has become a dumping ground for the unwanted.

"Yes! Harder!" I hear his voice, a guttural growl, and my stomach begins to churn.

Oh Lord, why me? I cuss, moving to open the door as I reach it, not breaking stride but instead plunging headfirst into his den of iniquity.

The scene would shock most people.

A nun on her knees, giving head to the god of The Underworld.

Haedes' face is contorted with anger and pleasure melded together, and Annie's eyes are wide and tear-filled, staring up at him as he continues to thrust into her mouth.

At the intrusion, they both turn from where they are positioned. Her at the foot of the bed, him towering over her, both hands grasping the black wood of the bedpost with white knuckles.

I cough, clearing my voice as Annie's gaze becomes terrified. She's bound at the wrists and ankles with black silk, unable to move, but clearly mortified. Her blonde hair falls from beneath the ceremonial wimple he always makes her wear for reasons I can't understand, as her jaw slackens and he turns to me, fully naked.

"Your daughter, and yes, she *is* your daughter— is under attack from the Demon Lords. She's coming to stay with us. Thought you'd like to know," I announce, keeping my chin tilted high and spinning on one heel.

I don't want him to complain, barter, or try to stop the motion of these events, I merely want him to accept them so Xion can get on with the job of protecting the girl.

"Luce— what— *wait!*" I hear him call after me but don't break my stride, letting the sound I focus on be that of my steps and the long silk skirt trailing in my wake.

I make my way down into the main entrance hall of the Exilia, treading across the smoky quartz of the floor at increasing speed even though I know there's no point, not really. If Haedes wants to catch me, he will, but it's something about the thrill of my heart beating so rapidly in my chest, my blood pulsating through my limbs as I flee from him that urges me on. Being mortal is something you just can't beat. Or at least, not in my opinion.

As I pass several envy sinners, women in heavy dark armour, they look me up and down and frown at their own lack of regality. I nod to them as I pass, hoping that my presence brings them one step closer to redemption, to leaving this place once and for all.

Finally, I reach the spiral staircase to my suite and alchemy chambers again, but before I climb the final step of the crystalline ascent, I'm shielding my eyes. He appears in front of my door in a plume of blue flames, still doing up the buckle on his slacks and buttoning his shirt. He's not even wearing any shoes.

He stares at me, deadpan.

"Well, how nice of you to finish on my behalf." I raise one eyebrow and narrow my eyes, tossing my blonde hair over one shoulder.

"Finish? After that intrusion? Don't be ridiculous! You're enough to make any man go limp," he barks, clearly angry. I don't flinch at the insult; instead, I smile.

"Well, at least I've had my curiosity satiated. I always did wonder if the carpet matches the drapes— if you know what I mean." I point to his hair, which is cobalt blue even still, showing a lack of rage despite his contradictory expression. I'd put that down to an influx of fear.

"Well, thanks to you, that's now not the only thing down there that's blue," he barks, and I chuckle.

"Oh, boohoo. I'm sure you'll make up for it another night. After all, you're never short of lust-filled sinners to screw. That in itself is controversial, to say the least— but still— that's not why you're here. Is it?" I push past him, taking a key from my cleavage and opening the door. I step across the threshold before standing aside and raising an arm to indicate he should enter.

"No. I'm not here for a lecture from you."

"I don't care. You're getting one. Sit."

Beelz stirs, rising like a silent shadow, watching Haedes with burning citrine irises, her tail swishing from left to right.

She doesn't like him, not that I blame her. If I was a cat, no matter what size, spontaneous flames from nowhere would freak me out too.

"You're not my mother, for God's sake," Haedes cusses, sitting down on the couch. I fold my arms across my chest after slamming the door shut behind me.

"Yes. Exactly. This *is* for your sake, and hers. Stop being such an asshole," I condemn him, and he sputters, almost laughing before his eyes widen.

"Look, I don't want to be anyone's father," he expresses.

I roll my eyes.

"From the way Sephy speaks, I don't think she wants you to be either. But she's in danger. We can't let her die. You owe her your protection, at the very least. Besides, maybe if you didn't sleep around so much, this wouldn't be an issue." I judge him, burning into him with the scrutiny of my pale blue stare as he exhales.

"Sleeping around with mortals you mean? I only ever did that once! And how was I supposed to know she could get pregnant down here? Time is supposed to have no effect on the human body, remember?" he shrugs, like a schoolboy trying to foist responsibility onto someone else for his missing homework.

155

"Yes. But— maybe this isn't such a bad thing — I mean, you *are* pretty miserable. Maybe having some fresh blood around here will do you some good," I suggest and he laughs.

"Trust me, nothing that reminds me of Demi Sinclair is going to do me any good. Make me want to drink myself into a coma— perhaps. But good? Definitely not."

I look at him, older than the hills and stubborn as a mule. He doesn't realise how isolated he's become. How he's addicted to nothingness. The nothingness of alcohol, the emptiness of a song when you have nobody to hear it, the absence of any feeling as he rams himself into yet another lust sinner, too afraid to feel, to make any real connection.

Yet, he cannot work out why he's so miserable. So alone. Why he clings to me so much for company at our weekly dinners.

He is flailing.

"Well, regardless of how you feel, she's coming here. She needs our protection, and I won't let her die," I state, firm in my conviction as I continue to stare down at him. Beelz sits at my heels, staring at him too with dark orange eyes.

"You always were one for charity cases." He says it to hurt me I think, but instead, I feel the truth of his words. It's no lie; I don't want to see people suffer the way I have suffered or die at the hands of those created by entities like my father. I don't want to see pain or torment. There's enough of that already in the world corrupting innocent souls. I don't need to be the cause of more.

"I suppose you'd know that first hand," I retort, and he looks to me with a surprised glance as he leans back, resting his hand loosely atop his crotch.

"I seem to recall it was I who saved you when you first fell," he reminds me of that day. The day I had woken in a pile of smouldering ash; naked, disowned, and alone.

"That might be true, but I've been saving you ever since. I'm even saving you right now," I reply, balling my fists at my sides.

"Oh, are you now? And how is that, exactly?" He gets to his feet, snide.

"I'm giving you someone to love, something to live for. Even if you don't want to. You will. When you see her. I know you will," I whisper as he closes the distance between us.

"Your youth is showing, my dear. Now go back to playing with your ragdoll." He gestures toward the bedroom where I know Thane is probably strewn naked among sheets, sleeping.

I scowl, but before I have a chance to retort, he's disappeared once more in a blaze of electric blue flames.

I exhale heavily as the smoke dissipates.

He needs saving more than I thought.

SEPHY

The sound of the seventies continues to surround me and Jules as the night wears on.

"So, did my father— did he really capture a Merman?" I ask, finding the walls of denial I've kept erected to try and protect myself crumbling at the edges. They're clearly not going to work any longer, not when I've got demons chasing me that have access to everything inside my head.

"Yes. He really did. Well, Haedes did the capturing part. I was a part of what transpired, I'm sad to say." Jules has a glass of cocoa too and has brought tollhouse cookies to aid my emotional state. He's sat on the floor, looking up at me with his shotgun resting still against his hip. Every time a roll of thunder sounds or a floorboard creaks with the wind, we startle, both on edge and too wired to sleep.

"Sad?" I ask him, and he nods.

"What we did. It was— unsavoury. I've carried that guilt for many years. It wasn't worth it— finding the science behind how to turn their tears into diamonds." He takes a sip of cocoa, and we both sit bolt-upright as the door behind us moves ajar, creaking loudly into the silence.

Jules grabs his gun, leaping to his feet, but quickly lowers it again as he realises that a worried Cerb is the cause.

"Awww, I think you scared him. Come here, boy." I pat the place next to me on the couch, and Cerb launches himself across the floor with only a few pads of his oversized paws. He's so large that I have to move over, the blanket still wrapped around me, before he places his large head in my lap, looking up at me with an anxious stare and one ear cocked. I place a mindful hand on the back of his neck and begin to stroke that place he loves whilst he warms my feet with his body.

"Did you torture him?" I ask Jules, face serious as I raise my gaze from the Leonberger in my lap.

"Yes," is his only reply. I nod, not sure what to make of that.

"I don't know how I'm supposed to react to all this. I mean— he was my dad. I loved him. Is that wrong?" I feel vulnerable in asking this, but I guess Jules is the best person to answer me.

"There is nothing wrong with loving your father. He wasn't all bad. He may have been infected by avarice more than anyone I've ever known, but his intentions started out good. I believe he made his first barter with Haedes to be able to provide the kind of life he knew he needed to win your mother. He was homeless for a long time," he enlightens me, and I raise my eyebrows.

My father was homeless?

Was that why he was always so wary of them, because he'd known that desperation on a personal level?

Jules watches my face and continues, leaning forward as he sits down again. "We must remember that it is perhaps not the person who attracts a sin but the situation in which they find themselves. People will do a lot when they're desperate. And once he had you— well, he became terrified of losing it all. Terrified of you growing up how he did."

He pauses watching my reaction.

"But— he *traded* my mother—" I say, wondering how this had made her feel. How lost had Adam Sinclair become, that he would sacrifice the thing he loved most? Then again, perhaps she hadn't been that thing. Perhaps money itself had filled that void instead.

"He became obsessed with increasing the fortune, with keeping everything secure for the future. He believed it was worth sacrificing everything, even his afterlife. He may not be a good man in the opinion of some. But he's done nothing wrong by you. Nothing at all. He sacrificed a lot to provide, even though I think he knew you weren't his child."

"You think he knew?" I ask Jules, sceptical.

"I think he did, or at least suspected. I mean, if you look at the dates from when Demi was with Haedes and when you were born, it's pretty obvious. Besides, your red hair—" He looks at me with a slight frown. "If you want some comfort Sephy, I'll tell you that he loved you as though you were his own. He wanted the best life for you," he adds, and I smile, contemplating the dregs of cocoa in the bottom of my mug.

"Thanks. For all this. I guess, I never wanted to ask Peter. I think he hates me," I admit.

Jules frowns.

"Peter hated your father. He thought he was no good for your mother. But don't tell him I told you that." He looks guilty now and I nod, not able to come up with a reply right away.

"I kind of figured. Didn't hate having this giant mansion to hang around in for the last eighteen years while he shipped me off to boarding school though, did he?" I say after a few minutes.

Jules' eyes turn angry, his jaw visibly tensing.

"No. He didn't."

Silence falls between us as I think about Peter, his connection to me, and whether I care if it is truly severed. On the one hand, he's my mother's brother, my last blood family—

No. He's not. A tiny voice whispers in the back of my head, but I ignore it, sure that the cocoa is causing me to become infected with all kinds of dangerous emotions.

The sound of an approaching yeti startles us, but soon I relax as I remember that there's only one demon I know so lacking in stealth.

"Xion?" I call out, just as he rounds the corner and enters the room.

"Hey, you were quick," I comment, looking up to the clock, also made of a large vinyl record, on the opposing wall.

"Was I? It's hard to tell," he's breathless, and his voice sounds strained.

"Yes, only four or so hours," I inform him. Jules looks between us.

"I better get to sleep. After all, I have the giant task of locking this place up tomorrow. Xion, you'll sit with Sephy until she goes to sleep?" he requests, and Xion nods, a slight smile tickling the edges of his thick lips where soft flesh meets stubble.

"You'll come back to tend to Nightshade, right?" I ask him, and he nods.

"Yes, though you should know she's also not from around here originally." He smirks, and I smile.

"Immortal pony. Cool," I express, relief flooding my gut.

I've lost enough things I love for a lifetime.

"Did you finish your drink already? I have something from Luce. I'm not sure what it'll taste like though— things from her cauldron tend to be a little— eh—" Xion pulls a face as he passes me a glass vial. Within the tiny bottle is a swirling silver fluid. It looks metallic, almost like liquid mercury, except there are tiny red particles floating at the bottom.

"Eh, it can't be any worse than Jules' hangover cure, cough syrup cocktail." I unstopper the vial and hold it up to the light.

"Bottoms up— wait, what's it for?" I ask, stopping the draft merely inches from my lips.

"It's to calm your nerves," Xion explains, and I narrow my eyes.

"And I won't grow horns?" I interrogate him, suspicious. His mouth quirks at the side.

"No. You won't. I promise." He reaches inside his jacket pocket, pulling out a thick black book. As he does so, I tip the contents of the vial back and let it trickle in a thick lump to the back of my throat. I cough, then swallow as fast as I can, trying to avoid the taste.

It's a concoction of what tastes like dead flies, which I've experienced before while running cross-country through the British countryside, and some kind of rotting tangerine.

"I owe Jules' hangover cure an apology. *Ew*," I sputter, eyes watering.

"Sorry. Alchemy isn't the most— appetising of dark arts." Xion gives me a sympathetic stare, and I start to wonder why he cares so much about me. I've given him nothing but grief since we first met, and yet he hasn't disappeared or walked away like I anticipated. He's still here.

As I'm staring up at him, pondering this, he hands me the book in his hand. I take it, looking down at the cover which is detailed with a seven-pointed star embossed in gold.

"What's this?" I enquire.

"A history book, a real one. It'll answer some of your questions," he answers, and my eyes widen.

"Oh. Thanks."

I let the book fall open to the first page. Here, a family-tree-type diagram in sprawling handwritten calligraphy stares up at me.

"Delyria, Moloch, Arachne, Leviathan, Nocturna, Sanguina and— Ra?" I speak the words like they're magic, like the pages of the book might burst into flames at the mere sound of my voice.

"Those are the seven Gods of Ancient." Xion takes a seat against the arm of the couch, just in front of where my feet are resting under Cerb's warm stomach.

"Oh right— they're not the Demon Lords? I haven't heard you mention them before—" I express, and he shakes his head.

"No— they're the gods who created them. One god or goddess to each Demon Lord. Except Ra. He's gone thanks to Anubis." The only sound that I can hear above my own heartbeat is the ticking of the clock on the far wall.

"There's so much to learn— this is all so different from what I've studied," I murmur, and he smiles.

"You're smart, you'll get it," he reminds me. I smile at the compliment.

"So, the Gods of Ancient— they're like— bad?" I ask and he shrugs.

"I guess it all depends on your point of view. Some of the gods agree with their anti-mortal policies. Some don't. Cronus and Rhea, your grandparents, didn't. They kicked them out of the Higher Plains. Uranus created the gods and then Mortaria from his own life force so they had somewhere to go after falling from The Higher Plains so they could reach their full potential." I accept this explanation, looking at the next line of names.

Some of them I recognise.

Barbas.

Lilliana.

"I recognise these two. So, these are the Demon Lords? Abraxis, Gorgon, Barbas, Lilliana, Katerina, and Kraken?" I demand, and he nods.

"Yes, that's right."

"So where does Haedes fit into all this?" I ask, almost calling him my father but holding the term back.

"Haedes, Lucifer, Thanatos, Yama, Muerta, Osiris, and Anubis are who you know as the Nexus. They rehabilitate human souls so they can return to the Crucible of Gaia. Before they ruled as a council, Osiris and Anubis were trusted to run things, having been close to Ra before his death at the hands of Cronus. Well— sort of death." Xion takes a deep breath.

"So, he's dead? Or not?" I ask, now curious.

"Not really—you can't technically *kill* a god or goddess. Their energy has to be dispersed or trapped somewhere. For example, Gaia's life force created the earth and then the crucible of Gaia. Uranus' life force created Mortaria and then the well of Eternal Torment, so the gods of Ancient could create their Kindred."

"So, what about Ra? If he can't be killed, what happened to him?" I enquire, hungry for information.

"His soul is floating around in this place called The Nether. Anubis trapped him in human form and then he killed himself. He didn't want to be in a mortal body. It destroyed her," Xion explains. My eyes widen.

"Wow. Dramatic."

"No kidding. That's why Ra doesn't have any Kindred like the other Gods of Ancient." The explanation suddenly slots into the bigger picture.

"The Demon Lords—" I finish his sentence, finally catching on. It's complicated, but there is a method here. "So— what happened to the souls before Anubis and Osiris?" I ask, kind of scared of the answer.

"They weren't rehabilitated; the Gods of Ancient just tortured them and kept them in Mortaria. It was their way of trying to get back to The Higher Plains."

"How?" I demand the answer in as simple way as I can, needing the information like a Yorkshireman needs beer.

Xion inhales.

"You see, if you have more darkness in the universe than good, it kind of hits this reset button. The walls between all dimensions dissolve and the power is up for grabs for anyone to take. It's dangerous, especially for mortals." Xion is watching me closely now, eyes intense.

"I see." I bite my bottom lip, imagining everything turning to chaos, to bloodshed. The thought unsettles me more than I'd like to admit.

"Too much?" he looks concerned, so I shake my head.

"Not at all. I'm just tired," I reply, yawning as I stretch up.

"Have you packed yet?" His voice is expectant.

"Not yet. What exactly do you pack for The Underworld? Like am I gonna need my curling irons? Tampons?" I ask, and he coughs.

"We have electricity if that's what you mean," he answers, ignoring my tampon comment.

"What about shoes? Stilettos or pumps?" I demand, husky in my tone, smirking this time as I flutter my eyelashes. The liquid Luce sent is working, making me more relaxed than I have since before the Banshee attack.

"Look, how the hell should I know? Just bring stuff that's functional and comfortable. If you need anything else, we have tailors and servants in no short supply. They'll be able to attend to your needs." He brushes me off in an exasperated and breathy tone. I frown. I know I have a butler, but the idea of being waited on by someone who's being punished for having a good time while they're alive makes me feel a little uneasy.

"Yes, Sir." I salute him, stretching my arms above my head yet again before placing them around the leather cover of the book and hugging it to my chest. "Thanks for this." I gesture to the book as I move my feet, causing Cerb to rise off my lap and thud onto the floor.

"That dog isn't coming with us you know—" Xion looks between me and then Cerb with a concerned expression, causing his brow to crease and eyebrows to lift at the outer edges.

"Of course, he is! I can't leave him here!" I bark, annoyed that he would imply that I'd abandon poor Cerb.

"Getting him in a carriage is going to be fun. He could practically pull the damn thing!" Xion complains, and I drop my arms in disbelief, letting the plaid blanket fall to the floor, crumpling in a heap around my ankles.

"If Cerb stays, I stay," I retort, and Xion rolls his eyes.

"Fine. The damn dog can come." He shakes his head, looking at me like I'm insane.

"This damn dog has more stealth than you any day, big foot." I walk past him, sending the insult flying over one shoulder.

"And a less annoying bark than you," Xion counters.

I should be offended, but instead, I just smile.

"I might be a bitch, but I'm your bitch now. So, deal with it," I call back again, a warmth filling my chest as I walk towards my room to pack.

"Gladly." I hear Xion laugh as I go.

I was scared I'd be alone, walking into a new world, a hellish one, nonetheless. But I feel better with the weight of the book in my palm, the consideration it had taken for Xion to remember to bring it back for me on top of everything else.

I've always been alone. For as long as I can remember.

I know I still am. I'm still an orphan without many friends or a family. But maybe, the thought occurs to me, just maybe, I don't have to be.

14

BOOGIE WONDERLAND

SEPHY

"HEY, UH, YOU THINK you can give me a hand with one of these?" I call down from the height of the staircase to Xion, who is waiting with an impatient look on his face, down in the lobby.

"Sephy, I said to pack *light!*" he complains, looking up at me and folding his arms across his broad chest.

"Hey, I might be meeting actual gods. *Actual* gods! I need more than one pair of shoes for that!" I complain, staring down at the two suitcases beside me. I've also got a cute leather backpack slung over my shoulders and a thick black overcoat with a large hood, just in case I want to disappear into a crowd. There's something else, latched through one of my pant loops, but I'll ask Xion about that after he's helped me with my luggage.

"You can bring *one* suitcase. The smaller one." He points to it and I sigh.

"What? Come on! I'm a woman. I need— stuff!" I express, whining.

"Okay, I'll do you a deal. You can substitute Cerb for one of the cases. How does that sound?" he barters, narrowing his eyes, and I give him an irritated stare.

"Fine. One case it is." I kick the case I won't be taking aside, filled with my favourite outfits for formal occasions, and descend, pulling the smaller case behind me, clunky as it falls down each step.

"Also, there's this." I push back the outer hem of my coat, reaching back into the loop of my leather pants and pulling out the opal blade.

"You can leave that behind," he advises. My mouth pops open in protest.

"What, why?"

"That blade held your powers once, it'll suck you dry. No using it. You haven't even bonded fully with your god half yet; we don't need you powerless *and* being hunted. One is quite enough." He's deadly serious as he takes the blade from my hand and places it on the table beside the front door as we pass, heading out toward the lawn.

As we open the front doors, I grab Cerb's black leather leash from the hook on the opposite side of the entrance before putting two fingers to my lips and sending a loud whistle bouncing through the vast emptiness of the estate.

A bark sounds in the distance and then the quick and heavy pounding of paws against carpet follows. Cerb comes blundering down the stairs so fast I wonder if he might not fall over his two front legs and cannonball the rest of the way.

"Come on, boy. We're taking a little trip," I whisper to him, latching the leash onto his black leather collar and feeling my arm partially ripped from its socket as he jerks forward.

"Hey uh, would you mind taking the case? I kind of need two hands to keep him under control." I shove the suitcase at Xion who sighs.

"Bodyguard and luggage boy. Jeez, I can't believe I'm getting a promotion already. And what, exactly, were you intending to do with two suitcases and the dog?" he asks me, and I give him a sly smile.

"Hey, you claimed the title luggage boy, not me, dude." I step out onto the mocha stone of the front of the manor's steps, letting Cerb pull me across the pristine grass and onward towards The Hollow. It's almost as if he knows where we're going, like he knows that it's where I need to be too.

As we approach the root-laden ground in front of the gnarled, charred tree, we pay the blood toll and walk, side by side, into Mortaria. Emerging, I step into the enormous gilded half-cage which surrounds the tree and suddenly find myself curious.

"Hey— if this is a portal to the mortal world— shouldn't it be, oh I don't know, guarded or something?" I question Xion as Cerb begins to leap upward.

He's growling, and I wonder what he knows that I don't.

"Oh, it is guarded. The guards are up in the trees." Xion points up into the bloody canopy of leaves, and I squint amongst them, trying to see who it is he is speaking about. After a few moments, I give up, not able to spot even the slightest flicker of movement or shadow.

"Well, they've got the subtle thing down. Maybe you could ask them for a few pointers," I quip as he begins to pull my case through the ruddy earth. I cringe as the wheels catch blackened stones and scarlet leaves, bouncing over natural mounds in the soil.

I keep a few paces behind him as he stalks off, taking me a different way than we'd walked previously.

"Hey, wait, don't we need to go to the river?" I ask, confused and anxious.

"You think you're going to get this luggage, plus you and me, and the monster dog into a gondola? Do you want to drown?" He looks like I've just suggested the most stupid thing possible, and so I give him a pissed-off glare.

"Well, I don't know; I'm not exactly local."

"We're taking a carriage. Now come on, we don't want to be out in the open all day. Not with me and my big feet." He brings the conversation back to my earlier comment, and I smirk. At least I know he secretly finds it amusing, even if he doesn't want to admit it.

Cerb sniffs the earth as we walk, his panting and wet nose hitting the ground the only sounds as we move, swift as ghosts, through the forest. I catch myself looking around, slowing up too often, and thinking that this forest is really kind of beautiful, even if it is soaked bloody.

Eventually, we reach a stretch of black road; it's empty, and Xion halts.

"Now, we wait," he informs me, stoic as usual. I stare down the road to the left, sure I can see an ocean horizon off in the distance.

"Wait— is that the sea?" I ask, confused, and he nods.

"Yes, it's how we bring in materials, livestock, food, that kind of thing. Stuff we can't get around here."

"So, the sea leads to— earth?" I feel ridiculous saying it, but he doesn't make fun of me, which I probably deserve after all the grief I give him. Instead, he continues to enlighten me.

"Not exactly. The devil's triangle— it's another portal. Luce set it up so we could have a better quality of life. Those sinners who were sailors or pirates in their lifetime meet with mortal merchants on the horizon and then bring back the stock." As I listen to his explanation I shift from foot to foot, mouth twisting with curiosity.

"And demons don't try to attack there?" I ask him, and he frowns.

"Of course. Leviathan's Demon Lord, Kraken, resides in those waters. But our ships are fast, and their residents un-killable. Besides, Kraken has been notably distracted lately. Nobody knows why. No doubt something to do with the Circle of Eight and their Kindred. We don't really get involved." He shrugs, kind of like he read this in his morning paper.

"The Circle of Eight?" I state the name, curious even still, and also bored of waiting.

"Yes, run by Poseidon. They manage the weaknesses between this dimension and the oceans of the mortal plain. Demons get through all the time. It's a big issue. I guess Poseidon is your Uncle, technically." He adds this in casually, and my eyes widen.

"So— I'll meet him?" I wonder immediately what it would be like to meet blood relations who are also gods I've only ever read about in stories. Will they have expectations of me? Will they hate my mortal side?

"No. Zeus and Poseidon, and most of the gods and goddesses, live in The Higher Plains. Where they belong." His explanation doesn't make sense, but shortly after the words leave his lips a carriage appears as it turns a corner onto the long stretch of road, pulled by two enormous black mares. I feel my next question is more pressing than any other so don't let it go as Cerb stands.

"So why isn't Haedes there?" I enquire, voicing my confusion.

"Haedes— the gods here, they're different. You should read the story in that book I gave you. It's called *Haedes' Descent*," he instructs me, and I nod. "You did bring it, didn't you?"

"Of course I did!" I snap, hating feeling like the idiot in all this. I just wish I had a grasp of the history of it all, the bigger picture, maybe then I'd feel safer in some way.

"Alright." Xion doesn't add any more to this, and I worry I've upset him. I don't have time to make up for my loss of temper though, as the carriage reaches us and Cerb backs away from the two enormous black Percherons with a wary eye. The driver looks down from his high seat behind the horses, eyeing my dog with a disapproving and depressed stare as Xion strides around the carriage, securing my luggage to its roof with provided chains.

"Get in." Xion opens the door for me, and I climb inside, handing him Cerb's leash as I take off my backpack and place it on the seat next to me.

Watching Xion begin to wrangle Cerb into the small carriage, I take in the interior. Almost everything is black, and tiny indigo lace curtains frame each window, offering privacy if one should require it. The seats are made from leather, dimpled throughout with enormous silver buttons, and are a similar colour to the curtains. The walls of the transport are covered in crushed black velvet, giving me the sense I've walked into some gothic scene from a horror movie set in Victorian England.

Once Cerb is inside, Xion steps up into the carriage, and the entire thing tilts sideways under his bulk. I think about commenting, but before I can come up with a witty one that's riddled with sarcasm, Cerb decides he's a puppy again.

Xion shuts the carriage door but is given no relief as the second his ass touches the dimpled leather of the upholstery, Cerb decides he is the perfect lap to sit on. Xion can barely see over his shoulders as he climbs all over him. Instead of scolding the dog, I simply watch on in amusement.

With a crack of a painful-sounding whip, the carriage lurches into motion, jostling to the sound of horseshoes clipping the road.

"Sephy, uh, can you get Cerb off me?" he pleads, but I shake my head.

"You have been chosen. You can't shrug off the chosen-ness." I shrug and let Cerb settle on Xion's lap. Sitting upright and looking out of the window, he doesn't realise there's glass and smacks his face trying to get his head out of the non-gap. I can't see Xion's face, but I can imagine what it looks like and it makes me chuckle.

"So how far is it to wherever we're going?" I demand, realising I have not even an inkling of our destination.

"Uh, not too far, maybe an hour, hour and a half. I'm taking you to the Exilia Multum, which is where Luce, Thane, and Haedes live. It's the best-protected place in the city." My heart drops in my chest at the thought of being in such close proximity to Haedes. I don't want to deal with any of that, I just want to focus on staying alive.

"I guess that's for the best then." I sigh, relinquishing the course of my life once again to his judgement and wondering if things are ever going to start going the way I want them to.

For a long time, all I can see out of the window is the vast, unending black sea. Xion says it's called The Sea of Shadows, which I think is totally unoriginal, but then again what do I know? I probably would have called it The Scum Sucking Demon Abyss of Doom, which surely does have a ring to it but doesn't quite slip off the tongue.

"We should be getting close soon. Or at least, that's my guess. It would help if I could actually see, though—" his voice comes, muffled from behind Cerb's thick fur.

My dog, bless him, remains glued to the window, watching this strange world pass by as we finally turn away from the black sands of the shoreline and begin to move inland.

I lean forward in my seat, staring out of the window as the city of Mortaria moves closer and closer. It's the oddest architecture I've ever seen, with a ghostly white nervous system, The River Styx, running through its heart. Into the sky, a smoky quartz shard rises, unmistakable as the focal point for the city. It is surrounded by slightly shorter skyscrapers, rising in what looks like bone.

"Hey uh, those skyscrapers— the weird spine-looking ones? What are they made of?" I ask, and Xion chuckles.

"I know what you're thinking, but it's Cinnabrite, a stone we have a lot of here," he replies. I exhale, relief flooding my gut.

"So, the sinners— they live in there?" I ask. His reply comes in a muffled huff from behind Cerb once more.

"Some do. It depends where they're assigned."

I don't reply, not wanting to ask any more questions.

Continuing to stare out at the sickeningly twisted spine-esque architecture of the buildings, I find my focus pulled down to the path as we move closer to the city. Here, I find black stone speckled with what appear to be garnets, causing the ground to look like it's been spattered with blood. The red sky above reflects in the many facets, giving the city the impression it's on fire.

I mean, it explains a lot because when you think about depictions of hell, fire and brimstone is usually the first thing that comes to mind.

"So, The Exilia is—" I ask, staring at the shard of smoky quartz gleaming high in the sky, hoping it's not that. It seems far too daunting, too intimidating, to call home, even temporarily.

"The large crystal building in the middle." I sigh as we move over a slight pothole and the entire vehicle jostles, causing Cerb to growl.

Dammit. I cuss internally, a little afraid of what living in such a place might mean.

"Don't worry. You'll have your own suite. Your every need will be met, I have no doubt."

Xion doesn't understand that I don't want my every need met. I want my freedom, and even though I'm being hunted, this place looks more like a prison than a sanctuary.

"I see." I wonder if he thinks I'm materialistic or spoiled. I mean, I can see why he'd think that; I have billions of dollars at my disposal. But in all honesty, I've never really put much stock in money. Not really. Time, and living my life to the full, being happy, have always seemed like the most important things.

Then again, perhaps I only see things that way because I possess wealth. "You know, I wasn't expecting a suite. I thought we'd be in a cave or something— or maybe your apartment. I didn't know you'd arranged something so fancy," I admit.

His voice is surprised as he responds.

"What— did you think I was going to just keep you hidden away all to myself down here?"

"No— but you know I would've been just as happy with that, or a cave. I don't want you to think I'm high maintenance," I confess, vulnerable.

"I'm shocked you care what I think. I'm just a bodyguard and part-time luggage boy." He sends the reply flying back like a boomerang.

I smile, glad he's finally recovered his good mood.

"It's not that I *care* exactly; I just have a reputation to uphold. Being a spoiled brat isn't exactly how I want to come off." I save myself, and I wonder if he's smiling behind Cerb's fidgety gait.

"Well, you don't need to worry. I don't think you are high maintenance," he replies, like he's doing me a kindness. Against my better judgement, I believe him.

Continuing to stare out of the window, we fall once more into silence. The carriage journeys beneath enormous pillars at last, and I gaze out as we pass multiple sinners wearing simple black armour, stationed at various posts, presumably as security.

The vehicle halts, and I hear the snort and pacing of the horses as the door is pulled open on my side before I'm ready to step out into the Mortarian air. I have no choice, slipping my backpack over both shoulders as I hear whispers coming from outside, presumably about me.

I duck beneath the black ledge of the doorway and step out onto smoky quartz flooring. The place I'm standing in, which has both roads and river running through it, is enormous and airy, with no walls, only pillars supporting a towering crystalline vaulted ceiling above.

My gaze falls onto two women as I walk hesitantly towards them. One has a clipboard, is tall, leggy, and unnaturally blonde with horn-rimmed spectacles and full red lips contrasting starkly against her translucent skin. Her body is curvaceous, with enormous breasts

170

that strain against the simple black blouse and an ass that's bursting against the seams of her pencil skirt. Standing poker straight in stilettos, she eyes me up and down with interest.

The girl beside her, however, could not be more different. She's wearing the same attire, but is wispy, with honey-blonde hair falling from beneath a wimple of all things, and what seem to be cornflower blue eyes. I can't tell for sure because her gaze is fixed firmly on the floor.

The woman with the clipboard and glasses takes a step forward.

"You must be Persephone. I'm Dolores, or Dolly. Whichever you'd prefer. I'm one of the main organisers of day-to-day operations here at the Exilia. I've got your room key here—" she passes me a chocolate-coloured, crystal key, before continuing, "—and Annie here will help you take your bags upstairs. She's the head of housekeeping." She's abrupt and pointed in her language, almost causing me to flinch.

I hear Cerb's ragged breathing coming up behind me and feel Xion's shadow fall over me as Annie and Dolores stare down at Cerb with wide eyes.

"Is that? Oh, it can't be—"

"That's Cerb," I introduce him, and they both fall to their knees immediately.

"Oh my Gosh, it is! Cerb, come here!" Both women hold out open arms, and Cerb gives a large bark, yanking on the leash until Xion has no choice but to let go.

The Leonberger makes a mad dash for the two women, tongue lolling out of the side of his mouth as he bowls into them.

"I guess you guys know each other—" I say out into the air, glad that I'm no longer the focus of attention. I notice the eyes of some of the people standing guard flitting toward me before returning to staring blankly at nothing. It makes me uneasy.

"Oh, yes! We've missed you Cerberus!" Dolores buries her hands deep into the fur around his neck and I roll my eyes.

"So— which way do I go? I'd like to unpack and get settled." I push on, and the two women rise to their feet in unison.

"Of course. Go with Annie; she'll take you to your room." Dolores indicates for me to follow the meek girl who is dressed like a nun.

Is she actually a nun? I wonder.

Perhaps, but I don't know if she would have ended up here if she'd been a good one. I conclude.

"Right this way, Miss." Annie's voice comes as no more than a mouse squeak, and as I stare at her, she shimmies past me. Blanching under my gaze, her face drains of all colour.

I grab Cerb's leash up off the floor, stopping its motion with the heel of my boot as he moves to run after her. Wrapping the leather around my wrist, I stall him, waiting a few moments for Xion to take my suitcase down off the roof of the carriage.

Once Xion is beside me with my case in tow, I look up at him, frightened to move into the depths of this new cage, no matter how gothic and stunning it might be.

"You don't have to come you know. I can manage," I whisper, but he shakes his head.

"I'm your luggage boy, remember? I might as well finish the job," he replies, expression stern. I know he can tell I'm afraid, and for once, I'm grateful for his persistence in sticking around even when I'm trying to push him away.

"Okay, let's go." I take a deep breath and step forward, following Annie who is waiting on the wide crystal staircase. It amazes me that so much is made from the stuff, and my eyes widen as I take in twisted metal climbing in vicious-looking vines before curling into gothic-style roses up the balustrade.

My feet are too slow for Cerb, who clearly knows where he's going better than I do. He rushes me through the many dark corridors illuminated only by alternating blue and red flames. Snaking up from sconces, I note they emit no smoke.

Finally, after climbing several spiral staircases and attempting to stop unsuccessfully to peer into some of the rooms with the morbid fascination of bumping into some death god, we arrive at what I suppose is my room.

Annie stands aside.

"If you need anything let us know. We'll be posting someone on guard outside your door; if you need something, they will come fetch us." Her voice is so small it's barely audible, but I nod, tired of the presence of other people. I just want to be alone now, even if that means saying goodbye to Xion for a while.

I palm the key I've been given, ramming it into the lock of a heavy bronze door and pushing it open.

Inside, a luxurious deep mahogany glow consumes my vision, and I'm left breathless at the decadence of it all. Chocolate diamonds shimmer, facets reflecting a warm glow from the agate fireplace.

The high walls are slick in what looks like tourmaline, and all the furniture is carved in gold baroque design. There's a cream rug near the fireplace, surrounded by cream leather armchairs, and Cerb takes flight toward it, stretching out like he owns the place.

In front of the right-hand wall, sporting a golden frame and carved to appear as though it is made from four wide trunked trees encrusted with dark topaz, a four-poster bed stands. It beckons, a mix of gold and cocoa velvets and silk atop the high mattress.

Opposite where I'm standing, a balcony extends, though I know the air will be less than refreshing.

"Should I just go?" Xion asks, and I gesture for him to leave, signalling my desire to be alone in not even wanting to speak. Everything is changing too fast, and I'm becoming quickly exhausted despite my usual high energy levels. I hear the door close behind me, and as I turn to say goodbye only too late, realising he's already gone, I see a golden envelope on the table beside the door.

Taking off my backpack, I take a few small steps forward, scared it's from Haedes, but as I grasp the thick paper in my hand and rip open the envelope, I'm surprised to find it's something far more formal.

Miss Persephone Sinclair,
You are invited by The Nexus to attend a formal ball, to be thrown this night, in your honour.
Please proceed to the Grand Hall when the sun is positioned outside your balcony.
We are eagerly anticipating meeting you,
The Nexus Council

I throw down the invitation.

I haven't even met my own father, but I'm supposed to go and make nice with a bunch of gods and goddesses who have no connection to me at all, first?

My heart becomes heavy so I walk the length of the room, throwing open the balcony doors and walking out onto the platform which overlooks the city.

Hanging my head over the ornate copper railing, the weight of change rests heavily on my shoulders.

Is it possible that this has all been one giant mistake?

I know I'm trying to push myself back into denial.

It doesn't work though as I gaze up to the violet sun overhead, burning despite everything in my head telling me it should not be possible. The sky should not be a smoky burgundy but instead blue, light, and airy, and yet it is.

The entire place screams oppression as I look down into the city streets, watching carriages move and people walk along the sidewalks like the insignificant ants they are. I too feel insignificant. I feel helpless.

Turning my back on the view, I don't bother to unpack.

Instead, I pull the book Xion gave me from my backpack. Launching myself into the deep and inviting hold of the four-poster bed, I flick through the pages, scanning for *Haedes' Descent*. It only takes me a few minutes to find, and so I begin to read, hoping that with more knowledge of this place, of him, I might start to understand who I am in all of this as well.

I wake with a start to the sound of knocking against metal and then Cerb's too-loud bark.

I must have fallen asleep after reading the tale of how Haedes had been expelled from The Higher Plains by his brother. My dreams became a morphed version of the tale, whereby my father condemned me to hell instead for his murder.

I'm coated in a layer of sweat, and the room is boiling from the heat being put out by the fire.

Groggy, I get to my feet and make my way over to the door, nervous as to who could be knocking.

Placing my hand on the handle, I take a deep breath before turning it. The door swings open, but it's not who I expect.

A familiar face at least.

"Sephy, you look terrible." Luce assesses me, pushing her way into the room and ushering in several sinners behind her. They bring in a dress form clothed in an enormous and overly decadent chestnut-coloured gown. It's dripping in stones, and I snort.

A panther follows closely in her wake, causing me to gape.

Surely that thing can't be domesticated?

Cerb, however, clearly knows more than I do, as he bounds toward the large black cat. I stare at the gown as it's set down upon the crystal floor, and the two animals begin to get reacquainted behind the brown monster dress.

174

"Uh, thanks for that. What the hell is this monstrosity?" I query, closing the door behind her and turning before placing a hand on one hip.

"It's your ball gown of course, for the reception tonight. You're the guest of honour." She looks at me with wide eyes, and I can't work out if her expression is as innocent as it seems. She seems so nice on the surface, but her reputation still irks me, and I wonder what secrets she has lurking beneath the pure white of her hair.

"Oh, I'm not wearing that," I state simply, a small laugh escaping my lips.

"Wait? Why not! I had our finest seamstress—" she begins, decadent red gown swirling around her as she turns to face me. The sinners leave, sensing an incoming wrath.

"Look, it's nice of you and all, but it's not my style. I don't wear dresses. Ever." I shrug, not expecting her to understand.

"But— but— you'd look so pretty— your hair!" she exclaims, astounded at my lack of wanting to play princess.

"I'm heading into a meeting with a council of gods made mortal, after being brought here because I'm being hunted by Demons. I do not want to look like a princess, damsel, or any other kind of thing that needs saving. I thought you'd get it, what with the horns and all." I gesture up to the two protrusions which rise from her skull, and she looks at me, eyes suddenly twinkling.

"You want to look strong? Fierce?" she asks me, and I nod.

"Exactly."

"Well then, I think I'd better take you shopping," she sighs, as if this is a chore and yet, behind her gaze, I can tell she's secretly thrilled.

"Alright— but let me just—" I begin, but she cuts me off.

"No time, Sephy. We have a lot to do," she promises, grabbing my elbow and pulling me out of the room, a wicked smile spreading across her bloody lips.

15

THRILLER

<u>SEPHY</u>

THE AIR IN THE carriage turns awkward quickly after our mad dash through The Exilia Multum into what I want to call the entrance courtyard. We move away from the palace, away from the glow of The River Styx, the only audible sound Luce's breathing and the horses' hooves falling upon crystal road.

"So— was it your idea to throw this party?" I don't like the silence, and I don't want things to be awkward. Out of all the people I've met so far, Lucifer seems like she's the one with the most knowledge and power. I'm curious about her, about how she came to be here, but I don't know if it's appropriate to ask.

"Not exactly."

She purses her lips, and I give her a questioning look, brushing my hair behind one ear. "It was Haedes' idea," she adds, watching my reaction as my heart becomes weighted like someone's tied rocks to it.

"He didn't think something less— I don't know, formal might be better?" I ask, and she laughs.

"You don't know him. He doesn't work like that. He will avoid getting visibly emotional at all costs. What better way than to surround you with hundreds of other people and make a giant impersonal display?" she snorts. I laugh despite myself. That sounds exactly like something I would try to pull. Maybe I have more in common with him than I realise.

"Well, I guess that there will be alcohol, so that's a plus, right?" I demand an answer from her, desperate to find a positive, and the edge of her lips twitch.

"Oh yes. It's Haedes. He's practically married to whisky." She crosses her legs beneath her red skirt, and I ignore the sentiment, mainly because she's making it evident that we have yet another thing in common.

"Isn't he worried that you know— announcing my whereabouts like this isn't such a great plan security-wise?" I demand, and she looks surprised at my forethought on this. I smile a little, glad that I'm not as oblivious as she originally assumed.

"We had a heated discussion about that, actually. I said that he shouldn't do it because it's a risk; he said that it's safe because we have so much security— I don't know. The Demon Lords had access to you somehow in the mortal world. I'm not convinced, but he's the boss." She shrugs, and I look out of the window as silence falls between us again.

Is Haedes putting me at risk in order to prevent having to meet me one on one?

I'm angry at this theory, mainly because I don't know why he's so bothered. I certainly don't expect anything from him, so I don't know why he's making such a big deal.

We pass old-fashioned streetlamps, flickering with a blue flame inside gothic-style glass cases. They stand upon black steel rods twisted toward the top. As I take in their oddity, I realise they look like the stalks of morbidly preserved, dead flowers.

The city streets seem familiar somehow as we pass strip clubs, coffee shops, nightclubs, and clothing stores. Sinners move along the sidewalks in a metronomic and uniform shuffle, mainly dressed in all black, all dead behind the eyes.

After a few minutes, the vehicle pulls to a stop, and the sounds of hooves cease. Luce opens the carriage door, impatient as the driver dismounts to open it for her slower than she can handle. I follow her out.

Standing out on the street, I gaze upon the innards of Mortaria. It's audibly less overwhelming than I expect for a city, with a lack of car horns and people talking on cell phones. However, one thing I can't help but smile at is the fact that slow jazz is ringing out through the air.

"Is that— live?" I ask, glancing around for the source.

"Yes. Music is good for the soul you know." Luce gives me a smile, and I smirk at the comment, grateful for the music as a distraction from how out of place I feel.

Looking forward now, I find myself outside a mystery store with a dirty black sign. The letters on its surface were bright gold once, but something has worn them down so they no longer make up legible text. I'm sceptical as Luce leads me forward and pushes down on the handle of a door with four dirty glass panes that make up a window.

A bell sounds out, unapologetic and tinny, as we enter.

"Hello? Sissy?" Luce calls out into the pokey corners of the tiny shop.

I'm comforted a little by the claustrophobic feel of the place because it reminds me of the rooms back in England. Here there's no high ceiling, no electric lighting, only more blue flames that illuminate the inside of the shop, casting shadows into the acutely angled corners. Desks littered with bolts of fabric, scissors, and scattered rogue buttons edge the room, and I look around in interest, finding, not surprisingly, only dark tones on display.

From the back room, a short woman in a simple black jumpsuit emerges. I can tell her hair was lustrous once, but now it's dull and frizzy atop her head. Her skin is pale and her green eyes widen as she sees Luce standing in the doorway.

"Oh, Lucifer! What a pleasure it is! Who is this?" she inquires.

Luce stands aside so I can step forward. I'm grateful she doesn't try to introduce me, instead letting me do it myself.

"I'm Sephy." I hold out a hand, but she merely looks at it, and then to Luce for instruction, fear evident in her worn expression.

"It's alright, you can shake her hand. She's demi," she explains, and I look back at her.

"They're not allowed to shake your hand?" I ask her, and she shakes her head.

"No. It's just an etiquette thing. It enforces respect," Luce informs me, and I nod, accepting this as normal. I guess they have to keep order in one way or another. After all, there are a lot more sinners than gods here.

"Sephy here wants something fierce for a masked ball tonight," she demands.

Sissy smiles.

"Alright. I'm glad to hear Haedes is throwing another. It's been a while," she notes, clearly looking for the reason as to why this is.

Luce doesn't smile at her, or give any more information, instead taking a seat on a large velvet pouffe of deep teal against the back wall.

I stand, uncomfortable, in the middle of the room.

"Do you like— you know, making mortals suffer?" I ask her, and she laughs.

"Oh, Sephy, this isn't suffering. What Anubis and Osiris had running before we took over, *that* was suffering. We have a system here. It's regulated rehabilitation. Sinners still have freedom; they can buy and sell time for things they need. Some are even invited to the ball tonight. This is a far better way of rehab than torture," she explains.

I frown even still.

"But why rehabilitate at all? Are the sins that bad?" I ask her, and she shakes her head.

"You misunderstand. It is not the sin itself but the darkness in the universe that an individual succumbs to in committing it. That darkness must be returned before a soul can be re-housed by the Crucible of Gaia. It is necessary for the survival of our universe. Trust me, I don't want to be the bad guy; I've had enough of being made out that way my entire life." Luce sighs, looking sideways into the room where Sissy is rustling around, impatient. She's clearly uncomfortable, but I don't let that stop me, more curious now than ever.

"Why is that, exactly? You don't seem bad to me. You seem— well, pretty sweet— if not a little intimidating. You've done nothing but try to help me so far— that's a lot more than Haedes," I compliment her, trying to be honest, and she smiles.

"Aww, thanks. Well, my mother, Hecate, she was raped by one of the Gods of Ancient, before they lost power. Moloch." She swallows hard, and I can tell she's deeply affected by her lineage. "He's my father. I was exiled from The Higher Plains for being half him, half inherently dark. My mother cut off my horns at birth— and I couldn't stop using Alchemy— couldn't silence the call to that type of magic. They were afraid of what someone with such a controversially mixed lineage could do in goddess form."

"Well, I don't care who your parents are. I care who you are now. People judging you for who you're related to is just them not having the open-mindedness to get to know you." I spit, realising that I mean it more than I thought. I want to ask if her horns grew back a moment later, finding them very much intact, but then decide against it, worrying she'll find me too intrusive.

My father was a businessman who captured and tortured a Merman, who traded my mother. Haedes is a god with less than a stellar reputation. But I'm not them. And anyone who thinks I am can shove it up their ass.

"Thanks. That means more than you know," Luce admits, swinging her feet as Sissy returns, measuring tape and black shimmering fabric in hand.

"Let's get you dressed for this ball then, shall we?"

Back in my suite, I'm fully dressed, ready and anxious to get this ball over with.

I'm wearing a glittering corseted suit jacket, which plunges low, revealing my cleavage, before flaring out at my hips and hanging far beneath my perky ass. Wide glittering black trousers hang from my hips, making me look dominant, almost like the ringmaster of a very kinky circus.

I complete the look with a top hat made of the same material, tilted on my head across from where my locks are pulled into a side bun just behind my ear. I've gone for dark makeup, making my eyes appear lighter than usual, and deep burgundy lipstick that plumps my lips. I bite the bottom one, checking myself out in the single mirror of the ensuite, fighting a fleeting curiosity regarding what Xion will think when he sees me.

Then it occurs to me, I don't even know if he'll be there.

I feel a little naked, vulnerable even, but as I slip on a pair of pointed stilettos, I shrug it off, knowing it's nothing more than longing for a familiar face in this brand-new world.

As the second shoe slips onto my slim heel, I hear a knock at the door, no doubt some servants come to collect me.

Pacing quickly across the slick floor, I'm determined not to be late as I shoot a glance at the violet sun over my shoulder. I find it hovering directly between my balcony doors as it continues in its eternal and unending circle across the sky, never rising or falling, but staying at the same height, always.

I pull the door open as soon as I reach it, the bronze handle cool against my palm.

"Oh— it's you," I stutter, shocked as Xion is revealed in the hallway outside.

"Yes— Uh, Luce asked me to come. For security reasons." He's wearing a thin black mask across the bridge of his nose, encrusted with red and black stones. His eyes shine out from the gaps in the fabric, molten as his heated stare traces me from head to foot.

180

"Oh. That's sensible I guess," I mumble, my heartbeat slowing in my chest for some reason unknown to me.

He holds out a mask, his body bulging against a tux which must have been custom tailored. I mean, there's no way he's buying off the rack with a chest that broad. His tie is scarlet to match the stones in his mask, and I wonder if he's noticed our outfits match perfectly.

"Here," he gestures for me to take it.

I grasp the mask in my fingers, turning it over. It's gold, with red and brown stones. Rubies and russet diamonds, I think. "The stones are representative of the sins of each person."

"Really? What's your sin?" I demand. His expression becomes slack, his eyes boring into mine and making the world around us temporarily fade into triviality. He replies, simply, his sentiment dangerous as it falls from his lips in a single syllable.

"Wrath."

The word causes a slight erotic shudder to wriggle up my spine.

"What about mine?" I query, slightly breathless and unable to tear my gaze from his as my heart begins to race in my chest for absolutely no good reason. I don't know why; I just can't seem to help it. He looks so caught off guard at my question, like I'm asking him the most intimate thing anyone has ever dared.

He swallows hard before continuing, "Well, I mean, for the most part, they represent sin. Yours is just decorative though. It went with that dress Luce had made up for you. I told her you'd never wear it—" he's rambling now, breaking the intense look between us as I tie the golden silk ribbon around my skull, tightening the rigid accessory against my face.

"Yeah, I'm not exactly the dress-wearing kind," I agree.

"It's a shame," I hear him mumble, but ignore this sentiment as he holds out an arm to me.

I swear I see his hands visibly shaking as I loop my arm around his, resting my fingers just above his wrist, but ignore this also. I simply want to keep moving forward through the night's forced conversation and choreographed interaction with as little emotional turmoil as possible.

"So where is this ball?" I demand, not remembering if the invitation had disclosed a location.

"That would be in the grand hall." Xion clears his throat; voice cracking with uncertainty despite the fact his answer is definitive. Is it possible he's nervous too?

"Are you alright?" I ask, voice harsher than I intend. He looks down at me as the question reaches him and smiles.

"Yes. I just hate formal occasions. They're so boring. Dancing is the only thing that makes it bearable if you ask me," he complains.

"I agree. Promise me, even if we have the worst night ever, we'll have at least one dance together towards the end. That way I'll have something to look forward to." I surprise myself with the offer, wondering if it's the nerves causing me to act so sentimental.

I'm never usually this weak.

"Alright. It's a date," he promises, causing me to blush despite myself. He also flushes at the sight of my reddening cheeks, and I cough as we both fall into silence for the rest of the walk through the sprawling labyrinth that is The Exilia Multum.

"There you are!" The striking of Dolly's metal-tipped stiletto heels against crystal ring out as she approaches in a flurry, her voice grating against my nerves.

"I'm sorry; there wasn't a clock in my room," I apologise. However, I can only follow the instructions, however vague, on the invitation I've been given. "You'll get used to that. It's packed in there already. Come, come, come!" She swoops behind me and Xion, still wearing her black shirt and pencil skirt. She's holding a slightly fancier clipboard, and there's a crystal pen hooked behind her ear, which I notice catches the light as she ushers us down the corridor. The persistent sound of her stupid heels sets me even more on edge as she quickens her pace, each step a countdown to my impending doom.

"Open the doors!" she screeches as we reach the height of the staircase I'd ascended upon arrival. At the top, though I hadn't noticed before, two doors which seem to fade out of existence and into the wall itself are hauled open by no less than six sinners.

They stare at Xion and me, though I can't tell what their expressions are supposed to convey. They look almost hungry, like I'm a meal.

"Don't make eye contact with the envy sinners. Come, come, come!" Dolly continues to screech in my ear and I roll my eyes. She's worse than my old dormitory mistress.

"Now, enter!" She gives Xion and me a firm shove, embedding several of her long nails in both our spines. I almost trip over the flared hem of my shimmering pants, but Xion catches me as a sudden hush falls where before there was small talk, the sounds of clinking glasses, and the slurp of what appears to be champagne.

The room, which we are unceremoniously pushed into, is as enormous as I expected. The facets of the smoky quartz capture the bright red light cast by many flaming sconces, turning the space cosy. I examine the space further and find silvery lilac and black drapes hanging from every wall. There are black tables full of silver plates and platters stacked high with food, and the glasses atop the trays of multiple gaunt-faced waiters gleam in platinum, throwing red light in random and sporadic flashes.

I want to spend longer looking, but I can't as the silence becomes unbearable.

Hundreds of faces turn to Xion and me, and I'm not sure what I'm supposed to do next. As I'm about to flush scarlet under their scrutiny, Luce steps forward out of the crowd to save me, dressed now in a plum gown with an onyx-spattered ivory mask resting over her pale blue eyes.

"I'd like you all to make the acquaintance of our newest demi-goddess, Sephy Sinclair." She holds out a hand, gesturing toward me like I'm some kind of amazing monument that's just been erected.

Suddenly, the room fills with applause.

I can't help but smile, feeling wanted at least temporarily. I scan the crowd, trying to find him, curious and wanting to rip off the band-aid. This waiting is slow and torturous. I wish he'd just make himself known to me and get it over with.

As the applause dies down, I notice that there's no music in the background. There doesn't even appear to be a sound system, only a stage at the far end of the room, covered by curtains that match the drapes.

An enormous crystal chandelier dangles and I watch it sway to and fro, hypnotised slightly, before realising someone is trying to talk to me as Xion gives me a slight nudge.

The crowd has surrounded me, not that I've noticed. I've been too busy trying to pick out anyone who could be Haedes.

"I'm sorry, what?" I turn my attention to the man who is directly in front of me, blinking once, then twice, wondering how I hadn't noticed him.

"I said, it's nice to finally meet my cousin—" He looks unimpressed, his blue eyes glittering against tanned skin that only makes his strawberry blonde hair lighter as it falls, long and feathered in a halo around his head. I don't understand what he's talking about, and so give him a questioning look as I examine his ridiculously over-the-top and muscular body.

"I'm Hercules— you know, twelve labours. My God, what do they teach you lame-ass mortals in schools these days? You've *never* heard of me?"

He's a smart ass, that's for sure, and his biceps seem to be larger than his brain. I cock an eyebrow.

"Oh sure, you're the son of Zeus, right? Aren't you half mortal?" I query, wondering why he hates mortals so much if he is one.

"Not anymore. My mortal half died long ago, I'm a Titan now, and it'd do you good to learn your place here and fast. You're just a demi-goddess. You have a long way to go before you even get to be in my meek position." He puffs his chest out with pride, and I give him a disinterested expression.

"Is that supposed to impress me? Like, I don't give a shit who your father is. Or whether you're a mighty Titan. As for you being my cousin, I can't see the resemblance. All I see is a jumped-up little jackass with bad hair, ridiculous muscles that make him look like a balloon animal, and someone in dire need of a mental upgrade." His mouth pops open as I push past him, making sure to use my sharp pointy elbows to knock his thick arm out of the way.

Xion smirks.

"I think you might be my favourite person in the world right now," he whispers, and I wonder if he might be attempting sarcasm.

"What? He's a prick!" I exclaim. Xion continues to laugh.

"Oh, we all know it, but nobody has the balls to actually *say* that," he expresses, amused beyond what I'd thought was possible for his usually stoic face.

"Well, I don't give a shit who you are. You don't talk to me like that, ever."

"I like that," he whispers in my ear, causing a shudder to run up my spine. There's a darkness to his comment, almost like he's making some sort of taboo promise that makes me squirm in the most delicious way possible.

It's been too long since I got laid; I'm getting restless. I curse, wondering how easy it is to pick up a guy in hell—

"Persephone." A familiar and entirely blue face enters my field of vision, spinning from my right to greet me. I turn, taking his hand in mine and shaking. His skin is smooth like a baby's beneath his bronze mask, and I make a mental note to ask him later if he moisturises or not.

"Yama." I nod, formally greeting him in return.

"This is Anubis, and her son, Osiris," he introduces the two figures who he's just been speaking with.

They take measured steps forward, the woman's golden skin shimmering orange under the light of a nearby sconce. Anubis has long inky hair and is wearing a floor-length white gown with a cage of gold wrapping around her torso over the top. Her son smiles at me, his skin a slightly dirtier shade of bronze. Both their eyes are wide and dark, surrounded by heavy liner with matching cobalt masks, and they have straight noses which define their profile more than anything else about them. Anubis is wearing sapphire-coloured lipstick, and the two of them examine me with interest as her lips spread over her teeth in a smile.

"Hello."

I give a small wave, not sure whether this is entirely appropriate.

"Welcome. I see that Xion is at your side— how wonderful," Anubis remarks, though there's an undercurrent to her tone that tells me she's not glad at all.

What, is she jealous?

I'd think as a goddess she could wrangle any man she wanted, even one who's half demon.

"Uh, yes, he's my security."

"And luggage boy," Xion adds with a smirk.

Osiris laughs behind his mother.

He's dressed in long white robes and his ears are pointed against his skull. His face is long, cheekbones sharp as razor blades. I feel like I could say something to him, and he wouldn't be entirely awful, but as for Anubis, I'm sceptical at best.

"How wonderful for your— luggage. You'll have to come see us at The Icon." She extends the invite, and I frown— wanting to ask what the hell The Icon is— when I'm interrupted by the beginning of one of the most familiar songs in the world.

The crowd turns, mirroring me as I spin away from the three Nexus members with whom I have absolutely zero in common.

Michael Jackson's *Thriller* blasts out into the room.

Overhead, from nowhere, a cloud of mist appears, hanging like a thick, magical fog canopy. I wonder if this is some kind of mystical flash storm but soon realise with surprise that it's the source of the music.

"Oh Jesus," Xion mutters under his breath. He clutches my hand in his suddenly, and it is with this rough touch that I'm immediately afraid.

What's going on?

The curtains at the far end of the room pull back, revealing a stage holding a troupe of dancers, all dressed in black with trilby hats. In the centre of them all, he stands, unmistakable.

Haedes.

My father.

He begins to move, grabbing an old-fashioned microphone and singing along with the words. His hair is an eccentric cobalt, slicked back against his skull, and his face is androgyny-made flesh. His body is edgy, too quick, slick even in its rhythm as he dances along with the nostalgic beat and the troupe works with a seeming effortlessness behind him.

I'm transfixed by his motion, by the way he moves, by his voice. The dancers behind him might as well not be there as he has undoubtedly captured the attention of every single person, mortal or god, in the room.

His suit is indigo, his shoes white, his mask slim and black, only highlighting the extreme architecture of his skull. I continue to stare, stunned as the musical number continues. It's utterly ridiculous, completely insane, and yet for some reason I can't help but grin from ear to ear. This is me in so many ways.

He leaps off the stage, bringing his knees high up to his chest like Swayze in *Dirty Dancing,* indicating that the crowd should part. Without argument, as he struts forward, it does.

I'm left, standing in the centre of an empty aisle that's formed by two crowds of guests. I want to move, to disappear into one of them, either one is fine, but it's too late.

Haedes' eyes rest on me, their depths stormier grey than I thought possible. He takes several strides forward, feet striking the crystal floor with each rhythmic beat of the song. He holds out his arms, and I'm helpless to resist. I pull my hand from Xion's nervous grasp behind me, taking a few steps forward toward him whilst keeping in time with the music.

His arms come up to my hips, and he begins to spin me across the floor as though it's no more than liquid smoke. In this moment we are weightless as the memories of those we've lost.

I look into his face, but where his body and voice are the most expressive entities I've ever seen, his eyes are not.

He looks tired as he stares back at me, devastated even. I wonder if I'm a disappointment, not that I care. I don't owe him anything.

Taking the situation for exactly what it is, a distraction from the pain of meeting an estranged daughter, I let go of trying to analyse everything and dance with him, enjoying every second without expectation until the final beat of the song is upon us.

I turn to him, slightly out of breath, and look him straight in the eyes. As the song fades to nothing, I introduce myself, realising I'm going to have to be the one to instigate this, even if I have no desire to.

"I'm Sephy." I hold out a hand, which he looks at blankly but doesn't take.

"I know who you are. Thank you for being here tonight. Now, I must go and greet my other guests. I'll be back to speak with you later." He is polite, giving me a dashing smile before strutting away and becoming but a head of cobalt hair in a sea of formal wear and fake smiles.

Xion rushes over to me, his face concerned beneath the bloody gleam of his mask.

"Are you alright— that was—" He has no words, and neither do I. What was that? Me meeting my biological father for the first time? Was that it? A cheesy dance number and then a formal brush-off?

What the hell?

"I'm fine. Let's get some alcohol and food— I'm starving." I find myself gagging for a drink, anything to rid myself of the hideous cold seeping through my entire body. I could mistake it for disappointment, but that would only be true if I'd been hopeful for something more than merely a man with no desire to know me at all. As it is, I was right on par with my expectations, so the cause is a mystery.

As I make my way over to one of the waiters, whose motion makes me question whether he's a zombie or the result of some trainee necromancer's failed entry exam, I hear my name called.

Reluctantly, I turn.

"Sephy!"

Xion pivots beside me, our eyes resting on two strangers heading toward us in black suits.

Two men, both with emerald encrusted masks, make their way through the crowd. I stare, trying to work out who it is I'm looking at but come up empty.

Should I know these people?

Xion stirs at my side, and within moments everything around me is in chaos.

Xion darts forward, grabbing one of the sinners by the throat. As he does so, he shifts, showing his true face and causing the buttons of his suit jacket to pop off as the seams audibly rip. His face is vicious, but before I can call out to ask him what the hell he's doing, the wind and my confusion are both knocked from me. My throat is in a blackened grasp before I have a chance to blink.

The second man has me, raised above the ground in a deadly stranglehold within seconds.

My heartrate skyrockets, unsure of what's going on, but knowing that I desperately need air. The person assaulting me looks like Xion, but it's not him, even though his face is marred by similar sooty skin. The eyes that belong to what I now suppose is a demon are a merciless lime green, full of hate, and laced with the intent to kill me as I struggle, helpless, a full metre above the floor.

"Stop!" Xion's deep growl thunders, and the crowd turns, further alerted to the commotion by his guttural and desperate exclamation.

"You kill her, and I'll kill him—" he threatens, squeezing his grip tighter around his captive's throat.

The demon who has me in his grasp tightens his fingers, crushing my windpipe. After throwing the mask from his eyes, he pulls out a knife from the inside of his suit, which is ruined from his shift to demon form, pressing the serrated edge to my throat.

"Try me, half-breed scum. There's more where he came—" He doesn't get to finish his sentence because his words are replaced by a high-pitched scream.

Flame blinds me, blazing hot against my skin as it consumes him one limb at a time, drawing out his death and causing as much pain as possible.

I'm dropped to the floor in a crumpled heap as he perishes, gasping for air in a cloud of his remains long after he turns to dust.

I look up from behind the pile of ashes as it finally settles, finding Haedes with scarlet hair now, pupils glowing bright orange around the rims like the sun during a total eclipse. He's looking down at me with an intense ferocity I've never seen from anybody, and it terrifies me.

Now, in this moment, as his chest rises and falls, straining, he is the most powerful, most pissed-off entity I've ever seen.

I tear my gaze away, letting my eyes fall on his hands that command two streams of fire like a dominatrix wielding their favourite whip.

His fury and his gaze alone could scorch even The River Styx dry.

Spinning on the ball of his dance shoe, he turns his back on me to attend to the other demon in Xion's grasp.

Xion steps aside, giving him a wide berth as Haedes takes out the second demon in seconds, leaving nothing but a pile of ash and the smell of barbequed flesh behind as the flaming vines extend and wrap themselves around the demonic body like a team of boa constrictors.

"Stay the fuck away from my daughter," Haedes snarls into the silence as the crowd watches on, shocked.

16

LOVE IS A BATTLEFIELD

XION

EVERYTHING IS TOO CLOSE to the surface, my rage, the demon part of me, my blood coursing hot and thick around my body. My anger is untameable as I watch her, wide-eyed on the floor amongst a pile of ashes.

She's looking up at him in wonder.

Of course, he leaps in to defend her now, making himself the hero, when really this is all his fault.

Did he plan it this way?

Who knows.

Either way, I cannot remain idle any longer. I don't care if he's a god or not.

"Haedes!" I roar, voice reaching a depth and level of projection I seldom find myself pissed enough to manage.

Taking several measured steps forward, I ball my blackened fist by my side, throwing down the mask from my eyes so that he's subject to the full force of my furious gaze. His hair turns from red to blue too fast, and it makes me feel like he's acting a part in all this all the more as he squares up to me.

"Woah, what's your problem?" Haedes snaps at me, the whips of fire in his palms diminishing. I don't know if I should take this as an insult or not.

Has he forgotten who I am?

What I am?

I know I've been in his service for decades, but has he really written me off as nothing more than a stray puppy? Has he decided I'm no threat to him or anyone, after everything I've done?

"This is your fault! You put her in danger! This ball was a giant neon sign announcing her location, for Christ's sake!" I raise my voice even further. Getting up in his face, my body casts deep shadows into the edgy design of his skull. He looks up at me, perhaps an inch shorter in height but clearly not intimidated.

"What did you just say to me, boy?" he snarls, and my eyes dart over his shoulder to Sephy's expression. I expect to find her scared of me, but instead, she looks like she wants to interject.

I keep my expression firm, staring down at Haedes and holding my ground.

"I said that if you didn't have such a fucking giant problem with being an adult and owning your shit, you wouldn't have nearly killed your only daughter. This is completely unacceptable!" I growl, defensive, as he raises one eyebrow and turns back to Sephy, offering her a hand. She refuses to take it as she gets to her feet.

"Are you alright?" Haedes asks her, and she looks between us both.

"Yes, no thanks to you. I'm fine." I want to smile, but I keep my expression stoic as she delivers this mighty blow in so few words. Haedes looks to me and then back to Sephy, eyes turning a multitude of hues before settling on outrage.

"But I saved you!" he exclaims, and Sephy cocks her head.

"No, Xion saved me. You put me in danger for your own selfish reasons." She spits her fury at him without mercy, and I watch on, my temper quelled by her straightforward attitude and bravery.

She definitely sees right through him, which I can't help but adore.

"But—" Haedes begins, but Sephy raises a hand.

"No buts. You might not know this, but fathers generally don't put their own needs before the safety of their daughters. Or at least not good ones anyway. I can't stay here anymore. It's not safe— thanks to you."

She shakes her head, looking at me with a kind of silent, desperate plea stirring behind her cognac irises.

"What? Where are you going to go? I'm all you've got here," Haedes stutters, hair tinging furiously scarlet at the root.

"I'll go with Xion," she announces, certain of herself.

I'm standing here, ready to fight for her, ready to defend her, and yet, she's taken the wind out of my sails yet again, reminding me she's no damsel.

"Yes. She'll be staying with me from now on," I confirm, causing a stir among a few members of the onlooking crowd as the family drama unravels before their eyes.

Haedes turns his head to stare at them, eyes narrowing before he bellows, "Get out!"

A sudden burst of flame explodes from his right hand as a warning shot.

I stiffen in place as the guests abort the gathering, well, all except a few Nexus council members who stand, unafraid and unimpressed.

"You want to go with *him*? This— *disgusting half-breed*?" Haedes asks her, tone laced with hate. I expect her to get angry, I mean she's great at losing her temper, but instead she smiles.

"Yes. I mean, after all, I'm a *disgusting half-breed,* too. So, I guess we should get out of your way, seeing as how we're so beneath you and your mighty intellect."

She takes a few firm steps past the man who is visibly crumpling under her words alone, though she might not see it. I, however, have worked for Haedes too long. I know he doesn't suffer fools; he refuses to suffer at the hands of anyone but himself, so the fact he's allowing her to talk to him in this way and not murdering her where she stands says more than she knows.

"If you leave this Exilia, don't even think about coming back," he threatens her, and I know that inside she must be hurting more than she visibly shows, too.

She doesn't hesitate in grabbing my elbow, still mapped with tattoos like rivers of molten rock, and turning her back on Haedes. She pulls me towards the exit where the last of the terrified guests are making their escape.

My heart soars more than I want to admit, more than it has in years, as I leave the hall with her on my arm.

As we go, she calls back over her shoulder in that way that always makes me smile, swinging her hips and simply saying, "Why would I want to come back? There's nothing here of value to me anyway."

LUCE

The doors echo as they slam closed in the wake of the pair who leave me and the rest of The Nexus council members stunned. My plum gown is pinching in against my ribs, and as I turn to Thane, mouth hanging open, I'm completely lost for words.

"Well, that was a disaster."

She rolls her eyes.

I hadn't even had a chance to introduce Thane to Sephy, but in watching how she'd handled Haedes, I can tell she's already earnt her respect.

"God dammit!" Haedes grabs a nearby waiter by the throat. Yanking a glass of whisky off his tray, he downs the entire contents before smashing it on the floor and throwing the unsuspecting gluttony sinner aside. Glass flies outward in a supernova of shards from the point of impact, causing Anubis to stir.

"That's enough, Haedes!" she scolds him, her acutely angled eye-brows sloping downward in the middle of her forehead toward her nose as she scowls.

"Enough? Enough? My goddamn *daughter* was just attacked in my own goddamn home! God damnit!" He's cursing, rushing toward the tables of food and beginning to smash up the ice sculpture of a cupid with his bare hands. I raise one eyebrow as the rest of us watch on in mild fascination.

Thane shifts her gaze to me from his outburst, expression fatigued.

"Should we do something?" she asks me. I shake my head.

"No. Just let him have his moment," I reply.

The rest of the council members move over to us and we gather in a circle, our finery lost on the lack of occasion as we ignore the smashing and crashing going on in the background.

"Did anyone try to tell him that this was a security risk for her?" Muerta enquires, moving to my side. Her magenta and scarlet dress has many ruffled layers and pulls in her waist. This, combined with the makeup upon her face, makes her look like little more than a skeleton in a lustrous raven wig.

"I did," I admit, remembering the conversation.

"It's not your fault, Luce. He doesn't listen to anybody. We all know that by now," Thane adds, taking my hand in hers. Osiris looks over his shoulder to where Haedes is now smashing every single champagne flute individually, a look of purposeful and demented malice plastered on his face.

Jesus. I think Sephy broke him.

"He said that we have enough security here. I mean— we do. We have a lot. I don't know how they got in. Have there been any breaches lately, Anubis?" I query the Egyptian Titan, her skin glowing golden and her eyes unmistakably harsh as they pop out of her face against her bold blue eyeliner.

"No. Not in years. You know that we're fastidious, Lucifer. I'm surprised at your doubt in my ability to keep the boundaries we've set intact." She's touchy about her competence, no doubt because she was a Titan before she came here, and has once again been put second to Haedes, a pure god descended almost directly from Gaia.

"I mean no disrespect. I am simply trying to work out how those Abraxians got in here." I frown at her defensiveness, and Osiris looks between us, uncomfortable as he shifts inside his lime and white robes that are embellished with gold leaf at the seams.

"How did Xion even know they were demons? I saw him take one of them out before they even shifted," he asks, thick lips caressing the words. I know that he and his mother have always been wary of Xion, but I won't allow them to muddy his name during this. If it weren't for him, Sephy would probably be dead.

"I don't know— but I'm sure his intentions were only in Sephy's best interests," I protest. I hadn't invited him tonight but he had come anyway, for her.

"That's yet another thing we're concerned about—" Anubis begins, but is interrupted as Haedes moves over to the group, out of breath. His hair has returned to its cool hue, and he looks calmer.

"Sorry about that," he mumbles, ashamed of himself as his eyes drop to the floor.

"So nice of you to join us, Haedes," Anubis scolds him yet again. He rolls his eyes.

"Oh, I'm sorry; did I inconvenience you with my personal anguish and devastation?" He's sarcastic, and I'm surprised he's got the gall after everything that's happened. Then again, he's constantly pushing the limits of everyone around him, so I probably shouldn't be surprised at all.

"No. You inconvenienced me with your stupidity. Didn't it occur to you that you were putting her at risk?" Anubis demands.

He only shakes his head.

"She wasn't at risk. I killed those demons before anything bad happened! I don't know what the big deal is?" He's denying he's in the wrong now, his go-to reaction for guilt.

"Regardless of that. We have two problems. One, we don't know how the demons are getting into both Mortaria *or* the mortal world. The second one is to do with what we have heard from The Fates." Yama is always good at keeping us on point. He's concise, logical, and I'm glad for it. I really can't stand watching the council bicker. It's bad enough at our monthly gathering, which I never attend without copious amounts of wine before and sex promised after, let alone bringing it into a party which was supposed to be a good time.

"Yes, as I was saying, I'm concerned about Xion and your daughter getting close. He clearly cares for her," Anubis announces. I don't change my expression, continuing to stand poker straight, but I'm filled with nerves.

"Jesus, Nu, I *just* found out I'm a dad. Can we please leave the mental image of her fucking some half-demonic asshole for another night? There ain't enough whisky in the world to erase that shit," Haedes cusses and Yama turns to him.

"Being serious for one moment Haedes, the Fates came out with some interesting phrases at her trial. Chimera being one of them. They said that a *Chimera of all souls* will rise from her ashes. They mentioned something called The Phoenix." His face is stoic, and I feel my heart begin to race slightly. I'd been hoping everyone had forgotten about that.

"What does that even mean?" Haedes demands.

"It means that letting a demon half-breed and a demi-god fraternise so casually is a disaster waiting to happen. Nobody needs some half-demon-half god being born into a mortal body. It could destroy everything." I blanche at this comment, feeling it stab me in the heart like a shard of ice.

I know Anubis isn't talking about me, but she's exactly the kind of person who led my mother to disown me.

Thane squeezes my hand and I exhale, letting the feel of her skin on mine ground me.

"Who said anything about them having a child? They're just friends," I interject.

Osiris looks between me and Thane, a look of incredulity plastering itself on his face.

"I'm not so sure about that. Did you see how he leapt to her defence… that's—" he starts, but Thane cuts him off.

"Exactly what a security guard should do. Do not forget that Xion has been charged to protect her." She is trying to remain on my side in all this, but I wonder what she really thinks. I know she has her own points of view about parents interfering in their children's love lives.

"Besides, Sephy isn't exactly the relationship type," I add, recalling earlier when I'd looked into my crystals and seen jumbled glimpses of her past. I'd been trying to see what kind of style I should go with for her gown. As it was, I didn't find her wearing so much as a skirt, but there were plenty of leather pants getting thrown asunder by an array of different men.

"You know, I find it creepy that you know that," Haedes snarls, trying to change the conversation back into an argument. He's trying to distract by pissing me, and everyone else around him, off. He gets off on the fight, the banter.

I ignore him, not having time for childish games.

"Haedes, your colours are showing," Muerta warns him, her voice half dangerous, half dreamy as she gazes at him with drooping lids. Her enormous brown eyes are sort of alarming when they look directly at you, evidenced moments later as Haedes turns to me.

"So, what's your take on all this? Exactly how screwed am I as a parent on a scale of one to ten?" he demands, laughing as though this is all one giant joke.

"I think you already know the answer. You don't need me to tell you that. Grow up Haedes," I spit, angry at his lack of trying with his only blood relative.

It stings deep, hurting me in a way closer to my heart than I want to admit.

"Ooooh, the Devil's got sass now!"

I wonder exactly how much he's had to drink as I watch him, noticing he's swaying slightly on the spot. His bravado and then anger had masked it before, but I know it takes a lot to get this man inebriated.

"Damn straight. Now go to bed. You're drunk," I order him.

The other members of The Nexus look embarrassed, not only for him but for me, having to once again act as his mother, even though I've never had a loving one of my own.

"Whatever," he mumbles like an insolent teen, turning on his heel with a swagger that makes it even more evident to me that he's tipsy.

I should've known that he wouldn't be able to handle being a father; he can barely handle being a mortal.

We wait until he's left the room, banging into things and creating a cacophony of clatter. He only makes it halfway across the hall before he convects atop the puddle of whisky from his prior outburst. It leaves a flaming pool in the middle of the floor, and as the remaining Nexus members turn away from it in disgust, I try to change the subject.

"I'll go and speak with The Fates, see if I can learn anything more about this Phoenix they've spoken of. I also think Thane should go and peek in on the Demon Lords. I know it's dangerous, but we need to find out how they're infiltrating not only here but the mortal world as well." I voice my plan and Yama smiles, content. He's a man of action, of absolutes, so forward momentum pleases him.

"I shall summon a carriage to pick up The Fates and bring them here." He nods at me, his approval evident. Thane comes in close, giving me a chaste kiss on the cheek, full of promise for when she returns.

"I'll go and ready for flight." My lover leaves without another word, clearly troubled by the turn of events in a way she will not vocalise until we're alone.

I look around at the remaining members.

"What about Haedes?" Muerta asks me.

The others look at me with expectant stares.

"I— I just don't know anymore." I sigh, disappointed to say the least.

17

FIRESTONE

PANDORA

WE WAIT. THE SIX of us gathered for the first time in longer than I can remember.

The five Demon Lords, Abraxis, Gorgon, Barbas, Katerina, and Lilliana give suspicious askance glances into the mirrors lining the walls of the main chamber of The Halls of Antiqua.

I am a patient person, but often I forget how waiting in Mortaria is one of the most torturous experiences that one may have the pleasure of enduring. There is no motion in the air, no breeze, nor evident movement of the sun above. There is no ticking of a clock or ageing of those around you. There is merely endlessness in all directions, with no indication of linear passage through that thing we call time.

Gorgon watches me with interest; he thinks I haven't noticed, but I'm far more perceptive than any of the five Lords give me credit for. His pointed long face is inexpressive, his large forehead plastered with greasy hair that's stuck to his pale and sweaty skin in wavy lines, snakelike and creepy. He's wearing all black, a slim-cut suit that makes him appear even thinner than Barbas. He's tall, with lime eyes that are covered by dual lids, one set which close vertically and the other beneath which slide shut like a set of too-quick elevator doors.

Katerina gives a deep exhale and then a painful sounding inhale, causing her ribs to jut out at odd angles from her spine as she twists in her stone seat.

Abraxis is the tensest of all, his glowing orange eyes narrowed and focused on the tiniest of details, trying to find any indication of change in my motion. His scrutiny causes his human features to become evil, highlighted in a tangerine glow. He's been waiting for his Kindred to return for a while now, perhaps too long.

I glance over to Barbas next, and well, he just looks plain furious. Ever since the Phobias failed to subdue one Miss Sephy Sinclair, he's been silently seething, and I'm sure harbouring an intense hatred toward me in particular. I mean, it was I who put him up to the task in the first place, and so it is I who caused him such humiliation in front of his peers.

Lilliana stirs, causing the rest of us to perk up. Her eyes widen, and I feel the box heat in my pocket against my thigh. Pulling it out without hesitation, I toss it up into the air where it slides open on one side. A portal explodes, breaking the tension and ending our limbo.

From within the sparking scarlet and spinning onyx smoke, a single figure falls. Landing on her haunches atop the table in a simple black ballgown, she straightens as the box drops back into my palms, hot to touch. Pulling a glistening jade eye mask from her face, she is breathless, almost like she's had a narrow escape.

My heart sinks.

"Alexis." Abraxis' expression is hopeful as she dismounts the table but soon changes as she simply shakes her head.

"Horatio and Paris— they didn't make it," she announces. Abraxis' disappointment quickly turns to fury.

"That's enough of this, Pandora. This is a wild goose chase!" he exclaims, phasing into his black and orange demonic form, trying to intimidate me. As if this is all my fault and not at all because the Kindred of the Demon Lords have become lazy and weak.

Gorgon watches us with interest as Barbas joins in the attempt at placing the blame entirely on my shoulders.

"It was a nice thought, but I am not willing to sacrifice any more of my Kindred to kill some girl just to hurt Haedes."

I sigh at this comment.

"You're all misunderstanding me. I wasn't going to *kill* the girl. I was going to hold her hostage so Haedes would have reason to hand over Mortaria. I've been trying to get your hunting grounds back." I keep my expression dead on my face, not showing how close I am to leaving and never coming back. These Demon Lords are too small-minded, too fuelled by competition amongst themselves, or a hunger that they cannot satiate. They cannot see the bigger picture.

"Haedes— he did defend her. He used The Eternal Flame to destroy my brothers. He was furious that she'd been attacked," Alexis adds.

Abraxis turns to her.

"Be that as it may, she's cost us a handful of Kindred already. Three of which cannot be resurrected because they were destroyed by The Eternal Flame," Abraxis barks, pectorals bulging as his orange eyes glow hot and dangerous, anger mounting visibly within him.

"You men! You know nothing of the suffering our Kindred have endured." Katerina speaks up now, rising from her seat and slamming her fragile-looking palms down on the table.

"It is alright for you; you do not need the Sanguine forest, or the Plains of Ichor to survive. Your Kindred are not hungry, are not starving—" Lilliana adds, moving to Katerina's side, her wild hair making her appear unhinged in her rage as her words fall like acid into the air.

The atmosphere among the group becomes tense once again, Gorgon still saying nothing as he watches the argument escalate from his shadowy corner of the room, irises popping neon lime against the dark.

"No, they are alive, and I intend to keep it that way," Barbas retorts, his shame at his recent failure only too evident as his eyes wash over me in frosty examination.

"I know you have lost, but the window to capture this girl is closing fast. I do not know when we will have another opportunity such as this one. She's still unsure of her powers, not yet fully bonded with the half of herself most powerful," I plead now, feeling pathetic, which makes me all the angrier.

"We have tried, Pandora. Three of us now have sent Kindred and lost those Kindred. We do not possess the resources to capture her or fight off the wrath of Haedes. It's a nice little dream of yours, but unless you have some magical way of getting to the girl when she's unprotected and weak, I feel strongly that it is a feat not worth pursuing." Abraxis brushes me off, pacing around the table.

"Even if gaining control of Mortaria could help free the Gods of Ancient?" I ask, and they look at me with only slight interest. Maybe they think I'm bluffing or desperate—maybe they think I'm overestimating my power. Either way, Abraxis isn't buying it.

"Even so," he replies, answer final.

I open my mouth to speak but close it again. Done with the conversation.

I am not wasting any more time trying to convince those who are too proud to risk failure to gain power in this world. Power is all that matters really, and I know more than I'd like to admit that if I was in their shoes, having been endowed with such primal energy and magic, I wouldn't be just sitting around waiting for the end to come.

"Fine. We'll discuss this again soon. I promise you," I vow hotly, turning and stalking from the meeting chamber.

My heart is pounding in my chest, beating hard against the thick boning of my scarlet corset. I'm betrayed, frustrated, and beyond anything once again undervalued and unappreciated.

As I walk down the eternally long passageway towards the exit of the crumbling ruins, I crave distance, some time to think. It is with this that I find myself casting my mind back to the last group of powerful beings who had refused to listen to me.

The Aetherial Court made me into what I once was. A Titan. But it was also they who had ruined me, used me, and spat me out once I was no longer of use to them and refused to be put in what they felt was my rightful place.

I had grown up in the Yorkshire Dales, long ago. Upon my mortal death at a young age, from being prostituted out by my father and made diseased, I had been chosen by Hera, made into one of her Kindred and given eternal life to fight for the protection of The Higher Plains in Aetheria.

My wings had been glorious, a gift from the gods, and I had felt sacred, special. I felt like I belonged. Then, during one particularly nasty altercation, I lost my immortal life and ascended, becoming a Titan and finally walking among the gods and goddesses I had so worshipped in my time as a Nephilim.

I wanted to help, to be a part of The Aetherial Court, to govern the lands I had so loved to defend as a Kindred, but he, Zeus, merely laughed at me. Telling me I was not pure. That I was not worthy of such an honour.

After everything I had done for him, for all the gods and goddesses in that damned court, even Hera, the woman who had chosen me, was made weak and subservient to the will of her husband.

For my pride, for thinking I was able enough to rule, having once been mortal, I was gifted the box, a great and terrible power all at once. I looked into it and saw horrors beyond what I had thought possible, the darkness that resides in human nature laid bare. I had fallen from grace that day, from The Higher Plains, and landed here, among the Kindred of gods who had once been dealt a similar fate, banished and powerless.

"Pandora?" A whisper reaches me, breaking through my recall of memories that never fail to kindle my fury. The place on my shoulder blades where wings had once flourished itches now, irritating me all the more.

"What?" I turn on my heel as I pass through the doors, continuing to walk backwards with no intention of slowing down to listen to more reasons why my plan was ridiculous and would never work.

"I want to help you." As I reach the cracked and disintegrating courtyard of the cathedral, I find Gorgon quickening his pace, trying to catch up with me.

"You couldn't have possibly made that little fact known in front of everyone else?" I scowl.

His green eyes narrow, his pallor and perspiring skin making him look dead or diseased.

"Do you want the assistance of the Gorgonians or not?" he asks simply, his skin flickering in and out of camouflage.

"What do you have in mind? And what is it going to cost me?" I retort, suspicious.

"I was thinking we do a little recognisance. If you send in a few of my demons, using that box of yours, they can sneak around and see what the weaknesses of The Nexus are. Perhaps one or more of them can be bargained with. You might discover that they're willing to give her to you, given the right incentive," he muses, and my eyes widen.

That's actually pretty smart.

"I'm shocked. That's very cunning." I plaster surprise readily on my face like thick jam on a scone. His eyes blaze.

"Do not mistake my silence for weakness or stupidity, Pandora." His lime irises glow brighter a moment, and I know he's trying to exert his will over me. I feel the tug from deep within but refuse to give in to it. His hypnotic charms might work on mortals and base demons, but on those of the more powerful persuasion, they are not as strong as he assumes.

"I would never do that. That being said, you must want something in return. Nothing that ever comes from you is free." I cut through the façade that I'm so weak and he's so generous. This is a trade, plain and simple.

"When you take Mortaria, I want her. Lucifer. My master would be greatly impressed if I could bring her to him." He reveals his intent, and I nod. This is certainly true. I'm sure Moloch could get a lot out of a little family bonding once he's been freed.

"I'm sure that can be arranged." I smile at him, my hopes of conquering the land once again restored.

I feel my physical self calm, my muscles unfurling as Gorgon looks to his left and then his right. His long tongue flickers between his lips, making a hissing sound, and his favourite demon Kindred, which I had known could not be far from his side, appear. They flicker into sight, their camouflage fading as their yellow, green, and orange eyes blink with unfeeling and reptilian subtlety. I watch as the snake-like demons slither around my feet, the hairs on the back of my neck standing readily on end.

I *hate* snakes.

"Very well," I begin, reaching into my pocket once more for the box, "You will go and discover what weaknesses lie within The Nexus council. Go fast, and do not return until you have something of use to me," I command them, Gorgon translating in an accompanying concoction of hissing.

I open the portal once more, allowing only a few Gorgonians entry, aware that the box can only withstand so much power moving between locations at one time. I keep a hold on the box's edges, making sure that the box itself is not swallowed by the portal as I allow when I travel, looking next to Gorgon.

"Come Pandora, let us walk a while."

He holds out an arm to me, and I press my hand upon his elbow, the black lace of my gloves becoming slick with the moisture seeping through his suit.

"Do you really think that they'll find something we can use?" I ask him, curious now. He smiles.

"But of course. After all, Haedes is perhaps the least tolerable man on earth. Wouldn't you agree?" he asks me.

I nod.

"Yes. Except for his brother of course," I reply, and Gorgon smiles.

"Pandora, you really need to let your vendetta against Zeus go you know. You are a smart beautiful woman. Wasting your time on one such as he is pointless. Everyone knows The Island of The Blessed, not The Higher Plains, is where the real power has always been and remains to this day."

As we walk around the rotting gardens, I think of The Island of The Blessed, of the place where the Gods of Ancient are trapped, waiting for the day when they will once again be free.

I can only hope that day will come to fruition at my hand.

SEPHY

As I stare out of the carriage window, on the move yet again, I see a raven fly overhead and frown. It seems out of place to say the least, with the rest of the sky noticeably barren of any wildlife. Xion catches the change in my expression and leans across the padded seat opposite me, staring out up to the skies, a small smile spreading across his lips.

"Thane is on the hunt for information again," he informs me, but I frown, having no idea who it is to whom he is referring.

"Thane?"

"Yes, Luce's lover, Thanatos. She's cursed to be able to transform into a raven. If they feel a threat is brewing, they'll usually send her over to The Fallen Kingdom to see what's up," he informs me in a small voice, tone lacking its usual volume.

"I see. Well, at least someone cares whether I stay alive or not." I roll my eyes, irritated. I've not got any of my belongings with me, and my dog is still back in the Exilia where I've vowed never to return.

"I'm sorry. About all of it," Xion mumbles, his eyes trying to catch mine and hold my gaze.

I don't reciprocate, turning once again to watch the city pass outside the window.

"It's not your fault. I should be thanking you for agreeing to take me in." I sigh, feeling more like an orphan now than ever. Undoubtedly being shuffled from place to place is even worse than being sent overseas to some stuffy boarding school. At least there, I'd known I'd have a warm bed to sleep in at night and breakfast every morning.

"You don't have to thank me for that. It's what friends do." Xion once again tries to make things emotional, but this time a single word of his catches me off guard.

"Friends?" I repeat the word, shocked to hear him using it.

"Of course. You don't think I stick around to carry your luggage because I have some sick sense of self-loathing, do you?" He tilts his head, heart-breaking in his ruggedness as a lopsided and entirely genuine smile takes over his usually stoic face.

"I don't have many—well, any friends." I relinquish this small truth, which bugs me more than I want to admit.

"I don't know why. You're not so bad." Xion places a hand on my knee and squeezes, causing tingles to run up the inside of my thigh. I pull back from him, vulnerable, and sigh as I let the dimpled leather of the seat cradle me.

"It's hard to make friends when everyone wants your money," I admit, and he frowns.

"Well, I don't want it. It means nothing to me. I like you. You're funny." His explanation is simple, and as the carriage hits yet another bump in the road and we both jostle atop our seats, we fall into silence once more. I have no idea what to say to him. As it stands, the sad fact is that he's probably the best friend I've ever had.

"Thanks," is the only word that I allow to pass my lips.

He doesn't respond, merely smiles, and continues to examine me as I go back to looking out of the window, feeling as though I'm trapped in a goldfish bowl, looking out upon Mortaria but not really a part of it. I'm supposed to belong here. This is where my mother had fallen in love with my father and they had made me. The real and true story of my creation. This is my origin. And yet, I feel like nothing more than a stranger in a strange land.

"Come on." Xion encourages me to move as the carriage stills upon the road and he opens the door, yet again not waiting for the driver to descend onto the path and do it for him. I step down the small collapsible stairs and out onto the sidewalk. We're dwarfed by an enormous skyscraper made from white stone speckled through with crimson spots and splashes. The construct twists upward like a mangled spine that's been contorted into a thick double helix, and I swallow hard as Xion leads me in through a set of tinted, spinning glass doors before we step through into the lobby.

"What floor are you on?" I ask him, feeling my stomach grumble against my will.

"The penthouse. Perks of working for The Nexus," he elaborates, and I nod as we take quick and careful paces towards a flight of stairs.

"Don't you have an elevator?" I ask him, and he shakes his head.

"This is hell, Sephy, not The Hilton." His tone is teasing, but I don't laugh, realising that I'm actually nervous, even if I can't put my finger on why. Could it be the fact that I've once again narrowly avoided being a demon entrée? Or is it that I'm entering Xion's personal territory for the first time?

I guess it might be the second one.

After all, I'm not used to having to rely on anyone for anything. Him taking me in is more than I could have expected, especially when I didn't exactly ask him first.

We climb more stairs than I would have thought possible and reach the top after around ten minutes of trekking.

"Jesus, where is your apartment? Heaven?" I ask him, out of breath. I bend over, hands on my knees as I try to catch my breath. He probably smirks, but I'm too distracted to see it because the boning of my corset is pushing into my ribs. After a few seconds, I start to feel faint. Shaking my head, my stomach gives another audible rumble.

Xion takes one look at me and strides across the brushed steel of the floor, his tread causing the metal to echo loudly.

Finally catching my breath, I follow him towards a door as he reaches inside his leather jacket for a key with which to unlock it.

I take the top hat off my head, feeling my stiletto heels pinching my feet, and quickly trail after him into the apartment as he steps aside just inside the door.

The place is simple — black stone floors, walls, and furniture, with only a dash of silver here and there. The torches on the walls burn blue, and I wonder why nobody seems to have electric lighting even though Xion had mentioned before that this place does have power.

The doorway is at the head of the apartment, and it spreads back in a single, long room, partitioned only by sliding glass doors that separate the open plan kitchen and living area from the enormous bedroom. He has a huge bed, but it looks like no guest room. So, I guess I'll be taking the couch if that's the case.

My stomach growls again and he stalks behind me, yanking open the fridge and looking back over his shoulder.

"How about we silence that yowling cat inside your stomach before it alerts the Demon Lords to your exact location— though with that volume it might deter them— Huh, maybe I should just starve you." He's sarcastic as he grabs a container from the fridge, opening it and throwing it into a black microwave with a tinted glass screen and neon blue dash.

"You cook?" I ask him, surprised. He doesn't seem like the domestic goddess type.

"No. I reheat. The gluttony sinners bring stuff over here from the kitchens in the Exilia. Luce knows I suck at cooking and also at being hungry. Demons don't do well when they're hungry." He gives me a wicked grin while I stand in the hallway, staring at him like a spare part. "Well don't just stand there. Come, sit down; you're starving, and I can imagine your feet hurt in those things. How's your throat?" He's suddenly in his element, looking after me in his own rugged, masculine way, and I can't stand it. I feel totally redundant and vulnerable.

"Fine," I reply, slipping my heels off and padding over the cool marble of the floor. The heat and ache ebbs from my feet before I jump up onto a silver stool across the kitchen island from where Xion is standing beside the humming microwave.

It emits a small ping and he turns, grabbing the container from the inside of the appliance and handing it to me with some cutlery.

"Eat," he orders, watching me with a caring but firm gaze. I indulge him this once as the smell of meat sauce fills my nostrils and I begin to salivate.

We don't talk again for a while, mainly because I'm too busy stuffing my face to speak. Xion gets me a glass of water and then moves back through the apartment, taking off his jacket and pacing noisily through to the bedroom.

He disappears for a while, but I'm too distracted by the spaghetti and bolognese sauce that's possibly even better than Jules' — though I'd never tell him that — to notice.

Once I'm finished, I stretch up to the ceiling, full and in the beginnings of sleepiness. I swivel on the stool so I'm facing the room, looking back into his home. Xion is setting up a pillow and blanket on the couch, and looks up to me with a jerk, as if he didn't realise I was watching him.

"I ran you a bath. I have a spa tub and figured you could use it. I'll take the couch," he announces.

I frown.

"I'm happy to take the couch," I argue, fatigue beginning to hit me hard.

"Look, I'm not letting a woman sleep on my couch when there's a perfectly good bed right there. You're sleeping in the bed. End of discussion," he growls, and I roll my eyes.

"You know I don't need you to take care of me," I snap at him, defensive. I'm in his place, eating his food and from the sounds of it, about to be forced into his comfy ass man-bed. He's making me weak.

"I know you don't need me to. I want to. That's what friends do. Now, go and get in the bath." He is saying this now through gritted

207

teeth, clearly aggravated at my lack of compliance. Mad, I hop down off the stool and move past him.

"You know just because I'm taking a bath doesn't mean I'm obeying you. I'm just dirty— that's all," I remind him.

He smirks and then shakes his head.

"Just get in the damn tub, and stop complaining," he retorts, not looking at me, but continuing to set up a makeshift bed on the sofa instead.

I pad through the bedroom, finding an ensuite connecting with the right-hand wall.

I push open the heavy black wood of the door, my feet finding yet more cool marble. The walls remain the same flawless black, as does the floor. The only difference in here is that there's spotlighting built into the ceiling, casting a stark white down onto me. I see a mirror above the vanity across from the door, so take a few steps forward after shutting myself in and examine my face, finding it too pale. My makeup only partially remains, clearly having been washed away by sweat from the dancing and then assault. The bath is steaming up into the air, and the jets are going as I take off my armour, shedding the glittering corset and pants onto the floor.

Stepping into the tub, the hot water causes me to relax, and I lean back into the bubbles, the scent of bergamot and Himalayan salt filling my nostrils.

I look down at my thin, pale body, finding it no longer strong as I had once thought, but now seemingly frail. That demon had the ability to end my life in the palm of his hand, and if it weren't for Xion's quick thinking—

Then something occurs to me.

How had Xion known they were demons before they'd even shown their true faces? Did he recognise them from before? Can he sense other demons like him?

I suddenly have a million questions and realise that for someone who claims he's my friend, I know very little about him. A wave of something like paranoia floods my gut as I sink back into the water, my mind racing over all our interactions. He offered his home to me. When he had no reason to— or did he?

Is he working with his father?

Am I just another target for him to annihilate?

What if I'm playing right into the Demon Lord's hands?

I should be afraid at these thoughts, but instead, I just float in the tub, numb as I let the water caress me and my anxiety bob away on a sea of steam and spa jets.

Once I'm out of the bathtub, I wrap a black towel around myself, realising I have nothing to wear. I pad through to the bedroom, looking through the still-open sliding doors to where Xion is sitting on the couch, looking through a book of some kind.

"Um— I don't have anything to wear," I mumble, knowing that if he is working with the Demon Lords, I'll definitely need clothes to flee.

Xion turns at the sound of my voice, looking at me, my face clear of makeup and my hair sodden through. He smiles a little.

"What?" I demand. He suddenly looks guilty.

"You look— well, a lot more like yourself," he admits, and I scowl. What does that even mean?

"Right— well, could I look like me in clothes?" I ask, feeling my vulnerability increase as he rounds the sofa quickly and approaches me.

"Of course," he replies, taking a right and opening a closet built into the wall right next to the ensuite door.

From inside, he pulls out a few black garments and then throws them at me.

"They'll probably be a little big, but I'll go back to the Exilia and get your stuff tomorrow. I'll check on Cerb too," he adds as I open my mouth to ask. I slam my jaw shut again, not sure what to say.

Standing, I hold the clothes in my pruning fingers as he moves back to the sofa without another word.

"Thanks," I call, turning on my heel and moving back into the bathroom to get changed. I normally don't care about people seeing me naked, but for some reason, it's different in his apartment. I don't have Jules, or anyone else to clean up after my decisions. It's just me, and well— me.

Dropping the towel, I pull an overly large black V-neck shirt over my head. He's also given me a pair of boxer shorts, unsurprisingly also black, and so I put those on too, seeming ridiculously slim in this baggy attire.

My hair hangs down over my breasts, dripping and ratty, my face pale with heavy bags that are all too evident beneath my eyes. I guess I really do need some sleep. It's been far too long. In fact, it feels like forever.

I quickly pick up my clothes and the used towel and fold them up, putting them on the floor so I can pull them on in a hurry if I need to upon waking. Stepping out into the bedroom once again, the hairs on the back of my neck stand on end. I know he's watching me, and it prompts me to ask the question that's been burning inside my chest since I first got into his tub.

"So— how did you know those two back there were demons?" I ask, hoping he has a perfectly reasonable explanation.

He twists to face me, arm flopping over the back of the couch, and says, "They weren't wearing pendants."

His explanation is simple, but it makes me frown as I hop up into the hold of the black leather sleigh bed. The sheets are black velvet, soft to touch, and my legs brush against them as I inhale the scent of pomegranates and spice from his shirt.

"Pendants?"

"Yes, all sinners in Mortaria have a sinstone pendant. Like this." He pulls up a shard of black crystal hanging on a steel chain around his neck.

"What's it for?" I enquire, curious now.

"Each sin has a different stone, but the intent is to pull the darkness out as a Sinner repents. Then the stones are thrown into the well of eternal torment and destroyed when they're full and the soul is pure," he explains away my doubt, and so I nod, paranoia defeated as I yawn.

"So why do you wear one?" I continue, shuffling up the mattress and pulling the sheets back so I can slide into the bed, the cotton under-sheet caressing my still sore feet. There are stacks of pillows at the head of the bed, all velvet, silk, or cotton, and I fall back amongst them, letting out a sigh as a fog of fatigue continues to roll in across the forefront of my consciousness.

"It helps me control the darkness. It gets cool when the dark part of me starts to overpower the light—" He looks sad as he tells me this, and I wonder why he's so ashamed to be part demon. He's not a bad person, well, not from what I've seen anyway. He's the first friend I've ever really had.

"So— you didn't recognise their faces, from before?" I ask, wondering exactly how much experience he has with the demons of which he is a part.

"No. Abraxians, well, full Abraxians, pure Abraxians, can take the form of anyone they've killed. I can't do that— I've just got my true demon face and my true mortal face."

"So, you got all of the fun burden and none of the perks of being able to look like Brad Pitt?" I ask him, and he shrugs.

"Yeah, well, if I had any desire to kill Brad Pitt, that is," he chuckles, clearly amused at this thought. I smile, glad I've been able to make him feel better.

"I don't know— his movies are pretty terrible," I admit.

Xion looks outraged.

"What— Mr and Mrs Smith? The Curious Case of Benjamin Button? Are you mad?! Those are great movies!" he exclaims, and I'm surprised as my mouth pops open.

"How would you know?" I demand, curious even still.

"I like visiting the cinema— in the mortal world, that is. I get to sit in the dark like anyone else and lose myself in someone else's problems. Plus, cinema popcorn is better than sex," he claims.

I cock an eyebrow, intrigued.

"You can't have had very much good sex then," I quip, intending it to be funny. Instead, his face falls serious and stoic.

"I, uh— I haven't. Not since— not since before," he adds, and things suddenly turn awkward between us again. How has he not gone insane by this point? I mean, he's either got a wicked case of blue balls or a hellishly large stash of porn hidden somewhere in this apartment.

"Well, goodnight. And uh— thanks for letting me stay. I'm glad we're friends," I confess, trying to subtly show my gratitude.

"Me too. Goodnight, Sephy." He moves to close the doors between us, shielding the bedroom from the blue light of the sconces.

I turn onto my side, finding a panoramic glass window that looks out over the ever-crimson sky of Mortaria.

Snuggling into the sheets and allowing Xion's sweet and spicy scent to surround me, I close my eyes, blocking out the view of The Underworld and slowly falling into a troubled sleep.

"Sephy! *Sephy!*"

I'm woken by the sound of screams and my body being shaken rapidly.

Looking up to the dark ceiling, the screaming stops as my eyes fly open.

Then I realise.

I was the one who was screaming.

"Jesus. Are you alright?" Xion demands, forehead glazed with a thin layer of sweat. His large eyes bore down into mine and I take a few seconds to process the fact that I'm not being damned by my Mother for hating Haedes, not falling into a fiery inferno, but rather lying in Xion's oversized bed.

"I'm fine. It was just a nightmare," I whisper, trying to convince myself of this fact. I'm shaking slightly, and Xion moves to sit on the edge of the bed as I prop myself up against the pillows, my breathing ragged.

"Well, I think you'd give a Banshee a run for its money with that scream. You sure you're okay?" he asks again, eyes filled with concern.

It makes me feel sick, the amount he obviously cares.

The velvet sheets cling to me, heavy, and I'm suddenly claustrophobic, not unlike the night I'd run into the forest back at the estate.

"I need to get some air," I breathe, and Xion turns to look out the window beside the bed.

I let my gaze wander too, finding the world outside alight with sparkling rain. Or at least what looks to be that way.

"Come on. Let's go up to the roof," Xion suggests. I nod, longing for fresh air but also somewhat curious about the state of the Mortarian weather.

My feet find the floor as I twist atop the mattress, getting out of bed and relishing the marble once as a sweet relief. I follow Xion out of the apartment, flesh riddled with goosebumps and legs shaky underneath my weight. I'm still exhausted, but now a lingering terror at the idea of sleep threatens to never let me feel fully rested again.

What is happening to me?

I have never been this needy, this scared, this weak, before. I've always tackled everything in life with relative ease.

Why is it that suddenly I feel so— mortal?

I sigh as we leave through the front door, walking across the landing at the top of the ridiculously long and winding metal staircase that leads down to the bottom floor.

Xion falls into a metal door and it groans beneath his weight, opening and leading to more stairs that presumably ascend to the roof.

At the top of the stairs, Xion walks through an archway, leading me out into the muggy Mortarian night air.

I stare up at the sky with wide, disbelieving eyes.

"What— what is this?" I ask, holding out an open palm. Tiny sparks fall into my outstretched hand, causing a momentary sizzle on my skin, which merely tickles before turning to nothing more than memory.

"It's a spark shower. The sun, it causes them occasionally," he explains, moving over to the corner of the roof and looking for something.

I gaze up to the skies where it appears as though stars are falling from the bloody heavens. As the sparks get closer to me, they brighten, as though moving through the air is only fanning the flames that drift like snowflakes, dancing a silent and stunning ballet through the night.

Turning from this supernatural wonder, I shift to see what Xion is up to.

"What are you doing?" I query, looking out over the city below as I take a few steps toward the cinnabrite railing.

"Looking for the on switch. Sometimes I train up here— I thought some music might help calm you."

He's so thoughtful. *Too* thoughtful.

"Oh," I reply, unable to come up with anything witty. I wonder if he realises how he's coming off. I mean, it's almost as if he actually likes me or something.

Surprising myself, I speak without thought.

"Well, I did promise you a dance," the words fall from me and he turns, a look of surprise, and then a smile, creeping across his face. Sparks fall around us, causing the scarlet sky to dim and our facial features to soften and accentuate.

"I don't have anything retro— I know you like that—" He sounds hesitant, but I shrug.

"That's okay. Maybe it's time for something new," I muse, my gaze falling upon The Exilia Multum as my hair is momentarily pulled back from my face, a slight and unexpectedly cool breeze capturing it.

As Xion fumbles with some kind of music player that's built into the wall of the building, I begin to wonder whether I'll ever see home again. If I do escape the Demon Lords, what will going back to everyday life be like? I mean, I know for sure that Xion won't be there. He has a job to do here and a seemingly important one at that. Once I don't need 'protecting' anymore, I guess I just won't see him around.

Sound sputters into the air that looks like it's been subject to a slow-motion firework explosion, and I turn as *Firestone* by Kygo seeps out into the air. Xion steps forward on bare feet across the rooftop, closing the distance between us.

"Madame?" He holds out a hand, giving me a ridiculously over-the-top bow.

"Oh god, I don't have foot insurance— I'm going to regret this aren't I?" I joke, reaching out and taking his hand.

He pulls me into his body as the modern melody pumps into the air around us. The bass is light but easy to dance to, and soon I'm caught up in a heady concoction of sparks crossing my vision and the scent of pomegranate filling my head.

He can move. Not like Haedes, but there's no denying that he can dance despite his usual lack of grace.

"I'm pleasantly surprised. You're not bad at dancing," I admit, smiling up at him and trying to keep things casual.

"I should be okay at it; I did grow up in the fifties," he reveals, and I smirk.

"Some people would call it wrong, an old guy like you dancing with a young pretty thing like me," I tease him, but as he spins me out from his body, his face turns grim.

"It is wrong. I'm a demon, Sephy," he reminds me of this painful truth.

"You're still my friend. You're like Casper the friendly ghost— only— with wicked swirly tattoo things." I try to comfort him, but he looks suddenly guilty.

"I'm sorry that you're having nightmares." He changes the subject, and I shrug.

"I'm sorry that you think you're less of a good person because of who your father is," I counter, trying to stop him from avoiding the subject. I should know his tactics; after all, I utilise most of them myself.

"You don't know what I've done," he replies.

"You've done nothing but be nice to me. That's what I know. I mean you're like Mary freaking Poppins with the spaghetti reheating and the bath and everything—" I tease him again and he laughs.

"Don't let my epic microwaving skills fool you. I'm dangerous. That's okay. It is what it is. But don't forget that. Please." He sounds like he's begging me now.

"Oh, don't worry, I still have my asshole detector," I retort, and he can't help but smile.

We dance the rest of the song, surrounded by falling sparks of fire in a multitude of hues, ranging from ruby red to cobalt and then finally to lilac. When the song ends, Xion looks down at me, his molten gaze consuming my field of vision.

"We should get back inside. If this shower gets any heavier, we'll be at risk for burns," he mutters, as if I've almost gotten too close to him.

"Okay," I sigh, dreading sleep.

He moves to turn off the music, and I feel myself getting panicked. As he turns to face me, his eyes widen, once again brimming with concern.

"What's the matter?" he demands.

"I'm scared to go back to sleep," I mumble. I know I sound pathetic, needy and weak. I know that in this moment, I'm losing my grip on what makes me Sephy, but I'm being hunted, and I could die. That's terrifying, especially to someone who's never truly feared death.

"I know. It'll be alright." He strides over to me, placing a hand on my shoulder and pulling me into his body.

"It won't be alright. What if I die? Nobody is going to miss me. Not even my own damn father," I whisper.

Xion snorts.

"Don't be so ridiculous. I'd miss you. Who would give me my daily slap of sarcastic disdain if you weren't around?" he asks.

I laugh.

How does he do that? Even when I'm flailing, he still manages to make me laugh, even when I don't want to. "I'll tell you what, I'll— suppress your sympathetic nervous system until you fall asleep. How's that?" he suggests, and I stare at him, totally puzzled.

"Excuse me? You'll do *what*?" It sounds kind of dirty when I think about it, but he merely rolls his eyes.

"When cattle are slaughtered, they're forced through a small tube; it stops them panicking or being afraid. The applied pressure on their bodies causes them to relax." He takes my hand and leads me from the rooftop as my face morphs into a scowl, trying to understand exactly what it is he's saying.

"Okay— so I think you just *tried* to say that you want to hold me until I fall asleep— then again that's the most freaking creepy way of describing a hug ever. Either that or you just called me a cow— I'm not actually sure," I retort, paranoid. It's such an odd thing to say.

"Sorry— I thought you'd find it forward of me if I said hug," Xion explains, and I sigh. He's right, I probably would have told him to grow some balls and stop treating me like some damsel in distress.

"Alright—we'll try the cow thing. But only until I fall asleep, okay?"

His eyes fill with anxiety as we walk back into the apartment under the glow of multiple cobalt sconces. We both look weary.

"I promise," he replies, looking hopeful, and I let myself smile as a feeling of contentedness floods my gut, extinguishing my anxiety faster than I'd thought possible.

But why?

We climb into the hold of the velvet sheets, and he holds out an arm for me to crawl under. I lie across his chest, his rapid heartbeat loud in my ear. He places a hand on the top of my head, and wraps the other around my shoulders, pulling me close.

I relax into him, inhaling his sweet musk as my eyes begin to droop at his proximity. It's almost as if he makes me feel safe.

I know it's wrong because I don't have feelings for him. I'm using him, and I feel guilty, but then again, I've used men before when it suited me.

Why does it bother me so much now?

18

LIGHT MY FIRE

SEPHY

I'M WOKEN BY THE sound of a harsh and unapologetically loud knocking at the door.

I stir, feeling his weight around me even still.

Oh crap.

We must have fallen asleep together, and that is just a little closer than I want to be to any man I have no intention of *actually* sleeping with. I struggle from his burning limbs, crawling out of his clasp and off the bed.

Xion doesn't wake, which surprises me.

Some security guard he is.

I roll my eyes, curious about who could be at the door.

As I tread with sleep still fogging my vision, I worry it's someone who could potentially be a threat, but as the knock comes again, I realise that I'm probably overreacting. I mean, what kind of demon knocks politely before entering to kill you?

Grabbing the door handle, I pull it open, utterly shocked to find none other than Haedes standing in front of me with a cool expression plastered atop his edgy features.

"What are you doing here?" I demand, my face falling into an expression not unlike the one I reserve for people who I actively want to punch in the eye.

"I came to— apologise." He leans sideways, cocking his angular hip and glancing over my shoulder to where Xion is still asleep on the bed. He looks at me once more, examining my attire, and then his mouth and eye both twitch on the left side of his face, an involuntary response which gives away discomfort.

"Great. Just what I always wanted. An apology from Haedes, god of being a giant prick." I slam the door in his face and spin in my fury, finding Xion has finally startled awake behind me.

"What are you doing?" he exclaims, totally disoriented.

"Haedes is back. He wants to apologise. So, I slammed the door in his stupid face," I explain casually, and watch as his sleepy eyes widen. Maybe I'm acting like a child, but seeing as how Haedes is just as immature, I guess it fits.

"Why did you do that?!" He looks outraged, getting up out of bed and moving swiftly over to the door.

"Um— because he's a jackass!" I retort, shocked he doesn't immediately see my side in all of this. After all, he was the one who went all *This. Is. Spartaaa* on him only last night.

Xion takes the length of the apartment too fast, suddenly in front of me with his hands on my shoulders before I have even had a chance to blink.

"Sephy, I know he's not the most— pleasant of people. But honestly, I think you might want to listen to him. He is the only one who can teach you to defend yourself," he's pleading with me now like my survival means more to him than it does to me. He walks past me, flinging the door open, only to find Haedes still standing behind it, unmoved, with a bored expression on his face.

"Hi," he says again. His eyes, dove grey, glow with a rim of slight electric blue.

"Sorry about that," Xion apologises for me, and I narrow my eyes.

"Why are you apologising for me? I'm not sorry. He's an asshole!" I turn on my heel, storming over to the couch and sitting down, trying to put as much distance between us as possible.

"She's not wrong. I am an asshole." Haedes shrugs, stepping over the threshold in his finely tailored black velvet suit. He's far too suave for a guy with blue hair, and I realise now this should have made me suspicious from the start.

Crossing my arms across my chest, I prop one foot on my knee and allow it to bob up and down, trying to indicate that I don't have all freaking day to waste on hearing his stupid-ass apology. Looking at me with an inexpressive stare, he takes a seat in an armchair opposite.

"This is uh— cosy." His grey eyes flit between Xion and me, both of us dressed in only underwear and t-shirts, both of which belong to Xion. He looks like he wants to say something, but I deepen my scowl to the point where my face actually begins to ache, and so he simply coughs before continuing. "Look, last night was— it was a disaster. I'm no father; I'm aware of that. But after some serious thought, I've come to realise that I can at least teach you to master your powers. I owe you at least that much. You can even come back to stay at the Exilia if you wish." He's trying to be sincere, but he's still coming off cold, calculated, almost like this is a business deal and nothing personal at all.

"You had to seriously think about teaching me how not to die? Gee, father of the year award goes to—" I know it's spiteful. I know that I'm showing now more than ever perhaps I really had been hopeful for undiscovered family, but still, I can't help it. I'm furious. "And as for the Exilia, I'm good here thanks. I really don't fancy being left homeless next time you have a little one of your outbursts," I add. He sighs, brow deeply furrowed.

"Very well. But you should still allow me to teach you how to wield The Eternal Flame and convect. It could save your life." He doesn't respond to my anger, though I note that the tips of his hair turn slightly orange. I'd seen him entirely redheaded, like me, last night, but I hadn't connected the fact he'd been mad then. I must be getting under his skin.

I smile.

"Sephy, I think you should go with him." Xion pleads once more with his gaze, and between the two of them, I feel utterly backed into a corner. I don't want to go, but I know, as I have known for a while now, that in this world it doesn't matter what I want.

"Fine," I bite out, pissed beyond what I'd thought possible for being awake merely moments. "I don't even know why the Demon Lords want me dead so damn badly, but it's starting to get on my nerves," I announce.

Haedes smirks at this.

"I can imagine. As for why they want you dead I'd say it's some sort of ploy to get to me; though I can't say what or why."

"Well, neither can I. It's not like they can use me against you. You'd have to give a shit for them to do that." My words cut him visibly like a knife, and he sighs once more.

"Either that or they simply want to kill you for parts; demi-gods have all the powers of a god with the bonus of mortal bone, flesh, and blood. Plus, you're weaker than a full-blown god, easier to pick off." He cocks his head.

"Well, that's just grand; I'm a demon Happy Meal." I roll my eyes, heart beating louder and louder in my chest the longer I'm talking to him. He certainly isn't a bringer of light or good news in any sense of the word. In a way, I can see why he got put in charge down here. He's brooding and cynical as they come, tortured even.

"I'll meet you outside," he relinquishes, but I glare at him, pursing my lips hard.

"No, take me to my suite now. I don't have anything to wear here. This is as good as it's going to get." I gesture down to my makeshift night clothes, and he raises one eyebrow.

"Oh, right, of course." He clearly hadn't thought about the fact that he'd left me without any form of clothing, personal artefact, or otherwise. Charming.

He takes my hand, pulling me toward the space near the kitchen.

"Hold your breath," he instructs.

I open my mouth to ask why, but before I can, my lungs are full of smoke and my eyes are streaming. The world is closing in around me, warping and twisting in a bright and paranormal cobalt light. I feel like I'm going to suffocate, until suddenly, in an instant, I fall forward. My hands don't hit the kitchen floor. Instead, they bury themselves between lush blades of green grass.

As I sputter, I wonder if I've somehow been brought back to the mortal world, but as I try to draw breath by leaning back on my haunches, I find that the sky above is still bloody, and the sun still ultraviolet in its unending burn.

"I did warn you," Haedes breathes out, grabbing my wrist and trying to help me to my feet as I continue to splutter.

"You call that a warning? What the hell was that?!" I yell, confused beyond anything. I see charred marks in a ring around Haedes feet where he's stood on a quartz-lined path and look up to find the Exilia towering over us both.

"We convected. Travelled back via fire."

So that's what convecting is. I realise, finally finding my feet and catching my breath, purposefully pulling away from Haedes' attempt at aid.

"Where the hell are we?" I glance in all directions, still dressed only in Xion's clothes as I turn on the spot, the baggy cotton tickling my skin. It's cooler here for some reason, and I can hear trickling, like running water.

"This— this was your mother's." He's reaching out to me, trying to be kind, or so it would seem, but I'm wondering how he thinks bringing up the fact that my mother had an affair with another man will be helpful. He might have loved her, but I loved her too, and I loved my father, Adam Sinclair.

"She— grew all this?" I gape around at the green grass, the tall, luscious trees boasting a variety of red fruits, and flower bushes blossoming sweet-smelling florals. When I take a closer look though, I see a more lethal light to the beauty of it all; poison ivy, deadly nightshade, and water hemlock can also be spotted, hiding among the camouflage of lush benign green.

"Yes, I made her a space for gardening, created a freshwater spring to make the soil fertile for her. Even in this place, she managed to nurture things to life, to make them grow where others have failed." He doesn't sound nostalgic, just heartbroken with a chill edge of formality.

"It's beautiful." I compliment the space, not for him, but for her, before turning to face him and realising that whether I like it or not, he's in my life right now. Maybe, just maybe, my mom would want us to at least try and get along. I mean, clearly, she saw something in him. Maybe it's just buried deeper now she's gone.

"Can you teach me to do that thing— you know, convect?" I ask, and he nods.

"I don't see why not, but first we need to get you producing the flame at will." He's all business again as he shuffles in his shiny shoes, kicking the gravel like a small fidgety child.

I look to the exit but merely find a gate, shackled in chains and heavy-duty-looking locks. This isn't a space he lets anyone frequent.

"I'd like to get dressed so we can begin." I try to keep momentum, not wanting to stop in this thriving memorial to my mother.

"Very well." Haedes once again takes my hand, but this time I'm ready. Holding my breath, I let the fire consume us both as we convect out of the living past and into my very uncertain future.

"Focus!" Haedes barks, sipping yet another glass of whisky as I hold out my hands for the millionth time this hour. My hair is yanked up in a high ponytail, and my yoga pants and black sports bra are soaked in sweat.

"I'm trying!" I exclaim, tired of his yelling.

"Not hard enough!" he calls back at me, causing my rage to grow. "A demon won't wait for you to be ready. You must be able to do this at the click of my fingers. You need to tap into what makes you produce the flame. What happened when you used it last time?" he asks. I can only shrug.

"I dunno; I was scared. Cerb was— I dunno— he was fighting with that thing, and—" Haedes nods, and before I can blink, he's gone. He returns moments later, having moved only an inch from where he was previously standing. Cerb is at his feet. I smile at the dog, but before I have the chance to call him to me for a reunion cuddle, Haedes shows me he has other plans in mind.

Twirling his fingers, he manipulates the eternal flame into a ball, looking at Cerb and then me with a malicious grin. Pulling his arm back, he turns his attention back to the Leonberger.

"Hey, Cerb, fetch!" he commands, throwing the ball of flame. I watch as Cerb willingly takes flight after the projectile, and suddenly my rage is unstoppable.

I feel it spark in my synapses, then rush through my veins as though, once more, gasoline has been set loose by my nervous system. The flame erupts from my fingertips as I throw it at the ball of flame Cerb is pursuing, without thought, causing both to collide and mushroom outwards. The Leonberger backs up at the flash of light, ears lowering in fear as he emits a whine.

"What the hell was that? You can't do that!" I yell, pissed he'd put my dog in danger.

"And yet, it worked. So, I guess I can." His face is calm as he takes another sip of whisky, his long fingers flitting my words away as though they're nothing.

"It didn't work. All that means is that if Cerb is in danger, I can protect him. I need to protect me!" I'm getting out of breath as I yell at him, beyond angry. He knows how to push my buttons, and it's driving me crazy.

"No, it showed me that your anger is where your power comes from. Just like mine," he explains. I roll my eyes.

"What a load of horseshit. I've been wanting to make that whisky in your hand catch light and burn your stupid blue eyebrows off for hours now. Anger isn't it at all!" I express, and he smirks.

"Oh, I'm sure you are angry at me, but I mean real, life or death rage. That desire to save someone, that anger that someone might take them away from you. You must harness that. Being pissed off isn't enough anymore. It may have been enough before, but now you need to learn to find it at will. To have that desperate fury on command," he explains, crossing his legs so he's leaning against the piano beside him where his whisky glass and bottle are propped.

"And how do you suggest I do that?" I ask him, serious now as I feel my rage wearing thin.

"You can turn pain into power Sephy. Trust me, it wasn't my happy childhood and great relationship history that made me qualified to rule this place. Real rulers don't avoid pain; they embrace it and turn it into power." He's becoming poetic, and I nod, wondering if he'll burst into song.

"So, what— I just— think of something that happened to me that wasn't fair?" I ask him, and he nods.

"Something painful. Something that hurts you deep inside." I know what this thing is immediately, and so recall the days following my parent's death.

Closing my eyes, I find myself reliving the memories too easily. Of standing over their coffins, of Peter forcing me into an ugly black dress with a stiff white collar for the funeral despite my kicking and screaming, despite my fear of putting them in the ground.

Opening my eyes, I find a flickering flame, hearty in my palm.

"Most magic is emotional. Never forget that. If you feel weak, your magic will reflect it," Haedes elaborates and once again I can't find a witty comeback or a snarky retort. He's disarming me somehow; despite the fact I feel nothing but resentment for his annoyingly relaxed gaze.

"You're a very brash person," I comment. He smirks.

"So are you," he replies. It's true; I know it is, but I don't want to admit it.

"Xion says the same thing," I blurt, not sure why I'm bringing him up. Haedes' eyebrows rise on his face.

"Does he now? Do you like him— Xion?" He takes a sip of whisky and watches me with interest as he swallows.

"We're friends. He's saved my life. I owe him a lot," I remind him.

"You're my daughter; you don't owe anyone anything." His reply surprises me even further, and he looks like it was not entirely thought through before he'd spoken it.

"I'm not your daughter. You don't—" I begin, but he interrupts me.

"Don't what?" he asks, dropping his gaze to the bottom of his whisky glass which is, yet again, almost empty.

"You don't know what being a father is. You've never been scared for me, never sacrificed anything for me— you're not vulnerable because of me. Not really. You put me in danger. What does it matter to you if I die? I mean, it's not like you'd care. After all, you're just going to keep on living. I'm sure you could make another daughter or even— I don't know." I think for a moment before continuing, "How can anything be precious to you when all you have is time? My mother, she was precious to you— or at least, I think she was once— and you lost her. Yet you don't even want to know me— Don't you care? I'm part of both of you, at least biologically. Just— stop acting like you give a shit if you really don't. I don't have time for your personal problems, and I don't deserve to suffer for them. I'm suffering enough because you're my father already." I'm out of breath, wondering why it is I'm suddenly saying these things to him. It could be because I'm tired or simply because I want him to cut the crap and let me know where I stand.

"Come with me," is all he says, leading me across the smoky quartz of the floor.

I tread after him, moving fast in my sneakers and watching Cerb as his gaze tracks my motion. Clearly not worried for my safety, he curls up in a ball in the middle of the enormous room, a puddle of fluff amid the gloomy sheen of the place.

Haedes takes me through a small golden door behind what had been the stage from the night of the ball. He doesn't use a key but instead, places a hand on a panel and allows the metal to glow orange before it slides open with a few clicking sounds. I watch, unsure of what to expect behind it as nerves begin to flutter around my stomach like bats set loose.

"This is my vault," Haedes announces, waving a hand and illuminating the space as many sconces flicker to light with a red flame. The walls are gold, and so is the floor, solid gold in fact. The entire room looks like it's on fire, and I inhale deeply as the contents of the place are revealed atop hundreds of shelves.

"They're—" I begin but he interrupts me.

"Hourglasses. These show the time left on any sinner's sentence here in Mortaria," he enlightens me.

I pass the hourglasses, all of which tinkle as stones move or still in their narrow waists. They have different coloured crystals within, which I assume links to which sin the sinner is charged with. Some of them have a mixture, but I'm getting the impression this isn't what Haedes wants to show me.

"Come—" he beckons me, moving deeper and deeper into the vault. I trail behind him, looking at a shelf of urns on my left. They look like they're filled with ashes or maybe something else, and one has a triangular symbol on that I've never seen before. I reach out to touch it, feeling drawn to the curve of the pure quartz it's carved from.

"Don't touch that," Haedes calls out, causing me to jump. I turn, finding him right beside me.

"Well, that's not creepy." I don't smile, biting my tongue to stop myself from saying anything further.

"Come on. Best not to dawdle. There's all kinds of magic you could be getting yourself into trouble with in here—" he makes this dark promise, causing me to become even more curious. However, I know I can't escape him, not with his ability to convect at will, and so follow him despite my desire to explore.

We reach another door, and this time, Haedes takes a key off a chain around his neck. It's tiny, and it barely looks like a key at all. I only become certain of its function when he slots the multifaceted crystal into a central hole in the door, bringing his hand up to a similar panel to the one I'd seen before and allowing his palm to heat. The door gives several audible clicks, and he withdraws the crystal key, allowing it to slide aside and stepping back so I can enter first.

A suspicious person would wonder if they were being lured into some kind of prison cell, but the second I'm inside, Haedes follows me in and illuminates the room, this time with a blue flame instead.

"What— what is that?" I ask him. He looks only serious as we gaze upon it. It's enormous, at least ten feet tall, and black, only visible in silhouette because of the flickering sconces that cast its many facets in a cool light.

It's an enormous, onyx hourglass.

"It's mine," he gives this as explanation.

"Well, I'd gathered that. It's in your vault. What is it? And why is it that enormous?" I ask him, and he sighs.

"No, Sephy, I mean it is mine. My hourglass," he reiterates his prior statement, and I frown, not sure what he's trying to insinuate.

"What— why do you have one? I don't understand—"

"When Zeus banished me here, he didn't ever intend for me to live this long. He wanted me to live out a normal mortal life in pain and die so I could learn about death. As it was, he forgot I have power over the resurrection flame— that's why I made the sun—" he expresses.

"You were afraid to die—" I say, realising what he's getting at.

"I still am. I'm afraid that Zeus won't have me back— up there," he admits.

"Why is it made of onyx? What use is that?" I demand, still puzzled by the object.

"That's another one of Zeus' little lessons. I'm not supposed to know when I die. That's the point. That's why I didn't go after your mother. When I'm in the mortal world— I age like a mortal but faster. The mortal body and my godly powers don't mesh so well," he informs me.

I frown.

"I see— why wouldn't Zeus let you back into The Higher Plains?" I ask him, and he shrugs.

"I don't know. We're not exactly close. He always hated me. So does Poseidon in all truth. I've never felt like a god, or like I want to rule. I just— wanted to be loved. I wanted to be happy. But when you're born as a god, especially one with my lineage, you're stuck." He looks sad, self-pitying almost.

"Well, I can see why you wouldn't want to return if Zeus is anything like Hercules," I comment. He stares at me with genuine curiosity.

"Not fond of your cousin?" he enquires, and I cock an eyebrow.

"I told him he needs a mental upgrade."

Haedes sputters in disbelief.

"I would have paid to see that. What did he say that warranted such accurate assessment?"

"He was bragging about being a Titan. Acting like me being a mortal made me slime off a slug or something—" I express, and he laughs, expression infectious.

"Oh, that's rich. He's not a Titan, Sephy. He's just like you. He's still a demi-god. Lying little shit—" We stand, staring at each other, cast in the intermittent flickering shadow of the hourglass.

"So— demi-gods are immortal? I mean if he's still part human, he must be—"

"Old enough to know better than to make a jackass of himself in front of family? You'd think so, but no. Hercules is a difficult pill to swallow. Then again, if I had Zeus for a father, I'd— well, I'd be drinking a lot more than I do now, if that's possible."

"Why?" I ask him, and he smirks.

"Zeus is a bastard and won't make his own son a Titan. He gave him this spiel about having to complete twelve labours. I mean he never thought Hercules would actually do it— but then, the boy proved him wrong. He's far too valuable as a half-mortal, and he hates his father for it. You're very much in the same boat too, now. I mean, Zeus would be mad to make you a Titan, I'm afraid that's my fault. But at least you have your immortality." Haedes looks highly amused by the whole thing.

"So— I don't understand— why is being half-mortal valuable?" I ask. He runs a hand back through his hair, making it spiky and wild.

"Well, neither gods nor Titans can move freely between dimensions. The only way gods or Titans can move between The Higher Plains and the other dimensions; is if they're put into a mortal body. Once they are trapped, they can't return until their souls are set free through the death of said mortal body." He takes a sip of whisky, his gaze holding mine. "As a Demi-God or a Kindred— well, you can travel freely through most dimensions. Hercules can frequent the Higher Plains, be it only temporarily and under the sanction of his father, as well as every other dimension, provided he has the means to get there. Gods can't travel freely like that between dimensions, moving their life force across the walls weakens them a hell of a lot. It's dangerous." He shifts on his feet.

"I see. So— that's why the Demon Lords want me?" I ask.

"I don't know— I'm sorry. I wish I did. But I know that's why The Fates are so shaken by this Chimera prophecy. Any being that is a Chimera of all souls, part god, demon, and mortal— well, it would be able to walk between all dimensions, all worlds. That's why you might have noticed a certain lack of joy at the idea of you getting friendly with Xion." He looks sad, causing me to succumb to slight empathy for him.

"Well, they shouldn't worry so much. Xion and I are just friends," I insist, tired of people assuming otherwise. He nods, cobalt eyebrows rising only slightly on his forehead.

"I see, well—" he begins, but I cut him off, deciding to change the subject. My personal life is nobody's concern, especially not his.

"Do you miss it— The Higher Plains?" I enquire, my curiosity allowing me to push past the disturbing fact that I'm having a civil conversation with him. Something I never saw happening only this morning.

"No. I'm under a microscope up there with Poseidon and Zeus being so close. I would have been happy to stay here forever had your mother returned. I think we could have been happy. But instead, I'm— I'm stuck." His predicament resonates with me.

"I understand that. My parents— they left me with a business empire, one which I have no desire to run," I express and Haedes smiles.

"I am aware. I was the one who built it."

I shrug.

"So— why are you showing me this?" I demand, and this time it is he who shrugs with a nonchalant and invisible mask slipping over his features.

"I just, I want you to know I'm not invincible. I have shit to lose. I feel just like you. I don't want you to think of me as some monster. I'm not. I am quite useless at emotions. Your mother was the only person ever to get that out of me, and now she's gone— I can't— I don't want to get attached like that again. I might die, or the other person might die— I don't think I can go through that kind of loss again and survive." He confesses, and I frown. Cocking my head, my face is cast in shadow as I look down at my feet, heart racing at his words.

It's familiar, too familiar.

"Me too," I admonish, knowing now that we're far more similar than I'd ever expected.

Damn it.

19

BOOGIE SHOES

<u>LUCE</u>

"YOU ALRIGHT, BABY? YOU seem rather distracted—" Thane coaxes me as the carriage we're inside quakes with the uneven pacing of the horses pulling it. The driver is evidently new.

"I'm fine— just thinking about last night," I admit, adjusting my horns on the top of my head. My meeting with The Fates had been concerning if not a little disappointing. The prophecy, which they've connected with Haedes' daughter, speaks of a being that will be part mortal, part demon, and part god. Meaning it can walk between all dimensions in both the higher and lower plains, putting everyone at its mercy.

Other than this, Layla, Moira, and Anya had no more information to give, seeming weary to say the least.

I'm wearing midnight blue today and find myself disheartened at the fact I'm heading back to the grind. Last night was supposed to be fun, but for some reason I've ended up more stressed than before the event, and to top it off, it's Monday damn morning and I'm anticipating a mountain of paperwork. Especially because there was a cruise ship that mysteriously vanished in the Pacific over the weekend. "You're sure you didn't see anything suspicious?" I ask her again, my anxiety surrounding the situation mounting more than is probably appropriate. I don't know, for some reason, I just can't stand the thought of Haedes having yet another relationship implode in his face. I mean, it's totally his fault, but I doubt he'll see it that way, and it's doing him no good being so isolated.

"I'm sure. I mean, there was a spark shower, so I couldn't hang around for that long, but it seems pretty quiet around there to be honest." Thane reaches across the space between us and takes my long fingers in hers, squeezing gently and running her rough thumb across the back of my knuckles.

She's dressed in a tight velvet indigo suit with a matching top hat adorning her head decorated with a plume of raven feathers. A white blouse hangs off her edgy frame with ruffled cuffs and collar, and an enormous sapphire brooch that dangles over her heart. She's beautiful, as always, and I can't help but stare.

"Here at last," she murmurs, clearly agitated by the new driver too. She opens the door and we step out, matching in deep blue hues, onto the dark soil soaked in both ichor and blood. We stand now at the convergence of the Sanguine Forest and the Plains of Ichor, the mass graveyard Golgotha, where doppelganger bodies are born from the earth. I let my gaze fall on the enormous torch that lies central to it all in the distance, burning bright blue and providing the spark of resurrection for all the doppel bodies waiting to rise beneath the dirty concoction of red and white fluids.

"Come on, we best not be late for those early risers." Thane hurries me forward as we move silently through the gargantuan steel gates, which look like thorny vines that climb from the earth in metal. Dead trees hang, limbs stiff with rigor mortis as the breeze finds them immovable and barren. Not a leaf rustles, nor a soul sounds as we tread across the soil, closing the enormous gates behind us and smiling at the two wrath sinners on guard duty on the opposing side.

"Morning, Nigel." I nod to one of them, but he doesn't smile, merely continuing to stare forward across the fields of headstones.

They span hundreds of miles, some crooked or cracked, some pristine, and some blackened or charred. They're squashed together in a messy and disorganised spattering, any semblance of order lost to the casual observer. This is my domain, my place of work, and yet I still find myself uncomfortable at the thought of so much rot, even in the face of resurrection and rebirth.

Striding across the dark, spongy, and fertile earth, I turn right and travel the length of the graveyard as quickly as I'm able. Soon, we reach the main office at the front of the place, a cosy mausoleum from which Thane and I conduct our business.

Unlocking the stone front door of the miniature marble house, we both step inside, finding Juanita already bustling around the misleadingly large space and organising everything for our arrival.

"Morning, Nita. Is the coffee on yet?" I ask, and she nods. Of course, it is. She's the best assistant I've ever had. Her mocha-coloured skin is paler than it would be if she was alive, but her Mexican heritage remains unmistakable as a frizz of dark hair is pulled up messily into a bun atop her head. She's wearing simple black slacks and a matching blouse, a sinstone pendant of jade hanging heavy around her neck, signalling her sentence here is for the sin of Envy.

"How bad is it? I heard about the cruise ship disappearance—"

She looks grim.

"Yes, *The Zenith*, bloody Poseidon's fault of course. Not that I'm cursing him or anything— but there's a lot of paperwork to go through here. That cruise was full of wealthy moguls, and you know how that usually goes," she sighs. I give her a sly smile.

"Between you and me, I find Poseidon and Atargatis utterly irresponsible. I mean, splitting souls? Imbuing your Kindred with darkness? They're utterly reckless— and you know who has to deal with the freaking paperwork? Me. That's who. Bloody muggings over here." I vent my frustration as I point to myself, and Nita giggles.

"Soulmates are great in theory, right?" She cocks her head, looking between me and Thane.

"Yes, because you can't possibly fall in love without being destined. Thane and I do just fine— Don't we honey?" I spin, looking over my shoulder to where she's examining an enormous paperwork mountain on her desk.

"Oh— uh, yes." She's not listening, so I turn back to Nita, rolling my eyes.

"Women," I mutter, smirking again before I turn, letting my skirt fall behind me, and move over to my desk.

The paperwork is an enormous mountain, files stacked upon files, stacked upon registers, stacked upon more files.

I sigh.

It's going to be a long day.

"Pass the coffee," I command, and Nita goes to grab me a cup as I take a seat in my red leather office chair. Looking over at Thane, who is clearly just as irritated as I am about the lack of help we have down here, I smile at her, trying to catch her eye. She doesn't notice, and so as Nita hands me my coffee, which is black to match my soul, I look ahead to the insane amount of work in front of me.

I take a sip from my favourite mug, which reads '*I'd tell you to go to hell but I work there and I don't want to see you every day*' on one side. Inhaling the sweet yet bitter fragrance as the hot liquid rolls down the back of my throat, I ready myself to begin yet another day in the afterlife of the damned.

"Here's another one!" Thane calls out.

I stride, sweeping through the rows of headstones, to stand beside her. Nita hurries in my wake, a pile of black jumpsuits stacked neatly in her arms.

We stand, surrounding the grave, or re-birthing site as some would call it. The soil begins to stir, heaving like muddy ocean waves. Dark flesh bursts from the earth, a hand, then an arm, then a head, and finally a torso. I watch on, semi-amused as the rising doppel struggles to climb from his own grave. There's no freaking mistake what this sinner is here for.

We let him struggle against the weight of his own burial for about ten minutes, but eventually, as Nita coughs, I roll my eyes, and Thane sighs out, bored. Grabbing him under the arms, I haul him up like a newborn baby, only a lot uglier and far larger to boot.

"You're— you're—" he stutters, realising what he's seeing.

"Yes, yes, I'm the devil, blah blah— can we get on with it? I don't want to have to stare at you naked. Nita give him a suit." I drop him onto his feet, brushing dirt from his shoulders and turning from him to look over my shoulder.

"Mr—" I gaze at Thane, who is holding a clipboard in her tense fingers.

"Bogarty," she finishes.

"Mr Bogarty. Please make your way all the way to the end of the row once you are dressed. There you will be sent for sentencing via gondola. Do you understand?" I ask him impatiently. His dark eyes are bewildered, like an animal caught in a trap, as he hastily looks down at himself and then grabs the jumpsuit being handed to him by my assistant.

He struggles into it, looking between us three.

"Sign here please—" Thane passes him her clipboard and then a raven feather quill, which he takes in a shaking hand before making a brief squiggle on the paper.

Thane snatches the clipboard back from him, and he continues to look around at us, then at the sky.

We all stand there, bored.

"What— what is this place?" he asks, voice trembling.

I move toward him, placing my hands on his shoulders and then turning him in the correct direction.

"No time for dawdling. It'll all be explained in your orientation packet. You'll receive it on the boat. Now please proceed to the end of the row." I give him a small shove, and he begins to walk, almost like he's a zombie, toward his inevitable fate.

We watch him go, calling, "Farewell, Mr Bogarty," in unison and giving a small wave with fake smiles, before smirking and trying not to laugh.

He doesn't look back; instead, he merely continues to stumble forward, one foot in front of the other, over graves and through mud, toward the river that runs directly through Golgotha, delivering souls to their waiting doppelgangers. Here, he will meet a ferryman or woman and be well on his way to repentance by noon.

Good riddance.

"Why do sloth sinners always manage to get themselves stuck? I mean come on; climbing out of a grave isn't *that* hard," Thane tuts.

I smirk.

"How would you know?" I demand, and she shrugs.

"Remember that time Haedes took me out drinking a few months back? Yeah, well waking up from that night is something I don't ever want to re-live— ever." She smirks at the memory, and I laugh again, imagining Haedes locking her in a coffin, drunk.

This also explains why she's been turning him down for drinks ever since.

"That's the last plus-size jumpsuit. I better go back to the office and get some more," Nita announces, and I nod, visibly dismissing her.

Once she's gone, Thane and I take a moment to stand amongst the headstones in silence.

"You feel bad for her, don't you?" Thane asks me.

"Who?"

"This Sephy Sinclair girl." She leans back against a headstone, crossing her ankles and examining her nails in the dim light.

"Of course, I do," I reply. She frowns.

"Look, I just— I'm concerned about you getting involved in all this. Please, don't try to force things between Haedes and her. If it's supposed to be a relationship that will work, they'll both make it happen on their own. I don't want the Demon Lords putting out a hit on you too."

My gut turns icy.

"I'm only trying to help. Besides, I think it's entirely unfair she's being put through all this because of who her parent is. Besides, I can look after myself; you shouldn't worry so much." I brush her off, irritated that she's treating me like a child. Her eyes narrow.

"Look, Haedes isn't exactly father material, Luce. I'm serious; I don't want any trouble for us. We've been through enough. I just want us to be together, without pissing off anyone else with serious power. This is nothing to do with us." She's cool in her tone. I scowl.

"It's everything to do with us. She's being hunted because Haedes is her father. I was banished and you had to give up your goddess form because of who my father is. It's not justified, and I won't stand for it. People need to see that you shouldn't launch a war on some poor unsuspecting child just because of their lineage," I snap.

Her eyes turn angry.

"You're right, I did give up my goddess form to be with you. I'd really prefer it if you didn't get yourself captured or killed by Gorgon over some girl who isn't even our problem. She's Haedes' mess; let him deal with it." She shrugs responsibility off as if it's nothing, infuriating me further.

"Thane! How can you say that? After everything Haedes has done for me! He took me in; he put me back on my feet after I fell. After my own family disowned me. I don't understand where this is coming from!" I exclaim, furious.

"What about everything I've done for you, Luce? Screw Haedes— what about me? You think I want to be stuck here alone without you?" she demands.

Suddenly I'm confused.

"Where is all this coming from? You were all for me going to the courts before? Who's been changing your mind about this?" I question her, suspicious.

"Anubis and Osiris—" she begins, but I cut her off.

"Of course! I should've known," I whisper in a harsh tone, and she scowls even deeper.

"Look, they make a really good point. They're concerned about her and what her existence means; they think she could be a threat. That girl might be being hunted, but she's also connected to a prophecy that is talking about bringing a Chimera forth. You're encouraging her to spend time with a man who's half demon. How do you think this is going to end?" she demands. I cross my arms just below the low square neck of my corset.

"So, what? Now they shouldn't be allowed to be friends because he's got demon lineage? That's fucking rich coming from you!" I yell, losing my temper. Her anger turns from explosive to reserved and cool within only seconds.

"You and I can't biologically make a child. That's different," she mutters.

I roll my eyes, flipping my hair over one shoulder.

"The fact is, Thanatos, you still haven't forgiven me for being half him— half dark. You still can't get over the fact you had to leave The Higher Plains to be with me. You don't want me to put anyone else through what you've been through, right? Because why would anyone willingly live in a place like this, even for someone they love, if they're half ancient dark god? *Right*?" I feel tears coming to my eyes now, my heart hammering in my chest.

Thane's gaze fades from intensity to superiority.

"I can't talk to you when you're like this, Luce. It's not about you. It's about her. It's about not getting involved. But clearly, you have some unresolved personal issues."

She turns from me, and within moments, I'm hearing the familiar crunching of bone and ripping of muscle. She cries out, but as the pain of her cursed transformation takes over her and she vanishes inside her clothes, my fury dwindles.

From within the folds of indigo velvet and soft white cotton, a raven appears, crowing once, then twice, before taking off into the crimson dawn.

Nita returns a few moments later with more jumpsuits.

"Where did Thanatos go?" she asks, and I shrug.

"None of your concern." I feel my eyes continue to sting with tears but wipe them away, straightening my horns. I can't appear weak in front of rising sinners; it's my job to give them the first taste of The Nexus' authority.

"Right, well, where to next?" she queries.

I pick up the clipboard from the ground where Thane has dropped it.

"There's a lust sinner due to rise over there, any second. Come on." I beckon her, realising that my day will be twice as busy now Thane isn't here to help. I'm angry at her, it's true, but I'm more hurt. Hurt that she doesn't understand why I care so deeply about Haedes and, by default, about his daughter.

I hear something, something I'm always subconsciously listening for, and stop on the spot. It's a slithering, the motion of scales moving through the earth in slick and fluid motion. I listen deeper for the hiss, wondering if it's just my imagination, as silence falls and the wind stirs the dead yew trees around the outside of the graveyard.

Maybe I just need more coffee— I muse.

Brushing it off as me being hopeful that Thane has returned from the skies to apologise, I continue to trek through the gargantuan graveyard under the violet sun, Nita in tow.

SEPHY

The flame extends out from my palm, climbing out from me in organic and fluid torrents, I slash it against the floor like a whip, exactly as I had seen Haedes do only last night. I'm sweating, though the perspiration dripping down my temple is not from the heat of the fire, which I barely feel. Instead, it's from the amount of effort it's taking me, even still, to muster this kind of flame and control it.

"Good!" Haedes praises me, clapping his hands together that are now missing his seemingly usual whisky glass. I let the flame extinguish at his compliment, my hands falling to my knees as I bend over, spent for energy.

"You ready to try convecting?" he asks, causing my eyebrows to rise on my damp forehead.

"You think I'm ready for that?" I'm surprised and he grins.

"Sure. I mean, it might be a while before you can do it on command. You're still bonding with your powers, as I understand it. It'll take a while, months even, before they're fully a part of you and you can control them at will. It'll be tiring, and you'll have to get used to it. I think we should try though." He rubs his hands together, almost like he's enjoying himself, and I see a twinkle behind his eye.

"What are you planning?" I smirk, still out of breath as he makes a tiny sidestep, dancing toward me.

"I know exactly how I'm going to train you for this,"

"Oh really?" I feel my mouth quirk at the edges, stopping my lips from twisting into an excited smile.

"Ever heard of K.C and the sunshine band?" he asks me, and I snort.

"Ever heard of K.C. and the sunshine band!? How is that even a question?!" I retort, exasperated.

"Good, because I own the voices that you've come to know and love. Got quite the sweet deal for them too." He clicks his fingers and a fog appears a few metres above our heads.

"You— *created* their voices?" I ask him, and he smirks.

"You can't honestly think there are that many people born with musical talent who just so happen to fall into fame and fortune. I love music, so I'm quite often giving those with great voices a leg up. For a price of course—" he explains. I blink a few times, trying to take in the information.

"That's insane," I mutter.

"I'd have thought you'd have realised I am utterly insane by now. Now, come on— dance with me." He beckons, clicking his fingers again as a familiar tune begins to ring out around the room, as sweet and pure as if it were live.

"Now, you gotta find that fire inside of you, then picture where you want to be, and close your eyes. Visualise yourself trying to move toward it." His hips begin to swing to the rhythm of the song, and I find myself taking his hand, spinning under one of his arms and smiling without being able to help it. He's a mean old bastard; that's for sure, a hard taskmaster, cruel, and beyond insufferable, and yet there's something about him— that's so utterly— well, *me.*

"Come on— that's it— feel the rhythm. Shake it." He urges me to loosen up and I feel odd. He dims the candles around us and clicks his fingers again. This time, sparks begin to glow within the overhead cloud of magic, causing a disco ball effect to bound from the multifaceted walls and ceiling. I grin.

This is too cool.

He pulls me to him and then pushes me out from his body again. As he does, he lets go of my hand and is gone in a wisp of blue flames, in perfect time to the song. He calls to me from the other side of the room as I let my feet continue to move and my hips continue to swing, the rhythm running through my veins, my heart beginning to beat in funky time.

Closing my eyes, I picture being in his arms, arriving there for the start of the next chorus so the dance can continue.

I ball up my fists and let the music take me back to my mother, to my father and how they used to dance with me to this song. I feel a pang of overwhelming guilt, but this is soon overshadowed as I feel the air around me heat and compress.

Haedes' arms come around my waist, and I open my eyes.

He smiles at me, his expression enough to break a million hearts. Glorious white teeth and eyes that explode in an azure glow from his face are overwhelming.

"I did it," I breathe.

"That you did— now, keep in time. Can't be doing *Boogie Shoes* dishonour, now, can we?" He spins me out from his body again and disappears, this time in red flames so he's at the other end of the room. He beckons me again.

I smirk; this time I know I can do it.

Convecting to him, I don't even lose a step as the song reaches the height of its glorious vintage funk, and I laugh out loud.

I feel *powerful*.

As Haedes dances a few steps in front of me, I convect, this time moving around the room seamlessly. The only thing I leave behind me is wild and loud laughter as I dance in and out of the flames that allow me to teleport anywhere in the room.

This is *fantastic*.

Soon, it's over, and Haedes is watching me, still dancing as the final few notes sound and the music falls away.

I stop, out of breath and grinning from ear to ear.

"That was fun!" I exclaim, and he nods, expression besotted at first but then cooling. The aftereffects of my quick trips around the hall suddenly catch up to me in a rush, and I'm lightheaded. I tilt on my feet, swaying from left to right before gingerly sitting down on the floor.

"Are you alright?" Haedes asks, clicking his fingers and dispersing the musical accompaniment from overhead. The lighting returns to normal simultaneously, and I find the room spinning ever so slightly.

"Just lightheaded," I sigh, pulling my ponytail from where it's stuck to my neck and sticky with sweat.

"Have you eaten today?" he demands.

I shake my head.

"Not since— damn it, last night," I recall, and he shakes his head.

"You need to be careful. To begin with, being in Mortaria will make you feel full-on invincible; you won't feel the need to eat or sleep as regularly as you should, especially as you're bonding with the goddess half of yourself. But you need to keep up your strength to avoid crashing out like this. You're not a doppel; you still need the regular things a mortal does to survive," he warns me, reaching inside his suit jacket and passing me a candy wrapped in clear plastic.

"What's this?" I ask him, and he smiles.

"Pomegranate sucking candy. My favourite," he reveals, and I stare at it.

"They were— they were my mother's favourite too." I blink a few times, hand shaking as I reach out to take it.

"I know. Who do you think got me addicted?" he mumbles, unable to keep a small smile from tugging at the edges of his thin and usually melancholy lips. "Eat that, then go get cleaned up. I'll take you for a real meal out on the town if you're not opposed to the idea?" he suggests, and I wonder if I want to go. The idea of a private meal with him is intimidating, even though it's probably how we should have started things off last night.

"Alright," I reply, unwrapping the candy and popping it into my mouth. After a few minutes, the sugar hits me so I can get to my feet, blood cooling close to the surface of my skin.

"No more convecting for now, alright? I don't want you to end up stranded somewhere. Especially not with the Demon Lords looking for you," Haedes calls out over his shoulder as he moves to walk towards the secondary exit of the hall at the back of the room.

"Okay. Is it formal— where we're going?" I ask.

I swear I hear him chuckling before he calls back, "Not exactly."

I step out of a carriage, and it's like I'm with Madonna or someone equally as famous. Everywhere we step, sinners stare at Haedes, as though he's a rare sight indeed. I'm wearing black leather pants and a black lace halter-top with elbow-length black lace gloves and knee-high leather stiletto boots. My lips boast a deep crimson, and my eyes are rimmed by dark, thick eyeliner. My hair is lustrous, having found pure magic inside the bathroom within my suite in the form of the most fabulous shampoo and conditioner I've ever used. My heels click sharply against the garnet-spattered sidewalk as we move from the vehicle, which is faster than any I've used so far, and eyes follow me as curious whispers catch in the stagnant air of the warm city streets.

"Where are we going?" I whisper to Haedes, who has an arm held out for me to hold onto. He's wearing a trilby hat and a tight silver velvet suit with a black waistcoat underneath. The hat is tilted on his head, and a hand, made heavy by thick silver rings, comes up, dismissing our transportation only moments before it pulls away from the sidewalk.

"We're going to a favourite little place of mine. The steak is to die for," he adds.

My lips tiptoe around the beginnings of a smirk.

"Is that supposed to be funny?" I demand, more at ease than I expected.

"A little pun never killed anyone," he smirks, too suave for his own good. I don't reply to this, letting him lead me across the pathway and toward a place with an extremely long line out front. If you ask me, I think it's a nightclub, but then I wonder if that's entirely appropriate for people who are supposed to be repenting.

The bouncer doesn't even pause as he catches the colour of Haedes hair in his sights, pulling the black rope aside for us before we've even reached him.

Haedes tilts his hat to the man, eyes lighting a cool blue and illuminating beneath the shadow of the brim.

"Okay, I'm getting seriously freaked out. I'm not about to find Hitler and like— Stalin playing cards or something, right?" I ask him as he brushes aside a thick velvet curtain that hangs across the doorway.

"Not exactly," he chuckles, but I don't have time to ask any more questions as the room and its purpose is revealed to me in an unapologetic and blatant flamingo pink light with spotlights focusing on cages.

"You brought me to a *strip club*?" I burst out laughing, and Haedes shrugs.

"Best steak in the city—" he reiterates. I move to examine the dancers in the cages more closely.

"They're all—" I begin, but he cuts me off.

"Men. Lust sinners who objectified women in their lifetimes to the point of harm." He waves the explanation away as unimportant, and I watch as women in leather corsets and tights wield whips, thrashing the dancers through the bars if they deviate from their dance. The air is laced with the scent of sickly-sweet body glitter, scented like peaches and cream, that shimmers upon the thick cut muscles binding the men in flesh.

"Wait, wait, wait—" I say as he walks me through the club. My feet tread across a carpet patterned with snakes and lips, though why, I couldn't tell you. The walls are draped with thick velvet in deep hues, and he doesn't seem to have heard me as he pulls me toward a table in the centre of the restaurant. It's cordoned off, presumably just for him.

"Wait, what? What's wrong?" He pulls out a chair for me, and I feel myself getting more and more confused the further down this Mortarian rabbit hole I tumble.

"I thought sinners came here to— I don't know— repent. Not get their skank on," I exclaim, taking a seat as Haedes chuckles to himself and sits down across from me.

"Well, I can see why you'd think that. But these men *are* repenting; they're being put in the place of the women they hurt with their lustful urges. You see, sin isn't sin unless it hurts another. Wrath isn't truly wrath unless it has a focus and that focus is badly affected." He's becoming philosophical almost. I nod, fascinated.

"So, it's more about the victim than the sin itself?" I ask him, and he nods.

"Oh, yes. Exactly."

"But wait— what about the other sinners? I mean, shouldn't they be off repenting too?" I ask him, and he sighs this time, raising a hand into the air. It shimmers with magenta and tangerine-tinted glitter that falls from above.

Within a few seconds, a woman in a reserved black dress and dark hair pulled into a high ponytail is at his side.

"The usual, Patricia," he orders, before blinking a few times.

"What are you drinking?" he enquires, and I stir at the thought of finally getting my hands on some alcohol.

"Whisky neat, please," I request. She looks at me oddly.

"So that's two of the usual. The 75 years matured. Bring the bottle," Haedes adds, all business, which I don't mind, seeing as how the subject of said business is fine whisky.

"So, as I was saying—" I begin, and he sighs again.

"Are you really interested in all this? It's so— boring." He scrutinises me, fidgeting in his seat.

"Yes. I really am. Like— I have so many questions. How do you have electric lighting down here— why are there sinners out enjoying fine wine?" I start to think of more questions, but he holds up a hand.

"Well, the first question is easy to answer. Sloth sinners on treadmills. We have them power the city," the explanation he gives is bizarre, and though I know I shouldn't be surprised, I find myself unable to stop my mind conjuring the image of humans running in hamster wheels.

"As for your other question— that's a little more complex. Basically, sinners repent best given small liberties. Before I got here and took over, the repentance rate was far too slow. People being tortured— well, it doesn't exactly help them let go of anger— if you get what I mean. Some of my colleagues would strongly disagree, but you must give these mortals enough rope to hang themselves with and teach them the strength to use that rope to save themselves instead." I feel myself turn surprised as I hear him out. That's a much kinder, sweeter solution than I've been expecting.

"So— what about if they don't move on in time— you have that balance to maintain, right?" I continue to grill him and he nods.

"Yes, Yama and I work with The Fates closely. It's all incredibly technical, but we have to stagger how many souls reach the stage where they move on. We need to purify souls, but we need to purify them at the same rate they're being housed in mortal bodies— so the cycle stays balanced. Does that make sense?" I frown, glad as my drink arrives. I take a sip.

"Kind of," I reply, and he smirks.

"It's complicated, but it's the balance of the universe. Did you expect it to be simple?" He gives me an expectant stare, and I shrug.

"Simpler. Maybe with like a spreadsheet or something. Or a soul chequebook that you gotta balance." I enjoy the feeling of slick whisky burning the back of my throat as I cross my heels beneath the table, which is covered in pink and silver linen. The flatware and cutlery seem to be plated silver too.

We fall into silence for a few moments as I watch the dancing asses of several ugly-faced men with ripped bodies. I catch the eye of one but look away, unnerved by the fact that they're so easily attainable. I mean where is the fun in having all catch and no chase?

"So, some of the sinners are kept back—" He smirks as Patricia brings us the menus.

"Yes, a lot of them are female lust sinners— I have a weakness for them," he confesses, and I choke on my current sip of whisky.

"That's a little— controversial, isn't it?" I query him. He sniggers under his breath, shuffling in his seat.

"Perhaps, but I suppose there are one or two things about mortal bodies that aren't so bad." I want to cover my ears and scream in this moment. "Too much?" he asks me as I bite my bottom lip.

vhisper, heart sinking in my chest, defeated by his unre-
ssion.
 right.
ed to tell you that this could be dangerous for us all, if you
lved with a demi-goddess, do I?" I stare at him firmly, and
s head.
t can't be allowed to happen. It's too great of a risk." He
with sadness in his eyes. "Besides, I don't think she feels
e're just friends in her mind, and I have no intention of
 She's not the relationship type." This time he says it as
tional in his reply. I nod, letting a slight smile grace my
f his restraint. At least he's sensible. I can't say if I'd been
n with Thane that I'd have been able to stay away.
u but be careful. Other members of The Nexus don't share
emind him.
bis and Osiris." He shakes his head, inhaling deeply. "I
lame them. A being created from a demi-goddess and
n would be able to walk in all worlds. It would be able
 all worlds." He voices the fear we've all been trying to
truth of the matter, that a love between he and Sephy
d bring about the end of all days.
I cross my hands in front of me as we stand, flattening the
irt, awkward as silence threatens to blanket us. "Anyway,
lk to Haedes about finding a permanent relocation for
he returns. I'm sure they'll be back soon," I promise him,
 a small, sad smile, that's almost a grimace.
Luce." He reaches forward and puts his arms around me,
ional despite his attempts to mask it. I've never seen him
t angry or stoic, so this is surprising for me to say the least.
oulder blades with my long fingers, inhaling the spice of
sk and wishing I could take away his pain.
elcome," I reply, watching him as he leaves me alone in
w of the alchemy chamber, amber crystals dotted around
tion flames turning the space emerald.
or closes with a slam, I sigh.
hane was right. I curse.
we her an apology.

oves me in red. Says it's my colour.

"Little bit— dad." I call him this to make a point, but I notice that he flushes at the term, and I find my own face heating too. Mumbling, he looks down at his menu, quickly changing the subject.

"You really should have the steak; it's extremely tender," he suggests, and I exhale, the awkwardness of sitting with my father, Haedes, God of The Underworld, in a male strip club, beginning to creep in on all sides. I kind of want to ask if the steak is whipped tender but button my lip, trying to keep things at least partially civil.

"Steak it is," I announce, glugging my drink and picking up the bottle Patricia has left between us, pouring generously.

There isn't enough time in the world to mature a whisky strong enough to make this shit any less weird, but I guess drinking a little more can't hurt.

Can it?

20

HUNGRY EYES

LUCE

I LET MY FINGERS stroke the spherical crystal of the eye, a gift from The Fates, as I watch Haedes and Sephy digging into tender steak. Glitter falls from the floors of many dangling cages as lust sinners gyrate against the bars, suggestive in every single motion. Some people would find it fun, provocatively dancing all day long, but if it's for just anyone, not the one you love, then it becomes a kind of job, like you're an actor and not entitled to your own emotions, preferences, or desires. You must continue to smile, to provoke, but not of your own volition.

I smile, watching the father and daughter get along.

I only wish I could use this eye to see what will come rather than what has already passed, and that the Demon Lords weren't so shrouded in darkness it obscures all vision I might have of them.

Sighing out, I feel the hairs on the back of my neck stand on end.

Turning to face the curved wall behind me with a paranoid glance, I brush a strand of pale hair behind my ear.

The vials of Aetherial roots and herbs, which line the top shelf, reflect my suspicious face back at me. I scan the chamber, the scent of preserves, dying flowers, and fauna of every variety filling my head and intoxicating me with the promise of magic.

Bottles containing Mermaid's hair, the odd scale, Kelpie mane, and the wings of a spring-born sprite lie to my left, and I let my eyes trail over them, listening carefully. I rotate then to the right, my gaze cast next upon the remnants of demons, spinal cords, and synovial fluid in jars. Dead eyes stare out at me, bobbing in thick, cloudy jelly.

Perhaps I'm being silly.

Maybe it's my guilt over the argu[ment]
continually look over my shoulder, [w]
right.

Then again, perhaps not—

I'm about to start brewing a draf[t]
a knock sounds at the door, echoin[g]
height of the turret.

I hope it's Thane and make quick [steps]
so often slick with the spattering of

Grasping the old-fashioned iron ri[ng]

"Xion," I say his name, surprised.

He looks anxious, like he's been w[aiting]
molten eyes are wide, his fingers scra[tching]
chin in the way they do when he's ag[itated]

The leather-clad bulk of his form [steps]
forward, looking into the depths of
for something— or more likely some[one]

"Where is she?" he demands, and [steps]
through the door to join me. Closin[g]
him, the dark blue of my skirt sweepi[ng]

"She's out to dinner with Haedes[," I sigh]
heavily, not satisfied with the answer

"I came to get the rest of her stuff t[o]
look after Cerb for her?" he request[s]
bottom lip and watching him as he shi[fts]
and beginning to pace around me in

"What's wrong?" I ask.

He stills, looking up at me with a
anxiety but failing miserably.

"I just— I don't know. I'm concerne[d]
place without any effort at all, or so it
exactly secure—" I frown as his brow

Taking a step forward, I place my ha[nd]
of his jacket, feeling the popping vein

"You care about this girl, don't yo[u]
pained.

"I— I can't help it," he admits, loo[king]
mouth presses into a thin line. He pus[hes]
hair, not meeting my gaze.

"I see," I
quited confe

Thane wa[s]

"I don't ne[ed]
become invo[lved]
he shakes hi[s]

"I know. I
looks at me
the same. W
ruining that
fact, not em[otion]
lips, proud o
in his positi[on]

"I trust yo[u]
my faith," I

"Yes, Anu[bis]
can't say I
a half-demo[n]
to destroy i[t]
ignore, the
Sinclair cou[ld]

"Exactly."
silk of my sk[irt]
I'll try to ta[lk]
Sephy when
and he gives

"Thanks,
clearly emot[ional]
anything bu[t]
I grip his sh[oulder]
his male mu[scle]

"You're w
the jade glo[w]
the resurrec[ted]

As the do[or]
Dammit. T
I guess I

Red. She

I stare at myself in the mirror on my vanity. I'm wearing a red bra, which opens at the mere pull of the ribbon tying the two cups together beneath my steep cleavage, and a matching thong to accentuate the curve of my ass. I smear my lips in crimson, fully intending to leave the colour all over her skin.

The candles I've lit around the bedroom incrementally flicker as she lands, her wings causing a slight disturbance in the air behind the closed French doors.

Stepping across the room, my black stilettos are harsh against the floor as I look down at the black stockings elongating my already lengthy legs. I sprawl out on the bed, grabbing the string of pearls I've got around my neck and draping it through my fingers.

Lying on my stomach, I face the door, ready for her to enter. Grabbing the surround sound system remote from the bedside table, I click a single button, allowing the room to fill with the sweet yet sexy melody of *Hungry Eyes*, Thane's favourite song.

The frosted glass of the balcony doors swings forward, revealing her.

"What's all this?" she calls, voice broken from her too recent transformation. Her skin is pale and milky, tempting me from afar. I gaze up at her through thick lashes.

"An apology— what else?" I purr, crossing my heels behind me as I tilt my head, silken hair falling lusciously over one bare shoulder.

"I see—" Her eyes narrow, and a small smile creeps onto her lips, despite the fact she might try to fight it.

"Come to me," I command, beckoning with a single finger draped in dark pearls.

"Yes, Ma'am." Her eyes blaze, and I lick my bottom lip, watching as she walks with feline grace across the slick stone and over to the sumptuous softness of our bed. Her angular face is erotic in its hunger, in its hardness and softness that roll into one another like a raging storm.

As she treads toward me, her body stiffens visibly before I've even laid a finger on her, goosebumps crawling over her flesh and making an only too obvious show of her arousal. I rise so I'm on my knees, meeting her with open arms as she crawls over the velvet sheets.

I waste no time in placing one hand on her breast, and the other on her cheek, wrapping my long fingers around the shell of her ear and burying them in her hair. I pull her luscious lips to mine, inhaling the taste of blackberries and pine like it's a drug, and I'm addicted.

"Mmm," I exhale, closing my eyes and running my fingertips down the back of her neck. I let my fingernails trail down her spine, tickling her silken skin and feeling myself becoming wet as I reach the delicious plumpness of her ass. I dig in my nails, pulling her into me and allowing my tongue to explore the inside of her mouth. I groan, and she echoes my pleasure as she falls on top of me. We tumble to the sheets, hair wild around our faces as we remain locked in a passionate stare.

"I haven't heard the word sorry yet," she teases, hovering over me and pulling at the red silk holding my bra together. I squirm under her spindled form, staring at her lips and licking my own.

"I'm sorry, baby," I whisper, eyes widening as she lowers toward me, placing my nipple into her mouth and causing my back to arch beneath the prowess of her ample tongue.

"I'm sorry too— I love you. I'd fall from heaven a million times for these lips. I'd burn for these tits— I'd die for you, Luce." She circles the outside of my plump breast with her lips, causing the apex between my thighs to burn tenderly with desire. I raise a hand to her collarbone, letting my fingertips trace a path from her throat, down between her breasts and then lower to her thighs. She gasps as I explore her, eyes widening and lips parting in a perfect 'o' shape I cannot help but want to devour.

I use my weight and top her, straddling her and discarding my bra by throwing it to the floor. Leaning, I bend over her and bury my fingers into her hair, pulling her head back and licking the length of her throat. I plant kisses across her skin, a blank canvas for me to paint scarlet with my lust, with my love for her.

Her eyes bore into mine, and I feel my hard nipples tracing her body as my arm curls to hold her in place. My hand slips between her aching wanton thighs.

She's soaked, and I smile down at her face, at her wild eyes and maddeningly gorgeous lips that constantly call to me as the tide calls to a Psiren. I feel my arousal becoming more than I can bear but remain in control. This is about her pleasure, not mine.

She exclaims a moan, and just as I'm finding a rhythm that I know will make her climax within seconds, her eyes turn wide, startled.

With a jerking motion, she's upright, breaking the connection between us and scrambling from beneath my touch.

She grabs the knife we use to peel lush, fresh fruit from beside our garnet fruit bowl, catching her breath and appearing partially feral as she stares up at the ceiling like she's gone slightly mad.

She throws it without pause, and as I watch, confused, the blade finds its target and a Gorgonian falls from the ceiling where it's been watching.

Hitting the floor in a scaly heap, it bleeds out onto the crystal, the camouflage of its skin flickering in and out of existence like an old TV on the fritz.

"Shit!" I exclaim, heart racing.

Thane continues to stare up at the ceiling, eyes sharp as razors.

"There were more— but they got away," she growls, and I blanche.

"What the hell is that thing doing in here?" I demand, and she picks up the fruit knife, now embedded in the centre of the Gorgonian's snakelike torso. It squirms, flopping once, then twice, before giving up and lying still. I think it's dead.

"I don't know. But I told you this would happen. Gorgon— he's the fourth Demon Lord to unexplainably get demons into Mortaria in as many days. This is a serious issue. It's not just a coincidence. We need to find out how they're getting in. It puts you at risk too. You know he wants you."

She's flustered, running her hands through her hair, stark naked as her chest rises and falls frantically.

I reach over to the pillow where I'd left the surround sound remote, turning off the music and killing the mood.

Our night of proposed passion is definitely over.

"We need to find Sephy and Haedes. We don't know where those other demons are headed. They could be looking for her," I fret, and Thane nods, staring at me with anxious eyes.

We both scramble to get dressed, and even though the day should be almost over, it feels like something bad is only just beginning.

No rest for the wicked.

PANDORA

I've been waiting for a while, nervous, concerned that the Gorgonian spies will find nothing. I've retreated to my quarters, a small, meek offering of a place to call my own, what used to be servant's quarters for those sinners who were not tortured or eaten by the Demon Lords and their Kindred. I have a single bed and a wardrobe with my gowns, the finest things I own and that I have collected from across the worlds I have visited.

My only other possession is the box, which I keep on my person at all times. It's a complicated little device to be sure, and even now, I'm sure I do not know all its secrets. It has taken me years to work out how to mentally connect with it, how to recognise its limits and respect them accordingly. It's taken me a long time to be ready to begin taking my revenge, but now that time is finally here; I'm utterly tired of waiting altogether.

I glance up through the disrepaired ceiling to the crimson sky and find my impatience growing. As though the box can sense this, it heats in my palm.

I turn it over in my fingers.

Throwing it, a stark beam of light and heat explodes from one side as a panel opens. Out slither the Gorgonian spies, their skin assimilating to the floor only too seamlessly. I feel the hairs on the back of my neck stand on end, I hate snakes.

"Go, find your master," I urge them.

I'm on my feet in a matter of moments, trailing after the faint outlines of the enormous snake-like demons as they slither through the doorway and out into the chasmic main hall of the building.

I pick up the box, which has tumbled to the floor, on my way out, maintaining pace as they disturb pools of coagulated blood, aiding me in keeping up with them as they drag the fluid along with their underbellies, staining the floor a stale burgundy in wavy lines.

Once they reach the main chamber with the cracked table, I take a seat, waiting for them to return. I glance at my reflection in the mirrors, making sure my hair is flawless as I wait on Gorgon.

After a few minutes, from within the emerald light of the Gorgonian wing, Gorgon appears. His pointed, pale face is plastered with a mask of wicked intent.

I smile.

"So, I'm hoping your expression means that they found something we can use?" I probe him and he relinquishes, smiling cruelly.

"Oh yes, Anubis and Osiris. They fear the girl and what her relationship with the half-breed might mean. They're your way in, if any," he announces.

"Well, that's easy. Anubis and I have quite a bit in common, I'd imagine she'll be willing to help. Especially when she discovers I'm still alive," I muse.

Gorgon cocks an eyebrow.

"Old friends, are we?" he enquires, genuinely intrigued.

"Yes, she's a Titan too. She has felt the injustices just as I have. He took away her Kingdom and gave it to Haedes. That's plenty of motivation for her to screw him over," I snarl, a smile twisting my features into something cruel.

"Very well then. You'd best be on your way. The early bird catches the worm as they say—" Gorgon flutters a graceful hand, and he watches me with a joyous and glowing lime gaze, the reptilian slits of his pupils narrowing.

"I'll be back before dawn. Don't wait up," I say, getting to my feet and leaving the room in a grand stride. I can feel his eyes on me as I walk away, grasping the box once more in my palm, and a shiver runs up my spine. Whether it be his raw power or the fact he seems not to underestimate me the way the other Demon Lords do, I can't help but enjoy his gaze on me.

I look back over my shoulder, giving him a sly glance as I throw the box up into the air and visualise Anubis' face before I step through.

Then, the golden whirring of the portal surrounds me as I make my way to bargain with a woman who has lost just as much as I, if not more.

I don't have to wait long, shielded from view in the shadow of one of the many thick golden pillars that line the walls of The Icon's throne room— well, I say throne room. It once held a throne, but that throne has since been destroyed, along with Anubis' entitlement to rule this place alone.

I watch as she and her son sit down to dinner; a gargantuan gold dining table spanning the entire length of the room. They are attended by sinners of envy, gluttony, and avarice, shirtless and adorned in only fabric wrapped around their genitals or breasts, sinstones hanging around their necks. This place has certainly remained timeless in its attire.

From the left side of the table, three Jackals bound down one of the twisting corridors toward them, no doubt wanting to share in the meal. As plates, steaming high with fine cuts of meat, are delivered, and Anubis and Osiris take golden cutlery in hand, the Jackals start to growl, the black sheen of their coats turning gold at the overwhelming and rich glow of the surrounding room.

I step out into the glow of Eternal Flames and the Jackals go wild, bearing their teeth and rushing toward me. I raise both my hands, an indication that I wish to get into no kind of fight. God knows I could not rival either Osiris or Anubis in battle, not with the loss of my Titan powers.

At the sight of my intrusion, Anubis and Osiris rise to their feet. Anubis' dark hair tumbles in a waterfall of black, draped in gold chains that act as a casual headpiece. Her dark eyes narrow, and as the Jackals near me, she clicks her fingers.

"Stop," she barks, the three animals heeling immediately, no question in their tiny minds who the master here is. The sinners dotted around the corners of the room have begun to close in, ready to defend the two Egyptian Titans made flesh. They are much slower than the dogs, perhaps even slower than Anubis herself, which makes them utterly useless if you ask me.

"Pan— Pandora? Is that you?" Anubis scrutinises my face, eyes reflecting utter shock back at me.

Osiris is on his feet too, face comically clueless.

"Mother, what is the meaning of this?" he demands, sounding pompous in his ignorance.

"Yes, Nu. It is I." I smile at her, and she comes forward, putting her arms around me.

"Praise Ra! I never thought I'd see the day! How on earth— how in the Heavens did you get here?" she enquires, looking to me and then to her son. "This is Pandora; she was a Kindred, just like I was. She, too, has been cast aside by the likes of Zeus," she explains, and Osiris looks dazed and unimpressed as he slumps down into his seat again and takes a sip of wine from the golden goblet in front of him.

"Take a seat; dine with us." Anubis snaps her fingers and orders the sinners to fetch a spare plate. I take a seat at her table, coughing, out of place in such grand surroundings. It's been so long since I sat in a chair like this.

"So, when Zeus refused my application to be on the Aetherial Court, he gave me this box— well, it's not really a box at all; it's actually a portal that was made from the wood of trees in the Othrysian Orchards. It allows me to travel anywhere I choose in The Lower Plains. I ended up here at first, but I've been around since," I express, not giving away too many details.

"I see, that's wonderful for you," Anubis replies. Taking a seat, the glistening gold of her gown melds seamlessly into her chair, making it appear as if she's merely a head and arms.

"It is. I'm still outraged at the thought of you losing rulership over this place to the likes of *him*, even if it was before my time—" I take a purposeful sip of the wine in front of me, looking at her over the rim of the glass with pity in my stare. I know it irks her, but I also want to build our camaraderie, to make her feel as though I truly understand her.

"Yes, well, we're all very democratic here now. It's become quite the way of life," she explains in a tone void of emotion. The jackals, begging for scraps as their bejewelled collars clash against one another, emit a slight metallic ringing into the air. Hushing them with authority, she waits for my reply.

"I see, you sound thrilled." I smirk at her as a thin man places a golden plate of lamb in front of me. The smell of it makes me salivate, but I don't take a bite, not yet.

"I am— making do." Anubis looks at me and then at Osiris.

"It is just such a shame for Osiris; he has never reached his fullest potential," she sighs, taking a bite of her food and chewing thoughtfully.

I watch her, her slender golden arms and thin face beautiful as ever.

We're all so beautiful, the ones they chose. It is a shame that beauty was not enough to stop us from being discarded.

"So, what brings you here?" Osiris asks, interjecting between our small talk.

Anubis is no fool; she knows I have an agenda, but it seems that her son lacks such tact.

"I have a little proposition for you," I announce, and Anubis looks intrigued.

"I'm listening." She takes a fork full of buttered green beans and stuffs them into her mouth.

"I'm working on— well, let's just say that I'm working on helping the Demon Lords survive. Let's just say you and I have some concerns in common. Or so a little birdie tells me," I explain. Her beautiful dark eyes become sharp.

"Go on."

"Her name is Persephone Sinclair. We have heard of the prophecy, the prophecy of the Phoenix, the Chimera. Quite frankly, the Demon Lords are concerned as well. She is a risk. One they don't want left unchecked." I word my proposal carefully; she need not know that I intend to take back the Demon Lords hunting grounds, nor need she know that I'm using her. She needs merely know that, right now, our agendas line up.

"I see. Well, that's difficult." Anubis looks to me and then to her son, weary.

"How so?" I ask, and she shrugs.

"The girl is well protected, and as my colleague so rightfully pointed out, there is no reason to believe that The Fates aren't seeing something which will not come to pass. You know as well as I that visions of the future are rarely certain, especially now they've been banished from The Higher Plains. She and the demon-halfling are merely friends. If that. Once you stop hunting her, I'm sure they will part ways, and she will go on with her mortal life. She need not be a threat to us."

I frown, Anubis has become comfortable in her age, a fat cat upon a gilded golden pillow who refuses to budge. The sparkling blue eyeliner rimming her dark eyes glistens as she tilts her head, waiting for my response, and the enormous golden earrings hanging from her petite earlobes tinkle against her jaw.

"I see. Well, I just thought we might be able to rid ourselves of the problem together. But if you believe she truly is no threat, then I suppose that's fair enough." I don't want to push my luck with her; after all, I don't need her asking questions about my relationship with the Demon Lords. Her expression is slightly stiff, stony even, and I watch her as she swallows hard.

"Why don't you just stop hunting her? I have no doubt she'd return to the mortal plain. Problem solved," Osiris interjects, and I look at him, readying to put this idea to rest once and for all.

"We cannot simply leave a demi-goddess out there unchecked. Having her return to the mortal plain is to leave a weapon in plain sight with little or no protection for anyone who plans to use it. She might have been safe before her trial, before the prophecy, but now the information is out, she's too dangerous to be left alive."

"It's you, isn't it? It's you who's been letting the demons into Mortaria. With that box of yours." Anubis is accusatory in her tone, but I merely smile.

"Perhaps."

"You must not want to be involved with the Demon Lords, Pandora. Their time has long since passed. They worship gods who are long since dead and banished. If you want a cause worth fighting for, the Demon Lords are not where to find it. I promise you." She's lecturing me like she's my mother, or one of them, one of the pure. Either way, she's acting like she knows better. Time has surely not made her meek or humble. Instead, her arrogance grows into that of those she once so loathed.

"Perhaps you have forgotten that even though you walk among pure-born gods, you are not one," I retort, getting up from the table.

"Perhaps you have forgotten that my god is long since dead. I must look out for the balance of the universe now in whatever way I can. Ra is dead," she repeats, and I smirk.

"Look, I'm sorry. I realise now that expecting you to betray them, the pure, was silly of me. I just didn't think you'd have forgotten the fact that they cast you aside so easily, Nu. I'm sorry about that. I truly am. Clearly, they're your friends now, and everything is perfect," I sneer at her.

"You better leave this place right now and tell the Demon Lords that if they know what's good for them that they'll cease this quest to capture that girl. I might not be sole ruler here anymore, but I still command the armies," she threatens.

"Are you sure that's enough for you?" I retort. "We could take this place and rule it together you know— it doesn't have to be this way. All you must do is open the gates," I tease her, knowing this will only infuriate her more.

"Did I think about rebelling, about fighting to keep Mortaria as mine? Yes, of course, I did. But you think that I could honestly do that without Ra?" she demands honesty. I merely shake my head.

"Of course not. But who said anything about doing it without him?" I add, and she purses her lips as her nostrils flare.

"He's dead!" she exclaims, and I shake my head.

"No god truly dies forever. You know that as well as I do. His energy might be scattered— but he still exists," I express, leading her on with half-truths that I spin as facts.

"What do you mean?" she demands an answer of me now, desperation rife in her voice.

"Nothing. It matters not. After all, why would I risk finding a way to bring him back with such a powerful and dangerous prophecy posing a threat?" I have my back turned to her now, having spun on my heel to leave, and smile, hearing her breathing quicken behind me.

"You're lying. No one has the power to do that, to resurrect a god," Anubis accuses me, nonchalant in her arrogance.

"We shall see," I mutter.

Pulling out a vial containing a tiny scroll from my cleavage, something that Gorgon had given me during our walk earlier, I turn back. "If you change your mind about the girl, you can summon me using this. You know the drill." I place the glass on the table where it tinkles against the metal surface, holding the gazes of both Titans as I smile.

Grasping the box from inside my dress pocket, I press into the desired panel, picturing the Fallen Kingdom, and walk once more into another whirling portal.

As I tread through the scarlet mist crackling with ebony lightning, I can only hope that the seeds I've sown have made Anubis curious enough to approach me again. I can only pray that she's more power-hungry than she seems, and as devout to her creator as I always thought from our time in The Higher Plains together.

As for me, I have done my job as best I can, and now I must merely watch and wait, yet again, for the opportune moment to strike.

21

ON THE ROAD AGAIN

SEPHY

EVERYTHING IS SPINNING, WHIRLING, and it's utterly freaking fantastic.

Haedes and I saunter down the street, which sways oddly as it's filtered through the whisky fog tainting my vision. The velvet of his suit feels soft, so soft, and I'm sort of debating asking him for a hug just so I can run my fingers all over it.

I'd been intimidated by him at first, but as I try, almost successfully, to put one foot in front of the other, I hear myself say, "You know, you're not so scary— you're like a blue care bear with explodey hands." I grin at him, and he chuckles back at me.

"How drunk are we?" he asks, voice slurred, and I giggle, taking more steps down the street and ignoring onlooking sinners. It would be the early hours of the morning by now if we were in the mortal world, and things would be starting to quiet down. As it is, we're not in the mortal world, and everywhere along the central street of the city is packed. I examine the sinners, their Victorian-era attire; only a few still sport black jumpsuits, and I wonder if these are the vanity sinners.

"God-level drunk. *Unholy God Level Drunk!*" I stammer, yelling into his face for absolutely no reason and staring with a sudden and overwhelming curiosity. This might be the drunkest I've ever been, and my only excuse is that I'm currently experiencing the most awkward identity crisis you can imagine.

"Hey! Where are we going? It's not a dungeon, is it?" I ask, suspicious as the world continues to spin. It makes my stomach churn, but my mind is saturated in happy, so I don't really mind much.

"Sugar— Skullz— and no— no torture for you. Not unless Xion sings—" He blows a raspberry and gives me a thumbs down as we stumble toward a building with a large neon sign.

"Sugar Skullz—" I read it slowly, almost like the neon of the sign is blurring and turning the words into a foreign language.

"Come on. Muerta has the best tequila." Haedes pulls me forward, and I pass a lot of pissed-off-looking faces as we enter the joint without having to queue once again.

"You're like— *famous*, you know that?" I ask him, frowning, and he smirks.

"Yeah, I know, right?" he giggles like a little boy, pulling me down a long black corridor lit in a bloody hue. My feet struggle to place themselves on the hard floor, and as Haedes pushes aside a dark velvet curtain, revealing the innards, I find myself wanting to wrap myself up in it and start my life over as a burrito.

The place has scarlet carpet and black walls; the tables are alabaster and look like they've been made from real human skeletons or animal bones, and I realise that I've seen this style of décor before. Each table holds a tiny flickering candle, putting the real focus on the stage where a single microphone stands next to an outdated and horrifically familiar-looking machine. A figure approaches it, and my stomach falls into my ass.

Haedes said no torture.

He lied.

"Wait— this is a Karaoke bar?" I ask him, and he nods. "Oh God! Why would you bring me here— this— it sucks!" I pout, glancing at the stage that's lit up in stark spotlights from beneath. Atop it, a sinner climbs, beginning to sing *Wind Beneath My Wings* before I can even try to assassinate him in a ball of fiery inferno.

As I stand, paralysed by his pitchy melody, I suddenly begin to feel the urge to vomit rising quickly in my throat.

"Muerta! Tequilllaaaaaaa!" Haedes yells, pulling me towards the glass bar that's decorated with hundreds of tiny dots, forming a macrocosmic and mind-blowing pattern. It's incredible, and I sort of want to know who designed it, how long it took them— must have been like *forever*.

I take a seat on a stool, looking down the length of the bar and turning my head so it's parallel to the glass, staring until my eyes meet with another pair.

"Oh look, a kitty!" I smile, seeing a cat wrapped around a skull that's sitting on the bar. Two candles, one in each eye socket, waver. I reach out to pet its creamy fur but am met with yowls as the evil ball of fluff reaches out and slashes at my hand with a hiss.

"No! Bad kitty!" I curse the creature and turn to Haedes. "Why does this cat hate me so much? Like— am I a bad person?" I ask him, and he frowns.

"Nah, Cassie hates everyone. Everyone except Muerta." He looks around once, then twice before losing his utter lack of patience and yelling out, "*Muerta!*" at the top of his lungs yet again. A rattling of beaded curtains parting sounds and shortly after, a woman who I have met twice now emerges from the back room.

"Oh, Haedes, it's you. I had a client. What's the matter?" she asks him, cocking a dark eyebrow. I look at the bony makeup covering her flawless skin and giggle a little. She reminds me of that book— *Funny Bones*— that my mom used to read to me when I was a little kid. That book was great; the skeleton family even had a little skeleton dog.

"Tequila, darling." Haedes clicks his fingers, and Muerta rolls her eyes.

"Seriously? You pulled me away from business so you could get inebriated with your daughter?" she berates him, spinning on one foot.

From behind the bar, which is covered in large backlit X-rays displaying some truly horrific breaks and fractures, she pulls out two shot glasses and a large glass bottle of tequila. Slamming it down on the counter, Haedes smiles.

"He's got the parenting thing down," I add, and she rolls her eyes at me, unimpressed.

"Thanks, you know you're my favourite, Muerta—" He can't think of a better compliment and so settles for this pitiful attempt. She rolls her eyes again and then looks between us, her glassy pupils scanning me with disapproval. I puff out my chest a little, not one to be underestimated, even if her cat did just try to assault me.

"Come on, Cassie," she calls the cat, who gives me the stink eye before jumping down off the bar and following her mistress. The tinkle of beads sounds once more, and then it's just me and Haedes, sitting alone with the sound of *Copacabana*.

"Does Muerta— ya know— what kind of *clients* does she see?" I ask Haedes, winking at him in the least subtle way you can imagine.

"She can see into people's souls, see their sins as you know. That power is amplified when someone sings— like even if they *suck at it!*" he yells at the tone-deaf woman on stage before continuing. "People who come here, they're often seeking advice about how to speed things along, or if they need to be reassigned. That kind of sinner crap." Haedes sounds like he's sobering up quicker than I am, probably because he's a god and all, and so pulls the stopper from the bottle of tequila and takes it to his lips, rendering the shot glass beside him obsolete.

"Will I end up here? I'd look bad in one of those jumpsuits," I ask him, confused as to where I fit.

"Nah, you'll go to The Higher Plains, or if you're not accepted there, then you'll go to The Nether Realm— kind of like limbo but without the pole," he enlightens me, mouth quirking up at the side.

"That's a shame, I do love a good pole. Wait— What do you mean? Not accepted?" I ask him, and he shrugs.

"I dunno. My brother is an asshole."

"I read about your dad— in that book Xion gave me. He seems like an asshole too." I take the bottle from him, tipping it up and downing the salty draft far too quickly.

"Oh yeah, I come from a long line of assholes." Haedes nods, pressing his lips together and closing his eyes.

"I guess that means I do too." I laugh, and he smiles at me.

"Well, you're lucky, you're only a demi-asshole. That'd be your mother, saving you once again from the torment of being completely made up of my genetic makeup— I should thank her." He takes the bottle from my hand again and holds it up above his head.

"Thanks, Demi! You made our daughter only part asshole, and for that, I am lucky. Miss you always, babe." He takes a giant slug of the alcohol once more, blowing a kiss into the air as he swallows, and I feel myself getting sad, untethered emotions rising to the surface because of the booze.

"It's my fault she's dead," I mutter.

"Yeah, well, it's my fault she got pregnant with you. So, I guess we're both to blame." He hands me the bottle again and I take another swig, my mind falling deeper into a fog of intoxication.

"Should've worn a condom." I look at him, smirking, and he laughs.

"Eh— then who would I be drinking with?" he asks me, and I shrug.

"I dunno — some dead chick — probably Marilyn Monroe; I heard she was fun," I muse, and he looks at me with a deadpan expression.

"She was until she got drunk. Damn. You could *not* get that woman to shut up," he complains. This time, it's my turn to laugh.

"You must have met so many famous people. What's that like?" I enquire, and he shrugs again.

"Boring. Famous people are just regular people, regular people with the same sins as everyone else. They're a tad self-obsessed too." I smile at his reply, mainly because I know it's true.

"I see. Well, I can imagine my mortal half you find horribly predictable." I sigh, and he shakes his head.

"Nope, you're too much like me. Volatile, like fire; the mortal half only exacerbates that." He takes in more alcohol, shifting atop the stool where he's perched.

"I am *not* like you. Not at all," I argue. He looks curious now.

"Why would you say that?" he asks, curiosity flickering behind the grey mistiness of his gaze.

"I'm not afraid to die," I enlighten him, and he cocks his head.

"How can that be?" He's seriously curious, leaning into me so I can examine all of his features, finding only more similarities between us.

"I don't know. Nothing and nobody keeping me here I guess." I shrug, and he looks at me again.

"What about Xion?" he asks me, and I sputter, almost choking on salty saliva.

"That great goober? Ha! No. I'm good there. Thanks though. I'd rather take a bath in lava." I laugh it off, and Haedes cocks an eyebrow.

"Seemed like it this morning with you being all cosied up together."

I snatch the bottle back from him, and he smirks.

"That was a mistake. I was tired from all the almost being killed that *you* let happen," I exclaim, but he doesn't reply, simply keeping his eyebrow cocked as he exhales.

"Mhmmm."

"What?!" I snap at him, and he shakes his head, pressing his lips together, trying not to laugh.

"Oh, nothing— nothing at all."

"Good. Let's keep it that way," I growl.

A few moments pass, and we sit, gazing at the wicked selection of alcohol hung behind the bar, each bottle wedged between the teeth of a skull, though whether they're real or not, I couldn't tell you. I look at the spirits, smirking at the names as I pick up a cocktail menu to my right:

Kraken's piss- Rum mix.

Banshee's blood- Bourbon mix.
Succubi's kiss- Sangria mix.
Abraxian illusion -Absinthe mix.
Tarantula Terror- Tequila Mix.
Gorgonian Venom-Vodka mix.
Haedes' torment- Whisky mix.

I frown, wondering if you become desensitized to the thought of demon horrors after so long. After all, how scared can these people be if they're branding alcohol after them?

"So, what was that you were just saying about Xion again?" Haedes asks as I take another slug of tequila, letting the salt burn the back of my throat.

"Jesus, how many times do I have to tell you people? We're *just* friends!" I exclaim, and he smirks, eyes flitting over my shoulder.

I twist on my stool, whirling around and coming face to face with the friend in question.

I don't know why, but for some reason I can't help but spit tequila all over him, baptising him in alcohol, the real fuel behind my belief that I, Sephy Sinclair, can do anything.

I stare at him, eyes wide, flushing bright red but unable to stop myself as I burst out laughing in surprise.

"Sorry!" I sputter, feeling the sting of the liquid as it creeps up the back of my nasal passages.

Jesus Haedes, you're such an asshole. I cuss, shooting daggers at him over my shoulder.

"What's going on here?" Xion demands. I turn back only to spot Luce entering the building behind him, Thane in tow. I wonder what could be the cause of such a gathering.

"Well, Mr Grumpy, Mayor of Grumpusville, we're having a drink. Want to join? Or will you be having— *a water?*" I berate him, and he rolls his eyes.

"You took her out drinking?" He looks over my shoulder in disbelief at Haedes with a disapproving glare.

"Hey, she's a grown-up. She can have a drink with her pops. Can't you?" He nudges me with the back of his hand, heavy silver rings clinking against the glass as he takes the tequila bottle in his palm again despite the grip I try to maintain.

"Sure pops. Whatever you say." I give Xion a look and place a finger up to the side of my head, whirling it around in a circular motion. "I think he's crazy—" I whisper loud enough so he can hear.

All I hear back from him is an audible, "Hey!", before he continues to suck down spirit like it's honey and he's Queen bee.

"Sephy, we have to get you out of here. There's been another attack, this time on Luce and Thane," Xion explains, tone urgent. I want to take him seriously, but as he grabs my arm, yet another giggle escapes my lips.

"Look at you, all— I am man. You woman. We must run into the dawn from bad demon men on epic adventure!" I mock him in a caveman voice, and he scowls. I look behind him now, craning my neck around his large torso to see Luce and Thane staring at me, shocked.

I wave at them.

"Hi guys— sorry about the demon attack. Guess I should have left them another home address." I spin around on my stool as more laughter hits me.

"Wheeeeee!" I exclaim, laughing as the room spins. Haedes joins me, laughing too, and I see his blue hair blurred as the room becomes a hurricane of colour and sound. This is the first time I've felt truly weightless since I can remember, but as Xion puts his foot on the bottom rung of my stool and stops me dead, the weight of being mortal, or at least partially so, comes back full force, thwacking me in the stomach and causing me to throw up down Xion's front. I look up at him, his eyes not full of amusement or anger but pity.

I scowl, wishing he would stop pitying me, stop caring, stop making me like him— just *stop*.

This is my final thought as he hoists me off my stool and over one shoulder, in what seems to be becoming ritual for us.

I lose consciousness in a haze of whisky, tequila, and giggles.

I am in constant motion; unending, rocking, rolling, churning motion.

I'm going to be sick.

Oh, my god, I *am* going to be sick.

I open my eyes, body coated in a slick layer of sweat. I'm laid on my back, head propped on my backpack, looking up at the red sky. The motion isn't the only thing that's woken me either, as a sickly-sweet scent like cream soda mixed with the scent of puss, of infection, fills the air.

I sit up at a right angle, like Frankenstein in that movie where he first wakes up and doesn't know what year he's in.

Crawling on my haunches, I ignore the sound of Xion's ragged breathing as he snoozes beneath his leather jacket, slumped against the high corner of the gondola. Making a dash towards the opposite side of the boat from where he's situated, I lean over the bow, inhaling and exhaling like my life depends on it— which it sort of does, I guess.

"Please do not throw up in my boat." The voice doesn't come from Xion but from the tall, cloaked figure. As she turns, she's revealed as Char, the ferrywoman from my first visit here.

"Huh— what?" Xion stirs at the sound of her voice. Then looks between the two of us.

"Did you make her speak?" he asks me, stunned, and I nod.

"She told me not to throw up over the side of the boat," I wheeze, sucking in the air through my nose even though it's making me feel even sicker than I already do.

"Yes, I'd think we'd all prefer if we could avoid coming into contact with any more of your vomit today." He scowls at me, but I'm not even sorry. I'm in too much pain to feel sorry for anyone but myself.

"What the hell is that smell?" I gasp, leaning back over the edge as my fingers dig into the dark grain of the wood. A bead of sweat trickles down the back of my neck, falling from the damp patch at the base of my skull where my hair clings to me and ending up right between my shoulder blades before it dissipates in the muggy heat. I shudder.

"We're now moving through The Plains of Ichor," Xion explains as I heave. Nothing comes up, which I'm grateful for as my eyes turn down, finding themselves reflected ghostly amongst the milky water.

"Which are?" I ask, feeling better now that I've wretched, and slumping back against the side of the boat. Xion hands me a bottle of water from a satchel he's got at his feet. I take it, grateful for his thoughtfulness.

"This is the place where sinner's bodies are returned to the soil. When you have finished your repentance, you have a re-burial. The hourglass, which is what keeps track of how much time any given sinner has left to serve in this place, is smashed, and the soul released. From here, the body decomposes and is recycled, and the soul returns to The Crucible of Gaia for rebirth." It's all so simple to him, but as I take a sip of water, I realise that being sick isn't my only problem; my head is pounding something awful, too.

"I see," I whisper, using my smallest voice.

He smirks a little, which I guess I deserve.

"Where are we going?" I ask, and he sighs as my drunkenness fades and my fear begins to clutch at me once again, bone deep. The stress of my situation returns too fast and wish I'd never stopped drinking as the boat takes an unapologetic twist and my stomach threatens to heave.

"The Icon. We have no choice but to place you in the highest security facility we have. That means surrounding you with souldiers," he admonishes, and I sigh.

"Great, even more freedom for me to not have," I grumble, leaning back against the wood of the boat and feeling the chill of the water seeping up through the wood of the boat.

"A lot of good freedom will do you once you're dead," Xion retorts, clearly not up for my sarcasm. I get it. I'm a pain in the ass, but if he'd met his biological father, who just so happened to be a socially inept God of The Underworld, and then been to a freaking strip club with him for dinner, he probably would have gotten wasted too.

"Well, once I'm dead, I'll be up in The Higher Plains or whatever—" I twizzle my finger, gesturing upwards.

"Not necessarily, you have to earn your place there. You have no idea what Hercules went through to even earn his visitation rights—" he begins to lecture me, but the thought of floating around in limbo isn't as fun as being in some heavenly realm, so I interrupt him, changing the subject to something I can handle in my fragile state.

"So, what's it like— The Icon?" I ask, unscrewing the cap off the water bottle and taking a sip. The bland nothingness of the cool liquid is a welcome relief— if only the smell would subside for just a few moments, too.

"Well, I'll tell you now that you'll have to be on your guard. Anubis and Osiris are harsh for a reason. The sinners here have committed some of the worst acts you can imagine. Don't try them, Sephy. I mean it. They might struggle to kill you, but they can certainly cut off parts of you and make you wish you were dead, given a dark corner and a semi-sharp object. Alright?" he warns me, and I'm too frightened by the terror in his stare to object. My head is throbbing, and the news of the fact I'm about to be housed in a sea of criminal psychopaths for my own supposed safety is less than comforting.

I stare out over the bow of the boat to the Plains of Ichor. They're glistening wet with golden spider lilies blooming sporadically. Distinct lines dissect the rich-looking soil, almost like someone has used a combine harvester or some other kind of machinery to turn the metallic sheen of the soil into neat columns that rise only slightly into mounds. In fact, the entire place looks like a geometrically flawless golden sea from a distance. The sun above blazes lilac, lighter than it was before. Perhaps that means it's dawn, or maybe not. In this place of so many still unanswered questions, I can't help but let little things like this slide.

We approach The Icon and, even from a distance, I can see it's earned its name. I'm starting to feel the worst of my hangover leave me as the journey has put the steel of my nerves to the test. With every bump, every turn in the river, every swell of the current, I feel the undying urge to puke my guts out, and yet, I somehow remain vomit free. I only wish I could say the same for Xion's shirt, which he's cleaned up as best he can, but is still stained and probably needs to be incinerated for good measure.

It's an enormous pyramid, gleaming golden beneath the red of the sky, only exaggerating its regality. It's unmistakable, iconic, and as the earth fades from gold to an ashy white, I feel dwarfed as its shadow falls over me.

The gondola comes to a halt.

Grabbing my backpack, I step off the boat, uneasy in my heels as they sink into the snowy dander. It's colder here, and I have the feeling that we've been travelling north.

I stare beyond the slanted edge of the pyramid to where a gargantuan obsidian wall climbs, immovable and shadow-esque in its infinite seeming height and length. It glistens as I move, turning light at odd angles from its flat surface and directing it toward the pyramid, making it shine like a beacon in the dark.

I'm gawping at men and women who surround the pyramid, wearing jet black, unmarked, military-style uniforms but with a little twist; these are covered in chains, making them heavy, making the wearer suffer.

I continue to stare but soon have my attention caught by Anubis and Osiris, exiting from an invisible and seamlessly moving door in the base of the structure. They emerge into the light of what I assume is early morning, looking at us both in surprise.

"What on earth are you doing here?" Osiris asks, long white robes sweeping the ground behind his even and graceful tread.

"We've been sent for sanctuary. There has been another attack, this time on Lucifer and Thanatos." Xion makes our intention clear, moving to stand next to me, his satchel slung over one shoulder.

"I see— which Demon Lord was it this time?" she queries.

Xion replies promptly, crossing his hands in front of him.

"Gorgon. We still don't know how they got into the Exilia, but if there's anywhere that's safe, it's got to be here; you have the men to protect her should she need it." He's acting like I'm not even here, and Anubis sweeps my form with her eyes. I wish she'd stop, let me rest a while. I'm exhausted.

"Very well. Follow me, and we'll get you each a room." She says this pointedly, as though we must be separated at all costs.

I frown but then desist, head pounding at an even greater frequency.

She leads us past the wrath and pride sinners and into the pyramid, through many sliding golden doors, and down countless winding and labyrinthine corridors. The walls are spattered with rich lapis lazuli, crafted into images or hieroglyphs, and the deeper we get into the place, the more I feel like I'm being caged by its thick, precious interior. Put into a safe of sorts, from which nobody can touch me and I cannot escape.

The lighting is dim, many Eternal Flames flickering and casting shadows, almost as though I'm in one of those movies about an ancient curse or something.

After what feels like forever, we halt outside two doors opposing one another. Guards are stationed outside each room, and I want to protest but find myself too tired. I just want to sleep.

Please, God, let me sleep.

"Here." Anubis gestures for me to take the room on the right.

I hurry past her, feet aching, heart numb, and head spinning. The inside of the place is simple. Gold floors and walls, no windows, and a lone flickering torch beside a single bed adorned in Egyptian cotton sheets. It's not what I expect, but I can barely hold myself upright as I pull off my shoes and hear the Egyptian goddess shut the door behind me without so much as a goodbye. I'm cut off from Xion, from the outside world, in a cocoon of hard shimmer.

I could be overwhelmed, but instead, I'm too tired to take any of it in. Dumping my backpack on the floor, I throw my jacket beside it and collapse, fully clothed, into an exhausted and all-consuming sleep.

I am woken, pulled from the depths of unconsciousness that's enveloped my brain like a too-warm blanket, by a screeching loud enough to wake the dead— quite literally.

I shoot bolt upright, covering my ears with my pillow.

It's dark, The Eternal Flame having been extinguished somehow, so I hold out a palm, letting the pillow fall from me and using my fear to conjure my own flame to light up the room.

There are no Banshee, which I partially expect to see crouched in the corner; there is only me, in my room, alone.

I get up, nerves frayed and paranoia creeping up my spine like a spider, neck hairs standing on end with each passing second in a wave of instinctual arousal.

I open the door, looking left and then right down the dark corridor. The guards have gone.

What is happening?

The wailing screech continues, over and over, like a fire drill that refuses to cease.

I tread across the hallway knocking once, then twice, before entering Xion's room.

"Sephy?" he calls out into the dark.

He's half asleep, lying on the bed, and my terrified face is illuminated by the small flame cradled in my palms.

"What is that?" I ask him, and he squints at me, leaning half up off the mattress. He's topless and I notice his chest is spattered with dark hair.

"It's okay, it's just the siren. There's probably a demon attack in progress close to the wall," he replies sleepily. I feel the chill of my own room at my back and the warmth of the one before me beckoning.

"You okay?" He rubs one of his eyes, which is bloodshot, with an uncoordinated hand.

"I'm just— I don't think I can sleep knowing that's going on outside. Plus, it's loud," I sigh, exhausted even still. "I'm just so tired," I complain, yawning.

"Come here." He moves over so he's next to the wall, making space for me and patting the crumpled cotton sheets beside him. I frown.

"I—" I begin, but he interrupts me.

"Sephy, it's alright," he promises me, and I willingly believe him.

Stepping lightly across the floor, I extinguish the flame in my palm and curl up next to him. He puts his fingers in my hair and rubs circles around my scalp. I want to protest further, telling him this isn't friend behaviour at all, but the scent of sweet pomegranate is too intoxicating to resist. I relax unwillingly at his touch, at the warmth of his arm curling around me protectively.

I don't know how he does it, but in the midst of a demon war, a blaring siren, and chill paranoia infecting my subconscious, Xion helps me find peace and then sleep.

I hear a knock and stir, skin on fire from his heated proximity.

I look up, then around. The siren has stopped.

Within a second, the door slides open, leaving our sleeping arrangements exposed.

Anubis stands in the doorway, eyes wide with disgust and horror.

Xion stirs only slightly beside me as I stare at her, worried she'll get the wrong impression.

"You weren't in your room. I thought you were dead. Breakfast is in an hour," she announces, turning from the door without another word and sweeping, in all her godly magnificence, away down the corridor, disapproval ringing out in every strike of her heel against cold precious metal.

22

YOU GIVE LOVE A BAD NAME

<u>PANDORA</u>

GORGON IS STARING AT me from across the table, drumming his long fingers against the stone. He's sitting sideways on his seat, feet propped up on the cracked surface, scrutinising me.

"And what makes you so sure, exactly, that Anubis won't just completely disregard your little offer and carry on killing our Kindred?" he asks me, clearly impatient.

"The fact she was so curious about the prospect of resurrecting Ra," I muse, also bored of waiting.

Gorgon laughs, his tight suit widening across his torso as he draws his feet back, straightening upon the stone of his acutely angled chair and leaning forward across the table.

"Yes, I meant to ask you about that part of your little trip. You know you don't actually have the power to resurrect anyone? Let alone a god. How exactly are you planning on getting around that little hitch? The only person with powers over resurrection who'd even listen to you is Moloch, and he's long gone to The Island of The Blessed. You know even I haven't been blessed with such an ability." He looks at me with dead eyes, and I stare at him with a smirk, amused by his challenge and lack of faith.

"I hadn't really thought that far ahead— but if I had, I'd ask you to remember that blessing is not the only way to possess the power of a god. Which has been so recently evidenced by the very person causing this conversation." His eyes widen slightly before he laughs as though I'm stupid.

"I think you're confused, Pandora. Lucifer can't resurrect the dead; she merely works in a graveyard where the dead rise into doppelganger forms. The Resurrection Flame is responsible. I thought you would at least know that." He cocks his head, greasy hair trailing down across his large forehead in vine-like curls, clinging to him.

"And I would have thought you'd know that I would not mistake re-birth into a doppelganger body for *actual* resurrection, Gorgon. I mean bringing them back into living, breathing, ageing bodies, or in the case of gods, bringing them back as a single entity, whereby their energies are fully intact." I smirk at him, and he looks curious, slit pupils narrowing even further.

"Lucifer does not possess such a skill," he scoffs at me.

Ye of little faith.

"How would we know? She's not exactly well acquainted with her Ancient half," I suggest. He frowns, looking stupid as he brushes away this idea without second thought.

"I see. Well, if speculation is your only foundation for making such a claim, I sincerely hope that Anubis can't tell you're lying." He licks his bottom row of teeth, sighing and looking at his knuckles with a half-bored smirk. I want to roll my eyes, to yell, bang my fists down on the table, and tell him to stop being so damn closed-minded. But alas, I am far too self-contained and in control for such a plight.

A few moments pass in silence and I concentrate on my breathing, trying to ignore the nagging feeling that every single person around me constantly underestimates my capabilities. I'm not merely a banished Titan with a box, because in travelling the lower plains unaided you must be more than that. It's not a safe place for someone like me, someone who questioned the gods and lost as I have lost.

"Ahhh— you are being summoned." Gorgon twists to where, in the stone of the floor beside us, a seven-pointed star — the symbol of the Nexus — is burning. I smile, content that I've already convinced Anubis to change her mind.

"I better be going." I get to my feet, and Gorgon slides something across the table to me.

"What's this? A parting gift, for me?" I place my hand across my heart in faux-smitten plight, unable to help but give in to my feminine side, smiling as I pick it up.

It's a velvet green bag and inside, as I loosen the drawstrings and pull the folds of fabric, I find something that causes me to gasp slightly.

"Well, I never— where did you get this?" I ask, surprise pleasantly marring my features.

"One of my children swiped it from Lucifer's alchemy stores," he brags, clearly pleased with himself. I stare into the vial; curious as the glistening powder shifts effortlessly like fine sand.

"It's very pretty—" I compliment, confused. "What's it for?" I ask him, and he leans back.

"It's ground fire opal. The finest powder," he explains, and I shrug, still not understanding.

"I don't—" I express, and he cocks his head.

"Pyromancers are susceptible to fire opal; it saps their powers. Thought it might come in useful. My children also tell me that the demi-goddess is convecting already, be it with limited capability," he adds, and I feel my surprise grow further.

"Well, then, this is the most thoughtful gift I've ever received." I take a step forward to shake his hand, but instead, he turns from me, standing quickly and moving fluidly across the room, avoiding contact.

"I'll gather the others. We'll be waiting patiently for your return," he informs me. I'm clearly not meant to take the gift as anything more than a tool with which to apprehend my target.

I don't say another word as he leaves the room, and I'm left with only the scorch marks of the seven-pointed star upon stone to indicate anything has changed.

Smiling and hopeful, I take the box from my pocket and slide the desired panel open, envisioning the throne room of The Icon once again and feeling my connection with the box grow. Watching the whirring portal start up, I step through to meet my summoner.

"You rang?" I call, finding Anubis standing, impatient, behind her three pet Jackals. Osiris is beside her, face uncertain. The dogs shift as the portal closes behind me, and I slide the lid of the box shut, replacing it inside my pocket.

"It has become apparent that you were correct, Pandora. This girl, she's dangerous. She cannot separate her head from her heart," Anubis informs me. Whatever the girl has done to inspire this change is well-timed to say the least.

"I see," I reply, trying to keep my expression stoic. I flip my hair back over one shoulder, waiting expectantly for her to continue. After all, *she* summoned *me*.

"I cannot see any other solution at this point other than to destroy her," she concludes with a pained look staining her flawlessly painted face. This time I smile without restraint.

"And how exactly do you plan to do that?" I ask her, and she sighs.

"A little doping should do the trick. I'll invite her to dinner and have her sedated. Once she's out, you can take her back to the Demon Lords." She's thought this through, which is hardly surprising; she's smart. "But my son and I will also be taking the same sedative. I do not wish to be implicated in this, Pandora. Do you understand?" She is firm, crossing her arms across the white-wrapped linen of her floor-length gown. I bow my head, acknowledging her desire.

"I understand. Haedes would not be best pleased if he discovered you were giving up his little girl, now, would he?" I ask, wry, and she shakes her head, causing her thick golden jewellery to clatter around her neck and against her jaw.

"I don't know how much he'd care to be honest. So, if you're trying to use her for any other reason than to ensure this prophecy does not come to fruition, then I'm not sure it's wise," she warns me.

I frown.

Does she know I intend to blackmail Haedes into handing me his Kingdom? Is this a trick?

"You have my word. It is merely for protection, for all our sakes," I lie, and she nods, eyelids fluttering. "I have something for you actually," I add, smiling, trying to keep things civil.

I pass her the green velvet bag, removing it from my cleavage where I placed it for the journey.

She moves forward, the Jackals parting before her as her sandalled feet step softly across the gold of the floor. Her eyes widen as she takes it in her palm.

"What is it?" she demands more information, peering into the bottom of the bag.

"Ground fire opal. It should weaken her. Just in case. Try mixing that in with the sedative," I suggest, and she smiles.

"That's very thoughtful of you. Thank you." She is only mildly grateful, as though I've just presented her with a new hat. We're demure, proper in all respects and etiquette, as though we're not discussing the subject of kidnap and murder at all.

"Well, we are in this together, for the greater good. Is that all then?" I ask, noticing she looks suddenly eager to have the conversation over with. Murder is so often misconstrued as unsavoury rather than necessity after all.

"Yes, we will eat later tonight. You should return and watch the dinner from nearby in sinner attire, if you come back just before, I will have a servant attend you," she decrees.

Simple.

"Very well, I'll make sure it's taken care of quickly. If you know what I mean." Her eyes soften, and I realise that she's probably actually torn up about this. Where Anubis is hardened, she is also a mother, and with that comes weakness for the children of others, even if that does include Haedes.

"You must leave now; they'll be here for breakfast soon. I don't want to be implicated. If I hear you so much as whisper my name, I'll have you slaughtered, and you should also know that while I might be unconscious, I'll also be surrounded by guards, so don't try anything funny," she threatens me, clearly uncomfortable with the arrangement but sure she's doing what is right and not what is easy.

"You have my word. Good day." I speak my words of parting, reaching for the box once more. I open a panel, the portal spilling from within as I picture the Fallen Kingdom clearly in my mind.

The Jackals bark at the disturbance in the air, and I hear Osiris scold them this time. If you ask me, this is the most control he's taken of any situation, ever. He's a mommy's boy for sure, though with a mother like Anubis, it's not hard to see why.

Back in the Fallen Kingdom, I step out of the mist of the box's innards and back into the mirrored chamber. Here, the five Demon Lords have assembled, waiting for me with bored expressions.

"That was fast," Gorgon observes, his expression momentarily worried.

The rest of the other Demon Lords are sitting around the table, except for Barbas who is standing. They all stare at me, expectant.

"Anubis and Osiris have agreed to sedate the girl; I will be bringing her here," I announce, and they all smile.

All of them except Lilliana.

"We're going to kill her?" It's more a statement than a question, but she poses it as if she's waiting for my instruction. I shake my head.

"No, we're going to use her as blackmail. Her life for Mortaria. Your children will starve no longer," I vow. They all look genuinely surprised, even if it is subtle.

"You truly think Haedes will hand over Mortaria for his daughter?" Abraxis demands.

"I believe he is weak, just as all parents are weak when it comes to their children," I make this pointed remark, noting how he sits back, as though defeated. I have studied these Lords for a while now, and this has only helped me in the long run. I know that Xion is a personal weakness for Abraxis, even if he would never admit it.

"Very well. Then it is done. What would you like us to do?" Katerina enquires, every breath she inhales painfully apparent as her ribs push against the boning of her corset. They all stare at me with unsure gazes.

Could it be that they're looking to me as their leader now?

I smile. This is exactly where I want them, exactly the power dynamic I have been craving, whereby they work for me.

"Now, you will go to the Dark Colosseum and ready the strongest of your Kindred to tear her apart should Haedes say no. The rest of your children should be sent to protect the perimeter, should anyone try to stage a rescue," I order them, looking to Lilliana now, "Except for you. You will give me two of your strongest fighters to accompany me when I go and deliver the ultimatum to Haedes, then go and dispatch the rest of your Kindred for the main event," I demand.

"Yes, of course," she replies, subservient.

I have broken them, shown them that I am smart, that I can bargain with gods who have taken so much from them in years gone past. I have shown them I can rule. This is just the first step of course, but it is an important one, for in convincing the Demon Lords that I am worthy of their respect, of their loyalty, I am one step closer to once again standing among gods. This time, though, it will be different—different gods, Ancient gods, gods to whom I will matter.

I will show them.

I will prove myself.

I will have my revenge.

SEPHY

What am I doing?

This is the only question I can seem to form as I sit on the edge of my bed, back in my room. I'd left Xion stirring in his sleep and been unable to fathom staying in the room with him a second longer. Having changed my clothes into the only other set I currently possess, which had been stuffed into my backpack, I lean back, letting my hair fall down my spine and looking up to the ceiling.

Why do I keep sleeping with him? That's so— not me. Like not even in the same zipcode as me.

Is it him? Or is it me? Or is it this fucked up situation I can't seem to escape, like some kind of nightmare that's come and infected my life, poisoning what I thought I knew and causing me to become victim to its potent darkness?

Ugh. I'm beginning to sound like a warning on a Ouija board.

I place my head in my hands, pulling my fingers through my hair as it falls forward in a fiery wave, and sigh out, trying to gain some kind of hold on reality, on what's really going on.

Why can't I keep my boundaries straight with him?

Is it Xion in particular? Or is it the fact that it seems like he's the only one who has my interests at heart without bias or ulterior motive? Surely it can't be anything *that* ridiculous or sentimental. I mean come on; I'd never be *that* chick.

A knock at the door startles me.

"Come in," I call, not bothering to move.

It's Xion.

He steps across the threshold and into the room, expression giving nothing away. I look up to him; his molten eyes are, as ever, full of concern for me.

Why do you do that? You're supposed to be a demon, not a freaking puppy! I cuss internally.

"What's wrong?" he asks me, and I shrug, not wanting to tell him just how confused he makes me.

"Just stressed. My usual tension-relief activities are kind of off the table for now." I exhale, bored of this place, bored of running, bored of being afraid.

"Which are?" he enquires, crossing his arms and causing the leather of his jacket to crinkle at his inner elbow.

"Quick and easy sex, beating the crap out of Jacque, my personal trainer— riding Nightshade." I list them off, and his mouth quirks at the side.

"Well, I'm sure I can help with at least one of those." My eyes widen at this sentiment, and my mouth goes dry.

"Excuse me?" I stutter, and he laughs.

"Training. We could go out onto the Ashen Waste, give you some more practice with your powers?" he suggests, and I exhale, disappointed for some reason.

"Xion—" I find myself more curious than I want to admit, unable to stop myself from asking the question.

"Yes?" he replies, his gorgeous ruggedness only exaggerated by the fact that he's just recently woken.

"You don't want to fuck me, right?" I ask him, trying to sound cocky, trying to remind him of who he is dealing with. I don't do relationships; I do quick, easy, and fun.

He laughs, though the sound is hollow.

"Don't flatter yourself." With this remark, his voice is somewhat pained, but I guess that's because I've taken him giving me comfort last night a step too far.

"Sorry, it's all this change making me act like an emotional psycho. I've been afraid. I can't be that way anymore. What happened last night— it can't happen again. I was being ridiculous," I announce, heartless, and he nods.

"Understood. Come on, it's time for breakfast." He doesn't wait for me to leave the room; he simply goes, leaving me trailing behind him.

After an awkward breakfast, where Osiris decides to inform me of exactly why sinners don't need to eat, or sleep, for that matter, Xion and I head out of the pyramid.

"You know I really could have done without knowing about how dead bodies work under The Resurrection Flame— like I know I asked about where the sinners were eating— but did Osiris have to get that graphic?" I complain to Xion as a final golden door slides aside in front of us.

Stepping out into the cool Mortarian air, I'm startled to find it snowing.

"His people used to pull brains out of dead guys' noses with steel hooks. Subtlety isn't his forte." Xion reminds me, and I muse over this momentarily. He does have a point.

"Snow?" I query the weather, quickly changing the subject, and he shakes his head.

"Ash. Though I can see why you would think otherwise." As he speaks, stoic in tone and expression after our prior conversation, I hold out a palm, letting a few flakes of ash fall upon my hot skin. When I examine our surroundings I realise the ground is covered in off-grey powder, not the pure white snow I had first thought, and kick at it with my boot. It moves like dust with hardly any weight to it, spraying up in front of me.

I sputter.

"Don't inhale that. It's not good for those of us still living. And while Osiris might not have the best table manners, it's important you know the difference between us and the doppels. We're alive. We need to eat, to sleep. They can choose to, but they don't have to. Some sinners aren't allowed to eat, gluttony sinners for example, while others are forbidden from sleeping; those would be the sloth sinners," he explains, keeping things factual.

"I see— any other differences I should know about?" I ask, trying to keep the conversation moving as we begin to tread away from The Icon.

"They can't leave. They need the sun. A few have tried to escape, but their blood won't let them cross any portal. They're stuck here until they're redeemed," he explains, and I nod. It makes sense.

"I haven't upset you, have I?" I ask him, concerned about what he thinks of me. This is, indeed, unfamiliar territory where I'm concerned, and I'm beginning to dislike it.

"Why would you think that?" He looks surprised, and I shrug as my feet leave imprints in the ash underfoot.

"I don't know; I came to you last night, and then— I don't know." I truly don't know how to express how I'm feeling to him.

He smiles, but sadness lingers behind his eyes as he runs his hand through his hair, dislodging a thick layer of ash. Unfortunately, it looks like he has chronic dandruff.

"Look, Sephy, you're scared and being hunted. I don't hold you to anything you do. You came to me last night, but I'm your security guard. It's natural. I know it doesn't mean anything. You don't have to worry. I'm perfectly aware that you don't possess a single shred of feeling towards me or any man for that matter." I'm slightly relieved, but then a heaviness fills my chest as his final words ring out in my ears.

"Thank you," I reply, but he doesn't smile, instead placing a hand on the leather of my jacket.

"Don't mention it. Now come on; let's go hitch a ride to the Waste," he suggests, lowering his hand down the length of my arm and grabbing my palm in his firmly.

"I could always try convecting—" I suggest, and he turns to me in surprise.

"I think it might be a bit much for you to convect us both. You're still bonding with your goddess half. I don't want to tire you out before we've even seen any demons." He reminds me of what we're here for, and I wonder why I'm willingly walking into The Ashen Waste with him. Why am I seeking out the demons that are already hunting me?

I know the answer as an open-top cart full of sinners in dark armour comes into view. We continue to move through the ash, which plumes up beneath our feet, toward it in silence.

It's because I'm tired of running. I'm tired of being afraid.

Do I have a death wish?

Maybe.

Or maybe I'm fucked up enough to think Xion will be there, muscles bulging, ass-kicking— defending me.

I momentarily consider slapping myself as this thought crosses my mind.

What have I become?

A woman who needs defending?

Not today.

Balling my fists by my sides, we reach the open-top trailer attached to four Percherons, standing in two lines of two. The armoured sinners turn, six women and four men, all staring at Xion and me as we step up into the crude wood of the vehicle. I sit beside Xion in the only remaining space, facing away from the horses, and as the driver senses that his load is full, he slaps a whip against the behinds of the Percherons, and we jolt into motion. The trailer reminds me of something I saw cattle transported in once, with dark wood railings and simple wooden benches lining the edges.

I pull my hood from the sweater I'm wearing beneath the leather of my jacket up over my head, knowing my hair is a dead giveaway of my lineage.

Xion's thigh and his shoulder push into the side of my body, squashing me against a woman with black hair beside me. I peek out from under my hood as we approach the large obsidian wall, noting a pendant of deep bloody garnet hanging around her neck.

As we reach the wall, I watch several sinners spin an enormous wheel made of the same dark crystal protruding from the base of the construct. The gate's crisscrossing metal bars lift slowly from the ash rising a few inches above the lowest hanging struts, allowing us passage to the other side.

With another crack of the whip, the horses' momentum begins again, and we lurch forward. I stare up, the aroma of the air stale in my nostrils like the scent of a bonfire long since extinguished. Crossing my legs, I twist atop the bench, gaping at the enormous archway we pass through without falter.

The wall is thick, extremely thick, and as we emerge on the other side, I can see why it's necessary. The sinners around us visibly tense, and I turn my gaze from the wall to the horizon behind me.

My eyes widen, breath catching in my chest.

They sprawl, in thousands, across the ash-smothered land. Demons fighting with sinners in a timeless clash to the death beneath the crimson endlessness of the sky.

"Wow," I express.

Xion nods.

"Now you see the need for the wall," he adds.

I look at him, peeking from beneath my hood and into the molten bronze of his eyes, which have heated considerably, reflecting the sky.

"I do. Have you ever— fought out here?" I ask him, and he nods again.

"I spent years here, learning to channel my rage, control my inner demon. In fact, I probably spent more than two decades in this crap heap," he sighs, and I wonder how he's not traumatised or permanently paranoid. Even from this distance, the scent of blood and metal is thick in the air, and the din of clashing swords and the smashing of claws and teeth against armour is loud beyond what I can bear.

The cart comes to a halt only a few hundred metres from the wall, for what I assume is the safety of the horses. The sinners depart first as I continue to gawp around, unable to take in the magnitude of the event before me, before Xion grabs my hand and pulls me along behind him.

Stepping down onto the ground, the ash is thicker here, and I note that the fall of it from the sky is heavier too.

The wind whips around me, a deep chill gripping my bones.

Wonderful. I cuss, wondering if getting out of the pyramid for some utterly stale air was the best idea.

"Come on, let's go toward the edge; that way we can find a few strays to practice on," Xion suggests, moving through the sinners who are drawing swords from their belts and pulling shields off their backs. I feel slightly naked without a weapon of any kind, but then I remember that I *am* a weapon. Xion pulls out the twisted obsidian knife from the back of his dark jeans as we move across the wasteland in silence. I stare at it, underwhelmed.

Well, at least he's not compensating for anything. I think, wondering if he shouldn't have brought maybe a sword— or a bazooka.

Unnerved by the battle taking place not a mile north of where we're trekking along the length of the wall, I can't think of anything to say that isn't laced with my own fears, so we move on in silence.

After what feels like forever, we reach a point far left of the main fighting. I'm worried we're too far away, but Xion stiffens momentarily in posture at my side almost immediately, and I know he's sensing demons approaching fast.

"They can sense your power. Prepare yourself," he warns me.

I grit my teeth, using my fear to ignite a ball of flame in my palm. I hold it up, squinting into the grey fog caused by the smear of falling ash, heart beginning to race.

Xion widens his stance beside me, his long leather coat blowing around him as the wind ruffles his dark hair and we stare out into the waste together.

The first demons approach, moving faster than I remember. They're Banshee, and I have flashbacks to the first time I'd seen one. To the way it screamed and smashed all the mirrors in my old ballet studio, to the way I broke its neck with my bare hands.

"Ready?" Xion asks as their tread becomes audible in my ears, a repetitive muted pounding getting only more insistent as they grow closer and closer.

"Ready," I reply, widening my stance and preparing.

Come on you skanky ass dogs. I curse under my breath, riling myself for the fight, for the struggle.

The three Banshees are about to reach us, but before they do, I take out one by hitting it with a ball of flame. It whimpers, falling to the ground and catching alight, clearly weaker than the one I'd fought before.

A second Banshee flies over the body of its packmate, soaring through the air, nine-inch claws outstretched and aiming for my throat. It knocks me back, and as I fall to the ground, not ready for the impact, ash flies up around us in a spectacular cloud of dove grey. I remember the weight of Cerb hitting me in a similar but much less lethal way, and so bring up my arms, shielding my face and holding back the head of the demon as I focus, recalling the funky rhythm of *You give love a bad name* in my head.

Snapping jaws come within inches of my face, but after only a few seconds, I've convected from beneath the body of the beast and am extending out a leash of fire, wrapping the burning flame around the Banshee's neck from behind. I yank so hard that the beast falls to the floor in a heap before burning to ash. It blows away, inconspicuous amongst the blanketed landscape around us.

I turn to find the other beast under Xion's knee, its neck thick, and yet no match for him even in mortal form. He gestures for me to assist, so I throw my arm around in the air like I'm bowling, hitting the incapacitated demon straight between the eyes with a perfect sphere of scorching fire.

Exhaling, he looks at me with a smile.

"Very nice."

I'm out of breath, my heart pounding and my adrenaline pumping in my veins. It's almost like I was made for this. Like fighting demons is what I've been missing all along.

"Who's up next?" I question, widening my stance and readying to fight whatever the waste throws at me next.

We've killed a good amount of demons by the time I find myself getting fatigued. It's been a constant ballet of fireballs arcing through the sky, the breaking of bones, and the blocking out of dying screams. Xion and I work well together, but as I finish off a particularly long-legged Phobia attempting to outmanoeuvre me, Xion's eyes catch mine.

His gaze travels behind me.

"Sephy, behind you! Watch out!" I spin, finding a demon I've never seen before, towering over me. It's ghostly white with glowing red eyes, gangly arms and legs, and razor-sharp teeth that could be as long as ten inches. It's like a vampire has bitten that creepy slender man from the horror stories I'd heard as a child, and I feel sick as I look up at it, dumbstruck.

Ew. Someone fetch this thing a paper bag, it's burning my eyes! Is all I have time to fathom as it moves closer.

I hadn't expected the demons to come at me from behind. Enemies never do that in movies; they only ever come from where the fighter can see them—

"Sephy, watch out!" Xion repeats, as though he thinks I haven't heard him. I can understand why as I'm rooted to the spot, examining the thing with morbid fascination.

The demon pulls back a long thin arm and brings it down. It's aiming for my face, but I raise an arm at the last minute so the long, knife-like nails of the beast slash through the leather of my jacket, my hoody and then the flesh of my forearm instead. I cry out, falling back to the ground and gritting my teeth after, trying to focus despite the pain as the unspecified demon moves toward me too fast.

I crawl back in the dirt, the ash cool between my fingers. My arm is bleeding, and as I try to raise a hand to summon a flame, defending myself, I'm eclipsed as a dark shadow puts itself between me and harm's way.

I watch as Xion transforms, skin rippling from white to black, glowing as it's mapped with orange swirling tattoos. Within seconds the demon is dead, slashed to pieces viciously by Xion's obsidian blade.

Exhaling, I feel the wind pick up, slowly getting to my feet and using my uninjured arm to summon yet another flame, this time directing it to the crumpled body on the floor, destroying the demon once and for all.

"What was that?" I exclaim.

Xion turns to me, looking down into my wide eyes with his own. They're entirely black with glowing orange pupils.

"A Succubi," he grumbles, demonic voice too deep. It causes a shudder to run through me as I step toward him, placing a hand upon his cheek and feeling the roughness of his flesh. He doesn't flinch away this time but merely stands, muscles pulsating and breathing ragged as I examine him with fascination. His alien pupils scan me, concern filling them despite their unnerving colour. I reach up, letting the skin of my entire palm blaze hot. I temper my rage, bringing it up to his face and letting the blaze illuminate his skin.

As The Eternal Flame lightens his charred flesh, it ripples, returning to that of a man in part. He inhales deeply as his orange eyes turn back to bronze, his skin tinged red by the sky above.

"What— what are you doing?" he sounds broken as his voice changes from demonic to human and back again.

"I don't know. I just had this hunch. Guess I was right," I express as he reaches up to touch the patch of skin that is now olive flesh and nothing more.

He sighs.

"You— you made the demon part of me—" he's almost speechless and I smile, pleased with myself.

"Recede— I guess." I shrug, letting my hand drop. As it does, his demon form completely dissolves, leaving him as the man I've come to know as my friend.

"Thanks for taking care of that," I sigh, frustrated that once again I'd been bested, but grateful he'd been there.

"It's my job," he replies, turning from me and cutting off the conversation. "We should get back; you're hurt." He gestures to my arm, which is leaking blood down my arm and dripping off my fingertips, staining the ground scarlet.

I guess playtime is over.

When we get back to our rooms in The Icon, a disapproving and divine stare is waiting for us.

"So nice of you to return. Where have you been might I ask?" Anubis' disapproving tone seeps through the air like noxious gas. My arm is throbbing, blood still leaking from the gash caused by the Succubi.

"We went out to the Ashen Waste, to train," I reply.

Anubis' expression turns incredulous.

"That's absurd. Why would anyone being hunted by demons actively seek them out?" she asks me, and I shrug.

"Maybe I'm just not all that afraid anymore," I retort, coming across braver than I feel.

"I see you are not without some consequence." She gestures to my arm. I roll my eyes.

"You know, I'm pretty sick of people treating me like some kind of a pet. You can't just stick me in a cage for my own damn protection and expect me to just sit inside. I'm a demi-goddess, and I need to keep using my powers. Haedes told me that," I argue with her. The flickering light of the sconces makes her look dangerous as her dark eyes flash and her high cheekbones are cast in shadow, making them appear sharp as razor blades.

"Well, I'm sure Haedes had your safety at the top of his priority list." She's being sarcastic, but before I can get into a full-on shouting match with her, Xion interjects.

"Just drop it, Anubis, it's done now. And she's fine. Now, what can I do for you?" he demands, irritated.

"I wanted to invite you to dinner. I left you both something to wear in your rooms. We'll eat in an hour," she decrees.

I nod, entirely not looking forward to more dead anatomy lessons with Osiris.

"I'd love to, thanks," I call after her in a fake happy voice as she's already turned and begun to stalk back towards wherever it is she's headed.

"You shouldn't anger her, Sephy. She's—" he begins, but I cock an eyebrow.

"A bitch?" I ask, and he smirks.

"Giving us her hospitality," he corrects me.

I sigh.

"Could've fooled me."

"We best get ready for dinner. Are you alright with dressing that wound? There are bandages and stuff in your backpack," he informs me, and I feel a little violated knowing he's been through my stuff.

"I know there is, I packed them. And you know you really shouldn't worry so much. After all, I'm a demi-goddess, right?" I remind him.

"That would be correct," he acknowledges.

"Then you should know by now that I can look after myself," I bite out, pushing him even further away. The way in which he so readily jumped to my aid before scares me. The way his expression fills with fear when I'm hurt or scared also frightens me. He's too close; pushing in on the walls I've worked so hard to keep strong all these years.

"Alright then," he breathes in a whisper, turning from me and putting his door between us.

23

WALK LIKE AN EGYPTIAN

SEPHY

I LOOK AT MYSELF in the mirror, impressed with Anubis' perception of my tastes. The woman might be mean as a snake, but damn has she got style.

I'm wearing a high-necked black tunic layered with hundreds of feather-esque leather pieces. I have tight-fitting black leggings on beneath and soft black leather boots with flat soles. My hair is wild and loose around my shoulders, curling slightly as the fiery auburn twizzles down into strawberry blonde at the tips. My eyes are surrounded by provided eyeliner, which is little more than a stick of charcoal, and my lips are slathered in deep plum lipstick that managed to survive the journey right at the bottom of my backpack. I hear a knock sound at the door and exhale, knowing that it's Xion, and ready to get this meal over with.

Checking myself out with one final glance into the reflective gold of the walls, I turn on the flat heel of my boot and move to the door, which slides aside, revealing Xion on the other side.

He's wearing a sleeveless black leather vest, the square cut making his biceps bulge against the seams of the shoulders. It's high-necked, causing his jaw to become more prominent than I've ever seen it. He's wearing black leather pants and black boots to match, too.

He stares at me as I come into view, eyes widening with approval.

"You look nice," he compliments me, and I smile, a little awkward after earlier, but trying to push on despite my attempts to distance myself from him emotionally.

"Thanks, you too— I guess Anubis wanted us to look like twins or something—" I conclude. He smirks, looking down at himself.

"Yeah, this cut-off sleeve thing really isn't my style," he sighs, and I look up at him with a cocked eyebrow. If you ask me, the cut-off sleeves are *very much* his style, but I don't say that. I simply try to keep a straight face, staring ahead as we travel through the endless golden labyrinth of The Icon's interior.

We're silent as we reach the dining room where we'd taken break-fast with the pair this morning, finding a more elaborate and far less casual set-up this time around. The smell of cooking meat, garlic, and cayenne fills the air, and I inhale deeply, not at all impressed by the aroma but knowing from experience that many delicacies taste better than they smell.

Anubis and Osiris sense our presence, but something I'd not no-ticed before catches my eye before they've fully passed the threshold opposing us. An enormous pendulum swings, torturously slow, be-hind the golden pillars that stand before a wall at the far end of the room. I wonder if it's there for any purpose other than to make time appear as though it's moving incredibly slowly, but then am distracted once again as Anubis coughs, causing me to turn and grace her with my full and undivided attention.

"Welcome. Please, be seated. Dinner will be served momentarily." She gestures to the table, so Xion and I waste no time pulling out our seats. I position myself at the foot of the table, opposite Anubis, who sits at the head, wearing a black and gold off-the-shoulder gown. The seats are high-backed in gold with cobalt velvet padding and sapphires embedded into the armrests. I place my elbows on the table, edged with a border embedded with lapis lazuli, and look down at my reflection in the gilded plate before me, decorated with intricate scarab designs around the rim. The cutlery is heavy, engraved with a pyramid on the hilt of each piece, perhaps a tribute to The Icon itself. I move them aside to get to what's underneath. Taking the thick, woven, midnight blue napkin, which feels like papyrus from old s, I open it and place it into my lap as I cross my ankles under the table. Glancing up, I find myself under the scrutiny of my fellow diners.

"Very nice— art," I compliment them, gesturing to several hiero-glyphic paintings on the wall beside me.

"I'm glad you think so. They're a tribute to the human suffering and pain that was inflicted under my rule," Anubis elaborates. I press my lips together.

Well, this isn't awkward—

287

"So, how are you two finding The Ashen Waste?" Osiris asks us, far more interested in making conversation than his mother. I'm grateful for the change of subject.

"It is startling, to say the least. I'm lucky Xion was with me earlier—I guess I had no idea quite how many demons there are out there," I admit, trying to come off humble, wondering if perhaps this will appease Anubis.

As servants, dressed in white cloth twisted artfully around their bodies for modesty, enter the room, the smell of something not entirely savoury fills the air, and then my nostrils. I wonder, trying to smile through my disgust, what exactly it is I've done to offend Anubis to begin with. Why is she so hostile towards me? Is it because of whom I'm related to? Or is it that she wants Xion for herself maybe? This second option seems less plausible than the first to me, especially as I lay no claim to Xion, despite what she may think.

"I'm sure you were glad to have him by your side, you two seem very close." Osiris looks between us, and I laugh.

"We've been put together in a very challenging set of circumstances. I have no choice but to be close to him. He's my guide here. I'm a stranger in a strange land so to speak," I remind him, trying to divert the conversation.

"But surely you must have some personal feeling toward the man, I mean, he has saved your life many times over, has he not?" Anubis asks the question this time as a trolley is wheeled in by a female server with pale skin and black hair, pulled back in a long braid. Her eyes startle me, their lilac pupils too pale, but I try to remain focused.

"He has. But I think if you'd ask him, he'd tell you it was more his duty than anything else," I express, looking to Xion for aid.

"Absolutely," he replies, and Anubis frowns as the sentiment reaches her.

"We've seen how you look at her, Xion. You need not conceal it," Osiris coaxes him, and he stiffens in his seat.

"You are correct. I need not conceal something that does not exist and is a figment of your imagination. I don't know where you two are getting this from, but I'm merely Sephy's security guard," he vouches, and for some reason, his response pains me.

I reach forward to a glass and gold goblet encrusted with sapphires as a servant comes over, pouring red wine from the depths of an urn. I frown at the custom but move to take a sip.

It's not whisky, but it'll do.

Anubis watches us, moving to give an order to the woman approaching me with a steaming cauldron full of what looks to be soup. It's a slimy green in colour, almost like someone has heated up pond scum.

Oh, sweet Jesus.

"What is this?" I interrupt her as she opens her mouth to speak before slamming it shut again. Osiris picks up the conversation.

"Molokhia," he replies, and I frown.

"Apologies for my ignorance, but what exactly is that?" I ask him, and Anubis interrupts her son again, clearly uncomfortable with being silent for too long.

"It is a soup, which can also be used as a dressing on certain meats, you may know it by the name the Jew's Mallow?" she enquires.

I raise my eyebrows. That does sound familiar.

"Is it an Egyptian staple?" I try to sound interested, and she nods. "I see. Well, it smells, interesting—" I feel my nostrils quiver as she smiles at me.

The sinner pushing the cart looks at me with a dead stare, moving toward my place setting and serving me before all the other guests. She takes an enormous gold ladle, pulls a bowl from the bottom shelf of the trolley, and places it atop my plate, a ceremony more than a meal if you ask me. Carefully ladling the green scum into the bowl, she gives me an odd smile before departing and moving to Osiris, Anubis, and then finally to Xion.

Anubis watches me expectantly.

"Go on— try it, you'll like it," she encourages me, suddenly calmer than I've seen her since we met. She takes a sip of her wine, as I pick up a heavy golden spoon, leaning forward and taking a decent sized scoop of the dish before me. "You may leave us," Anubis orders the servants, pausing before taking her own food into her mouth, watching me intently. Her scrutiny scorches me, leaving me annoyed and helpless all at once. It'd be rude not to finish what I've been given, an insult to their heritage or something equally as ridiculous, so I figure I might as well try and get this over with in as few mouthfuls as possible.

Lifting it to my lips, I take it into my mouth, letting the slimy texture coat my tongue. It's gritty too, almost like someone forgot to filter out the sand.

"Is it meant to be gritty like this?" I ask, mouth barely opening and closing as the stickiness attempts to wrangle me into lockjaw.

"Oh yes, that's quite normal," Osiris assures me, tucking into his own bowl with fervour. I watch Xion, equally as hesitant, placing his spoon into his mouth as the woman with the trolley walks away slowly. We eat in silence, my mouth working hard to avoid the vinegary, yet somehow bitter, taste of the dish. I want to wince, to spit it out, but I'm also at the table of a Titan and her son who are keeping me safe from demons who want to kill me, so I guess throwing up is probably a no-no.

I watch the pendulum swing behind Anubis' chair, the torturously slow to-ing and fro-ing of the golden pendant causing my pupils to swing with it. I continue to chew and swallow fast, the only sounds that of clattering spoons and working mouths as conversation ceases.

The pendulum sweeping along its slow and precise path is the last thing I remember seeing, the effect of its motion hypnotic and calming to me. I hear the spoon fall from my hand, feel my body go limp, but cannot utter a single plea.

Blackness shortly follows.

XION

Darkness has fallen over everything, I'm paralysed, and my demon self is stirring, struggling even, beneath the effects of something— something wrong, something chemical. I open my eyes.

The hands sprawled out on the table before me are black, charred, and popping with veins.

What happened? What did I do? I wonder momentarily, getting déjà vu from the many times I've come to after killing or something equally as deplorable.

I look to my left.

Anubis and Osiris are being shaken awake by servants, their eyes bloodshot and their faces confused.

"What—" I begin, looking down at the bowl of now cold green soup before me. Then I look to my right.

She's gone.

I'm on my feet before I know it, staring around the room for any hint of her. My demon self becomes untameable beneath my charred flesh, the red mist coming across my field of vision as the swirling tattoos burn my flesh with the heat of my temper. I throw my chair aside, gritting my teeth and feeling my heart breaking inside my chest.

I failed.

She's gone, maybe even dead.

Storming across the dining room, I grab one of the servants by the throat and slam him against the far wall. The pendulum, swinging across its path, smashes into the side of his body without mercy.

"*Where is she*!?" I yell, fingers tightening around his oesophagus. Blood pounds beneath my fingertips, hot and vital. His eyes widen as he struggles for breath, dark skin and equally dark eyes becoming damp as I continue to assert pressure.

"I— I—"

"Xion! That's *enough!*" Anubis screams.

I drop the man to the floor, turning and rounding on her instead.

"*Where is she*?!" I bellow in her face. My voice, deeper than thunder, ruffles her hair.

"I don't know! We've all been drugged! I have no idea where she could be! The only thing I can think is that she's been kidnapped by the Demon Lords." Her eyes are full of fear, causing me to relax; she's as confused and disoriented as I am. "Abdul, go and check on the rest of the guards, see if anyone found anything. Sergei, go and ready my chariot; we're going to be needing it for our journey to The Exilia." She speaks calmly, but her words are simply fuel to my temper, which explodes once more in a burst of heated conflict.

"The Exilia? What about Sephy!? What about The Fallen Kingdom!? We can't just leave her! She's going to be slaughtered, Anubis!" I exclaim, and she narrows her eyes.

"Look. I don't know what to do. But I know that if we're going to try and rescue Sephy at all, you, Osiris, and I aren't enough to take on Five Demon Lords and the hordes of Kindred they have at their disposal. Even the sinner forces I have here aren't enough. We need a plan. We don't even know if she's still alive." She's speaking sense, which makes me want to hit her, makes me want to shake her so she realises the urgency of the situation.

"She's alive," I snarl, balling my fists at my side, my rage refusing to quell within my veins.

"You don't know that," Osiris replies.

I emit a growl.

"Oh, but I do. She's a survivor. She's alive. Now let's go." I storm from the room, making my way back to the outer layer of the pyramid. My hands are charred, I'm showing my true colours to the world, but I can't calm myself, can't maintain the façade of mortality I'm so used to.

As I hit the outside air, the ash falling around me in thick clouds, I look around, desperate. There's no way anyone could see anything out here. My heart sinks even deeper, and I wonder how much further it can fall before shattering on impact. I know that the guards won't have seen anything.

So, she's just gone, as though she never was.

I stand, stiff in posture, breathing raggedly like a hungry, primal beast as I try not to think about Sephy being tortured, being hurt. Sephy being killed.

"Fuck this," I spit, moving to turn, deciding that I may as well try to take on the entire demon army outside those gates. If there's a chance I can get to her, even a slim one, I'll take it. It's my duty, and I've failed her, I'll never forgive myself for that.

"Xion! Get in!"

As I'm about to take off into the greying fog, a glint of gold and the glowing outlines of twelve skeletal jackals come into view. It nears me, the familiar chariot of Anubis, moving at great speed through the ash. She's wearing a long golden cloak and a headpiece with a snake, her expression refusing even a hint of compromise. She glares at me in warning as I too refuse to move. Staring at her and then back to the wall, back to where Sephy is probably now moving closer and closer to the final beat of her heart.

"Xion! Get in!! We need Haedes' help! None of us can muster the flame, it'll be a bloodbath—" she pleads with me, looking deeply into my eyes as ash continues to fall between us, dark pupils scorching in their intensity.

"I can't leave her—" I breathe, my voice lost on the wind.

"You're not leaving her. We're going to save her," Anubis promises me, holding out a hand. I frown, wondering why she's being so kind. She's normally so stoic, but behind her dark irises, there's pity there, guilt even. Maybe she feels bad that she gave me such a hard time about protecting her before.

I take her hand, and she pulls me up into the golden chariot. Osiris looks at me, expression emotionless as the ash continues to fall in heavy sheets.

Anubis snaps the whip against the hipbones of the closest jackal, emitting a loud whistle from between her plump lips.

The red sky begins to move in a blur as the phantasmal animals pull us, their bony heels barely touching the ground as we pull away from The Icon and begin moving away from the wall.

With every mile we travel beneath the burn of the violet sun, away from the wall, I feel her fading, feel her slipping. I should've been more vigilant. Should've done more—

The wall becomes but a speck in the distance and my rage leaves me as I stand, body jerking with the motion of the chariot, my human form returning. I stare down at my hands, at the pale flesh that has taken the place of the demon's true form. I've never met anyone like Sephy, never met anyone who could physically banish the darkness that has raged within my soul at just the touch of a hand.

Perhaps she'll be okay. Perhaps she's just as strong as she always claims.

I hope she was right. I want to believe she was right. I want to believe in her.

After all, what else is there if I can't believe in the one person who has made me feel truly human after all this time?

24

CRY LITTLE SISTER

<u>SEPHY</u>

I AWAKEN TO THE back of my head throbbing. It's resting against something unknown and hard.

I sit up, my surroundings shrouded in shadow. My fear grows, clutching at my gut. I hold out a palm, trying to summon The Eternal Flame to shed some light on the situation.

Nothing happens.

"There's no use you trying that." A chilling voice comes from the darkness. I shift, wincing as my body aches in protest. I've been moved here without my consent, and whoever's done the moving hasn't been gentle. I reach up to touch the back of my throbbing skull and my hand comes away sticky and wet as I flinch on contact.

Shit.

"Who's there?" I call out, trying to stand before I realise that I'm only inches from the top bars of what appears to be a cage. I reach up, wrapping my hands around the rough metal and rattling them. They don't move, not even an inch, and I begin to panic as I realise I can hear my blood pumping in my ears.

I squint into the dark.

A single match is lit, a face illuminated. One that I recognise.

"You— but— you're a servant," I call out stupidly. The woman in an enormous and billowing black leather ballgown looks down at me, her lilac eyes intelligent. Her hair is loose now, no longer swept back from her face in a braid, and her hollow cheekbones and eye sockets make her look as though she exists in a permanent state of aggravated superiority.

"I was once— but not any longer it would seem. My name is Pandora." She introduces herself in a tone laced with grandiose expectation, and I frown, crawling closer to the bars so I can get a good look at her.

"Pandora? As in that idiot who opened that stupid box and unleashed all the world's evils?" I size her up, and she stares at me deadpan as I feel my fear begin to fade.

"You can't seriously be trying to anger your captor? Really, Sephy?" She looks at me incredulously, pacing upon the stones scattered across the floor. The match she's lit finds a home with a single stubby white candle, placed in a bronze holder atop a wooden table. The room illuminates a little more as the flame grows slightly and Pandora sits on the wooden chair, looking down at me through the bars silhouetted on all sides.

"Why? What are you gonna do to me? Kill me?" I ask her with a cocked eyebrow and she smirks.

"Perhaps. Does that bother you?" she asks, and I shrug, realising that the best tact is to relinquish control and stay logical.

"Not particularly. It's been coming for a while now. Being hunted sort of takes the shock and awe out of it," I retort, trying to rattle her, to make her see I'm unafraid.

"I see. Well, if it was my aim to simply kill you, you'd be dead already. As it is, I have something a little more specific in mind for you." She crosses her legs beneath the folded leather pleats of her skirt, a killer heel exposed beneath.

"What did you do to me?" I question her, willing myself to convect, to produce a flicker of flame, anything.

"You've been weakened. Can't have you messing with the Demon Lords and their Kindred. Your brand of magic— makes death so permanent after all," she enlightens me, and I frown again. "Fear not though, you may be perfectly fine. Right as rain in fact. Provided your father hands back that which he and his family took from the Demon Lords, of course," she threatens me, and I raise my eyebrows, chuckling as I shake my head from left to right yet again.

"Ha. If you think Haedes will trade Mortaria for me, you're insane. We met all of two seconds ago. Besides, he thinks I'm an asshole, and I think he's an asshole. It's this whole thing we've got going on." My mouth twists at the memory, and she narrows her eyes, trying to work out if I'm lying or not.

"Well, either way, I get something out of the deal; Mortaria, or causing your father great anguish. After all, the suffering of a god of his lineage cannot be overlooked as a consolation prize." She strokes her chin with long, dark fingernails sharpened into stiletto points, sighing out and looking down on me.

I lean up, wrapping my fingers around the bars of the cage I'm trapped in, slightly disgusted as I realise that the stones crunching underfoot aren't stones at all but the leftovers of human remains devoured whole.

"Why do you want Mortaria anyway? Why do you care so much? It's not like *you're* a Demon Lord. You're just one of those people who has more curiosity than good sense."

Her eyes widen at my audacity.

"Well, seeing as how I can't make you see the seriousness of your little situation, perhaps I'll send in some real Demon Lords. Maybe you'll respect them. Though I doubt it. The apple never falls far from the tree, and your whole family had little respect for anyone other than themselves," she spits, and I fight the urge to stick out my tongue at her. I'm not afraid. I probably should be. But this seems like an inevitable ending to the road I've been travelling down since the day I signed those stupid contracts against my will.

If I die, at least I'll be free of the pain of being mortal. At least the ache in my chest that my parents left behind will finally dull. Maybe, maybe I'll even be happy.

All I know is that I'm numb. Numb to fear of the end. Numb to the pain of my broken identity. Just numb.

I sit in the cage, back against the bars, in a mood because I'm being kept waiting. If they're going to kill me, they should have the fucking courtesy to do it quickly or at least give me a copy of *Villains in Vogue* while I wait.

I sigh, looking at my feet and bobbing them to an invisible beat in my head. I debate having a little dance by myself to loosen up, but then wonder whether the Demon Lords would be more inclined to kill me if they saw my attempt at twerking. I mean, if I saw someone twerking, and I was evil, I'd probably get all kinds of stabby impulses too.

For some reason, no matter how hard I try, I just can't seem to take this whole being captured and murdered thing seriously.

Is it because I've become desensitized?

Or is it really because I don't give a crap?

I could spend more time pondering this, but instead of becoming one of those self-reflective assholes, I spend my time trying unsuccessfully to summon a flame in the palm of my hand.

I should've known some stupid moron would have pyromancer kryptonite. It seems just too unlikely that I'd have such a powerful skill without there being something to take it away from me.

"Persephone." My name comes from the shadows, and a tall man with waist length, poker straight, white hair steps in through what I assume is a doorway. Either that, or he's been watching me from back there for longer than I've noticed, which is creepy.

"Ugh. It's Sephy," I complain, and he laughs slightly.

"Pandora mentioned you were— un-phased. I'm here to see if that's really true. If you really are— fearless." It clicks with me at this inference that this man must be Barbas. His eyes are white, his skin papery as it creases in the corners of his eyes and mouth. He is tall and skeletally thin beneath a long black overcoat and worn suit. He treads carefully and with purpose towards me.

"Well, before we get to that, can I ask you something?" I query him, and he cocks an eyebrow.

"I don't see why not," he replies, gaze momentarily curious.

"How the hell do you get your hair so lustrous? I mean, damn. Not a single split end. What conditioner are you using? Like— Garnier?" I compliment him with a cocky grin, and he looks alarmed by my candour.

"You pretend as though you're not afraid, but I can smell the fear on you. And yet— it is perhaps not fear of death. But rather—" he sniffs the air, exhaling deeply like one of those creepy serial killers in a thriller flick. "The fear that no one will come for you. The fear that you have pushed people away so far, that now, no hero will come to your aid," he guesses.

I snort.

"Not likely. I mean, who needs someone to come to my aid when I have me? I'm pretty capable you know. It's actually kind of sexist that you assume I need a man to save me." I cross my arms and push my nose up at him, trying to keep my cool and not let him get to me.

"You use humour to hide your fear, but I am the master to which it answers. You cannot hide your fear from me, Persephone," he declares, taking a single step forward and glowering at me, eyes ghostly in the dark.

"I don't know, you're not that scary. In fact, you seem deaf to me. I told you before, I'm Sephy. Not Persephone. So, are you deaf? Or just stupid?" I ask him, cocking my head again and wondering exactly how much I can get away with before one of them just goes ahead and kills me for good measure.

Then I realise that they're probably not under orders to kill me until they've tried to blackmail Haedes. I guess I have at least an hour or even more to kill, causing me even more stress than I'm already under.

I relax into my cage, staring with a dead gaze at Barbas and waiting for him to answer me. He looks exasperated, frowning and turning, seeming to leave the room after a few moments as his footsteps fade into nothingness.

Ha.

Sephy one.

Demon Lords a big fat zilch.

XION

The Exilia approaches, but not fast enough despite the blur of the streets around us. Anubis is beside me, Osiris watching my expression like a hawk. We stand in the chariot, moving through the city as the heads of sinners turn to stop and stare.

"Can't this thing go any faster?" I grumble, voice deep as I continue to allow my short fingernails to dig into the palms of my hands. The blood rushes to my biceps, causing them to bust against the leather of my jacket.

"We're pushing the Jackals as hard as they'll run, Xion. Patience please." Anubis is snarky, and I momentarily consider strangling her, but then I realise I have no way of controlling the chariot without her, so smack down the violent urges threatening to take over. I haven't felt this out of control, this volatile, since long before I took to slaughtering demons out on The Ashen Waste for anger management under Luce's advisement, and it's in this second that I realise perhaps Sephy means more to me than I'll ever admit.

We finally make our way underneath the hollow archways that surround the open lobby of the Exilia and I sigh. The chariot screeches to a halt beside the river, and I leap over the side of the golden contraption, my feet hitting the ground not moments before I begin running up the steps.

"We'll be back!" I hear Anubis call over to me, but I disregard her entirely as I continue to move only forward.

They have the authority here, after all; they're Titans made flesh, but I don't have time to waste sorting through this diplomatically. I only have the unending action that comes from desperation. The necessity that has become protecting this girl at all costs, whether she needs me to or not.

Having taken the steps four at a time, I make a left at the top of the staircase before dashing past the startled eyes of envy sinners, dressed in thick armour, my steps clattering heavily against the smoky quartz floor. I reach the bottom of the staircase leading to Luce and Thane's suite, the scent of something Alchemic drifting down the stairs and filling my nostrils with a pungent tang.

I make quick, effortless work of the spiral staircase, speeding to the top and wasting no time in bursting through the door and into Luce's apartment. She's not here as I should have guessed from the aroma floating downstairs, but Thane is, lounging out on the couch with Cerb and Beelz on the floor in front of her.

"Xion, what's wrong?" She notes my startled expression and gets to her feet, causing both animals to shift, becoming stiff and alert at her sides.

"Sephy, they took her," I stutter, and her eyes widen.

"Well shit," she cusses.

"Where's Luce?" I demand, and she looks anxious.

"In her lab; I haven't seen her since I got home about ten minutes ago," Thane informs me, wasting no time as she moves into action. She storms past me, knocking on the door of Luce's alchemy chamber without pause. Her knock echoes out, acute and unapologetic, around me like a warning bell, only exaggerating the urgency of the situation.

There are a few minutes of silence as Thane continues to tap her bare foot on the stone. Her hair is dishevelled, and she's wearing pinstriped black slacks, braces, and a white vest. She sighs impatiently before giving another few knocks on the door.

Before her knuckles strike the wood for the final tap, concluding her usual rhythm, the door swings inward, revealing Luce in a deep green gown. Plumes of smoke billow out from behind her, filling the space between her lab and the suite with the scent of something that's been singed beyond what's natural.

From behind her, The Fates emerge.

"I know why you're here. The Fates arrived half an hour ago." Luce's tone is urgent, her eyes worried as she looks up into my face.

"I need— I don't know— I need something to help her." I barely make a sentence. Luce looks serious.

"First of all, how was she taken?" Luce demands, and I breathe out.

"I don't know. We were having dinner with Anubis and Osiris inside The Icon. We had the appetiser, and the next thing I know we're unconscious. When we all woke up, she was gone," I explain.

Luce frowns, troubled.

"That's strange. As for something to help, I have it right here. This draft, it's the most complex thing I've ever attempted, but The Fates have assisted in the brewing. It will bind Sephy's powers to her fully. No waiting. It'll be a rough transition, but she needs to be alive more than she needs not to have a wicked migraine so—" She's rambling, trying to stay calm, keep things casual.

She holds out a vial to me, dark fingernails clinking against the glass as her pale eyes glisten with pride.

"Thanks." I grab it hastily, moving to turn and begin my descent back down the stairs.

"Xion, wait!" Luce calls after me, scowling at my impatience.

"What? Why?" I exclaim, heartrate heightening and blood beginning to boil at the interruption.

"You are going into this all wrong. You can't just walk across The Ashen Waste. She'll be dead before you even get halfway," she protests, so I take a large stride, edging on inhuman speed, getting right up in her face without a care for the consequences.

"What do you suggest then, Luce? That I give up? Let her die?" I growl, and she smirks, rolling her eyes.

"No." She reaches down into her cleavage, only accentuated by the pinch of her deep green corset. "I suggest you take the car." She pulls out a key that hangs on a silver ring attached to a small pair of fuzzy blue dice.

"Wait— is that— does Haedes know about this?" I ask, and she shakes her head.

"Nope. I had the key copied for emergencies. This constitutes an emergency. Now go before anyone else hears about this and decides to stop you," she warns me. I shoot her a grateful glance.

"Thank you. I—" I begin, but she pushes me back.

"Go! Her time is running out." She reminds me urgently, placing a hand on my broad chest and pushing me away.

Spinning on my heel, I grip the vial in one hand and the outdated keychain in the other before dashing back down the spiral staircase and into the lobby. I don't still for even a second, counting each moment now as precious, as if it could be her last.

As my eyes dart around the lobby, I realise I have no idea where Haedes keeps his car, let alone the kind of security measures he has around it. I mean, he probably loves his car more than most people. In fact, I'm absolutely sure that's true.

I see Annie coming towards me, eyes down on the floor, posture slumped as I store the car key and vial in my pocket. She's holding a bottle of polish and a cloth. I can only hope she's moving to polish the car as is Haedes' daily request. Perhaps this is fate, me bumping into her at this exact moment, some greater orchestrating force that knows I need to get gone and quick.

"Annie!" I call, taking fast and purposeful steps toward her. She takes one look at me and then moves to switch direction, eyes widening as fear sheens wet across their surface. "Hey wait!" I exclaim, using my inhuman speed to catch up with her and place a hand on the simple black cotton of her nun's uniform. I don't know why Haedes makes her wear it, but to each their own I suppose.

"W—Wh—what?" she whimpers, looking up at me like I might hit her.

"Are you heading to polish Haedes' car?" I ask her, and she looks left then right before nodding as her left eye gives a nervous twitch.

"Yes. Why— Why would you ask that?" She straightens her shoulders, trying to appear brave, but the way her hands tremble, making the polish slosh about in its can, makes me aware that she's anything but.

"He was telling me I should check out the engine— you know, for explosives or anything like that. Can't be too safe with the Demon Lords attacking Nexus members. I mean, they got in here once. They could be using anyone— I mean—" I lean in, getting close to her. "Even you might be a suspect—" I know I'm playing on her anxiety, but I don't have time to mess around and twist her arm slowly.

301

"M—me?" she stutters, showing that her mental resolve is weakening, I smile.

"Well, you are close to Haedes. You'd be the perfect suspect," I elaborate, and she shudders.

"But— but— it's not me. I'm innocent, sir." She bows her head, subservient as always. It makes me feel a little nauseous actually.

"I'm sure you are, but words are easily misleading, actions— well, not so much. I'm sure it would restore faith from the entire council and staff if you were to assist me in checking the car over. After all, you probably spend the most time down in the garage, other than Haedes of course." She looks as if she'd chop off her left arm to help me as she nods, moving around me in a scurry. I follow her across the lobby, walking back in the direction I've just come.

We make pace past envy sinners, their jade pendants gleaming cruelly in the dim light of the Exilia, and move past the spiral staircase leading back to Luce and Thane. She takes me down a dark corridor lit by a multitude of sconces with flickering blue flame. As we reach the halfway point of the long corridor, she makes a sharp right, slipping down a staircase I've never even noticed in all the time I've spent here. It twists back on itself, creating a slither of rock that maintains the façade of a continuous wall, and I look on as we descend together, impressed with the design.

At the bottom of the staircase, Annie proceeds through a silver sliding door, which she heaves aside with much effort. I follow her, moving into the space where Haedes' beloved 1932 Ford Hotrod Coupe sits upon a revolving platform, cast in a deep blue hue. It's sleek black with electric blue neon flames bursting from the hood, faltering where the bare engine is exposed, and then continuing down the body of the car in a fluid design that hugs the vehicle's front and back wheels.

"Here we are," Annie whispers, stepping to the left so I'm towering over her right shoulder. She pivots fast as my shadow falls on her, taking a few steps before opening a cupboard to fetch something, though I don't know what.

I take my chance. Moving in from behind, I give her a small shove.

"Sorry," I mutter, slamming the cupboard door shut and barricading it closed with a nearby mop handle that's been left so the floor can be kept in its unmistakably pristine condition. In fact, when I look around this place, it barely looks like a garage at all, more like a showroom.

I hear Annie struggling to get out of the cupboard, wondering how long the mop will hold such a petite and seemingly fragile woman inside.

Not wanting to stop momentum for a second, I run to the exit, finding the garage door can be opened with the spinning of a wheel, reminding me of how the gates open at the obsidian wall.

I turn it as fast as it'll go, raising the garage door, biceps burning.

Not wanting to take the risk that Annie will escape, I move across the silver floor, which has better grip than I expect, plunging my hand deep inside my leather jacket pocket and pulling out the fluffy dice keyring. I launch myself up the small incline and onto the revolving platform, plunging the silver key into the lock of the door before slipping inside the car. The black leather interior is lined with more silver, and the driver's seat cups my back as I push the seat away from the wheel so I have room to drive, only slightly smug that I'm taller than Haedes. I shut the door, causing the sound of a cupboard refusing to open to fall silent.

Feeling comfortable as I take the key and start up the engine, I jump at the immense roar it expels. The exposed engine shudders visibly in front of the windscreen, the vibrations thundering through the bottom of my seat.

Placing my hands on the steering wheel, I plunge my foot down on the clutch, find the bite point, and then move to accelerate out of the parking space. The car has more of a kick than I thought, and so I pull my foot back as I move too fast off the revolving platform. The car stalls.

Crap.

Sighing, I try to focus, try not the think about the fact that she's in pain, dead, or worse. I need to get to her, to save her, and to do that, I need to not be hideously maimed in a fiery car wreck.

"Okay. Easy does it," I coax, placing my foot back on the accelerator as I restart the car, finding the bite point much easier this time.

After a few careful metres, I see envy sinners becoming suspicious of my exit and so decide to throw caution to the wind. I plunge my foot down on the clutch and let off the gas, hearing a squeal of tyres on crystal and the shudder of the engine as I push up to a higher gear.

In a cloud of tyre smoke, I burst through the lobby of the Exilia, finding that the garage lets out on the far side, and lurch forward out of the place, not so much as looking back. The speed is comforting; it means I am moving closer to her, to saving her.

With every mile that passes, my hold on the wheel tightens, my changing of gears becomes more aggressive, and the demon within me stirs, impatient.

As I reach the Hotrod's top speed, a thought occurs to me, niggling away like a parasite in the back of my mind.

I creep closer and closer to The Fallen Kingdom, to putting an end to my suffering, but a single question still remains.

Is the demon in me rooting for her survival or theirs?

25

ISN'T SHE LOVELY

LUCE

THE LAST THUNDERING ECHOES of Xion's footsteps upon smoky quartz fade into nothing and I exhale heavily, relieved he's gone.

"Layla, Moira, Anya, follow Thane into the suite, she'll make you a cup of tea. I'll only be a moment," I instruct them, trying to be polite but knowing that the situation is time sensitive.

Spinning on my heel, I feel the weight of my deep-hued skirt shifting around my waist. The hem becomes damp around my ankles, absorbing the glaze of alchemic precipitation that's fallen on the floor, making it slick. The Fates bumble around me, glancing back with wizened and concerned stares as I return to the alchemy chamber, slamming the door shut behind me.

Most people are surprised, especially the sinners that clean the place, to find that my cauldron is not a giant vat, the kind you could boil a child in, but rather a small pewter pot with amethyst around the base for protection. I don't know why everyone assumes I would have an enormous cauldron for brewing, I mean, how is anyone supposed to produce anything with any potency in such a large vessel? With potions, you tend to find that the smaller the amount produced, the more powerful the effects.

Taking several strides across the cobblestones set into the floor, I stare down into the depths of the petite pewter cauldron.

Just enough, I breathe, picking up a copper ladle lying beside the vat on my left, and a vial from my right, scooping up the glowing bloody orange liquid and carefully delivering it into the hold of the glass. I inhale the sweet scent of the brew, the tang of cinnamon, a hint of crushed firefly wing, and a splash of luciferin, brought to the boil before stirring in Dragon scale and a pinch of ground Unicorn horn.

It's not an easy potion to make, and many of the ingredients I've used today will be difficult if not impossible to replace. Still, one cannot be frugal when it comes to saving lives, especially when that life belongs to Haedes' daughter.

I stopper the vial, content if not weary from the task of creating the potion in the first place, unused to calling on such dark powerful magic and ingredients. I'm barely above making sleeping drafts and natural remedies to calm the nerves, so this is far from what I usually make. The thing about alchemy, of course, which makes it so dark and dangerous, is the way it produces forces or effects that go against the natural order of things.

Striding back out of the chamber, I close the door purposefully behind me and make my way across the hall to the suite. Inside, the three Fates are sat on the sofa, admiring Beelzebub and Cerberus as they sleep beside the fire on the dark rug. Thane looks like she might stab somebody as they continually ask her the same question they manage to squeeze in every single time they're around us.

"When are you making an honest woman of our Luce? We need this information you know Thane; it's not easy to find something formal to wear that we all agree on," Moira says. Layla speaks up next, crossing her ankles as Thane moves to pour them all tea out of a black china teapot with copper accents.

"It's not fair; you two have always had the worst aesthetic taste, and I'm the one who loses my sight. It's typical," she complains, causing Thane to roll her eyes. We've discussed marriage, of course, but neither of us has felt it necessary to make that kind of declaration, especially when the thought that neither one of our families would be there is painful to stomach, as well as the fact that we'd not be permitted to marry in the Othrysian Orchard. It's sad, the fact that I've always known that's where I'd like to tie the knot but that it will never happen.

I blink once, then twice, as Thane looks at me, still standing in the doorway. The vial is clutched tight in my hand, and I realise I am getting off-topic. Time is valuable to us, and I'm wasting it thinking about a stupid wedding.

The Fates really have a way of making all my insecurities rise to the surface. I muse internally as Thane tilts the teapot a third and final time, delivering Hibiscus tea into the black and copper china cups that The Fates gave me as a gift upon my arrival here. They'd been for reading tea leaves, but I've never used them for anything except entertaining.

She carries a copper tray across the room, setting it down on a black crystal table beside the couch and handing each of the women a teacup. I watch them sip a moment before turning to Thane.

"Can I get you anything?" she asks me, face concerned. I shake my head, blonde locks bristling against my ears with their silky soft touch.

"No. But there is something you can do for me." I hold up the vial, and she frowns.

"But— I thought you'd given that to Xion already?" She looks confused, and I sigh.

"I gave him one vial. This is the backup. He won't make it to the Fallen Kingdom or, at least, not in time to do any good. You'll be able to make it to Sephy much quicker, and you'll be able to drop it in from above. I don't know where they're keeping her though—"

I look to The Fates, wondering if they might have anything to add, but unfortunately for Sephy, the Demon Lords, specifically Abraxis and Barbas, make seeing anything to do with them unreliable at best and lethal at worst. The three old women remain silent as they sip on their floral tea, as ever, the calm within the storm.

"You don't think he'll make it?" She cocks an eyebrow at me.

"When has running off half-cocked into The Ashen Waste ever worked for anyone? I mean, I know he's half Demon, but he's also half human. His emotions are clouding his judgement; he's bound to be reckless," I rationalise, and Thane continues to look at me quizzically.

"So, he *does* have feelings for the Sinclair girl. I knew it. And— you just let him go anyway?" she sounds incredulous.

"Were you going to stop him? Besides, he's better off out of the way. I'd rather have him off messing up Demons than screwing with the political implications of this kidnapping, which are no doubt about to implode around our ears," I sigh.

Thane's lips twist into a grimace; she knows I'm right.

"I'll go right away." She holds out a palm, and I take a piece of dark string from my pocket. Wrapping it around the vial, I then bend to wrap the vial around her ankle.

"Be safe. I love you," I confess, kissing her on the cheek as I rise.

The Fates stir behind us as she stalks back into our bedroom, stripping as she goes before sliding shut the partition and shielding her transformation from the rest of us. I ignore the cries of my lover, the snap of her bones and the unmistakable prickling of feathers bursting through skin. The Fates continue to drink tea, looking up to me as Layla says, "So— there's not going to be a wedding?"

"No, Layla. No wedding, but there may very well be a blood bath if I don't find Haedes and come up with a plan," I admit.

Anya shakes her head, eyes saddened.

"Well, we'll be here should you need anything, dear," Layla replies.

"I'll lock you in," I promise them, turning on my heel once more to leave. I'd like to rest for a moment, sit and drink tea with them, but once again I'm in the middle of events which could affect more than anyone can digest.

Shutting the door behind me as I step out into the hall, I lock in The Fates, hoping that if anything should happen, Beelz and Cerb will be enough to protect them.

Wishing for Thane's safe return, like a wife waiting for the return of her soldier from yet another unholy war, I spin on my heel and begin my quick descent down the spiral staircase in search of Haedes.

I can only hope I find him in an agreeable state. Though, for Sephy's sake, I'm also sort of hoping I don't.

The sound of a saxophone's hollow call travels throughout the hallways of the Exilia Multum, bouncing from the walls and floors and surrounding me in a hurricane of spontaneous jazz. Haedes must be upbeat, because I haven't heard him play something like this in a long time. I listen carefully, smiling; he's playing *Isn't she lovely*, by Stevie Wonder. I don't halt in my tread, giving my steps a small but jaunty rhythm as I enjoy the melody of the song, sad that I'll soon be completely ruining the mood.

I slam both palms into the double doors of the grand hall and find Haedes hopping on one leg across the room in the middle of a saxophone solo, his eyes glistening. If I was the kind of person to make assumptions, I'd say he was playing in honour of his relationship with Sephy, but then again with him I never can tell.

He takes his mouth from the Saxophone, licking his bottom lip and cocking his head at the intrusion as he waves a hand, silencing the soulful accompaniment that's hovering overhead.

"Luce? What is it?" he asks, not as grumpy as he would usually be about me interrupting him mid-tune.

"Sephy. She's been kidnapped," I announce, not pausing to try and break the news softly. He drops the Saxophone to the floor, letting it clatter and not even trying to save it. The tips of his hair, which today is spiked straight up in a fauxhawk, turn scarlet.

"I'm going." He turns, but before he can convect, I grab onto his elbow.

"No! You can't just go in there! That's what they want you to do!" I hiss, and his entire head finishes the move from cobalt to fire-engine red in a matter of seconds.

"Luce! I'm fucking going! Let go of me!" he spits, feral in his desperation.

Sephy got to him faster than I thought.

"No! You're not! Or— Or—" I begin to threaten him, but I don't know what to threaten him with. The man has one thing he cares about, and it's already under threat.

Shit.

"Look, at least take the Furies with you!" I plead as he moves to pull away from me. He stills mid-motion, the deep navy cotton of his suit crumpling as my grip comes loose from his arm.

"Good idea," he breathes.

I sigh out too; at least, he still has some sense of mortality about him.

"Alright. Let's summon them." I swallow hard, trying to stay calm, scared that he'll convect out of here any moment and all will be lost. We have more to lose if he's murdered at the hands of the Demon Lords, so much more than is worth thinking about.

I follow him, the only sound our steps and the audible drag of my silk skirt against the floor. I push my pale hair behind one ear, biting down on my bottom lip and wishing Thane was here. She'd comfort me, know what to say to make Haedes heel.

"Do we know how she was kidnapped?" he asks me as we make our way over to the golden door of his vault. He lets his palm heat against the magically activated locking mechanism, and after several audible clicks, the door swings open. I clear my throat to explain.

"She was taken from within The Icon. Something was slipped into the food or drink at the dinner. Anubis, Osiris, and Xion were all rendered unconscious also. When they woke, she was gone," I explain as Haedes leads me into the vault.

"That makes no sense. You're telling me that they got in and out of the pyramid and no one noticed? Nobody?" he asks me, and I shrug.

"I don't know— maybe the Abraxians—" I suggest but he rounds on me.

"Yes, but even then, how the hell would they be able to haul out a five-foot-eight redhead without anyone noticing?" he continues to interrogate me, and I shrug yet again.

"I don't know. It's terrifying. That's all I do know," I admit, and he sighs.

"Why hasn't she convected out of there?" he asks, cocking his head.

"I don't know that either. Why? You think she chose to go with them?" I ask him, and he shrugs.

"I don't know, if I was her, I might be curious. I'm not exactly the most hospitable host—or father. I don't even remember what happened that night we went out." He visibly shudders, and I smirk.

"I think that might be for the best." I give him an amused smile. "Anyway, we can stand here guessing all day, or we can summon The Furies and go and find out." I remind him of the plan, and he nods, moving across the floor in suave motion and over to the shelves housing urns where dangerous or volatile souls are housed for safekeeping.

I look upon the urns, one in ruby, one in sapphire and the final one in amber upon the top shelf.

They stand, the promise of power noticeable from here as the air around me becomes statically charged. Haedes removes each one in turn, carefully placing them on the floor. Deemed too dangerous for The Higher Plains after the brutal ways each of The Furies had lost their mortal lives under the crushing weight of patriarchy back when they had lived, they were banished here long ago.

Haedes steps back, looking at the urns and narrowing his eyes.

"Right, so— Erin, Ericka, Erlea?" he asks me, pointing to the ruby urn, then the amber, and finally, the sapphire.

"Yes, I think that's right," I agree, looking at him quizzically.

"They hate it when I mix them up, something about me not seeing them as objects— I dunno, some feminist spiel." Haedes flutters his fingers in the air.

"You know, for someone who is a great lover of women, you surely must support the idea of their equal rights—" I whisper, and he shrugs.

"Oh sure, equal rights are great; being beheaded by a pissed-off Fury— not so much. They're easily offended. Hence the title," he elaborates, and I nod. I haven't had many dealings with The Furies; none of us has. They're only brought out when absolutely necessary, and that hasn't been in aeons.

"Do you want to do the honours?" he requests, gesturing to the urns. I roll my eyes.

"Don't tell me you're scared?" I scoff at him.

"Hey, if you'd seen what these women can do with a set of testicles and an iron vice, you'd be terrified too." I cock an eyebrow at him. Does he even hear himself speak? "Or— maybe not. Look, just open the damn jars," he exclaims, tapping his foot impatiently.

I give him a mock salute and kneel, slowly taking the crystal lid from each urn in turn.

Stepping back, we watch as dust rises from each one in serpentine succession, curling and fading in different coloured streams. They intertwine, gold, red, and blue, twisting and turning like a vice, before separating and billowing forward. Once they've moved free of their crystal containers, each different colour stream of dust moves forward in the air and into the form of a woman.

They solidify, inhaling sharply in a cacophony of expanding lungs trapped within narrow ribcages. Standing before us, they bow their heads to me before turning to Haedes and staring at him without blinking or greeting. He straightens under the scorch of their feminine gazes, surprising me, considering he was acting like a complete coward not five seconds ago.

"Erin—" he holds out a hand to the first Fury, a woman with dark skin, lush full lips, and wild curly black hair. Her body is voluptuous, clad in brown leather that folds around her, making her look primal and ready for bloodshed. Her eyes are round and dark, made only more apparent by a slash of red war paint that's been smeared over the bridge of her nose and around her eyes like a mask. She takes Haedes' hand, shaking once, then twice, and I watch as her free hand brushes the handle of the sword hanging down by her side, short and broad, perfect for her height

"Erika," he greets the second Fury in line. She has glossy black hair that falls in two long braids down past each of her shoulder blades. Her skin is tanned, her features Native American. Tangerine war paint is slashed between her thick eyebrows and her body is coated in a similar leather wrap with a skirt, but this has thick and noticeably dark stitching around the hems. It is more makeshift than Erin's attire, but beautiful, nonetheless. A myriad of knives hang from the belt of her skirt, each sheathed in matching stitched leather. She's slender, but her arms give away dense muscle as she grasps Haedes' hand.

"And Erlea." Haedes holds out his hand one last time to a woman with brown eyes and pale skin. Her hair is dark and her features fiercely Asian. She's got an angry look about her and refuses to take Haedes' hand as the other two women smirk. Her body is wrapped in brown leather, the same as her comrades, her body spattered all over with sapphire blue paint. Her stance is broad, her posture stiff, and Haedes merely brings his hand back, not one to be left hanging, brushing it through his spikey hair and spinning around to face me as he rolls his eyes.

"Right, well, the reason you're here," he begins, but suddenly his voice is no longer the loudest thing in the room. Another voice, belonging to Osiris is shouting over him.

"Haedes!" he barks.

At his derogatory tone, the three women leap into action, moving in front of both Haedes and me before shoving us backwards. We narrowly miss one of the shelves stacked high with delicate hourglasses, and I frown, irritated. Maybe Haedes wasn't so stupid to be afraid of these maniacs after all.

"Woah, woah, woah!" I call out, putting my hands up as Osiris walks into the vault, his hands coming out immediately as Erlea moves forward to strike him with a Katana she's pulled from seemingly nowhere.

"Do you know who I am?" Osiris squeaks indignantly as Haedes convects between The Fury and the Titan, an unimpressed look plastered on his face.

"Easy there, Tiger," he purrs, grabbing the sword from Erlea and cutting his hand in the process. He winces, looking increasingly annoyed with each passing second.

"Who— who this?" Erlea asks, her English broken.

"This is Osiris. Son of Anubis. Member of The Nexus Council. Aka. Your Boss. No slicey. No dicey. Got it?" He lets go of the sword, and she scowls at him, turning on her heel and returning to her two partners, who have relaxed in posture, putting away their weapons.

"Can we wait for some kind of *actual* threat before attacking just anybody? It's so hard to find good help these days, and the last thing I need is you hacking up my staff. Capiche?" he asks them all this time. They nod, collectively sour-faced and lacking in reply.

"Right. What is it, Osiris?" Haedes asks, looking at me and rolling his eyes yet again.

"The Nexus Council has assembled. We need to speak with you; it is about your daughter," Osiris decrees.

Haedes doesn't argue, which surprises me. He simply leads the party out of the vault and out into the hall where Muerta, Yama, and Anubis wait, eyebrows rising on each of their faces in turn as they catch sight of The Furies.

"Right, let's get this over with. Sephy's been kidnapped. We're going to stage a rescue," Haedes announces, gesturing to himself and The Furies.

"Excuse me? Are you utterly mad, Haedes? You can't just go galivanting off to The Fallen Kingdom! You'll be murdered— and then, what? Mortaria will lose its Resurrection AND Eternal flames— you know, the flames *you* keep up and running? Without them, we have no defence against the Demons at all, and no way to resurrect sinners. You can't just leave!" Yama is furious, his blue skin turning a light purple as his blood comes closer to the surface. His glistening gold cornrows expose his skull is masked in a light sweat as his body stiffens within his gold and emerald robes.

"She's my daughter. What the hell am I supposed to do?" Haedes exclaims, the tips of his hair turning scarlet again.

"Oh, I don't know. Maybe not care, like you were not caring when you announced her location with a giant flashing neon sign?" Muerta barks.

I'm surprised; usually, she's one of the more sympathetic members of the group.

"Why are you being like this?" Haedes asks them, sounding like a teenager as his shoulders rise in two jagged hostile peaks.

"Because we've been screwed over enough being stuck down here with you because you were too proud to accept our help all those years ago Haedes. We won't be screwed again so you can go off and get yourself killed. We'll be overtaken by the Demon armies in days, maybe weeks if we're lucky, and then what? We die? The scales tip, and the walls of this dimension and every other bleed into nothingness? No, thank you," Muerta continues, crossing her arms over her chest which is covered in a black and white corset that looks like a ribcage. She brings a thin hand to her face, brushing her long raven hair back behind her ear where a dying poppy is placed, withering.

"So, what do you expect me to do? Negotiate with them? They're Demons!" he implores them to see his side.

At these words, a blinding light explodes throughout the room. The Nexus members leap back from its source and The Furies leap forward as I stumble back, lifting my skirt with one hand and shielding my eyes with the other.

Where before there was nothing but thin air, a woman now stands, a wooden box clutched in her hand and two enormous Banshees at her side. She fiddles with the box, and the light flooding the space is captured within it, disappearing and leaving her for me to inspect. The Banshees cling close to the sides of her wide skirt, baring their teeth. She's wearing a black leather ballgown with a high-pointed collar. Her eyes are lilac, and I swear I've seen her before.

Hair pulled up in a topknot, her skin grows even more stretched over her skull as she smiles with plump, plum-coloured lips.

She speaks, and suddenly I realise where I know her from.

"Did I hear someone say negotiate? Now we're talking," she purrs.

I gape, only one word escaping my lips into the silence.

"Pandora?"

26

I NEED YOU TONIGHT

<u>PANDORA</u>

HIS REPUTATION PRECEDES HIM, and as my eyes caress his angular figure, I can't help but feel my heart skip a beat. I might hate his brother, but there's no denying that Haedes is hot as hell.

My words ring out, bouncing from the crystal of the grand hall. It might not be The Higher Plains, but it's worlds away from the crumbling ruins of The Fallen Kingdom. Lucifer recognises me, my name falling from her lips and into the stunned silence shortly after my own verbal invitation.

The Nexus Council stares at me, and the Banshee at my side edge forward as three women I've read about only in myth, leap into action to defend their charges. Their growls are audible and make everyone, except me, in the room incrementally twitch. I myself am practically immune to Banshee screams by now.

"Pandora—wait, aren't you that Kindred of Hera—" Haedes begins, raising a hand and halting the forward motion of the three female warriors. His voice is smooth with an edge of rugger, like duchess satin when it slides through your fingers the wrong way.

"No. I *was* a Titan. But your brother—" I begin, and Haedes raises a hand.

"Look, if you're here to put me in the same boat as my brother, then you've got the wrong one— in fact, you and I may have more in common than you think." Haedes grins, charming as he steps forward before looking to the rest of the Nexus council members.

"Leave us," he commands them, sending the three wicked-looking women to usher the other gods made mortal from the room. They look back over their shoulders to him, their eyes wide with some expressions turning from shocked to irritated quicker than I can fathom. I wonder if Haedes is about to make my job far easier than I have anticipated, but as I take a few steps forward, he raises a hand.

"One moment," he promises, lifting a finger. Raising his hand, I feel the Banshees stir at my sides as I still, their loyalty to me as good as it ever has been to Lilliana. They shift, claws tinkling against the crystal of the floor as I stiffen, preparing for a fight.

He clicks his fingers, summoning a mist above us. A funky beat begins to emit, stirring my anger.

"What do you think you're doing?" I demand, scowling.

"I am setting the mood for civil negotiations. Not for you to threaten me as I know you intend to." As the words travel above the ambience, he smiles, flashing his white teeth and causing me to falter slightly in my scowl. As I'm staring at him, he unleashes two projectiles of red flame at the Banshees by my side. They perish before me, and I step forward toward him over their ashes.

"That wasn't very hospitable," I bite out, and he cocks an eyebrow.

"You don't bring dogs to a dance—" he whispers, closing the distance between us.

"Dance?" I query him, heart racing in my chest. I don't want to get close to him, and yet, I can't help but inch slightly closer. After all, I have his daughter— do I really have anything to fear?

"Yes, would you do me the honour?" He bows his head as a man's voice, low and seductive, echoes out across the room, filling my mind. I shake my head a moment, letting a loose lock of blue-black hair fall from my up-do and tickle the back of my neck. Reaching into my pocket, I pull out the box.

"Wait. I have something to show you first," I promise, picturing Sephy in the Dark Colosseum.

A portal bursts into life, causing Haedes to take a few steps backwards, his long legs making short work of the distance. The air in the middle of the room breaks apart, rippling and giving a view into The Fallen Kingdom.

Haedes' eyes widen, looking at the box in my hand.

"That's— an Othrysian portal box. How did you get it?" he asks, brow furrowing. His hair remains cool blue, and he runs his fingers through the spikey style, clearly perplexed by my mere existence.

"Your brother gave it to me. Nice little consolation prize for not being worthy of a seat on The Aetherial Court," I explain, unable to keep the resentment from my voice. Haedes rolls his eyes.

"Typical Zeus. So that's how you ended up here?" he asks me, and I nod, surprised how civil this all is.

"Yes. He couldn't see my worth. As you can see, though, I'm far from benign." I gesture through the portal, to where we can see Sephy being dragged by Abraxians toward the pit of the dark cylindrical structure. There, the strongest Kindred the Demon Lords have to offer lie in wait.

"It is a shame he underestimated such a beauty as thee." Taking a few steps forward, he nears the portal. I promptly slide the panel of the box closed, causing the window into the Dark Colosseum to dissolve as though it were never there.

"It is not my beauty that I want him to value. I am worth more than my pretty face. In fact, I'm worth more than most women." I slide toward him, and he puts a hand possessively around my waist, pulling me close with almost feral power. I had expected him to be furious, violent even. I had not expected him to be charming, devilishly so in fact.

"I can imagine you are. You had me fooled. All of us. I suppose that box of yours is how the demons have been moving between dimensions and past the wall so seamlessly?" he purrs, appreciating my body as his gaze falls over it like a tropical waterfall in the midday sun. Steaming and powerful, the look bites into my hardness repeatedly, eroding my refrain.

The music plays on and we begin to move, his mouth moving closer to my ear as we glide across the crystal in harmony, my heels tinkling against the two-dimensional and flawless facet. I breathe him in, the smell of heady fragrant smoke and dark chocolate filling my nostrils.

"But of course. The Demon Lords aren't powerful enough to travel across dimensions. You know that." I look up at him, raising my jaw as he spins me out from his body before pulling me back to him in a sudden jerking motion. I feel my breathing accelerate, lungs drawing the scent of him in deep. "Careful now," I warn him as his mouth comes close to my ear once more and his arms cage me in close to him. I can feel his cold and even breathing on my neck as he whispers, "What? Can't handle a little rage?" He's entirely suggestive, and I watch as the cold glow of his hair turns orange, indicating his anger is bubbling ever so incrementally closer to the surface.

"Of course, I thrive on rage. I'm built from it. It was the only thing powerful enough to keep me going after I fell from The Higher Plains," I recall, and I feel him smile.

"I know that to be true—" he whispers, twisting me underneath his arm. My skirt flares around me, creating a wicked pinwheel of dark leather and shadow as I twirl.

"There is, I fear, one thing more powerful than rage though—" I muse, pulling his body closer to me now as I take the lead from him. We turn circles in a figure eight across the room, not a step out of place nor a beat missed between us.

"And what, my dear, would that be?" he asks me, hips swinging in time to the song which is sexual to say the least. I look up into his eyes, knowing that now is the moment I must play just right.

"Love. Especially that between a parent and a child. Don't you agree?" I ask him, and he falters in his step slightly. "Careful now." I usher him back into the dance, letting him grip me with long desperate fingers.

"I do," he replies, causing me to smile.

"Then we should discuss why it is I am here. I have a proposition for you, and you alone," I whisper to him this time, coming close to the shell of his ear that boasts a single silver stud.

"What do you want, Pandora?" he speaks now in a firm hush, causing me to grin, unrestrained and fully, for the first time I can remember. The tension, the drama, it's all just too delicious.

"I want Mortaria," I whisper back, and he snorts.

"Why would you want this dump?" he asks me, arched eyebrows rising on his forehead in surprise.

"The Demon Lords need their hunting grounds back," I reply simply, and he frowns.

"So, you're doing this out of the pure evilness of your heart then?" he observes, tone dripping with sarcasm and disdain.

"Maybe I am." I play innocent, and he shakes his head.

"I'm not stupid. You want revenge on Zeus, right? You want to use Mortaria to screw with the balance of the universe and him?" he guesses, astute, looking bored and as if I'm too insanely predictable for his liking. I sigh, rolling my eyes.

"Obviously. Your brother deserves to be slaughtered. Preferably at the hand of a woman he has screwed over. You cannot deny he has it coming." I tempt him, wondering if having him on my side would be such a terrible thing.

"Oh, I don't deny it. He utterly deserves his comeuppance, but why on earth should I give you that opportunity? He's my brother. If anyone should fuck him up, it should be me." Haedes sounds jealous, almost as if he's been plotting something similar.

"Because if you don't, I'll rip your daughter limb from limb. I won't even leave you with a carcass to bury. I will have her devoured," I let the promise fall from my lips, encased in darkness and malice.

Haedes doesn't falter in his step this time, instead moving me faster and more passionately around the room.

"What makes you think I don't know that you'll just kill her and me the first chance you get after I hand this place over? After all, I'm related to Zeus," he queries, and I laugh.

"I have no intention of killing you. Well, not by the standard means. Wouldn't you like a normal life Haedes? A mortal life? A life free from all this responsibility, free from demons, from the sinners? A life with your daughter?" I coax him, knowing that this is exactly what he desires. His eyes widen slightly, but then darken as we continue to move. He smiles down at me.

"That does sound rather nice—" he admits, bending me backwards and placing his hands behind my rear. I feel him grabbing at me, desiring me, but then, all of a sudden, I'm on the floor. He's dropped me stone cold. "For you." He grins, clearly not welcoming my proposal.

In his hand, he clutches the box, my box. The box that I've spent half my life bonding with.

"Wait— what?!" I cry out, flushing with humiliation.

"Oh, come on! You can't be that stupid. Anyone who knows me knows that I didn't make a sun that could keep me young forever because I want a *normal* mortal life," he smirks.

"So, you'd rather have your daughter become demon food?" I ask him, shock resonating throughout my tone as I scramble to my feet.

"Of course not. But I'm not destroying the universe for her either. If you think I'd be bought so easily by the life of one girl because she's a blood relation, then I can see why Zeus didn't want you on The Aetherial Court. There's a bigger picture here. A picture you can scarcely comprehend, Pandora. No one life is worth the destruction of this universe. Or handing one of its most important strongholds over to the Demon Lords once more," he chuckles, eyes dead but expression mocking.

"You— you're a monster!" I narrow my eyes, alarmed by his callousness. I had thought he would be different, thought that because Zeus had slighted him, he would be sympathetic to my cause, share in my hatred.

"Actually, yes. But that's fine. As long as I'm still pretty." He smirks, and I feel my fury boil.

"You and your brother are exactly alike!" I exclaim, holding out a palm and willing the box to me. It leaps from Haedes' palm, flying into my hands as I lay, sprawled out on the floor.

He doesn't look impressed at this, but simply sighs, looking down on me like the pure-blooded and entitled god he is.

"Look, I get it. You hate Zeus. I hate Zeus. We all hate Zeus. He's an asshole. But you know what I don't hate? Being alive. Having a warm comfy bed and some whisky in my glass. Why would you think I'd destroy the peace that's governed this universe for centuries now? So, what? You can show him you're so powerful? I might be irresponsible, but I'm also selfish. Selfish enough to not want to be dead, or back in The Higher Plains with my brother who, as I've already stated, I hate quite a lot." He cocks his head, causing me to ball up my fists.

"You're really sentencing your daughter to die— just like that?" I ask him, and he nods.

"Just like that. I don't like it. Actually, I'm quite pissed about it and plan to open my finest whisky in her honour later tonight, but you know, that's the difference between someone like you, a Titan, and someone like me, a full-blown god. I was born with the understanding that this universal peace comes at a price. We all pay it at some point." His breathing is noticeably heavy, and he's pacing now. "Just look at you. You paid it by succumbing to the lie that you were anything but a piece of fodder for The Aetherial Court to use and discard. If I must pay it by losing my daughter, then that's something I have to bear." He sighs again, bending down and staring deeply into my eyes. "Being a god, being a ruler, it means sacrificing the things you love so that other people can continue to have the things they love."

"You're heartless," I spit, furious that he's not succumbed to my demands.

"No. I'm not. I just— I know that Sephy takes after me. I do not doubt that you'll have trouble killing her. She's stubborn, also like me. So, I wish you luck with that." He wipes imaginary dirt from his hands like I'm filth, standing and holding out a hand to me. I take it despite the fact I want to cave his skull in on the way up. Why is he being a gentleman despite the fact I'm about to kill his only child?

"I want you to go— go back to the Demon Lords and tell them that they will never possess Mortaria again. Their time is done. And you, Pandora, would be wise to quell your lust for revenge. No sin ever goes

320

truly unpunished. You should know that by now," Haedes warns me like he's doing me a kindness, and I shake my head.

"I don't care about punishment or sin, Haedes. I lived by the rules for too long, and I was still punished."

He stares at me with an amused expression as he places his hands in the pockets of his pants.

"Maybe you weren't as innocent as you thought. Sounds an awful lot like a deadly case of pride to me." He turns, flitting his hand in the air as a casual dismissal, as though he dictates my comings and goings.

"Now, you have a murder to attend to, but be warned, if I see you again, ever, in this place, even your ashes will not survive my fury. You are taking from me the last thing in this world that means anything to me. And you know what they say about a man with nothing to lose," he threatens me.

My lips uptick into a smirk.

"Sounds to me like you're afraid of dying. Which is not even mildly ironic. So— there's still that for you to lose." At this observation, he has no reply, so I smile wickedly at him over my shoulder as I picture the Dark Colosseum in my mind, sliding the correct panel of the box open and stepping inside the portal.

I don't turn back, don't look to see Haedes disappear, but I'm listening hard for a mangled cry of grief, the smashing of something as a bout of full-blown rage hits him. Instead, before the portal closes behind me, I hear nothing. Only self-contained silence.

I remain unsatisfied.

27

Ain't No Mountain High Enough

LUCE

THE NEXUS COUNCIL MEMBERS look to me as though I'm his mother, his keeper. I'm not, but for some reason, whenever Haedes does something nobody approves of, it's my fault.

Guilty by association I suppose.

"Lucifer, this is ridiculous! Why on earth would he need to be alone with her? You don't think that—" Anubis insinuates that which is entirely ridiculous, and I turn on her, my fury reaching its peak point of intensity.

"What? That he had them kidnap his daughter? Um— are you insane, Nu? Seriously, I know you're not that fond of the guy, but come on; she's his kid. Why would you even suggest something like that? Anyway, she was kidnapped right under your damn roof!"

"Then, why does he need to be alone with her?" Osiris asks, his golden skin boasting a small layer of sweat under the flickering torchlight of door-side sconces. His expression is confused, not confrontational, so I don't bite his head off like I instinctually want to.

"Has it ever occurred to you that in a situation where someone has something precious to you, you don't want that person to feel threatened? Or ganged up on? I think Haedes is simply giving himself maximum control over the environment and situation. Don't you think?" I ask them.

Yama stirs, nodding at me.

"I agree with Lucifer; I believe Haedes wanted privacy so he could speak with her and find out exactly what her game is. He's a mess; there is no doubt in my mind, but you cannot deny he's smart, manipulative even, at times. He's been the ruler of The Nexus Council and Mortaria for centuries now. The city has flourished under his rule. He's just having a hard time recently." Yama stands up for his friend, and I'm grateful.

"Of course, you would say that. Don't think we don't all know you're right in his pocket with your weekly chess nights," Anubis snaps and Yama rolls his eyes. I want to laugh, but I know it's not appropriate; instead, I go for sarcasm.

"Ooh, because chess is *so* taboo," I comment, shaking my head in disbelief.

Are we actually having this conversation?

Yama speaks up.

"You know, being a bitch isn't a good look on you Anubis. Besides, I speak not from a position of personal preference but from fact. Even you, yourself, cannot deny Haedes has brought wealth and riches to this place with the bargains he forms with mortals before their deaths. He is not stupid. It would be nice if you would perhaps give him the benefit of the doubt, would it not?" He folds his hands in front of him, blue skin shining out lilac against the red light of the hallway as an expression of serene calm remains, blanketing his features and masking any feelings he must have.

"What do you think it is that she wants?" Muerta queries me, turning from the other council members as though disgusted by the entire conversation.

"I believe it would have something to do with Zeus. I remember Pandora's case; it was some time after I fell from The Higher Plains. She wanted to be on the Aetherial Court— I recall The Fates telling me about it," I answer. Yama lets out a small laugh.

"That's rich. She's not even a pure Goddess. She was a Nephilim, a Kindred, wasn't she?" he asks, causing Anubis to scowl.

"Might I remind you that not everyone on this council is a pure God or Goddess either," she snaps.

Yama turns to her, face as inexpressive as ever.

"You, Anubis, were a Queen of Ancient. You also aided Cronus in ending your very own god for the wellbeing of the Higher and Lower Plains alike. Even as a blessed mortal, you sacrificed for the greater good. You cannot begin to believe that you and Pandora are even close to being the same," he retorts.

Anubis remains silent, pursing her plump lips together. I'm sure she's wondering whether to be flattered by Yama's acknowledgement of her duties to Gaia or pissed that he's prejudiced against her origins as a mortal princess.

"Yes, well, regardless of all that, do you think Haedes would strike some sort of a deal to save his daughter's life?" Osiris asks me.

I shrug.

"I have no idea, but I think the music has stopped playing. I'm going to look inside," I announce, taking steps across the length of the hall and opening the heavy door. I peek inside, a crack of light from the hall falling onto the smoky quartz of the floor. Here, I find Haedes standing in the middle of the room, ghostly pale and alone. His hair is deep cobalt, making his skin seem almost translucent as I pull the door fully open and hurry across the room to him. My steps echo out into the silence, eerie, and as I reach him, I place my hands on his shoulders.

He looks completely out of it, pupils glazed, mouth slack.

"Haedes— what happened?" I demand. His eyes move from glassy to cloudy fast, and The Furies follow in through the open door behind us, scouring the room and finding nothing else but two piles of slightly disturbed ashes.

He looks over to them, calling out in a hollow voice, "She's gone. You don't have to worry."

"What happened?!" I exclaim, shaking him.

"She wanted Mortaria in exchange for Sephy's life," his voice is cold, distant, and his body is stiff.

"What— what did you do?" I demand as the other council members follow me into the room.

"What do you think I did? I told her no." He turns away from me.

I watch his figure slump, losing its resolve as all suave swagger and rhythmic feeling dissipates. I haven't seen him this way in years— not since, well— not since Demi Sinclair died.

"So, you just— you just handed her to them? You sentenced her to death?" I ask him, realising immediately that this is the worst thing I could have said.

Haedes' hair morphs scarlet in a flash, eyes burning orange as he turns on me with a feral and distraught expression, the first recognisable emotion of his I've seen since entering the room.

"Yes, Luce! I fucking handed her a death sentence, alright! What the hell was I supposed to do? Doom the universe for her? This is why I didn't want to know her, and *you* insisted I get involved. This is *your* fault!" he explodes at me, and Anubis comes between us.

"Haedes stop! What did she want?" she asks, and Haedes exhales, trying to tame his temper.

"She wanted me to give her Mortaria." Anubis' eyebrows rise on her forehead, but before she can make comment, Haedes snarls. "Don't worry; I told her no. Sacrificed my daughter for the universe. Are you all happy now? Am I grown up enough for you?" he spits, turning on us collectively.

"So— she's going to die?" Osiris asks, finding his backbone at last. He, as usual, has remained almost completely silent during this entire event.

"Yes. Well done, Osiris. She's going to die. None of us can get there in time without risking being killed, putting Mortaria at even greater risk. I can't convect because they've already got her surrounded, and I can only convect a few people with me at a time, and that's at a stretch. Besides, if anything happens to me, as you've all already pointed out, the sinners will no longer be able to resurrect, and the universe will go to shit. No one person is worth the risk, yada, yada, yada. It's all utterly hopeless." Haedes throws his hands up in the air, and I take a small step forward.

"Not *utterly* hopeless," I interject, and Haedes raises his gaze to me from the floor where it's fallen.

"What did you do, Luce?" He implores me to deliver an answer, and I take a deep breath, calming myself and trying to remain level-headed.

"Xion is currently speeding towards The Fallen Kingdom in your car. And Thane is on her way over there too. They both have potions that will help Sephy fully bond with her goddess half at an accelerated rate. I brewed it myself this afternoon with the help of The Fates," I explain.

Yama's expression turns troubled.

"You brewed a potion that powerful? Are you sure that's wise, Lucifer?" he asks, and I scowl.

"It's only this once. It is an emergency after all," I retort, and Haedes looks between me and the rest of The Nexus.

"Thanks, Luce. I don't know if she'll make it out of this alive, but you did more than I've been able to. You gave her a chance at least." Haedes looks miserable, and I know he must be wondering exactly how he could have gotten around making the decision he's come to.

The answer, I feel, is that he couldn't. Every single option, including having him go in to collect her, is too risky, especially now that we know Pandora has full access to the entire Nexus Council and Mortaria with that box of hers.

Without Haedes, we have nothing in the form of real firepower, and Pandora full-on knows that. If Haedes dies, The Resurrection Flame goes out, the sun goes out, and our entire army of sinners will be reduced to nothing more than inanimate corpses littering the ground.

I wonder momentarily if Zeus thought about what he was doing when he sentenced Haedes, Yama, and Muerta to join Anubis and Osiris in mortal bodies, more powerful than any demi-god to be sure, but also a risk in security to The Higher Plains. I was banished not long after, and Thane made her choice to be here too, but we're vulnerable, all of us, especially now.

A shudder runs through me as we stand in a circle, the six of us staring at one another with grim expressions. We've been through a lot, fighting, wars, capture, but it's never been like this. We've never just been waiting to hear about the death of one close to us. I mean, even when Haedes had lost Sephy's mother, it had been sudden, unexpected, tragic.

With every moment that passes, I'm suddenly conscious of the fleetingness that constitutes each and every one. Each beat of my heart within my chest, each opening and closing of my eyelids, and each breath that escapes from my lips.

We stand in silence for a few moments, letting the severity of the situation fall over us like a cold wet blanket, watching Haedes like he's a bomb that may go off at any moment.

He turns to me, a sudden look of outrage on his face. I wonder what it is he's going to say, what blame he'll put on me now.

His eyes narrow, and his eyebrows rise on his forehead as he cocks his hip, troubled.

"Wait a minute— what do you mean Xion took my car?"

XION

I honk the horn, startling the many horses that litter the roads attached to carriages. I know it's cruel, but I really don't care at the moment; I'm trying to get to her, my only thoughts consumed by reaching her, saving her, protecting her. I need to do my duty. I am nothing without it, merely a monster with a pretty face.

I let out a final long blare of the horn and rev the engine again, this time, giving it everything I've got. The drivers finally get the message and part, veering from their courses so there's a clear path down the main street that runs through the heart of the dark city.

Wasting no time, I put my foot down, feeling as the turbo kicks in, and I'm pushed into the black leather of the seat. I race down the street, watching the cityscape turn to fields of gold and then to ash-scattered flat plains that expand out in endless grey.

I've been all over Mortaria today, and the journey back here has been quicker than the journey into the city by half. My heart is hammering in my chest, more aware now of time than I've ever been in my life, especially as I have spent most of it in a place where time has little or no effect.

Finally, reaching the place from where it seems I've only just come, I pull up to The Icon. I open the car door where sinners are already approaching to open the door for me; undoubtedly thinking I'm Haedes.

As I emerge, my leather jacket billowing out behind me as a gust of cool wind catches me by surprise, I walk toward the two sinners closest to me. One of them has a garnet pendant, for rage, and the other a clear quartz pendant, for pride.

"I need weapons," I growl, balling my fists at my sides. I widen my stance, not wishing to get into an argument.

"What's your authorisation?" The pride sinner asks me, scrutinising my form with wide blue eyes.

I sigh, *this guy must be new.*

Urgency growing, I allow the rage within my demon soul to burn bright and let my true face show. Their eyes widen, and without another word, they turn, leading me into The Icon. This time, though, we don't ascend to the height of the pyramid. Instead, we descend into its bowels towards the armoury.

I hear the clang of hammers on molten metal and anvils long before I see them. As we enter the space where wrath sinners pound the hardest substances into weapons of mass slaughter, I feel a wave of comfort from the familiar surroundings, from the smell of hot coals and hydraulically cooled steel. I know this, this world of desperate pain, heat, and the forge; this is the place where I was made strong, where I was forged into a being of unwavering self-restraint. Or I was— until her.

Moving quickly over to the far wall, I take up a handful of swords. Long swords, broad swords, and light needle-esque swords clatter to the ground as I haphazardly destroy the display of freshly moulded weaponry, not caring for order, just caring for efficiency.

"What do you need all this for anyway?" The wrath sinner demands, curious.

"I'm heading out to The Fallen Kingdom. Crossing The Ashen Waste," I explain, and the pride sinner snorts.

"Not bloody likely, mate; they've doubled in number in the last hour alone. It's a massacre out there!" he exclaims, and I shrug, the weight of hard and heavy steel in my hands comforting me.

"It doesn't matter. I've got to go," I mutter, pushing past them.

"There's a woman isn't there?" The pride sinner calls after me, but I don't wait to respond nor feel inclined to.

Yes, there is a woman. A woman in my charge, a woman who is stubborn as The Eternal Flame that she wields with such raw ferocity that it's a wonder I haven't been burned to a cinder in getting close to her.

"You know, I'll bet you ten years' service that there's a woman." I hear the pride sinner's voice follow me, echoing throughout the corridor as they trail in my wake, unable to keep up. I hope, for the wrath sinner's sake, that he doesn't take that bet.

Emerging from the labyrinthian decadence of The Icon, I find the sky beginning to fall cloudy with black smoke once more. I fear spark showers may be on the cards, but then again, this may move in my favour as demons don't do well under the natural phenomenon, though neither do I if it gets too heavy.

"Hey, look— wait!" I hear one of the sinners call after me. I believe it's the blue-eyed pride sinner and turn, rounding on him, frustrated I'm being halted once again.

"What?" I snap, arms full of metal.

"You're not hearing me! There are too many of them! You'll never make it through! Not with swords alone! You need— I don't know— something bigger!" he exclaims, and I look at him, eyes widening.

"What do you mean, bigger?" I ask, and he stares past me to the car, which has the engine still running, behind us.

"Do you know who this car belongs to?" I query him, and he shakes his head. "That would be Haedes," I inform him, and he gets a pained look on his face.

"I'm just saying, if it's really that serious, the reason you're going over to that place, then you're going to need more than a puny sword." He cocks his hip, staring at me. He's arrogant, which I should have expected, but he's probably also right.

"I suppose Haedes would prefer his daughter remain alive, even if his car does end up destroyed." I frown at them both and the pride sinner does a small fist pump.

"Ha! I *knew* there was a woman!" he announces, and I roll my eyes.

"Yeah, that's great. I have somewhere to be. Go and get them to open the gate," I command them, and the two men nod, jogging away and leaving the sound of clattering chains ringing in my ears long after they've become lost in the grey smear of heavy falling ash.

I open the door to the Hotrod, sliding in and dumping the swords on the passenger seat. Leaning back into the hold of the driver's seat, I take a deep steadying breath. This is possibly the most stupid thing I've ever attempted to do. I mean it'll be me versus hundreds if not thousands of demons, but I have to try. How can I possibly live with myself if I do nothing? I have enough guilt already on my shoulders to last an immortal lifetime. I'm not about to add more.

The engine is still running, blowing steam out into the surrounding cold air, the rumble causing my seat to vibrate beneath me. Shutting the door, I place my hands on the wheel, steadying myself and preparing to drive like one of those crazy people with a death wish.

Maybe I *do* have one of those after all.

I decide to turn on the stereo, looking for rhythm by which to act, something to psych me up for the journey.

As the enormous steel gates about a mile away begin to rise, I put the car in gear and ease off the clutch, pressing down on the accelerator and easing the car forward through the ash. I put on the windscreen wipers, as the stuff soon starts to pile up, and slouch, trying to see as well as I can in such unnatural driving conditions.

Moving forward at increasing speed, wanting to get this over with, I press the play button on the stereo after finally discovering how to turn the device on.

Ain't no mountain high enough floods the interior of the car.

I smile; this is definitely perfect for the insanity I'm about to attempt.

329

After a few minutes, I reach the gate that's now risen to its full height. I see the wrath and pride sinners by the wheel, pulling the hefty portcullis up into the air, and they both give me over-enthusiastic thumbs up. I smile sheepishly, not wanting to pretend like I'm friends with them, or that this entire ordeal will have some picture-perfect happy ending.

I pull through the gates and out onto The Ashen Waste, beyond the shadow of the wall, turning the car right and deciding that going directly through the thick of it is going to leave the car in ruins and me dead at best. I race along the length of a battle raging on my left, letting my hands tighten on the steering wheel as I go, thinking about all the ways this can possibly go wrong.

Either I'll die, Sephy will die, or I'll survive but then be murdered by Haedes when he finds out I've either not saved his daughter or trashed his car. All in all, after some serious thought, I come to realise that I'd rather be dead than explain the probable wreck that will be the Hotrod after this trip.

Then, as I turn to face the immense shadow cast by Mount Mallum underneath which The Fallen Kingdom lies, I wonder what will happen after this is all over.

What if both Sephy and I do survive?

She'll go back to her normal life— and then, what about me? I'll go back to chasing up leads like some morbid debt collector or fighting off demons in my spare time just so I can get remotely close to feeling something.

No.

The thought depresses me so deeply; I wonder if it might not be best if I don't return from this trip. I've known Sephy for such a short amount of time, and yet— I simply cannot imagine my life without her.

It's ridiculous.

Insane.

She has no interest in me; she's made that perfectly clear, and I'm no good for her. I'm no good for anyone. So why is it that at the thought of us parting and never seeing each other again, my long life seems more like torture than ever before?

I push my foot down harder on the accelerator, causing the car to reach the height of its potential speed. The engine roars loudly, no doubt alerting nearby demons to my location, but they were going to find me eventually, so it might as well be now.

I want to be in the thick of it already, into the adrenaline-pumping, heart-pounding, mind-numbing funnel of vision that comes only from a steely determination to survive despite the ever-increasing odds of death.

My fingertips turn to the colour of soot but I hold back my rage, knowing I need to save my strength for hand-to-hand combat, should it come to that.

The first of the demons catch my trail, several Phobias coming up in the rear-view mirror. I check my peripherals swerving left, then right, in a wavy line, trying to confuse them and prevent them from gaining traction on any part of the car that they can destroy.

They're soon joined by several Banshees, running in a pack, the smell of their sweet marrow-scented saliva filling my nostrils as it is brought in, pungent, through the car's vents. They near the car too fast as I've slowed slightly in swerving, leaping over the roof and landing right in front of me as I plough through them with no intention of stopping. They hit the bonnet, which crumples only slightly, before being tossed under the wheels like no more than puppies turned roadkill.

The song continues to ring throughout the car endlessly. To be honest, I'm beginning to wonder if the CD or cassette is stuck on repeat because it's not the first time I've heard this verse, I'm sure of it.

The lyrics give me strength, make me grit my teeth, and I swerve the car once more as a Succubi latches onto the roof with its long sallow fingers. It appears from nowhere, causing me to jump in my seat as the sound of nails on metal elicits a cringe. The sudden sideways motion of the car successfully dislodges it, leaving it in a miniature mushroom cloud of ash as it hits the ground. I'm triumphant for but a moment before continuing to steam forward, not looking back.

The volcano looms overhead, nearing at an increased speed as I smile, optimism growing with each mile that passes under the tread of the tyres.

I'm going to make it. I'm going to make it!

As I'm about to start singing along to the song, tapping my fingers on the steering wheel, I hit a pothole beneath the layers of ash and the car judders. I fly upwards in my seat, banging my head on the roof of the car. As I'm regaining my focus and my seated position, trying to get my feet back on the pedals, I realise that the Banshees lagging behind me have called their packmates for backup and are catching up quicker than I'd like.

Damn their telepathic links, I cuss, watching as a large group of beasts block my path.

I brake quickly, realising that I cannot possibly mow down so many. They surround me on the right, layers upon layers of the motheaten demons with white eyes, long claws, and hungry dripping jaws. Within moments, the left side of the car is also surrounded by Abraxians with wicked gleams in their eyes, and the intermittent flickering of Gorgonian camouflage adapting by the second. I swerve the car as I begin to slow, pulling on the handbrake and slamming the rear end of the vehicle into several of the onlooking Abraxians, trying to clear some semblance of a path.

They are sent flying, only making the surrounding demons more ravenous, more desperate for revenge as they close in tighter.

The car stops, right in the middle of the demon ring that's formed, all focused on me, right in the middle of the battle, which they seem to have abandoned at the realisation of where I was headed. This has been organised, and they've been given orders not to attack but to protect the last place they have to call home.

I'm so close to The Fallen Kingdom, *so close.* I can see the entrance to the old cathedral-esque hub from here, the silhouette of the crumbling walls, feel the heat coming off the volcano and the darkness thick in the air.

This was a very stupid idea, I cuss again, wondering why the hell I attempted this in the first place.

Then, amid my panic as the demons begin to place limbs and claws onto the metal bonnet and trunk of the vehicle, I reach over, grasping a sword in my palm. As I relish steel in my palm, I remember the only reason good enough for me to have done something this insane.

I need to prove I'm not all bad. If I save her, then maybe, I'll be worthy— Duty is all I have, and now saving her life is mine.

The thought of being so weak, so pathetic and vulnerable to my own instincts, ignites a fire in my stomach, a rage in my soul, and I watch my skin scorched demonic as my darker self presents. It's as though in my hating that very part of myself, I've brought it forward, made it strong.

The Banshees' cries echo, rippling through the air, an invisible and lethal weapon. The noise would be enough to kill any human at close range, now they're together in a pack, and certainly enough to send the glass windows and windscreen splintering before they explode around me.

I cover my face and eyes, waiting for the rain of glass to end, waiting for the fighting to begin.

As the demons close in, surrounding the car, I think of her and hope that she's as strong as she's always claimed to be. After all, I've never met someone who can tame the rage and shadow within me like her, and that is just a little too precious to lose.

28

BACK IN BLACK

PANDORA

MY FEET TOUCH DOWN on the black stone of the Dark Colosseum floor, the crumbling structure casting shadows across my unimpressed expression from above. The air is chill on this side of the volcano; perhaps because the wind is blowing in the opposite direction, and I feel the eyes of the five Demon Lords turn to me, ranging from milky bone white to onyx-tinted crimson, expectant. I place the box safely in the pocket of my leather skirt, bracing myself for their questions.

"Pandora. What is the word?" Barbas demands, poker straight white hair billowing around him as cool air wafts inside of the entrance chamber to the arena. There is no light here, only the dark outlines of dead carcasses that've been dragged along the floor for disposal, leaving the stains of bodily fluids behind.

"Haedes will not trade Mortaria for his daughter's life," I announce, my irritation growing as the five figures visibly slouch, their eyes narrowing and mouths becoming thin grimaces.

I have failed them, and now I have no doubt they will make me suffer.

"Well, I could have told you that," Barbas laughs, cocking a smile. I narrow my eyes at him.

Did he want me to fail?

"What do you mean?" I snap, short, and he smirks.

"Well, Haedes' ultimate fear is death, isn't it? There's no way he'd ever give up control over the one place keeping him alive," he elaborates.

"You couldn't have possibly mentioned this to me before?" I catechise him, but he only shrugs.

"I wanted to see what would happen; can't blame an old cat for being curious," he sniggers.

"Haven't you ever heard of the phrase curiosity *killed* the cat?" I mutter, digging my long nails into the flesh of my palm and letting them draw blood. The bite of a sharp edge on flesh gives me a small rush, boosting my confidence.

"Now Pandora, it wouldn't be wise to threaten the Demon Lord of fear and terror, would it? After all, I know exactly where your deepest fears lie," he taunts me, clearly aware of my weaknesses. Perhaps that's why he's done this, knowing that inadequacy is my greatest fear. In making me look stupid to the others, he's proving just that.

"Why are you all standing here anyway?" I demand, changing the subject and trying to reiterate my new authority.

"We're trying to decide whose Kindred should attempt to kill the girl first," Lilliana informs me, turning in a long and rugged gown of black taffeta that looks like it's been put together by a seamstress turned blind. The top of the dress is little more than two bunches of netting barely covering her breast, plummeting to where her protruding ribs can be seen moving in and out in an irregular and feral rhythm.

"What do you mean, first? This isn't a game. All the Kindred shall be set on her together. Why would you even consider sending them in separately?" I interrogate them, mystified, as I take several steps forward, allowing the lilac sunlight to settle over me as I still, finally, beneath a hole in the roof.

"Our demons don't work together. Everyone knows that. They turn on one another within only moments, particularly when they're hungry." Gorgon makes this clear, cocking an eyebrow and smiling at me, revealing a forked tongue as he licks his bottom lip. It's almost as though in this look, he's encouraging me to pursue the issue further.

"Well, they should work together! What, you don't have enough control over them to stop them from killing one another? That's utterly ridiculous. What kind of Lords are you?" I demand, and they look affronted. "Has it never occurred to you that you could use Banshees as mounts, have your demons move on their backs at the same speed? That you could have Gorgonian's infiltrating buildings and letting the others inside?" I put this idea to them, and several eyebrows rise on foreheads. Eyes twinkle, and then Abraxis speaks up, pushing his dark hair back on his head with one hand. In full demon form, his scarlet tattoos shine, swirling in the dark like molten rivers as his eyes burn into me with an amber glare.

"This is not the way it is done," he begins, looking at me with a grim expression, but then turns to the others, "but perhaps, it is the way it should be done from now on," he suggests.

Gorgon nods.

"I agree; if we cannot control our own Kindred, then we should not be in control. Period. We must work together. I feel Pandora may have ignited my hopes that we may reclaim Mortaria, however ill-informed her intent may have been, but perhaps there is still a chance. What if we ask the girl to join us?" Gorgon suggests, and I sneer.

"Excellent idea. If we can't persuade her father, I'm sure the one with her life on the line can be swayed," I agree.

Katerina speaks up, her deep rust-coloured gown rustling around her as she turns to me.

"What gives you such sudden faith, Gorgon?" she presses him to justify his claim as he spins to face her.

His suit is made from velvet that's pressed to look like snake's skin in a deep bottle green. He's wearing a pristine white shirt, a miracle in itself considering the state of the other Demon Lords and their attire. I mean, Lilliana looks like she desperately needs a bath for a start.

"Things are changing. My children can feel it, something in the shadowy waters of the mortal world. They have been in touch with the children of Kraken, and heard of a weakening in the walls between dimensions. An act of The Circle of Eight. It may be that we can bring back one of the Gods of Ancient after all," he whispers, causing me to blink not once but twice. Could it be that he's realised my assumptions about Lucifer may be correct?

"Which god would that be?" Barbas enquires, superior in his tone and doubting in his expression.

"The only God of Ancient who was not banished to The Island of The Blessed," Gorgon elaborates, causing Abraxis to stroke his chin in thought.

"Ra? But— he owes us no allegiance. He has no Demon Lord here, and his soul is floating around in The Nether, forbidden to return to The Higher Plains. You know this," he reminds me.

"This is true, but he cannot be successful alone. He will be able to help us free the others. Or so I believe. If things align properly," I interject now, making sure that I am not forgotten about.

"This is a lot of speculation," Lilliana voices her own doubts, and I turn to her.

"Perhaps, but it is also the only chance we have to reclaim what is rightfully yours. Wouldn't you take such a risk?" I demand, and suddenly, she looks meek.

She backs away, whispering only, "Perhaps," in response.

I straighten my spine within the boning of my corset, taking a shallow breath and pressing onward, not wanting to stop in my momentum, knowing that if I do, then my faith in my plan may falter.

"Regardless of this, we must first deal with the demi-god. You are happy to have your Kindred work together?" I look to them for confirmation, and they all nod in unison.

"Very well then. Let us proceed to the arena. We have an execution to spectate."

SEPHY

The lilac sun burns bright overhead, creating a glare that leads me to wish I could raise a hand to shield my eyes as my pale skin sizzles. Abraxian guards surround me, their black skin swirling with variations of Xion's coloured tattoos. They're varied in colour, and I find myself wondering if it means anything as I stand, bored and waiting, examining them.

Xion is definitely more attractive, and the female demons among the troupe look very masculine indeed.

I should probably be scared, but I continue to be simply impatient. Is it because I think Xion or Haedes or someone else is most definitely on their way here right now to set me free?

Perhaps.

However, the longer I'm stuck in this nightmare, the more I'm starting to think that it's because I've just given up and want them to kill me already. My hands are tied behind my back, utterly useless to me, especially seeing as I still can't muster so much as a spark. So, thus far, I've become less useful than a match with nothing to strike against, and I'm supposed to be a demi-goddess. Maybe this is just how it's meant to be, given my newfound discovery that Fate does exist and, apparently, can knit a badass afghan to boot.

The demons around me stir, alerting me to some sort of change in the atmosphere of my surroundings, almost as if they've become suddenly nervous.

I look up at the high edges of the pit. They're made from flawlessly slick stone, making escape impossible.

I shuffle on the ground, the hideous crunching of small animal bones, or maybe even the skeletons of some sort of infant, sounding underfoot. It's disgusting, and the entire place absolutely reeks of rot, of decay.

As I'm pondering maybe dancing to pass the time, shadows appear on all sides, and I find myself with the commercial slogan for Clorox stuck in my head. I roll my eyes.

Of course, at a time like this, I'm thinking *'For life's bleachable moments'*, as if I'm not already suffering enough.

"Miss Sinclair, welcome." Her voice comes from above and I glare, finding myself surrounded now. There are six of them, the Demon Lords I assume, towering over me as I stand in the pit, helpless. They are ceremoniously equidistant as they watch me from every angle, making me the star of my very own morbid stage show.

Maybe it could be a musical? I muse.

"Just call me Sephy; you know, the surroundings really aren't so formal," I call back, cocking my hip. Pandora glares down at me.

"Okay, Welcome Sephy," she corrects herself, and I immediately feel the power dynamic between us shift.

If she's acknowledging my request, it means she wants something from me.

I'm still wearing the outfit Anubis provided and wonder if she had me fighting for my life in mind when she picked it out. I look fierce and can only hope I feel the same ferocity when it comes to the fighting.

Flipping my hair over one shoulder, I scowl up at my captor.

"Can we get this over with then?" I challenge her, seeing the faces of the other Demon Lords examining me with curiosity. I stare right back, narrowing my eyes and looking up at their pale demonic faces.

One looks like a snake, another like a feral child who's been raised by wolves. The others appear terrifying in their own right, blood-thirsty faces and poker-straight white hair ingraining into my memory. I never want to forget them, even if I'm not alive for very long.

The final Demon Lord I lay eyes on stirs something within my gut. It's Xion's father. I know it is.

His eyes burn into mine, and I shudder slightly; the similarity is uncanny. Xion has barely mentioned him, and with a face like that, it's not hard to guess why. He seems utterly evil, and I haven't even heard him speak.

"We want to offer you the chance to save your own skin, seeing as how your father has sentenced you to death," Pandora announces. I blanche slightly.

"Are you kidding me?" I ask her, scowling. She went to ask Haedes to save my life, and he did *nothing*?

So much for parental instincts, I grumble, realising I should have known better than to trust anyone with blue hair.

"No. He really left you to the demons. Stings, doesn't it?" she goads me, but I shake my head. "Unbind her. I want to see her fight back before she dies." Pandora commands the surrounding Abraxians, who move forward, taking the irons from around my wrists. I rub the flesh there, red raw and tender from my rebellion, trying to keep the conversation going. I'm hoping if Pandora has a point, I might start to see it on the horizon at some point soon. This death thing is becoming a far more longwinded affair than I'd bargained for, that's for damn sure.

"Look, whatever; guess I'll have to whoop you myself." I feel like a teenager again, like she's my dormitory mistress, except a lot more vampy and with worse dress sense.

"Whoop me?" Pandora asks, her mouth twisting into a smirk.

"Yeah, you know, kick your ass." I raise my hands like a boxer, and she laughs.

"Without your powers, you're nothing more than a little lost girl in hell, Sephy. I'm really not scared. Now, will you join us, and aid in our cause to take back Mortaria from your father? The one who sentenced you to die at our collective hand?" she asks me. I shake my head without missing a beat.

"I'm not lost. I'm home. This is where I was created. And I'd never help you take control of it. You look like something out of last season's Goth rejects bin," I quip.

She frowns.

"Stupid girl! You'd rather die?" she demands.

I simply shrug.

"What can I say? I guess seeing all this I'm just not that scared of death anymore. I mean, any Nether Realm or Higher Plain has got to be better than listening to you drivel on, ain't it?" I ask her, smirking, and she looks like she might hit me.

"Very well, then. Release them," she commands, frustration obvious in both her expression and tone.

The Abraxian guards, who have me surrounded, dash to the edges of the arena, and from five different corridors around me, pointed steel gates rise under the actions of their soot-coloured hands. The clinking of chains being pulled through steel rings is the only thing I can hear as my heart begins to unwillingly pound.

The gates lead into five dark holes in the otherwise seamless wall, and I don't know where to look first. They're shrouded in abyssal dark, but I can feel the demons getting closer as my skin prickles, hairs rising on the back of my neck at a barely noticeable change in the air.

I tense my muscles, knowing I have no Eternal Flame at my disposal, but wondering if I can outwit the demons using speed and what little natural strength I possess. The odds may be stacked against me, but I won't go without a fight. After all, I always knew I'd be dragged from this life, kicking, screaming, and cursing. It occurs to me now that fighting, whether physical or mental, seems to be what I'm designed for above anything else.

The first demon enters the pit of the colosseum, its tread rapid on the alabaster bones littering the floor, each step leaving a crackling echo behind. It's a Banshee, my oldest demon friend, followed quickly by a slender Succubi, two reptilian creatures that slither, flashing intermittently in and out of camouflage, and several phobias. I look each of the beasts in the eye in turn, before the Abraxians, who have raised the gate, turn on me too.

The odds aren't that bad— are they? I count them. There's— twelve demons and one— well, me.

Well, shit. I hiss internally, tensing my arms and readying to throw a punch or something equally as futile. I glance up to the shadowy outlines of the Demon Lords and Pandora, who glower down at me, fascinated by the spectacle, and feel like a bug under a magnifying glass.

"Come on then!" I yell, trying to psych myself up but realising quickly that egging on the demon hoard is probably a stupid thing to do. Twirling on the ball of my foot and beginning to run from the demons, I watch them launch forward.

Hindsight really is wonderful.

The Phobias are by far the quickest, catching up to me in only seconds. I rotate, using the curved wall as an aid as the first leaps toward me. I inhale sharply, waiting for the pain, but it doesn't come.

I've caught it instinctually by two of its legs and let my arms buckle underneath its weight before bench-pressing the spindled legs backwards. The Phobia's body buckles as I push its legs back the wrong way, snapping them from its skeleton and feeling blood drench my forearms as it falls from me, lifeless.

One down.

I spin, narrowly missing a Gorgonian that flies toward me, smashing its head into the wall with no arms to stop its path through the air. I duck under the swing of the Succubi's long arm, narrowly missing the clutch of its four-inch-long bloody red claws and falling into a forward roll across the gravel.

As I stand firmly on two feet, flipping my hair back, I'm tackled straight on by the Banshees, who I seem to have oh so conveniently forgotten about.

The smell of death envelops me as my field of vision is consumed by the red of the sky above, before the snapping jaws and gnashing teeth of the demon eclipse it from view. Its fur is slick with moisture as I ram my palms into the cheeks of the beast, holding it back with mere willpower and what little energy adrenaline is providing.

My heart is racing.

I guess this is it.

This is the end.

This is how I die.

I look into the eyes of the Banshee, into the white emptiness of its soul as it jerks within my palms, bucking like a wild horse, snarls rumbling from within its chest. Its entire body weight is on top of me, and as I'm losing distance in the struggle to keep it from ripping out my throat, I momentarily consider just letting it have me, letting it kill me so it can be over.

A tinkling reaches my ears, and a flash of scarlet catches the corner of my vision.

Concerned it could be another demon, I turn my head for just a moment, finding not a demon but a small bottle that's fallen upon the sharp white unevenness of the ground.

Feeling new strength and adrenaline flood my body, I give a final shove of my hands and take the small amount of space to pull my knees up and plant my feet firmly on the Banshee's chest. I kick out with all my might, rolling sideways and out from under the heavy weight of the body in the small window of time I've managed to salvage.

I reach out, grabbing the vial in my hand.

God, I hope this is from Luce, I pray, pulling open the stopper as quickly as I'm able and chugging the contents like it's no more than a shot of tequila at Retropolis.

The taste is freaking awful, but I bare it, screwing up my eyes and letting it burn down the back of my throat as I swallow, gasping for air. Within seconds, my entire body is on fire and I'm whimpering, praying for death to come as my veins run wild with liquid fire, my heart ready to combust in my chest.

My ribs constrict like they're made of metal and someone is heating them with a blowtorch, and my lungs cease in their ability to take in air as I had attempted at first, as though I'm afraid that adding oxygen will only fan the flames raging within my chest.

The scent of gasoline fills my nostrils from nowhere, and suddenly, as I think I can take no more, my eyes fly open and my lungs fill with cool, healing air.

Finally.

Rolling over, I feel energy injected into my limbs, my muscles, like someone has doped them with amphetamine. Heart pounding, this time hopeful, I feel more alive than I ever have in the mortal world. It's better than drinking, or dancing with strangers, sleeping with strangers, riding—

This beats all of that, hands down, without a shadow of a damn doubt.

I'm on my feet in a single motion, only to find my hair is alight around my face. I stare at it, catching my reflection in the shiny slick stone of the round wall caging me in.

I smile, clicking my fingers.

Where I will it, flame erupts.

"*Ha!*" I exclaim, excitement clutching at me.

The Demon Lords look confused as I stand, hair blazing, hands conjuring increasingly ferocious flames as I let the magic flow through my body.

Muahahahaha. I cackle in my head. *You better run you little shits.*

I turn on the demons, no longer afraid, but empowered.

Taking out the Banshee closest to me in a single stream of flame, I spin on my heel in an artful pirouette, landing a spinning kick directly in the gut of the Succubi. Approaching me from behind, I catch it mere moments before it lunges for my throat, having felt the air stir. I wrap a tendril of flame around its neck and decapitate it, watching as it disintegrates to ash, burning up in my merciless clutch.

I take out the remaining Phobia with a simple, beautifully formed fire orb, which I bowl with exceptional accuracy, hitting the demon right between the eyes.

"Strike!" I call out, doing a little dance and smirking up at the Demon Lord with a thin face and long white hair. If I had to guess, I'd say he was Barbas, and it was his demon I've just eviscerated, but who knows? Either way, I'm bragging.

The Gorgonians present a greater challenge, and I'm wary of them and their camouflage as I kick one Abraxian toward his fellow fighters, causing them to tumble into a disorganised and glowing pile of scorched flesh. Using both of my hands this time, I form a ring of fire around them, letting them burn slowly. I allow my irises to reflect the flames up to Xion's father, a smirk of victory only too evident on my face.

Should I be this cocky? I wonder momentarily, but then shrug to myself, realising that I'd rather be cocky than weak. Rather be strong than dead.

I guess I have more of a desire to live than I thought, I realise, wondering where this sudden love of evading death and shooting fire has come from.

I don't know why, but I'm loving this, enjoying the heat, the scent of burning flesh and the feeling that no one and nothing can stop me from exerting my will. I'm turning into a right little pyromaniac.

I've been drunk before. But this is drunk of a different kind, and it's addictive as hell.

Once only the smoke from the Abraxians' bodies remains, rising around me like a dramatic effect in a music video, I stand, looking around me and trying to locate the final obstacles. The Gorgonians.

I glance over my shoulder, closing my eyes and trying to listen for any sound that would indicate the movement of snake-like demons. The slithering reaches me, and I push my palms out, one on either side, firing a line of eternal flame from each. I spin, creating a two-spoked pinwheel of blazing fire, trailing it along the edges of the pit and encasing the entire area in flame. I leave only a small ring of earth around myself, savouring the heat. The two Gorgonian demons slither, trying to escape. They fail, perishing, one on either side of me, clambering to ascend the wall lining the pit, fleeing for their lives in fear, like animals in a trap.

The hissing of the demons makes me feel sick as I smell the burning of their flesh, but my heart continues to beat rapid in my chest. I'm breathing calmly, but inside my mind is racing, senses acute and body oiled slick like one fluid machine of destruction.

I look up at the Demon Lords, finding all of them gone, all of them except her, Pandora, who remains.

I curtsey to her.

"Is that all?" I cock my hip.

She opens her mouth to speak, but no sound comes out.

"I thought so," I continue, a smile tugging at the corners of my lips.

I take a few steps backwards, ready to get the hell out of here. I picture where I want to be, my body humming and alive with power, hair still alight and glowing around my face.

Everything is so clear now, every movement in the air, the uneven, distressed breathing of Pandora as she watches on, her lack of power more evident to me now than ever.

I smile, contented.

"Sephy, out." I give her the peace sign and convect from the Colosseum, leaving only ash, bones, and smoke in my wake.

I don't make it as far as I'd like.

In fact, despite my cocky exterior, I wasn't even sure I'd be able to convect. I'm running on fumes, I can feel it as I rematerialize, surrounded by flames, on the outskirts of some crumbling ruins.

Stepping up and over a pitiful excuse for a wall that had once been grand, I feel the sunlight on my skin, the cool ash falling from the sky around me, and the heat of the volcano at my back. The smell of sulphur, of burning, is strong, and I wonder how anyone lives here without needing air freshener at least.

The first thing I notice as I step into deep ash piles on the other side of the wall is a demon hoard clambering to get at something. The second thing I notice is the sound of Marvin Gaye being drowned out by an extremely loud and grating car alarm.

What the hell is that? I wonder, mustering the energy to form an enormous fireball, which I can scarcely contain, in one hand.

I can feel the heat coming off this one and know that my energy is waning fast but that I need to hold on. I'm not out of danger yet.

My hair is starting to extinguish too, with only small flames, like those belonging to a candle, coming off the ends of my locks. All in all, I guess I'm not looking too bad when you consider I've spent the last few hours in a cage and then almost been eaten.

Running forward, I throw the fireball, killing four demons in one blow and causing the others to scatter. I see the source of the commotion, and as I take out several more demons with some effort and what little firepower I can manage, I find a wreckage that was once a pretty nice car.

"Sephy?" I hear my name called, a familiar voice that makes me want to smile and laugh all at once.

"Xion?" I call back, finding him scrunched up in the driver's seat with a sword in each hand.

"What are you doing here?" I ask him, grabbing a sword through the smashed-in window from the passenger seat and spinning, thrusting it into the pale flesh of a Phobia that's decided to launch itself at me from atop the exposed engine.

"I came to— save you, actually," Xion admits, decapitating a Gorgonian that's trying to slither into the car with him.

"Oh. Huh. How's that going for you?" I demand. He smirks.

"Great actually," he grumbles over the siren and the sound of the stereo. I reach through the window, smashing in the dash with my fist and stopping the car alarm without a second thought. Unfortunately, Marvin Gaye just carries on singing.

"Ah, so I'll uh, let you get back to it then. Exilia this way?" I point back across The Ashen Waste, and he rolls his eyes, exasperated and grumpy. Drawing his sword back from the Gorgonian body, he takes his feet off the dash, where he's been holding back something that has been trying to kill him through the smashed windscreen.

"Get in," he demands, and I do as he asks, glad to be off my feet. This whole being a badass thing is tiring, no doubt about it.

"Marvin Gaye?" I ask him as the music surrounds me.

"The damn stereo is stuck on repeat," he cusses and I give him a sideways glance.

"You know if you like Marvin Gaye, I won't laugh— this is very— inspirational." I try not to laugh but can't help it as a small smile creeps across my lips.

"It's stuck!" he protests, and I shake my head.

"A likely story."

"So, you're okay?" he asks me, and I nod.

"Yep. I told you I could look after myself. And yes, I will be saying I told you so a lot more in the coming days. So, prepare your bearded self," I inform him. He grumbles, rolling his eyes yet again.

"That's great, I'll remember this conversation the next time you need saving." He says this like there will be a next time. But I know that this is it for me. I can't go through this again, powers or not.

"Well, at least I have a ride home. I'm not sure I could've made it by convecting. I'm feeling a little drained," I admit, and he smirks at my sentiment, though the concern in his eyes flickers to life almost immediately.

"Adding chauffeur to my list of titles wasn't really on my to-do list today, but it's fine. I'll take what I can get." As he turns to me, waiting for a quick-witted response, my heartbeat slows and everything around me fades to black. I go to reply to him, but my lips won't move. Energy is sapped from me as quickly as it came, and I feel my grip on consciousness slipping from me too fast to reclaim.

I crash out in the passenger seat next to him, exhausted, battered, but undoubtedly alive.

29

WALK ON BY

LUCE

I STAND ON THE balcony, long fingers wrapped around the wrought iron railing. It twists artfully like vines studded with large thorns. I exhale heavily, tired of waiting, of always looking to the skies, hoping to hear the caw of a raven, the rustle of feathers, or the beating of wings.

The sky has turned deep burgundy; like someone has murdered the gods and their blood is spilling down into this place. Dark, sooty clouds billow, eclipsing the sun from view, and whilst the wind catches a lock of my hair, my heart still beats, a metronome, a timekeeper.

I hear him crashing around through the open, frosted glass doors, even though he'd promised he would behave himself. I realise now though that trusting Haedes was a mistake; his word, when it comes to me, holds about as much weight as a cloud-formed feather.

"Luce!" he calls to me, and I exhale, frustrated. Why is it that he somehow always manages to make it about him? His pain. His suffering. What about Sephy? The girl who is probably being digested right now. His very own daughter.

I breathe out, calming myself.

It was the right decision, I remind myself.

Regardless, I find myself slightly sick at the fact the decision was one made with such seeming ease by her own father.

I rotate, letting both hands grab the rail before pushing away from it and turning my back on the skies to tend to Haedes, yet again.

"Haedes, what is it now?" I demand, crossing my arms across my chest and blinking a few times. He's pacing from one side of my bedroom to the other, biting his nails down to the quick. His blue hair is paler somehow, less vibrant, and his eyes sheen dull grey as they catch mine in their lacklustre charms.

"Where's your alcohol?" he asks me, and I shrug.

"I don't keep any around here. Thane and I aren't big drinkers, you know that," I remind him. His mouth falls slightly open.

"What? So, you're telling me that with your parental lineage, you don't drink?! How?!" He looks astounded, and I shrug.

"As I taught Xion many years ago, those of us who are susceptible to darkness are at the disadvantage of having to maintain strict self-control. We don't let go. It causes accidents," I warn him, but he only rolls his eyes, unimpressed and not willing to entertain my feelings for a second.

"You know what that sounds like to me?" he asks, and I raise an eyebrow, "An excuse for being boring."

"I could say that you use emotional turmoil as an excuse for being a drunk, but I suppose that would make me insensitive," I mutter, and he smirks at me, though his eyes are a little desperate.

"You must have alcohol somewhere? Anything! What about— I don't know, wine for cooking?" He pleads with his gaze, moving through from the bedroom in a few suave steps and making his way past Beelz and Cerb, who lay asleep together in front of the fire.

The Fates remain on the black velvet sofa, exactly where I left them before all this began, and they turn in unison, even though one of them is blind, as Haedes begins to rummage through my kitchen.

Coming up empty, as I knew he would— mainly because I have removed all the alcohol on purpose— he takes strides across to the other side of the room, opening my drafts cabinet to fiddle with vials.

"Hey! No!" I scold him, rushing forward and slamming the doors shut, almost trapping his hands.

"Luce! Come on! I'm dying here! This waiting is torture!" he pleads with me, but I shake my head.

"Nope. Absolutely not. You have an addictive personality for a start. I'm not dosing you up on ancient magic. End of story." I shake my head, crossing my slender arms across my chest and letting my long nails bite into my elbows as I scowl at him.

He opens his mouth to protest, but before a single syllable can fall into the frustrated atmosphere between us, the sound of wings beating in the air distracts us both as we rush back through to the bedroom.

Thane has returned, landing on the railing of the balcony before she hops down, still in raven form, to the floor. Her silken black feathers are ruffled, and her beady black eyes find mine as the bird waits for me to attend her.

I sweep across the dark floor, placing a cloak on the floor outside and closing the doors to give her privacy as she transforms. I hear the familiar cries, morphing from raven squawk to woman's agony as I sit down on the edge of our neatly made bed, crossing my legs beneath the many layers of my skirt and observing my stomach tie itself into knots. I hate this, hearing her cry out, hearing her pain. It breaks my heart every single time without fail.

"How long does transforming back to a sack of skin and bones take?" Haedes growls, impatiently tapping his foot on the floor as he sits down next to me on the bed. I momentarily debate turning to punch him in the face, but I know he has the power to kill me and send me back to my mother, or worse The Nether Realm, even if he'd never use it.

I hope.

"Give her a second," I grumble, biting down hard on my bottom lip and watching as Thane's silhouette reforms from where before there was nothing. Wrapping the cloak around herself, the doors open, and she steps through, slightly out of breath. Her long slender legs protrude forward and out from under the black velvet of the garment wrapped around her shoulders, exciting me when I should be anything but. Her hair is a spikey halo of disorganised black strands, and her eyes move to us both as we stare at her, expectant.

"Well?" I ask, and she takes several delicate steps forward.

"They're alive. Both of them. Sephy got the potion from me, took it, and now they're on their way back; she saved Xion too." She sums up the results quickly and with short-cut sentences, putting us out of our misery as quickly as possible.

I jump up, clapping my hands with childlike excitement.

"What about— my car?" Haedes asks, and I turn, gawping at him in disbelief.

"Seriously? *Seriously*?!" I yell, placing my hands on my hips and giving him a glare that could wither even the deadest of souls.

"Well, there's no harm in asking— now I know they're both alive." He tries to justify his lack of caring for his daughter, but a part of me wonders if it's not so much her life he couldn't stand the thought of losing but his own sense of contentment. The guilt of such a choice would eat any man alive, but perhaps Haedes was, as always, more concerned with his problems than with those he has inadvertently caused. I really can never tell.

"Thanks for saving my daughter, Thane. Gee, you're so welcome, Haedes—" Thane puts on a breathless mockery of Haedes' voice and then reverts to her own, scowling at him. I move across the slick stone toward her, my bare feet enjoying the cool relief it provides, and kiss her on the mouth.

"Thank you," I whisper. She beams.

"You can thank me again later," she winks, and I hear fake retching coming from behind us where Haedes is pretending to be sick.

"Oh, fuck off," Thane barks at him, sweeping him out of the room and slamming the sliding doors shut.

Shedding the cloak, she proceeds to dress in front of me.

"He's unbelievable," she growls.

I nod.

"What do you expect? He has the emotional maturity of an egg," I state with blunt certainty, and she laughs.

"I don't know. I guess I expected him to give a shit about his daughter," she shrugs, and I mirror her action as she begins to button up a simple white cotton shirt over her milky white navel.

"I think he does; I think he does more than he'd ever admit, but he's scared. After today, I can see why. He can't be a parent. Not like anyone expects him to be. Being a parent makes you weak, weaker perhaps than being in love romantically, and they've already put him in an impossible position with her. They wanted him to choose between sacrificing her and losing Mortaria. He turned them down, Thane," I express, and she gapes.

"He— he really chose the universe over himself?" she asks me, and I nod, watching her stunned expression as her hollow cheekbones cast shadows over her parted lips. "Well, I'll be damned," she exclaims, and I feel my mouth twist into a smile.

"You are my love. We both are. But yes, he would have sacrificed her to do his duty. I think that gives him the right to be a bit of a jackass," I sigh, and she frowns, pulling on a pair of high-waisted black pants that hug her buttocks and accentuate the little curve her willowy form possesses before tucking in the shirt for good measure.

Turning from her as she finishes dressing, I move out to the balcony once more and look down upon the city, a sound alerting me to Xion's possible return. Correct in my assumption, I spot the remnants of

Haedes' beloved mean machine, trundling down the road, the engine smoking and the stereo blaring out some hideous song at a volume that is far too acute. I can hear it from all the way up here, and it's ridiculously cheery considering where the vehicle has just come from.

I shrug.

Maybe that's Xion's thing then? I wonder, hurrying past Thane and opening the sliding doors that partition the apartment, revealing Haedes bickering with the Fates.

"They're back. Come on." I move around the furniture, grabbing Haedes by the crook of his elbow and pulling him with me out of the door. We journey down the spiral staircase together, feet bare as they pad against the cold stone.

We fall into silence, and Thane can be heard locking the apartment door again as she follows us out.

As we hit the main level of the Exilia Multum, nervous eyes of envy sinners follow us and I wonder what rumours have been spreading. Try as we might, the sinners are never out of The Nexus' political loop for long. Perhaps that's why so many of them harbour strong yet secret opinions about us, maybe even loathe us a little.

The flickering light of sconces casts a red hue over Haedes' worried expression as we race to the main staircase, though out of concern for his daughter or his car, I couldn't tell you.

Thane grabs my hand as she catches up to us, just in time for us to turn at the height of the double crystal staircase. We descend together, side by side, our tread synchronised effortlessly as she smiles at me.

"You saved her, Luce," she whispers to me, kissing me on the cheek. I well up inside, heart sporting a happy glow as she looks at me like I can do anything, *be* anything.

"I couldn't have done it without you." I smile at her, sweet in expression, and she blushes slightly.

"I guess we make a pretty good team."

"I guess we do," I reply, squeezing her hand in mine.

We don't have to wait more than a minute and can hear them coming long before we can see them. The blaring of an inspirational and extremely inappropriate song echoes out in the gargantuan hollow of the entranceway, and soon after, the rolling of the flat tyres squeals up in front of us.

Xion gets out of the car, face stern as Haedes moves to scold him. Moving forward, Xion bravely hands his keys back to him, closing his palm around them as Haedes stands, shocked.

The windshield and all the windows have been shattered within their frames, there's a hole in the roof, multiple scratches and dents on both sides, flat tyres, a crumpled bonnet, the engine is smoking visibly, and the smell of oil leaking from somewhere fills my nostrils.

"You might want to have the stereo looked at; damn thing is stuck," Xion announces, cavalier as he stands before the black and blue smoking wreck.

Haedes looks like he might cry.

Returning with haste to the passenger side, Xion opens the door, pulling out Sephy, her red hair vibrant and definitive. I exhale. She doesn't look too badly injured.

As Xion shuts the door of the mean machine, causing a few intact pieces of window to fall out and clink against the floor, Haedes physically winces. I ignore this on purpose. My most pressing concern now is Sephy's reaction to the potion.

What I've given her is potent, and as a demi-god and not a full god, it's bound to have some kind of side effect.

I watch as Xion walks straight past Haedes, not making eye contact, not trying to talk, with Sephy in his arms. She's limp, like a red-headed rag doll, and her eyes are closed, her mouth slack. Her chest rises and falls in long deep breaths, showing me that she's still alive, but for how much longer?

What if the potion has caused her damage? I wonder as we move in a single line behind him, following toward the main staircase.

What if I have put her in a mystical coma or something worse?

I start to feel fear creep in at the corners of my mind, emerging from the shadows as the words of my mother come back to me.

You're a danger, Lucifer. Dark, ancient magic is a danger to us all, and that, my child, is half of who you are. You can't be trusted. It's nothing personal, it's just the way it is.

Hecate's dark and seductive tone echoes throughout my memory as I turn and follow in Xion's wake. My expression, which had been so full of hope just moments ago, is now laced with anxiety and worry.

Haedes may have sentenced his daughter to die, but I bet he'd kill me for poisoning her by accident.

I swallow deep, squeezing Thane's palm again as we begin to climb the spiral staircase. Thane drops my hand, right when I need the feel of her skin on mine the most, speeding ahead as she takes two steps at a time with her long legs before letting Xion into our apartment.

He travels the length of our dark luscious interior in only seconds, speeding through the space and laying the demi-goddess atop our black velvet sheets. Her red hair is fiery in contrast to her snowy skin, and she looks porcelain, fragile like a doll.

"What did you do to her?" Xion demands, tone accusatory.

"I don't know. That potion was strong. She's been through a lot," I express.

Xion scowls.

"Don't give me that. She just single-handedly fought her way out of the Dark Colosseum. She's not a child, you— you must have screwed it up!" He's getting angry now, and Thane places her hands on his shoulders, stilling him as he begins to pace with mad rage around the bed.

"Xion, stop. Let her rest. You've done the hard part, now we just have to wait. Sephy has to come back to consciousness on her own," she explains, taking the heat off me, for which I'm grateful.

Haedes hovers behind us, looking timidly at his daughter, late to the party as always. He isn't angry; he just seems out of place, melancholy, like he doesn't know what to do with himself.

"That's not good enough," Xion snarls, and I feel his rage getting out of hand.

"Xion! Enough!" I bark, my voice coming out louder and more feral than I intend. I feel the dark side of me present, and my heartbeat accelerates.

I'm scaring even myself.

"Look, Luce, I'm sorry. I just— wait and see isn't good enough." He looks at me apologetically, but he's still not willing to back off.

Sitting on the edge of the bed, I take Sephy's hand in mine, looking deeply into her face. She's scorching hot to touch, and her entire body is limp. I scrutinise her, watching and praying that she comes back to her body soon.

I turn to Xion, trying to make my agony over the choices I've been forced into making evident in my gaze as I speak.

"Unfortunately, waiting is all we've got."

SEPHY

I'm dragged from unconsciousness, much as I thought I would be dragged from life; kicking, screaming, and in great pain.

I open my eyes, finding myself in unfamiliar surroundings. As I let my fingers splay out amongst onyx-coloured velvet sheets, I exhale into the muggy air of the room, blinking once, then twice.

At least, this is comfier than the cage.

I breathe, relieved that my escape hadn't been some flight of fantasy concocted by my imagination.

"Sephy?" I hear Luce's silky tone calling my name and find her at the foot of the bed. Thankfully, she's not wearing her horns.

"Mhmm," I reply, groggier than I have been in forever, perhaps even groggier than when I woke amongst the golden Plains of Ichor. At least this time I'm not nauseated.

"Do you know who I am?" Haedes asks, peering into my field of vision from the left side of the bed. He's at my bedside, like he actually cares, making my rage kindle despite my lack of energy.

"Of course, I know who you are. You're that guy who just won the worst dad ever award," I scowl. He winces.

"I guess I deserve that," he admits. I continue to scowl.

"Yeah. You really do. Like you also deserve a kick in the googlies so you can never reproduce ever again," I inform him. A small smile traces itself over the firm set of his mouth, almost like a memory has him in its clutches.

"How do you feel?" the familiar voice asks, one that I actually want to hear, and I turn this time to my right where Xion is towering over me.

"I'm alright. Not Marvin Gaye standard alright. But it'll do." I struggle to prop myself up against the pillows, my muscles regaining strength quicker than I'd imagined considering how chronically shit I feel.

"I'm glad you're not dead," Luce announces, and I narrow my eyes.

"Why would I be? Wasn't that potion you gave me safe?" I scowl at her.

She bites her bottom lip.

"Well, that's just great. Feeling the love from you all right now," I mutter. One of them sentenced me to death, and the other tried to save my life with a potion that could have also killed me. What a crack team of geniuses. Aren't they supposed to be gods?

"I'm sorry, I didn't know what else to do. Do you feel dizzy, sick? Are you having any sudden violent urges?" Luce asks me, and I stare at her again.

"The last one has nothing to do with the potion, I can assure you of that. But I'm fine really; in fact, I think I'd better be going." I swizzle around on the bed, stretching upward and yawning. I may have woken up fuzzy-headed, but being unconscious was the best quality rest I've had since before I got here.

"What do you mean, *go*?" Haedes' voice is the one that vocalises the outrage at this suggestion first.

"I mean leave, go back to Chicago," I say it as simply as I'm able, treating him like a child.

"But— you can't just— *leave!*" Haedes sounds like someone has him in a chokehold, and so I twist, glancing across the width of the enormous bed and finding his gaze angry, with a hint of melancholy.

"Look. You're my father. I get it. But you're not my dad. Adam Sinclair was my dad. He would have died for me. He risked a lot to give me the future he wanted me to have. You— you're the God of the Underworld. How can you possibly be anything to me other than that?" I put this question to him, and he slouches under the weight of my words.

"I'm not trying to be spiteful or unkind; even though after the fact you almost got me killed I kind of have the right to be. But I don't think that I can be in your life, or you in mine. It's too much for me. Too much danger, too much of a risk." I exhale deeply, trying to make him understand without incurring his wrath. "I don't want to die. I thought I didn't care, but I realise now that I've got to continue doing what I did before I knew who I was. Taking care of myself. Because nobody else can do that; it's just me. If nobody else is going to put my interests first, I have to leave. Or I'll end up in a coffin before I've even had a chance to live," I state, candid.

He doesn't reply right away.

After a few moments, his head rises from where it's been bowed, staring at the floor, and his eyes sparkle slightly.

"You can't leave, Sephy. It's too dangerous. The Demon Lords— they'll hunt you down now, perhaps even harder than before. Am I right?" He looks to Xion, then to Luce. They both frown. "Xion, what do you think?" Haedes asks him, overlooking me and my opinion, like it doesn't even matter.

"I think the fact that you're asking me shows that you don't realise just how capable Sephy is. You're demonstrating that you are in no position to make her decisions for her. If she wants to leave, you have no right to stop her," Xion replies, and I want to kiss him.

"But—" Haedes begins, but Xion continues as I turn to face him where he hovers just behind my shoulder.

"Haedes, I didn't save Sephy from the Demon Lords. She defended herself. She doesn't need anyone's protection. She can look after herself. That's the honest truth," he states, folding his arms across his chest. I smile up at him, grateful.

"Very well then, I guess if that's the case, I have no choice but to let you go." Haedes doesn't stop for a goodbye; he merely storms out of the room, though his hair doesn't morph to orange, so I wonder if he's angry or devastated.

Against my better judgement, I find myself curious. Sometimes, I wish I knew what was going on in his head, what he really thinks of me. I guess I'll just have to settle for repressing this entire experience with him like I do everything mildly stressful and completely unpleasant.

"You're sure this is what you want?" Xion asks me.

I nod.

"I'm sure. I just, I don't think this life is for me. I like the demon fighting part, for now, and I'm pretty psyched about being a demi-goddess, because, you know, I'll never have to buy matches, pay for a cab again, or worry about anti-ageing cream, but other than that, I just want to be happy. I don't think that I'll find that in The Underworld— funnily enough." I quirk an eyebrow, and Xion nods, looking a little sad but firm in his expression. The rugged lines of his masculine face look down at me, capturing light and shadow and manipulating it so he looks both intimidating and besotted all at once, though that could be entirely my misinterpretation.

"So, I'm not going to just keel over from this crap you put in my veins, right, Luce?" I ask her between gritted teeth. She looks sheepish.

"Uh, no. You should be fine. Do you feel— I don't know, more goddess-ish than before?" she asks me, and I shrug.

"I don't feel like I've almost been eaten by a hoard of demons after being kidnapped and drugged."

"We'll say that's good enough for now. If you have any problems, you let me know." She gives me a wink, and I can't help but feel my frosty reserve toward her melt. She has saved me, risk or no risk, after all.

"I guess we better get going." I look at Xion, and he cocks his head.

"You want me to walk you out?" he asks, and I nod.

"Seems only right. You walked me in," I counter, and he smiles, though I can tell he's trying not to.

"Cerb!" I call out, and at the sound of his name, the Leonberger leaps right over the couch in the other room, almost knocking it and The Fates completely asunder. The three women rise to their feet as I greet my dog, running my fingers through his thick fur and inhaling the woody damp scent of his mane.

"I missed you, boy." I look into his round dark eyes and smile. Things are going to be just fine, for us both.

"Goodbye, Sephy. See you again soon," one of The Fates calls to me, though I can't remember which one.

Not on your freakishly old life, lady, I think, bending at the knee as I take Cerb by the collar before striding over to Xion.

"Should we get a carriage?" he asks me, and I shake my head.

"Nah, I got this." I give a small wave, grabbing his hand in mine. His skin is rough and calloused, and he holds onto me tightly.

"Hold your breath," I instruct him. "On three."

I give him time to prepare himself, smirking as I do.

"One—T—" Before I've finished the count, I convect us out of Luce's suite, ready to claw my way back to the real world.

As we materialise in a fit of flame and smoke atop the ruddy earth of the Sanguine forest, Xion sputters.

"Dammit! That wasn't three!" he coughs, and I laugh.

"Yeah, I know. Haedes did that same thing to me the first time I convected," I smirk. He rolls his eyes.

"Nice," he retorts, brushing himself down as the smoke dissipates into the air, and he stands up straight.

Cerb whines at my side.

"Gotta give you something to remember me by, don't I?" I ask him, my heart becoming heavy in its beat. I've known this moment was coming, but I haven't wanted to face it. I just can't stay in Mortaria and play demon hunter. I need to have a life, the life I was supposed to have. The life my father gambled so much to create.

The trees rustle around us as a stiff breeze causes the red leaves to shake, allowing lilac sunlight to fall, dappled, through the bloody canopy.

"I don't think I'll forget you," Xion mutters, his eyes crinkling at the edges.

"Well, you might, but only after like— a hundred thousand years. I'll just be that redheaded girl," I chuckle, but the thought makes me sad.

"Nah, you're too Sephy to just be some redhead." He smiles, and I wonder if either of us is going to move.

I spin on my heel, finding the gothic metal cage of The Hollow towering behind me.

I guess it's time.

"So, I'll not see you around then?" I ask him, semi-hopeful.

"No, my job is done with the Sinclairs now. Your debt is written off, and as a demi-goddess, you won't wrack up anything new. Your soul is safe. You're free," he reminds me.

"Freedom, huh? That seems to be the thing I've wanted most of all, ever since this all started," I admit as he hands me the Obsidian Dagger from the belt loop of his jeans. I feel the weight of it in my palm, reminding me of another weapon.

"Well, now you have it. Go and enjoy it, Sephy." He places a hand on my shoulder, and I take a small step back from him, trying not to get emotional. I slit the skin on the palm of my hand open, barely feeling it. I'm numb as I hand back the knife, grabbing Cerb by the collar once more and turning to walk towards The Hollow.

Pressing my hand against the tree and letting my blood feed the wood, I look back at him over my shoulder as crimson leaves crackle under the tread of my boots.

"Thanks, for uh, being my luggage boy," I call, waving, but he doesn't wave back, simply standing there, stance wide, watching me go.

"It's been my honour," he replies, unfeeling and stoic as though smiling will crack his mask of reserve.

Then again, maybe I'm merely duty and nothing more.

I turn from him and begin my journey toward freedom and future.

30

SHOULD I STAY OR SHOULD I GO

XION

I UNLOCK THE DOOR to my apartment, stepping inside to familiar silence as I return after a few nights at The Exilia. Luce and Thane have had me looking for potential weaknesses in their security, and it's been beyond stressful with the new knowledge that Pandora can walk in any time she likes.

The cold blue light of flickering sconces is melancholic as my tread echoes out across the stone of the walls and floor.

I'm home, alone once again.

The place is chill, and I exhale heavily as I slip off my leather jacket and walk over to the bed. Collapsing back onto the unmade sheets, I smell her familiar scent, cinnamon, as it envelops me.

I have done my duty by her. She is safe, and hopefully, she will go on to live a happy and carefree life. That's what she deserves. She's suffered enough with both the loss of her parents and in being hunted by the Demon Lords to last a lifetime.

So why do I feel so— empty?

Is it a loss of placement? Not knowing what my next assignment will be, or who I'll be hounding next? This has surely been a change, protecting someone and earning their gratitude, rather than condemning them to hell.

I stare up at the ceiling, bored without her witty retorts or sarcastic commentary, thinking about my life before.

Would Sephy and I have ever been friends in a world where I was mortal?

Probably not.

When I'd been human, I was preparing to enlist in the armed forces. I wanted to fight, to be a man of honour, then my demon self presented, and well— that was the end of that dream.

I ponder if perhaps I'm so down because in attempting to rescue Sephy, in guarding her, it had been like I was the hero for once and not the bad guy. Maybe it's because I felt a real sense of purpose with her, not that she needed my protection, but it was nice to pretend, at least for a while.

I sigh, wondering what Alex Johnson would think of all this, what I would have thought about Sephy before I changed my name and lost that part of myself. The naïve part, the safe part, the truly human part.

Alex Johnson would have found Sephy Sinclair to be brash, arrogant, rude, and quite possibly intolerable, but I'm no longer him, and she's no longer here, so all this speculation matters very little.

So why am I speculating at all?

Why do I care so much?

I haven't even known her that long. We've been through a lot together, that's true, but she's not my problem anymore.

As though this thought has summoned someone who *is* very much my problem, I'm blinded momentarily by a flash of blue flames. I blink once, then again, trying to clear the floating spots from my vision where the flash fire has burned my retinas.

"Damn it!" I exclaim, disoriented as I sit up on the bed.

Where the flames have died away, leaving no scorch marks because thankfully I don't have a carpet, Haedes now stands. "Don't you knock?" I complain, and he glares at me, clearly furious. His hair is scarlet, and his eyebrows, which slope down at acute angles, match.

I take a deep breath.

This is going to be fun. I groan, wondering what he's doing here.

"No, I don't knock on the doors of people who betray me," Haedes snarls.

I roll my eyes. He's drunk— I can smell it from here.

"You've been drinking," I state, and he smirks.

"How observant of you," he replies, cracking his bony knuckles like he wants to wrestle. I get to my feet, towering over him by several inches. I don't have time for this crap.

"I didn't betray you. I don't know what the hell you're talking about. Go home. Go to bed." I brush past him, trying to move into the main room, to get away from the scent of cinnamon, the scent of her, but he grabs the crook of my elbow, growling at me.

"You stood up for her! It's because of you that she's gone!" he informs me of his warped assessment, and I want to laugh.

"Haedes. Come on. Have you met your daughter? If she wants to leave, then there's no keeping her here. Besides, I stand by what I said; she can take care of herself. She's more than proved that despite the decisions you made putting her in harm's way." I remind him that the real betrayer here is not me, but him.

He betrayed Sephy.

My hands curl into fists at my sides as I wonder what the chances are that Haedes will let this go.

"I didn't do anything of the sort. What was I supposed to do? Sacrifice the universe for her?" he asks, spitting each word like he himself is a bonfire.

"No. You were supposed to find another way. You're telling me right now that if you were in the same situation with her mother, you wouldn't have raised heaven and earth to save her? Wouldn't have worked night and day to find a solution? I don't buy that. Not for a fucking second," I spit back, bringing up Demi in the hope that he will see the error of his ways.

"So, what? You're saying I don't love my daughter now?" he hisses, beginning to pace in circles around me. I track his motion, wary but ready to fight if I must.

"I'm saying you love yourself more. You're a selfish bastard. You loved fully once, got hurt, and now you'll never take that risk on anyone again. Even if they're worth it." Even I'm surprised as the words hit the air.

"And how would you know if she's worth it?" he demands, fury boiling through his blood. If I didn't know better, I'd think he was about ready to implode.

"Because anyone who knows Sephy Sinclair knows she is worth that and more. She's worth your respect. Your time. And your love. If you knew her, really knew her, you'd know that," I snap.

"And I suppose *you* do know her, *really* know her?" he mocks me, and my heartbeat begins to sputter. His tread is like that of a wild cat, soft, yet deadly in intent.

"I know her, and I respect her," I state simply, and he smirks.

"And I suppose you love her as well? Stupid boy! She can never be with you. You're nothing but a monster. You'll doom us all." These words are the last straw, and I feel my rage untamed as something within me snaps. My demon form presents, busting out my clothes as a roar comes from deep within my chest.

Hurling my body forward, I wrap my charred hands around Haedes' pale throat. He laughs, wheezing within my clutch as I smash him into the wall.

"Well, well, well— your colours are showing—" He copies something Muerta always says, and I wonder why I shouldn't just kill him right now. Then I remember, Mortaria would most certainly fall.

Restraining myself, I let him drop to the floor.

"Stay away from my daughter," he growls, voice gruff as he coughs several times. He summons a ball of Eternal Flame in his hand, leaping to his feet and coming up close to me, letting the fire tickle my face as I feel the darkness recede slightly against my will.

Fear doesn't clutch at me. If he were to do it now, that would solve problems for far more people than just us two.

"You stay away from your daughter, and me, for that matter," I counter, bringing my fist up and throwing a punch. It hits Haedes directly between the eyes, and he stumbles back, flame extinguishing, his coordination impaired by drink.

"Xion, you are forbidden to go near that girl, do you hear me? She's not your concern any longer." He sounds desperate now.

"And you are in no position to forbid anyone from doing anything regarding Sephy. You lost that right when you willingly gave her life over to the Demon Lords," I retort, and he looks at me, eyes blazing.

"If you go within five hundred feet of her, then you're fired. No more Resurrection Flame. No more immortality. You can return to the mortal scum you came from and die like one," he threatens me.

I straighten, letting my demon form recede now, narrowing my eyes.

I think carefully before I speak next, trying to work out all the possible results that might occur. He stares at me, silence falling between us as my mind ticks, knowing it is time I make a choice.

The choice is obvious; it is the why of the matter that is not.

I suppose the only way to ever know why I feel this way is to act and hope for the best.

"I quit," I announce.

Haedes looks mortified.

"You're quitting? Quitting so you can go and fulfil some prophecy and doom us all? And you think I'm selfish!" he chuckles, maniacal and insane looking as his mouth stretches too wide on his skull, white teeth bony bright in the dark of the room.

"No. I'm quitting because I just realised I'm following the orders of a hot-headed jackass who I have no respect for anymore. I don't serve assholes, and I don't fear death either. Besides, if you did kill me, I'm pretty sure Sephy would never speak to you again, if she ever does decide to return, which I doubt," I exclaim, cocky.

Haedes scowls, looking like he might say something, but then decides against it. I wait for him to erupt, to scold me, to scorch me dead with his wrath, but instead, his eyes glaze over, and he disappears in yet another flash of blue flames.

I look around my apartment, realising now the impact of what I've just done. This can't be my home anymore.

I need to go back to the mortal world— but do what there?

Get a regular job? Live a regular life?

This is all I've known for as long as I can remember. The only thing I'm good at is killing demons and, on a good day, restraining the one living within me.

I guess I might not have anywhere to go, but I have someone who I can go to.

A friend.

I begin to pack up what few belongings I own, a sense of relief settling over me as I pull leather jacket after leather jacket down from the coat hangers inside my closet and shove them into a black leather duffle bag.

I know at the presentation of this emotion I've made the right choice. I just hope she doesn't turn me away.

SEPHY

It's been exactly three days since I returned to The Sinclair Estate, and things are finally getting back to some semblance of normal life.

However, whilst the daily comings and goings of the estate may be returning to normal, I am changed, as cliché as that may sound.

I dress in a white cotton blouse and loose-fitting jeans, pulling my hair back off my face and into a high ponytail. I hear a knock at the door, and so call, "Come in!" as I place some neutral lipstick onto my lips and pucker them in front of the mirror.

I'm going for the conservative look, the clean look, the mature and sophisticated style I feel that my parents would have wanted to see me in, and in some respects, I'm sort of unrecognisable from the woman I was merely a few weeks before.

I still see them when I sleep, crawling in and out of dreams and slithering around the dark corners of my subconscious, The Demon Lords.

Sleeping has been rough in general, but I'm trying to keep things together, especially now I've seen just how chaotic my life could become given my lineage.

It's certainly true that after fighting for my life, running a billion-dollar company seems like small fry. I could probably handle it with my eyes shut.

Jules opens the door and comes through with my breakfast tray, the usual silver cloche and white rose in a glass vase, the paper folded across the top. His shiny black shoes pad across the thick lilac carpet, and I turn to him. His expression is surprised as our eyes meet.

"You look— beautiful," he compliments me.

"You seem surprised." I cock an eyebrow, taking several steps forward in bare feet, picking the single white rose, clipped from the gardens below, up between my fingers, careful of the thorns.

"You seem different. That's all," he corrects himself, and I smirk.

"You know what I realised?" I ask him, and he shakes his head.

"What's that?"

"I realised that whether I wear black leather or not, I'm still a badass," I announce, cocky even still, reminding him that I've not totally changed. He stands, not sure whether to laugh or not.

Instead, he keeps things formal, *what a surprise.*

"I see. What are your plans for today?" he asks, and I exhale heavily.

"Actually, I want to deal with the business today. I also want you to call me a lawyer," I request, and he cocks his head.

"You want me to tell Peter? You know he got in last night?" he suggests, but I shake my head, spinning the stem of the rose in between my fingers.

"No. I can handle it. It's my family name. I'll take full responsibility," I announce, certain in my tone now. This time Jules *does* smile.

"Very well— oh and—" he begins, but then flushes and looks down at his feet.

"Well go on, spit it out!" I bark, not completely having lost my impatience.

"I'm very proud of you. If your parents were here, they would be too." He takes several timid steps forward and plants a soft kiss on my forehead.

"Thank you," I whisper back to him, heart swelling.

"Anyway, I'll go and make some calls."

"Alright, I have something important to take care of first, but I'll be back soon," I promise, walking past my breakfast tray, rose still in palm, and out of the pink early morning hue of the room.

My hand caresses the deep mahogany of the balustrade as I run my palm along its polished length. The chandelier overhead refracts light in multi-coloured specks around the hall in the sunlight of dawn, which pours in through the high windows of the front of the house, as I reach the top of the landing.

I walk down the centre of the long staircase, reaching the lobby as my bare feet touch the soft velvet of the runner before taking to the cool chequered marble of the lobby floor. Taking a right, I proceed to the east wing, taking long strides through the quiet that's fallen over the house in my absence, heart pounding in my chest as I near my destination. The tall deep aubergine walls of this wing of the house rise around me, pictures of me and my parents when I was a child littering the walls on both sides, making me nostalgic.

I know it's long overdue, I know that I need to do this, but I can't help but feel more vulnerable than I have in years as I step closer and closer to that which I have dared not enter.

Even Demon Lords could not have this kind of effect on me.

I reach the French doors that lead out onto the lawn and tread out onto the grass, my ponytail blown from my neck, a cool breeze catching me in its clutch as it swirls around the grounds. The sky is clear baby blue, airy, and welcoming, unlike the oppression of bloodier tones.

The blades of slick wet grass caress my feet, and the bottoms of my jeans become sodden with early morning dew.

My heart grows heavy as I approach the weathered white marble mausoleum, keeping my eyes fixed on my feet and the fine white petals of the rose in my palm. I exhale, trying to calm myself, trying to ready myself, but I know deep down there's no way I can ever be ready.

As I climb the two small marble steps and pull open the door into the tiny structure, grateful for the cooler temperature within the walls, my blood is scalding in my veins.

Entering, I see the graves in the floor.

There are sconces surrounding them, all of which are barren of flame, of light or warmth, so I wave a hand, lighting them all with red fire and giving the place an intimate glow.

I take a step forward, dropping to my knees before the brass plaques set into the floor, one for my mother and one for my father. Reaching out, my fingertips trace the curve of the font engraved into the metal, allowing the cool substance to comfort me as I stare down at their names.

"So— I know I haven't visited in a while— well, ever. I've been afraid. Afraid to miss you more than I already do," I whisper, placing the rose in the space between the plaques, wondering if I'm crazy for talking to two people I know are gone. Maybe I am, but it's making me feel less devastated, so I guess there's that.

"I guess, I just wanted to say— well, thank you. For everything you did and sacrificed to build my future. I didn't know what that meant before. But now, I know the truth, well— I know that you did all of that for me. So— thank you." I'm repeating myself, so I turn, making sure that the door of the mausoleum is closed. The last thing I need is someone observing my pain.

"Mom— I also know about Haedes, and while I don't think I'll ever love him like you did, I know he's not a bad man. But— he's not my family. Dad— you did terrible things. Terrible things. But you did them for me and out of love. So perhaps— perhaps they're not so terrible. I love you both, and I'm sorry about the fire." Tears run down my cheeks, cleansing me of the guilt that's been lying beneath the surface for quite some time.

I sit and cry for a moment, letting the last twenty or so years come back to me in a flood of isolation and loneliness. I am an orphan, and nothing will ever change that or make it less devastating, or less a part of who I am.

"Anyway, I just wanted to let you know, I'm going to do my best to keep the business going, maybe even do some good. I just want to make you proud." I wipe under my eyes, heart breaking in my chest as I place a kiss on my fingers and then press them to each name in turn.

"I love you," I whisper, getting back to my feet.

I stand for a while in the glow of flickering sconces, wondering why I've been so afraid to come in here for so long. I don't feel worse. I don't feel the loss. I feel better, like they're here almost. Like I'm the closest I've been to them since I was six years old.

Turning my back on their graves, I walk from the mausoleum and back across the lawn, heart finally starting to heal after all this time.

I sit at a conference table in the east wing, looking over the mail that's come through since I've been away. Large cerulean curtains frame the windows, open for the first time in forever, and the candle-studded chandelier is lit with The Eternal Flame, courtesy of my newfound powers. The room is covered in dust covers and is in disuse, but if I'm going to run this business, then Jules and I will have to change all that. In fact, I have half a mind to redecorate the entire estate. I need to make it my own; I need to start living in the present and not in some shell of my childhood memories.

Pondering the many interior design possibilities that could be tackled with my enormous amounts of spare cash, I turn on my cell phone for the first time since I got home, finally ready to face my responsibilities.

I haven't seen Peter yet but expect to find apologetic texts or calls from him, pleading for my forgiveness. Instead, I find nothing from Peter. The only notifications for about two hundred missed calls from the same number that had call-bombed me before my little trip down under— like, *really* down under.

Who on earth wants to get in contact with me so badly they'd call so many times?

Curiosity piqued, I press the redial button, putting the phone up to my ear as I start to open legal documents from my lawyer's office. They'd arrived while I'd been out taking my run.

The phone rings several times until someone on the other end picks up.

"Hello?" I call into the speaker, the sound of heavy breathing coming from the other end of the line. After a few seconds, the caller hangs up, and I take the phone away from my ear, frowning down at it in confusion.

What the fuck?

Blocking the number, I go back to opening my mail, ignoring what's just happened and scanning through some documents about foreign assets involved with The Sinclair Estate.

Jules, carrying my breakfast tray over to me from earlier, comes in through the wooden doors.

"You should eat something," he scolds me, so I give him an appreciative and thankful look.

"Good idea." I agree, lifting the cloche as soon as he places the tray down on the long table and picking up a fork. Today he's made me pancakes. I can't help but smile, knowing he's trying to make up for my lack of food down in Mortaria.

"Oh, these also came for you," he states, walking out of the room. He returns after a few minutes as I'm shoving blueberries into my face, an enormous vase of red roses in his hands.

He plops them down on the table, water jiggling, and I cock my head, confused.

"Who are they from?" I ask, and he shrugs.

"I don't know; there's no card or note. Not even the delivery guy knows. This is the third delivery we've had this week," he expresses.

I frown.

"That's weird. Maybe they're from— Haedes?" I guess, wondering if they're supposed to be some kind of apology. I mean, they're phenomenal flowers, even if they are littered with romantic connotations, and so I wonder if he'd cut them from my Mother's garden. A form of apology perhaps? Lord knows Haedes could never apologise to anyone face to face, let alone me.

"Maybe. I don't know. What would you like to do with them?" he asks me, and I shrug.

"Put them on the mantelpiece in here. I have a feeling I'm going to be spending a lot of time at this table; there seems to be a ton of paperwork to go through. Did you call the lawyer?" I ask him.

"Yes, he'll be here at six o'clock this evening. May I ask why you need a lawyer?" he enquires, but I shake my head.

"You may not," I reply, not giving anything away.

"Anything else I can do for you then?" he enquires, and I smile.

"You can start unpacking all the rooms. I'm sick of the dust covers— and, well, the dust that comes with them. I want this place to be my home, not just a fancy ass building filled with shitty memories. Got it?" I assert myself.

"That is a wonderful idea," he agrees, pivoting on the spot like a soldier and bustling over to the door. "I'll just go and get my feather duster. Anything to drink?" he asks me, and I grin.

"I'll have water, thanks."

The meeting with the lawyer seems to take forever, but after it's all done and I've signed on the dotted line, I'm glad it's over and taken care of. I return to my bedroom, thoughts of the last few weeks stirring slowly in my brain. I haven't had any alcohol since I got back from Mortaria, and I wonder why I no longer find it appealing.

I change into white silken pyjamas, petting Cerb as he curls up on the end of my bed, and I turn in for an early night.

A knock at the door comes, startling me.

"Come in," I call, as the door swings open and Jules steps inside. The entire room is overcome with a warm glow; I've got my bedside light on and am perusing some interior design magazines with my laptop open beside me, looking at colour schemes and ideas. I'm thinking that the pink definitely has to go, and black definitely needs to make a comeback.

"Oh— I thought you'd be heading out." Jules looks startled, and I shake my head.

"Nah, I have a lot of work to do if I want to redecorate this place and start taking over the business," I remind him. He nods, mystified but content as he straightens inside his suit.

"Everything go alright with the lawyer?" he asks me.

I smile.

"Yes, fine, thank you," I reply, still not giving anything away. It's none of his business, after all.

"Right, well uh, I'll see you in the morning?" he asks.

"Yes, I have a director's meeting at seven, so I'll need an early breakfast and some coffee," I inform him.

"Goodnight." He dismisses himself, leaving the room and shutting the door behind him as I go back to looking at the magazines and my laptop screen. Cerb snuggles up to me, and I smile.

"See, boy, normal can be kind of nice," I admit, realising that perhaps drama and excitement were just a way to put meaning into my life because I had nothing more fulfilling.

My thoughts flit to Xion. I've been trying to avoid thinking about him by keeping as busy as possible the last few days. I miss his stoic presence, his unwavering calm even though things are always uncertain. I even miss his crappy taste in music and his ridiculously uncouth demeanour, as hilarious as that sounds coming from me who had taken the piss out of him at every opportunity.

He had been there for me with unwavering loyalty at a time when everyone and everything else seemed hostile, and now I'm taking a new direction going forward. I know I'm doing the right thing by including him in it, even in the smallest of ways.

I wish he was here, in fact, I kind of wish that I'd met him under different circumstances. Perhaps if I'd met him in a night club, though I would never have seen the duty-bound rugged strength of the man he is, I'd never have known what an amazingly dark sense of humour lies beneath his handsome exterior.

I don't need him. I've perhaps never needed him.

The question remains though, unanswered in the back of my mind, niggling away day and night. It is only now though that I let it rise to the surface.

But do I want him?

I sigh as I shut down my laptop and toss the magazines to the floor.

He got to me, no doubt about it. I do care about him, even if I'd rather that I didn't.

Unfortunately for me, we're dimensions apart, and I'll never see him again.

Perhaps it's for the best.

After all, if there's a prophecy telling you to stay away from one person in particular, you should probably listen.

31

SEXUAL HEALING

SEPHY

THE MEETING LETS OUT, at long last, and I walk from the conference room, sweating at the unexpectedly non-existent heat of the day. I don't know whether it's the fact that I've got fire running in my veins now or if it's because the high collar of my blouse under my new tailored suit is choking me out. Either way, I feel a desperate urge to strip naked and lie in the middle of a frozen lake. Though this might scare onlooking Eskimos.

Peter ambushes me in the hallway.

"Sephy! There you are. I just wanted to let you know that I found uh—" he lowers his voice as several directors walk past us, greeting me as they go, "my opal dagger. I found it on the table. I've returned it to the higher security confines of the room upstairs, the one near my office. You shouldn't just go leaving that around you know." I give him a blank stare, confused as to why he's telling me this or why he's giving me a damn lecture after everything. Not a word of greeting or apology for his behaviour, just some useless information and a scolding I don't want or need.

"Alright. Uh, thanks," I reply coldly, brushing him off and walking past before he can say another word.

I make my way up the grand staircase, seeking the solitude of my suite after a long day of hashing out business, which is seemingly the slowest moving on the planet. I mean, it's no wonder half the people on my board of directors look ancient; I have no doubt that they're probably having the very life sucked from them by the mere amount of paperwork they look over every day.

I turn left at the top of the staircase and proceed through to my suite. Here, I instantly unbutton my blouse, pick up a glass of chilled white wine sitting on a silver tray by my bedside, no doubt a thoughtful touch by Jules, and move over to my Vinyl record player. Opening the cabinet on which the turntable stands. I browse the collection inside, a smile gracing my lips as I come across one record in particular.

Marvin Gaye's Greatest Hits.

Shrugging, I slip it out of the cardboard case and place it onto the black platter, moving the cartridge and stylus so it's able to track the grooves of the vinyl.

Marvin Gaye's sweet, soulful voice echoes out into the room, and I stand against the door of my walk-in closet, sipping white wine and closing my eyes as I cool off in just my black lacy bra and long black slacks.

It's a rare moment of calm in this new world where my phone is constantly ringing and people are looking to me for all the answers. Hell, I've only been doing this like two days and I'm already exhausted.

I sigh, opening my eyes as a familiar voice calls my name.

"Sephy?" I jump, head turning, and find Xion tentatively looking through the gap where I've left the door ajar.

"Jesus! You scared me! What are you doing here?! What, does playing Marvin you now or something?" I exhale, giggling as I'm unable to help but grin the most genuine smile. I take several strides forward, practically skipping over to the door to let him in.

This really is a surprise I didn't even realise I needed today.

"No— I, I quit, working for Haedes," he explains.

I see the bag on his shoulder.

"Planning on renting out my bathtub now? Because you know I'd rather you take one of the spare rooms." I offer him nothing less than what he'd shown me, hospitality in my time of need. He sighs, relieved.

"Oh, I was worried you'd turn me away," he exhales, and I feel my expression drop.

"I'd never do that to you! Come on, Xion. I know I can be a bitch, but Jesus, I'm not having the man who tried and failed to save me from a demon hoard, and trashed a perfectly nice car in the process might I add, out on the street. What kind of monster would I be?" I cock my head, letting my hair tumble down from the clip pinning it loosely off my neck.

"I shouldn't have doubted you; it's just— I don't know. I don't fit into this world anymore. I'm actually terrified," he admits.

I grab his hand, pushing him to sit on the bed.

"Listen here, it may have been the Marv that brought you here—" he scowls and interrupts me.

"Actually, that was just a coincidence."

"Mhmm, you keep telling yourself that." I take a deep slug of wine and smile at him. "Anyway, you do have a place. I've got a vacancy for a security guard slash luggage boy slash chauffeur open right now. My last one left me high and dry. Asshole."

I wink at him, and he exhales.

"You're offering me a job?" he asks, and I nod.

"If you don't mind playing security guard for a girl who can look after herself, mind you," I remind him.

He exhales heavily.

"Thank you." His gratitude is more than evident as he slumps like all the tension has suddenly left his body.

"Look, it's okay if you missed me; you don't have to come to me with some sob story ya know—" I tease him, and he rolls his eyes.

"Actually, you *are* the reason I quit. Your father paid me a visit and left with a black eye," he reveals. I try not to laugh.

"Oh Jesus, did you take them out and measure? If so, I wanna know about his lower body hair situation because you know I'm still curious about that—" I'm flying high on a concoction of wine and feeling comfortable in my own skin. My life is heading where I direct it, I'm finally becoming the woman my parents knew I could be, and more than anything else, I'm actually happy to be alive, know it's worth, and don't see it like a punishment. To top it all off, my loneliness might even be coming to an end as Xion makes one hell of a partner when it comes to banter.

"He tried to blame me for you leaving," Xion explains, and I snort.

"You're kidding, right? He sentences me to death at the hands of some raging demons, and it's your fault? Wow— mature." I feel the shock of this settle in.

Why can't Haedes take responsibility for his own screw-ups?

"Besides, you're the only person who could have made me stay," I admit, biting my bottom lip.

At this, I hear a knock at the door, interrupting the flow of conversation between us. I turn, leaving Xion perched uncomfortably on the end of the bed, still in only my bra and suit trousers, and move over to the door.

Opening it, Jules is revealed.

"Hey, I uh, saw you have a visitor; anything I can get for you?" he asks me.

I nod as he stares at my attire with a cocked eyebrow.

"Anything you need?" I ask Xion, shooting a glance back over my shoulder. He looks nervous but then sighs.

"You know I'd love a drink," he admits with a guilty glint in his eye.

"Yes! Bring out the Bolinger, Jules. We have something to celebrate. I just hired me a luggage boy slash security guard." I gesture back to Xion with my thumb, and Jules looks surprised but happy.

"Oh, that's great!" He nods at Xion. "Congratulations, young man." Xion laughs.

"You know I'm old enough to be your father, Jules. Just call me Xion," he reminds him.

Jules looks perplexed.

"Can you make up a room for Xion too? He'll be staying here for the foreseeable future," I request, and Jules' eyebrows rise even further on his forehead, so much so that I wonder if they might not go into orbit around his moon-ish head.

"Very well! I'll be back with champagne!" he calls and totters off down the hall toward the wine cellars in the basement.

"You sure you can handle champagne?" I ask him, trying not to laugh. "After all, I am a billionaire; I'm sure we can special order you a great vintage bottle of water if you'd prefer to be totally boring." I tease him even still, unable to stop my happiness spilling from my lips with its usual sarcastic charm.

"No. I think I can manage, thanks. Besides, what's the worst that can happen?"

Three bottles of Bolinger later, Xion and I are strewn out on the floor of my suite, relaxing together as Marvin Gaye continues to croon out into the room.

"This is really good champagne," Xion expresses, and I look at him with a confused frown.

"How come you aren't drunk, then?" I ask him, and he shrugs.

"I don't know, maybe because I'm half demon and weigh more than you?" He's stoic still as he lifts a bottle to his lips, gulping the contents.

"You know I would've brought out the cheap stuff if I'd known it wouldn't get you hammered," I snort, brushing my red hair behind my ear and looking at him with interest. I pucker my lips, giving him some smoulder as we sit across from each other, surrounded by the empty bottles.

"Hey Xion, can I ask you a question?" I enquire, and he nods.

"Shoot."

"Did you really quit, over me?" I ask him, and he nods.

"Yeah, I did," he replies, scratching his stubble in the way he does when he's thoughtful.

"But— doesn't that mean you'll— you know, die?" I ask him, and he nods.

"Yup. I mean, not like tomorrow. But yes. As a half demon, I'll die. Not all of us got lucky with the immortality thing. It's the bodies of demons which are so sturdy, not so much the souls I guess," he replies. He doesn't sound particularly upset about this.

"That's gotta be a tough pill to swallow," I comment, but he smiles.

"Yeah, I'm just restless. Want to get on with the living now. If I've only got so much time left, you know?" he asks me, and I nod.

"I do. I feel like before the whole Demon Lord thing, I was just— waiting to join my parents. I felt like this life was a punishment for what I did to them. It all made sense. Now, I realise that this life itself is their gift to me. I don't want to waste it," I express, my guard down as the alcohol causes my mind to become buoyant and calm.

"Me neither. But I don't know where to even start— I mean, what makes someone's life worthwhile?" he asks me. I can only shrug.

"You are asking the wrong girl. I still don't know. All I know is that if you're willing to sacrifice anything for it, you're probably heading in the right direction." I shrug again, blinking once, then twice.

"This is a very personal conversation. Perhaps the most personal you and I have ever had," Xion observes.

"Yes, well, I trust you. Besides, I feel different," I admit. His eyes become glassy.

"I can tell—you smell different too."

This comment, the fact he's noticed, makes me smile.

"That would be my new intense moisturiser conditioner. Having flaming hair is a bitch for hair care, I'm telling you now," I complain, smiling at him.

"I can imagine," he laughs, swallowing hard before crossing his legs in front of him and staring at me intensely. "Can I ask you something now?" he requests.

"Shoot," I reply, curious as to what he'll say next.

"Why do you trust me?" he asks.

It takes me a minute to work out how to reply.

"I don't know. You've never lied to me. I mean, other than obviously lying to me when we first met, which I get was sort of for my protection looking back. You just tell me the truth when I ask. That's rare for me. When you have money, everyone just tells you what you want to hear to further their own agenda," I explain. He looks guilty.

"What?" I ask, leaning up, worried that I've misplaced my trust after all.

"I did lie to you. Once," he admits, eyes burning into mine as the mood between us becomes suddenly intense.

"When?" I ask, scared of the answer.

"Back in the pyramid. You asked me if I wanted to sleep with you." His gaze drops to the floor, guilty.

"— you said no," I remember, heart rate heightening.

"I know. I lied. Since the moment I first saw you, I've felt this protective urge. I thought it was a sense of duty— but I think now it's something different. I think— I think I'm attracted to you." He looks so ashamed of himself.

"How long has it been since you were last with a woman?" I ask him, unapologetic.

"Since the first time— I— since I lost my virginity." My heart palpitates at his innocence, and I wonder why it is I've been restraining myself when it comes to him.

"You know— I *am* on birth control. Bet the prophecy didn't include that little detail, did it?" I inform him. One of his beautiful eyebrows arches.

"Sephy, that's— I can't," he says this, but his actions tell a different story. He's flushed, his breathing has deepened if only slightly, and he can't help but bite down ever so slightly on his bottom lip. I know the signs; I know he wants this. *Needs* this.

I kneel up, crawling across the floor towards him and place a finger upon his lips.

"But— Sephy— the prophecy. I'm not the right— I'm wrong for you." He looks terrified as I climb into his lap, brushing my hair back behind my ear yet again as I watch his pupils dilate, taking me in.

I feel him stiffen beneath me; his arousal only too evident despite his claim otherwise.

"Fuck the prophecy. No one gets to say who's right for me but me," I whisper, leaning in and placing a hand on the rough, stubble-clad skin of his jawline. I rise on my knees, bending down and kissing him like it's his first.

I want to make it unforgettable.

The scent of pomegranates fills my head, and my heart flutters in my chest as the rough skin of his lips begins to move against mine. A small groan emits from his throat as I run my fingertips down through the stubble, which fades to smooth pale skin, tracing the length of his neck.

I end the kiss, both our breathing becoming ragged as he buries his face in my hair and pulls me to him. I wrap my legs around his waist, the feel of his warmth addictive. He lets out another feral, guttural moan, almost as though in trying to restrain himself, he's becoming physically pained.

I kiss him again, this time slowly, teasing him with my tongue, feeling his erection continue to press against me as I let my fingers wander through the dark lusciousness of his hair.

"Sephy— I— I—" he's desperate, confused, not knowing what to do with the feelings that are moving between us in such a physical manifestation.

I hush him.

"Shhh. You're safe. If you get too carried away, I can calm the demon— remember?" I whisper, reminding him.

Kissing him once more, I try to stop his hesitancy and dissolve his fear.

He moans again, getting to his feet as I remain wrapped around him. His hands come up and cup my ass, fingers digging into the plump flesh and causing me to cry out. This is more intense than any one-night stand, and it hasn't even started yet.

I get excited, anticipation pooling in my stomach in a heated torrent as he continues to French kiss me, walking around to the edge of the bed and laying me down before climbing on top of me. I take off my bra as he wriggles out of his black t-shirt, the heat coming off his chest bathing my pale skin as I lay beneath him, exposed.

I continue to breathe deeply, slowly, running a hand down from my collarbone, past my cleavage and then my navel as Xion's eyes trace me hungrily.

"Let go," I command, exploring myself with expert fingers. He does as I ask, face finally becoming determined rather than afraid.

I know it's been a long time, longer than I can possibly imagine, since he last slept with someone, so I can't even grasp how he must be feeling. I unzip my suit trousers, sliding out of them and pulling myself up amongst the white sheets so I'm in the middle of the bed, watching him.

His gaze is enough to burn the house down as he takes his jeans off and releases his pleasing length for me to ogle as I toss my panties to the floor.

My mouth floods with saliva, and he wastes no time taking his hands and running them from the apex of my thighs up to my breasts as he pushes my legs apart. I shudder, needy and greedy for him as he kisses my chest with rough and passionate lips, causing my pale skin to flush as he towers over me.

He bends down, initiating the kiss this time and running his hands back down the sides of my waist, causing me to inhale air in a sudden and desperate gasp. His hands come up fast and into my hair, pulling my neck back and exposing me to him as he kisses my throat roughly, desperately. He's animalistic in his sounds, in the instinctual way he takes my nipple into his mouth next and bites down, breaking our kiss for only a moment before coming back up to my ear and whispering.

"I'm going to make you sore, Sinclair." The words surprise and arouse me all at once as he growls, no longer unsure in any sense of the word.

The rough fingers of his spare hand fall to my breasts again as he buries himself into me with a single unrestrained grunt. My eyes widen and my mouth parts in a surprised expression as we meld together like two forms of molten hot metal, melting into one another under little more than the pressure and heat of our untamed animal desire to be close.

I'm already slick with need for him, and soon he's looking into my eyes with intense and unwavering loss of control. It seems to mount, unstoppable, with every touch that passes between our scorching wanton skin.

His expression is becoming increasingly more desperate with each passing second, the glow of demonic power set loose behind his irises. He doesn't stop, his muscles overpowering me with every single movement he makes, as I lay splayed out beneath him, helpless. I watch him struggle to stop the darkness from taking over, this battle growing the closer he grows to surrender.

I raise a hand, letting the eternal flame simmer on my palm and caressing his face with the back of my hand. The orange glow that's begun to spark in his irises diminishes within seconds, and I continue to kiss him, running my nails down his back and pulling him into me as deeply as I can.

It's perhaps the best sex I've ever had, if for no other reason than the fact it's the most intimate I've ever been with anyone. Xion kisses my neck as yet another feral groan escapes his lips, causing me to follow in a feminine echo of his pleasure.

His hands never stop exploring me, not for a second, and I let the growing tension between us build naturally as he continues to writhe on top of me, gentle, yet rough in all the right places.

The moment arrives. My muscles clench and the floodgates open as I climax. The act itself, my cries of unrestrained pleasure, tips him over the edge too, and we both meet for a final and mind-blowing kiss, as he grabs my hand, lacing his fingers between mine and calling out my name against my lips.

His mouth continues to possess mine as we still, his hands coming up to caress my face.

He pauses a moment, soaking in my look of pure bliss, before rolling over and bringing his arms around me. I rest my head on his chest, right over the rapid pounding of his heart, and feel my limbs turn to non-existent ghosts, floating separate from my body.

His touch haunts me before it's even left my skin as he runs his fingers down the curve of my spine. I look up at him, trying to process what's just happened.

We don't say anything; we don't talk.

We don't have to.

Some things are better left unsaid.

I fall asleep in his arms, another rarity for me, but we've been unable to stop touching each other for more than a few moments, self-restraint non-existent, and eventually exhaustion takes hold. The three times that followed the first had been just as intense, if not more drawn out, and when I open my eyes again, it's dark outside my window.

Why aren't I kicking him out yet? I ponder, knowing that this is not normal behaviour for me. Usually, I'm ready to have Jules dispose of my conquests by now, but this is different. It's Xion.

I can't just ask him to leave.

Then it occurs to me.

I don't want to ask him to leave.

I wrap the sheets closer around myself, and he stirs beneath my motion, the heat of his body seeping through the mattress and into my body as he turns to face me. His eyes are open, their metallic depths relaxed.

"I need to go," he whispers, half asleep. I exhale, feeling my heartbeat slow in my chest and my blood chill ever so slightly.

Of course, he does.

"Oh. Uh, okay." I sit up, feeling a little stupid.

What the hell did I think was going to happen? We'd sleep together once and be instantly in love? That doesn't sound like something I'd do— *ever.*

I've had too much to drink. Stupid champagne. I determine, rolling my eyes at myself.

Clearing my mind of such ridiculous ideas, I shake my head, my tangled red hair falling down my bare back from my shoulders. It tickles, more than usual as I'm sensitive after Xion's agonisingly delicious clutch.

Xion sits up, spinning so he is sitting on the edge of the bed, stark nude and accentuated as the crescent moonlight falls across his form from the window. I reach out, placing my fingertips on his trapezius muscles and letting them fall to his ass as I tease him, trying to tempt him back into bed.

"Sephy— I think—" he begins with a sigh, staring back at me over his shoulder.

I withdraw my touch.

"Look, it's okay. I understand. This doesn't have to mean anything," I finish his sentence for him, and he shakes his head.

"Sephy, this means everything to me. More than you know. But I need to run an errand. I wouldn't leave unless it was important. You understand that don't you?" he asks me.

I wrap the sheets around me, getting to my feet.

I feel beautiful as I step across the plush carpet and over to the door, draped in white silk like a Greek goddess. He appreciates me as he dresses, and I watch as his seductively hard body is covered in layers of black leather. I bite my bottom lip, which is red, raw, and plump from his kiss, every single inch of my body humming.

He takes several steps over to me as I lean against the wood of the door, blocking him in.

Placing a gentle palm on my cheek, he runs the fingers of his free hand through my hair.

"I'll be back; I promise," he whispers against my lips as he kisses me, and I feel my body relax as he holds me like I've never let anyone.

"This better be one hell of an errand." I glare at him, sulking, and he smirks.

"It is. I swear," he vows.

I blush under the intense intimacy of his stare.

"Alright. I'll be waiting. Take Cerb with you, too. I haven't had much time to walk him lately, what with me being a responsible adult and all," I reply, and he smiles as I step aside.

"Okay, I will. Leave some candles burning for me," he requests.

I smile, a wicked thought coming to mind.

"You bet." I give him a seductive glance, fluttering my lashes as he steps through the door, looking back over his shoulder at me and giving a smile that would melt the heart of a lesser woman. Some might say it would make such a woman swoon.

XION

I walk back through the Exilia Multum, glad to know that this may very well be the last time I'm within these high crystal walls, beneath the bloody weep of the sky. Cerb trots along beside me, sniffing my hand. He knows I've been with his mistress. I probably smell of cinnamon.

Tonight has been— well, it's been the best night of my life.

Being with Sephy isn't like I have imagined; it's better, raw, like she's just as scared of everything igniting between us as I am. She's such a firecracker, and I've discovered that the way she laughs and how she kisses is enough to bring any man to his knees.

What would it be like if I could never touch that body again? Kiss those lips, feel her trembling beneath me with need?

It doesn't bear thinking about, but I suddenly find myself feeling sympathy for the guy I'd punched back at Retropolis that night.

I realise now she's enough to make any man go insane, if they can get past the myriad of personal defences she throws up at first meeting and then restrain the undoubted sense of wanting to gag her, of course. She's a goddess with the temper and demeanour to match, and it's a wonder nobody has noticed she's so clearly different from your average woman.

I don't know what it is about her temper, the way she goes after what she wants no matter what, but it's set alight something in me that I thought long dead and buried.

I need her to be mine and mine alone, and that means I need to be able to keep her needs satiated. Hence the reason I'm here.

I ascend the spiral staircase to Luce's chamber, knocking three times on her door as I exhale, knowing I'm in for some kind of scolding. Cerb stirs at my side, sitting and cocking his head as we wait patiently together. I wonder if he knows what's going on.

The door opens after a long few minutes as I stand, looking down at my feet while anxiety creeps into the forefront of my mind. I want to be back in her bed, back in her arms, and yet I am here. Here because I cannot continue to feel guilty about an act I'm so helpless to resist.

"Xion?" Luce's voice reaches me as I look up and find her standing in the doorway. She's dressed in a scarlet silk floor-length night gown, rubbing her eyes, and wrapping a long, black, kimono-style robe around her waist with a silk tie.

"I'm sorry it's so late—" I apologise as she yawns, a black silk eye mask that reads *Wake at your own peril* slid up on her forehead.

"It's fine. I've been listening to Haedes spanking Dolly for the last three hours. I swear to Christ, if she yells *harder* one more time, I'm gonna go over there and show her damn harder. I'll spank her off the top of that freaking tower," she grumbles, opening the door so I can step inside.

Cerb makes himself right at home in front of the fireplace, but I feel awkward, knowing this is necessary but wondering why everything in my life is so damn complicated.

"What is it?" she demands.

I look through to the bedroom, where from within the crumpled black velvet of the bedsheets, a pair of yellow eyes burn out into the dark. Beelz blinks once, then twice, before going back to sleep.

Luce follows my gaze. "Thane isn't here. She got sick of the yelling too. Went on a flight to check on the Demon Lords." She gives another yawn.

"Coffee?" she asks me, and I nod, feeling a chill as she brushes past me.

"That would be great," I reply.

Luce takes a second to stare at me.

"You look tired. Not much rest for you either?" she asks.

I can't stop myself from smiling.

I straighten my expression quickly as she looks at me curiously, images of the last few hours flickering through my mind.

"No, not much," I express, coy.

"Sit," she commands me, so I do, her bare feet poking out from beneath the scarlet of her silken nightwear as she treads across the floor like a pixie or something equally as nimble. She begins to bustle through the kitchen, getting out two novelty coffee mugs and setting the coffee maker up.

"So, what are you doing here?" she asks me, and I sigh.

"Well, I came to ask you for a potion actually," I admit, and her face goes part excited, part judgemental.

"I'm not a magical milkshake bar, Xion. If you can't sleep, I suggest a gin and tonic. Or a mallet to the head. You can take it; you have a rather thick skull, after all." She's not amused, but I refuse to drop my gaze as my face remains relaxed in expression. I need to keep my cool,

"No. Nothing so simple. I want—" I begin, but I can't say the words.

"What? What is it? Spit it out? I don't have all night," she barks, impatient.

God, she's so cranky when she's kept up all night.

"Alright look, I'm going to level with you. I want you to sterilise me, alright?" I spit it out, feeling better once the words hit the air.

"*Excuse me?*" Her eyes widen in alarm.

Rounding the dark crystal of the kitchen island and moving over to me as the coffee maker begins to drip into a glass pot, she drops down onto the sofa, getting close to me so I can see her pale eyes are visibly concerned.

"I want you to sterilise me. You know, make it so I can't have any children. Not a vasectomy; that's not foolproof enough, not with my magical genetic history. I want something permanent," I explain. She cocks her head.

"What, you want me to make you— like a eunuch? I'm not following." She's still confused.

"I slept with her. With Sephy, and— I plan on doing it again. A lot. I can't have that stupid prophecy getting in the way," I explain.

I watch as her eyes slowly widen with outrage.

"You did *what*?!" she yells, putting her hands on her hips.

"I slept with—" I begin, but she hurls herself forward, picking up a black throw pillow and smacking me over the head with it.

"I heard what you said! I just can't believe you'd be that stupid! Xion! Didn't I teach you to keep blood flowing in the upward direction? Didn't I?!" she yells, hitting me again and again with the pillow. I laugh, unable to let my good mood break under her faux abuse.

"Yes! Alright, yes! You did. But you don't understand. She keeps me grounded, Luce. She has The Eternal Flame— it kind of, placates the demon half of me," I continue, and she stops hitting me for a second, pondering this.

"Stupid. Stupid. Stupid!" She thwacks me three more times, her words a staccato of irritation before she collapses next to me on the sofa again, out of breath.

"It was good?" she asks me, curious now with a reserved gleam of mischief in her eye.

"The best night of my life," I admit, guilty even still.

"Well then, I guess I might be able to help. But it won't be easy, Xion. That kind of potion requires some rare ingredients, and I've already brewed one potent draft as of late, as you might recall." She looks wary, and I frown. I know the dark arts are addictive. I know it's a risk, but she doesn't understand.

"Haedes fired me. I'm going to live out my life with her as a mortal and die, Luce. I can't not sleep with her. I just can't. You know I'm as restrained— more so perhaps, than any other man that you'll ever meet. But with her, I just can't. She makes me crazy." I'm rambling now. Luce rolls her eyes.

"Alright, *alright*. Fine. I'll help you get your freak on! Stop with all the confessions of love," she complains.

My heart stills in my chest.

"It's a little soon to be saying that word; let's not push the boat out quite yet." I glare at her, and she looks infuriated.

"So, let me get this straight. You want me to help sterilise you, like actually make you infertile, just so you can get your bone on with a girl you're *not* in love with?" She reaches round for the pillow again, and I raise my hands, ready to defend myself as she sighs.

"You're freaking impossible," she curses me.

I shrug.

"Sorry," I mumble, and she gets to her feet, moving to the kitchen to pour the coffee that has now brewed.

"So, why did Haedes fire you?" she changes the subject.

385

"Actually, I kind of quit. He threatened me, so I took myself out of the equation," I admit, and she looks surprised yet again.

"You want me to talk to him? You know what he's like; he says one thing when drunk and then another when sober. I'm sure it's just a misunderstanding." She looks hopeful, but I smile, shaking my head.

"Actually, I think I'm good. I think— I think I might have a good life waiting for me," I confess, and she smiles.

"I was afraid you might say that." She looks sad despite the curve of her lips, and I know I'll miss her.

"I'll miss you," I express the thought without pause.

"You're always welcome in my home; you know that, right? I don't care if I have to beat Haedes to a bloody blue pulp," she states, and I let my expression transform into one of gratitude.

"I know," I say as she moves forward and hands me a coffee cup, taking a seat beside me and looking into the fire in front of us, not making eye contact. The coffee in the cup's depths is black, just the way I don't like it.

I take a sip, glad for the caffeine despite the vile taste as Luce sips her own steaming brew and tucks her feet up under her.

"I'm happy for you," she announces finally. I smirk.

"Liar," I accuse her, and she scowls, running her long dark fingernails over the red silk of her sheath skirt.

"Is it that obvious?" she demands, and I look her deeply in the eyes.

"Just a bit," I admit, unable to keep the grin off my face.

"We need good men around here, and you, Xion, are a good man, despite your own beliefs. Sephy knows it too," she compliments me, and I put my hand atop hers, relaxing into the hold of the sofa.

"Thanks, Luce," I whisper, becoming choked up, almost as if the sex I've just experienced has broken some emotional dam inside my chest, and now the flood waters are rushing through me in every direction.

We stare into the crackling of the fire, silence falling over us as we sip bitter coffee, and I cast my mind back to who on earth I would be if Luce hadn't saved me all those years ago.

I might not always believe I am a good man, but I know now, for certain, that I am a lucky one.

32

EVERY BREATH YOU TAKE

<u>SEPHY</u>

I'VE LEFT THE ROOM blazing with almost fifty candles, lit by my power over The Eternal Flame. I'm dressed in white silk pyjamas, snuggled under the sheets as I continue to inhale the scent of pomegranates that Xion left behind. I drift slowly, closing my eyes and relaxing into sweet dreams of his return, when he'll undress me again, and we'll spend the next week in bed, shirking our responsibilities and the outside world. Maybe I'll take him away somewhere— on vacation; maybe we can just become sex hermits together.

These are the dreams and thoughts I become lost in as sleep takes me, and I surrender to the exhaustion I'm so grateful for. It would seem that everything in my world is changing for the better, and unbelievably, at last, I feel like I've found some semblance of peace.

I awaken, eyes still closed and barely conscious, to the sound of the door opening. My heart swells.

He came back, just like he promised.

The candles are still burning, and the night outside continues to fall, deep and blanketing, only dim crescent moonlight bathing the world outside. I'm ecstatic as I roll over, ready to be in his heated clutch again, ready to lose myself to some amazing sex and then have more amazing sleep right afterwards.

What's come over me? I wonder, feeling my heart flutter with anticipation.

It was never like this before, never this enjoyable, never this— *real.* Everything about this is fragile, delicate almost, in its realism, as if one wrong move from me or him and the illusion of actual happiness may shatter. I don't want to open my eyes, don't want to leave this room ever again, as long as it keeps this dream alive. This is because, eventually, it will all undoubtedly come crashing down or fade slowly into nothingness over time.

The thought depresses me as his weight hits the mattress, climbing up from the foot of the bed and over me. I stretch upward; willing to let him ravage me all over again.

Opening my eyes, I smile, ready to take in his face, to recharge the happy glow that has taken over me.

I open my mouth to scream, but his hand comes down to stop any sound escaping my lips as a sharp serrated edge pushes into my throat. My eyes widen.

It's not Xion.

Brad?

It's the man who I slept with all those weeks ago, the one who Xion had punched that night in Retropolis. I struggle under his weight, but as soon as I move an inch, the blade threatens me with its bite.

Terror fills my head, no cognitive thought able to make any kind of linear sense as Brad's cold voice fills my ear. He bends down to me, kissing my forehead before he whispers.

"You're a bitch, Sinclair. And a whore. What do whores get?" he asks me. I watch him raise the knife, fury so unmistakable on his face it's as if the emotion is wearing him as a mask and not the other way around. The knife comes down in my chest, the crack of my ribs and the puncturing of my lungs causing me to scream out. I raise a hand to fight back, to summon some form of The Eternal Flame, but nothing comes to me, and soon I see why. As he rips the knife from my body, its bloody blade catches the light, scarlet but unmistakably opalescent in the stark glow from the crescent moon outside the window.

How did you get that? Is the only thought I can form as the scent of my own blood fills my nostrils and my attacker's eyes gleam with pure malice.

I struggle, heart frantic and wounded in my chest as the knife comes down again, straight into my gut this time. I wriggle, feeling the blade turn in my stomach as he wrenches it out yet again.

I scream, but his weight is too much for me to fight. His rage has made him too strong. The candles around us extinguish, and I know that my magic is gone, my power is gone. I lean back, eyes filling with tears as I realise only too late that I've been careless with my heart. Careless with this life.

He takes his good time, not slitting my throat until the very end. Every time the knife makes a new dive for my flesh, he twists it, looking at me and watching as I writhe in agony. He smiles, getting off on my pain, on his revenge.

Dismounting me, he cuts off a single lock of my hair before he goes, bringing it up to his nostrils and inhaling deeply.

I lie among the white sheets, stained burgundy through and through. He stares at me, no trace of guilt in his eyes as his lips form the word *bitch* before he leaves the room, his tread softer than Xion's by far.

If I hadn't been so elated, so happy, perhaps I wouldn't be here. Perhaps if I had sent Xion to bed in his own room and we'd never fallen into mine together, I would have had time to save my own life. Instead, this relative stranger has come into my home, a thief in the night, and stolen the thing from me that I've held for so long, but have only just recently found worth in.

Silence falls over the room, just as darkness had when the candles flickered dead. I lie, waiting for death to take me, waiting for the end. Who knows, I might even see a familiar face.

Drip, drip, drip. Red on white. The blood runs down, flowing from my slit carotid like merlot from a casket of 1947 Cheval Blanc let run. I gasp, clinging to life in these final moments, struggling against the ice-cold grasp of something after as I finally give in to terror.

I have aged to maturity it would seem, becoming fine and rich in fragrance with a fiery kickback that no one can contain. Not even me. The fire had consumed Xion and me, but I had not cracked and flaked away at the imminent, self-appropriated, heat of his closeness. My fire had not consumed him either, turning him to ash, but rather we had walked into the flames together and arisen as a Phoenix, unstoppable as we burned.

I am not though, alas, invulnerable to the most mundane of human crimes. The most domestic of violations. The very pinnacle of mortal nature.

Letting go of everything, of the hopes and dreams I'd had for my future and accepting the grim nature of my real fate, I exhale my final breath and leave for something after.

XION

I emerge from The Hollow and into the new light of dawn, it's a new day here in the mortal plain, and I'm more than a little sad the night is over. Cerb trots along at my side as we make our way through the copse of lusciously green trees, emerging at the edge of one of The Sinclair Estate's many sprawling lawns now bathed in fresh morning dew and sunlight. The day seems brighter to me now, and I wonder if this is because I'm heading back to bed with a beautiful woman, or whether the seasons are changing and I just haven't noticed.

Cerb takes off in front of me as my feet hit the lush grass, bounding towards the main house without pause. He starts barking, clearly excited to be home.

I feel the weight of several dozen vials of temporary mystical contraceptive in my pocket. Luce hadn't been able to offer me a permanent solution, she doesn't have the ingredients, but has been able to give me something temporary so Sephy and I don't have to restrain ourselves in the meantime.

I smile to myself, relishing the memories of last night as I reach the stairs of the estate and climb, slipping inside the front doors, which are unlocked.

I frown.

Definitely need to start talking to Jules about locking up better, I muse. I mean, I know we have an enormously long driveway and a gate at the end of it, but with demons having access to this dimension, we can at least pretend to care by locking the damn doors.

I take step after step across the chequered marble floor, and then climb the staircase, anticipation building within my chest to the point where I wonder if I might stop breathing altogether. I haven't felt emotion this deeply in a long time; not positive emotion, not happiness. I've let myself forget that life can be good, can be wonderful even.

I tread along the corridor towards Sephy's suite, heart racing as I hear Cerb barking. He's probably woken her up, and she's probably fuming. I know how her temper can be.

I turn the corner into her room, heartbeat so loud it's audible in my ears, heat flooding me at the thought of climbing back into bed with her.

The scene that greets me turns my very core cold, my heart freezing solid in my chest.

Blood. Blood everywhere. This is all I can process as the smell of old rust hits me full force. I feel my face drain of colour, my body become numb as if I've left it temporarily and become a ghost.

Cerb is nudging her cold lifeless body with his nose, whimpering, trying to wake her.

I step forward, not able to speak, or let my breath calm me for even a second as I find the carpet stained red. The white sheets are scarlet and her skin is pale.

I fall to my knees, the only sound I'm able to hear my patella as they impact the floor. Her eyes stare out at me, lifeless, glazed, and brown. The fire from the cognac of her irises has long since diminished, and her hair is strewn, a mess of matted auburn strands and clotted blood that's flooded from her carotid in a torrent.

I let my eyes trace over her, the white silken pyjamas stained scarlet, ripped in places.

A knife. The word comes to me, the abrupt syllable only bringing visuals of it slicing into her skin.

I turn, finding the culprit on the bedside table beside several candles that have long since diminished. The candles she lit for me.

The opal blade. The object which had started Sephy's fight for her life had been the very same weapon that has ended it.

I don't know how to feel.

What to do.

I can't bring her back; she's too far gone. Rigor mortis has already set in. She's stiff now, like a doll as I reach out to touch her hand.

I immediately recoil. The flesh of her body is cold, wrong. Not hers anymore.

Who would do such a thing?

Demons?

Pandora?

Why?

After everything she's been through, everything we've both done to keep her alive. It ended like this. In a puddle of her own blood, no magic, no defender lying next to her. She died alone and in pain. After everything.

I'm on my knees, unable to stop looking at her, afraid that if I do, then she'll really be dead, really be gone. I can't speak. Can't breathe.

I do the only thing that I can. The only thing I can remember how to do.

I hold back my head and let the tears flow from my eyes as I cry out at the top of my lungs. Shocked, beyond what I'd thought was possible for someone without a fully mortal soul to feel.

33

WE'VE ONLY JUST BEGUN

<u>LUCE</u>

I HAVEN'T SLEPT IN days. Though whether this is because I am grieving, or because I know Xion's heart is broken, it's hard to tell. Everyone has fallen silent in a suspended state of shock after the news of Sephy Sinclair's murder. Particularly Haedes. I haven't seen him, nor heard a word from him since the news, and I wonder if he's finally gone truly off the deep end and drunk himself to death, though, the practical entanglement of killing yourself in Mortaria makes this seem unlikely.

I've been walking around my apartment for the last week, not going out or doing anything, really. I've just been thinking, pondering, wondering whether this crime is as human as it seems.

Could it be that Sephy Sinclair invoked the wrath of Pandora or the Demon Lords, even after her show of defiance? It seems likely, but in a world where everyone tells you to think horses when you hear hooves, I tend to look for zebras.

I stand on the balcony of my suite, looking as ever to the skies, waiting for Thane's return. The silence that's fallen over this place is uncanny, and I wonder if Haedes really is okay.

I'm worried, and the longer I enjoy the peace which I have so desired all those nights when I couldn't sleep due to the world's most irritating roommate, the more I realise I need to hunt him down.

Once again, I find myself unable to stop helping someone who doesn't want to help themselves, but I suppose that's just a character flaw of mine. Perhaps I'm just a sucker for a lost cause.

Turning on my heel, my simple black dress of Chantilly lace blooming around me as the skirt billows out, I spin away from the Mortarian horizon and stalk through the apartment. Slipping on some black velvet ballet pumps, I open the door, not bothering to lock it behind me, and descend the spiral staircase in haste.

I pass through the entrance hall, wondering where to start looking first. I could try Haedes' suite, but the thought of walking in on him in some kind of grief fuelled sex rage makes my stomach turn, so I decide to try my luck in the grand hall first.

I reach the entrance, pulling open the large double doors that are cool beneath my fingertips. The sconces inside are bright, lit by The Eternal Flame so I know he's nearby. I can't locate him anywhere in the hall, and yet I can hear his mad ramblings from all the way across the spacious chasm of the room.

"Haedes?" I call out, nervous as to what state I'll find him in.

"Luce! I'm in the vault," he calls in reply. I frown, puzzled. He doesn't sound intoxicated or even slightly tipsy. This is a pleasant if not slightly shocking discovery, and my stomach unfurls as relief blankets me.

I tread fast across the smoky quartz of the floor, my reflection intimidating as I'm dressed all in black today, the lace appearing delicate but on closer inspection has been crafted in the silhouettes of Venus fly traps, one of my favourite plants. My white hair is brilliant in contrast, my skin ghostly pale against my bloody red lips as I reach the golden-plated entrance of Haedes' vault.

Stepping inside, I find him on the floor with his legs out in front of him, leaning against the wall. He's surrounded by books, hourglasses, and magical artefacts that I've never seen, nor would ask to see. Haedes has acquired some truly dangerous magic in his time as head of The Nexus Council, and there is certainly more than one reason why he had this vault built in the first place.

"What are you doing?" I ask him, trying not to sound judgemental. He raises his gaze to mine, tired but electrically charged, sprawled out on the floor in a black velvet suit that's too short in the leg where he's sitting. Bright red socks are exposed underneath and his jacket lies at his side. His torso is covered in a crumpled red silk shirt, and his braces have been detached and are hanging down behind him. His hair is wild, and it looks like he hasn't slept in days.

"I'm—well, I'm trying to solve the mystery, aren't I?" he laughs, and I cock my head, confused as all hell.

"What?" I exclaim, wondering momentarily if his calm has deceived me. Perhaps he has, in fact, gone truly and utterly mad.

"I'm trying to solve the mystery of how to get to The Nether Realm. There must be a way." His words form a linear sentence, and yet the content still fails to abide by any kind of logic.

"Haedes— look, are you alright? You know there's no way to get to The Nether Realm. You know that— don't you?" I bend down, letting my skirt pool around my ankles as I sit on the floor.

"Look, I saw Hercules today. She hasn't risen from the Divine Pastures— they're not letting her, because of me. I can't just— I can't just—" He sounds like a record stuck on repeat.

"Are you coming to the funeral?" I enquire with haste, cutting him off. His eyes glaze over, spark diminishing as quickly as it came.

"No. I am not," he retorts, and my heart sinks. This isn't going to end well for anyone. He was too late to attend Demi's funeral too, and decades later he's still a broken man.

"Look, I think you should. It's good for closure," I explain my reasoning, and he suddenly looks angry as his hair tinges oranges at the tips.

"You don't get it, do you? I'm not looking for bloody closure! I'm looking to bring my goddamn daughter back!" he growls. I exhale heavily.

"You know better than I that resurrection, true resurrection, hasn't been attempted for aeons— not since, well not since my father stole The Book of The Dead," I recall. His eyes widen at my candour.

"Right— that was when Anubis was tricked by Cronus into putting Ra into Horus' body? Wasn't it?" He waves his index finger as if I've suddenly oiled the cogs working in his brain, making them slick and fast once more.

"Yes, that's right. Ra took his own mortal life and dissipated his energy; he was enraged at Anubis for promising Cronus his loyalty." I remember the tales from when I had been a child in Othrys, moved there with my mother for business, the talk in the Higher Plains of the wars that raged below. "But Moloch— he had special talents when it came to resurrection," I remind him, trying to get rid of any insane ideas that may be forming in his brain.

"True—" Haedes' gaze lingers on me, and I stare back at him, narrowing my pale eyes as I feel my heart rate accelerate.

"Before you say anything— No. I couldn't possibly do something on that level. Besides, The Book of The Dead has been lost for centuries. You know this, Haedes," I express, and he shrugs.

"You know what Xion said to me before she died?" he asks me pointedly, and I shake my head.

"No. I don't," I state, and he looks ashamed of himself.

"He said that if it had been Demi in that colosseum, then I would have tried harder—I would have found a way to save her. I would have broken all the rules," he looks miserable and I scowl.

"Xion was mad. People say a lot of stupid crap when they're mad." I remind him of his own words at the confrontation, the way he'd apparently threatened Xion, and he shakes his head.

"No. You misunderstand. He was right," he admits. My eyebrows rise as I push my hair back behind one ear.

"I'm not sure—" I begin, but he cuts me off.

"No, Luce. I *would* have risked my life for Demi. I would have died for her. I would have found a way. I'm *the* god of The Underworld, this is my domain, and I've become this— shell. I'm weak. I drink too much. I just try to get around my pain without going through it. I can't do that with her. I can't get around how badly I've failed her as a father. So, I am going to find a way to bring her back. I owe her that. I owe her every last ounce of effort I have. She deserves to live. Not to be stuck in some limbo void because her uncle hates her father." His speech makes me realise that perhaps Sephy's death has had the opposite effect on him that I'd anticipated. It hasn't destroyed his grasp on reality and his desire to truly live; it's reignited a passion within him I haven't seen for years.

I can't help but smile, despite the fact my soul remains heavily shrouded in the dark veil of grief that has fallen over us all.

"Well, I can't resurrect her. I can't, Haedes. I'm serious. An act of that magnitude and intent is rooted in darkness. It would— it would put me at risk. You know how susceptible I am —" I warn him, fearing for my goodness as he looks sad.

"I know. It's too much to ask. But if I can find this book, then maybe there's another way. Maybe I can figure it out. I am a god myself, though I know I haven't been acting like one lately, and I'm directly related to Gaia. If I don't have the power to do it, there won't be many people who do." He sounds more hopeful than I've heard him in forever.

"Alright. We should talk to Anubis." I suggest, and he nods.

"Good idea. I'll light a scroll in a few moments. I just want to brush up on my Gorgonian and Egyptian history first," he explains, and I agree.

"Very well. Do you really think this will work?" I ask him, and he sighs.

"Have you been keeping abreast with The Circle of Eight at all?" he enquires, and I shake my head.

"Well, Hercules was telling me that they've had to intervene in a serious situation in the Pacific. Poseidon's own stupid fault of course, but they moved their essences collectively from The Higher Plains to the mortal plain, just for a short time of course. As you can imagine, their recklessness with the walls between dimensions has left us with a certain weakness between this world and The Higher Plains, including The Nether. This might, in fact, be the perfect opportunity. If something like this is going to work, it must be attempted soon." Haedes informs me of his logic, and I roll my eyes, taking a moment to lament the carelessness of other gods.

"Are you serious? We're all down here trying to keep the balance perfect, and they're just transferring essences between dimensions? Seriously?" I cuss, fuming at the risk they've taken.

"It was 'imperative', whatever that means." Haedes rolls his eyes, mimicking my expression as his fingers form air quotes around the word. "You know, sometimes I think you and I should just rule the entire universe. I mean, it would be far more fun," he adds. I smirk.

"You've got that right."

"We are the life of the after-party." He smiles at me.

"And you're sure you wanna bring your daughter back to the party?" I question him. His eyes blaze.

"Have you met my daughter? It wouldn't be a damn party without her."

XION

We bury her on a Wednesday. As the rain pours down from the grey heavens of the Illinois sky, the coffin is lowered into the dark dankness of the ground.

Luce stands at my side, her hand, covered in a black lace glove, gripping mine as if both our lives depend on it. Tears fall down her porcelain face, her light eyes wide as I lean on her for support. Thane is here too, though she has given us both space and stands on the opposite side of the grave as we huddle beneath an enormous black umbrella, next to the mausoleum where Sephy's parents were laid to rest all those years ago. The trees rustle, the sound of rain hitting each individual leaf too obvious as the space surrounding the funeral site is filled only with sniffles and silence. This is a void of feeling, and numbness tightens its hold on me as I think of her body, still and cold, lying in the earth.

I don't know how to feel, where to look, how to act. I know I must look guilty in all this, especially to the police. A man with no identity, a man with no social security number or proof of his whereabouts, having shown up, having bedded the murder victim only the night before. Claiming to have found her the next day.

They took her body away right before I smashed up the interior of her suite during a three-day bout of demon rage I can scarcely even remember. Lost in a sea of demonic anguish, I had gone over the scene, the night, repeatedly, until it lost meaning.

But it wasn't me.

Not this time.

Jules believes me because he had found me, staring at her, sobbing, crying out at the injustice of it all. I must have seemed pathetic, a grown man on his knees in a puddle of blood, falling apart at the seams, but I can't say I would react any other way if I was to go back and relive that same moment. I catch his eyes over the six-foot-deep pit as the minister continues to talk about gods he knows nothing about.

I'm still buzzing with the shock, and a part of me wonders how quickly the memories of our night together will fade. It had been the best night of my life, and for a single glistening moment, my future had appeared as though it could be bright too. Bright with her.

Unfortunately for me, demons, even half demons, don't get happy endings.

Peter steps forward, and the minister falls silent after asking for sentiments about Sephy, about who she had been. Not that Peter actually knows. If he did, he never would have insisted they dress her in a floor-length white gown for burial, something angelic and pure. Sephy would rather have been buried in leather with a bottle of whisky beside her for good measure anyone who knew her knew that.

399

"It is with great sadness that we are here today at the ending of a life which was filled with good intent and potential. I only wish she had reached that potential before her life was stolen from her. Sephy Sinclair will never be forgotten, but I think we can rest easy knowing that she is with her beloved parents, my beloved sister, once more," Peter speaks the words like he's reading them off a teleprompter, and I feel like I might punch him, breaking his glasses right into his nose.

He doesn't deserve to speak for Sephy. Sephy hated him, and he didn't like her that much either from what I've come to understand of the matter.

The rain pitter-patters atop the umbrella as people begin to take handfuls of dirt and drop them on top of her. My heart wilts.

I don't want to say goodbye.

I only just met you. And I have so much more I need to say, need to show you. I lament, feeling sick as dirt hits the top of the mahogany casket with a dull thump. She shouldn't be in the earth; I've said this too. She would have wanted to be cremated so she could blow away on a breeze and be free as a bird— as a phoenix.

I drop in my handful of dirt, trying to be as careful as possible, not wanting to but knowing it's a part of this ridiculous mortal tradition.

The crowd scatters, and I realise I have no idea who half of the people present are. I wonder if Sephy did either.

I recognise a lot of her board members, which makes me want to laugh, but other than me, Jules, Thane, and Luce, I can't see anyone who she'd really want to be here at all.

As we turn, walking across the lawn and back up to the house for the mandatory wake, I continue to wonder about who is responsible for this.

Who killed Sephy?

Luce has considered the same thing, but she also makes a good point, which is that if it had been the Demon Lords or Pandora, they probably would have made it known to someone. After all, killing a demi-goddess is a bold move and one any dark creature would relish taking credit for, especially one with the hatred for Zeus that Pandora harbours.

I also can't imagine the Demon Lords would have used a knife. They seem to be far too clean-cut and calculative for such an underwhelming yet brutal act. It's almost as if the killer knew Sephy personally. Especially with how she'd been stabbed multiple times, more times than necessary to kill her, that's for certain.

Whoever had ended her life had been angry, furious perhaps.

I wonder who would harbour such an intense rage against her but can't think of anyone. Certainly, no one who would know to use the opal blade— unless the killer didn't know the purpose of the knife but found it lying around somewhere in the lobby.

I left the blade on the foyer table.

Is it my fault?

As I make my way inside the estate, I continue to make myself insane with questions, putting them to myself over and over as I make pointless small talk in my new tailored suit and sip rancid wine.

The wake passes in a blur of condolences and fake pitied glances. I hate it. Hate the stiff actions, the forced small talk, the ridiculously tiny finger food, which is soggy and makes me feel like a giant. Luce leaves eventually too, taking Thane with her, and I'm left, sprawled out amongst empty trays, bottles, and glasses on a sofa located on the right side of the grand staircase. It's upholstered in dark fabric that is soft to touch.

"Are you alright?" Jules' voice calls out to me from the other side of the hall. I shrug.

"Nope." I sip more rancid wine, cringing at the taste but continuing to drink it anyway.

He comes around the corner with a cart to take away the rubbish and the glasses for cleaning. He hasn't stopped working since the morning I'd found Sephy dead in her bed. He's like a fly on acid.

"Jules—" I sigh out, and he looks at me, instantly alert. "For the love of God, please sit down and have a drink with me." I hold out a glass of wine to him, and he shakes his head.

"I'm not drinking that crap." He disappears, returning a minute or so later with a new bottle.

"Why are we serving this, by the way? Don't the Sinclairs own a vineyard?" I ask him, and he rolls his eyes.

"Peter's orders. He's been tight with money for the funeral. He's been waiting for the Sinclair funds to transfer to his name, which still hasn't happened," Jules explains and I nod, amused by this, though I know I shouldn't be.

"Ah, I see," I express, wondering why exactly it is he would scrimp on his own niece's funeral. He really is a complete tool.

Jules opens the wine with a corkscrew that he magically procures from the inside of his suit jacket. Pouring us both a glass, he collapses onto the sofa opposite me across the littered coffee table.

"I keep thinking— if I'd have been here— If I could of—" I begin, but he waves his hand, taking a slug of wine and closing his eyes as he savours the flavour.

"Don't you dare. It's not your fault," he whispers, voice hoarse like he might start crying.

"I'm sorry. I mean, I was close to Sephy, but you— you've known her since she was born." My heart breaks yet again, this time for him.

"Yes. I just don't think this has all quite sunk in yet for me. I love her. Like she's my own daughter," he admits, and I smile at him, sadness lingering in the back of my eyes.

"I know; anyone who saw you two together could tell. She loved you." He smiles at me, looking like he could sleep into next week, and takes another sip of his wine.

"Thanks— I—" he begins but is interrupted by a knock on the doors.

"It can't be anyone for the wake, can it? It's far too late," I conclude, and he shakes his head, getting to his feet slowly and walking over to the door.

His motion is odd, kind of like a clock that needs rewinding.

I hear him mumbling to whoever is on the other side before the door slams shut and echoes out into the room. He returns several moments later with a large wodge of papers. He's got them open in his hands and is scanning the document like it's a matter of life or death.

"Xion—" he breathes.

I sit up, straightening and becoming attentive as his expression turns shocked.

"What? What is it?" I ask him, intrigued.

"It's— Sephy's will. She made me her power of attorney." He sounds delighted, and I frown, confused as I put my glass down in front of me as gently as I can.

"What does that mean?" I demand, and he takes a seat, this time in the armchair beside me.

"It means that she entrusted me with the job of making sure her will is carried out as she wished," he explains.

I nod.

"Oh, I see." I don't know what this has to do with me.

402

"Xion, she left it all to you." He hands me the papers, and I scan them once, then twice.

She did what?

"What! Wait— I don't understand?" I exclaim, and as I shuffle through the papers, a small white envelope falls to the floor. On the front of the thick white paper, the letter is addressed to me in only one word.

Bigfoot.

My heart begins to race as my fingers tremble on the paper. Slipping open the back, which is sealed with wax, I pull out a single thick sheet with trained cursive scrawl upon the front.

Xion, Aka, Bigfoot...

I know that you probably don't remember me, or— if you do then good because you know I am pretty awesome. The reason I'm writing is both terrible and fantastic, terrible because I'm dead (boo) but fantastic because I want you to have my money.

I know this might come as a surprise, but without you, without your efforts, I would never have made it back from Mortaria alive. This, I feel, entitles you to my fortune. Think of it as back payment from Haedes for all those hours you worked without pay down in Mortaria— I mean, he must owe you a lot by now!

So yep. That's it. You're a billionaire, so I'll be finding my tiny violin up in heaven to play for you as I watch you on your adventures.

Perhaps take up some ninja lessons? Get some less stomp-tastic shoes? I dunno.

Just please, stop feeling guilty about the past. I want you to take my money and do whatever your demonic heart desires. Go on adventures, see the world, spend it on a million identical leather jackets (this last one seems like you), but don't sit in Mortaria and rot. Don't let your soul wither and die. There is so much to live for, especially when you have limitless funds and the world at your feet. So please, take the same freedom that you gave back to me, and make it yours.

Sephy x

P.S. I'd kind of appreciate it if you set Jules up in a really nice place— perhaps the Bahamas?

P.P.S. Please, also take care of Cerb; he's my best friend, and I don't want him to get lonely.

I stare down at the letter, then at Jules, handing it to him. He snorts as he reads, undoubtedly because the tone reminds us both of the sarcastic spitfire Sephy really was. He gapes at me once he's done, and I stare back, neither one of us sure what to say.

"Well. Peter is going to be pissed," I comment. Jules smirks for a millisecond before he straightens his face, though I notice he can't resist getting a rather amused twinkle behind his eye.

"Well, I don't know about you, but I think she's bloody brilliant," he adds, and we both sit and smirk in silence, stunned.

"Yes," I agree. "She was."

34

YOU BELONG TO ME

XION

I DON'T KNOW WHAT to do. I no longer have any reason to stay here. Sephy is dead, and Peter no longer wants me here. If he hadn't had a reason to hate me before, he certainly does now after discovering that he's been once again legally inched out of his sister's fortune by the skin of his teeth.

I don't know how to feel about The Sinclair Estate. I don't want to sell it off; Sephy would probably never forgive me, especially if Peter made a bid for it, but I can't stay here either. The memories are too painful, not to mention the fact that Sephy's suite is in ruin after my demonic fists have taken to it.

The police tape has finally been removed and I'm concerned, to say the least, regarding the current ongoing investigation. Sephy has taken care of my biggest problem unknowingly, as with the Sinclair fortune she's also had my identity made real for the world, no doubt utilising her cash to buy such a luxury.

For the first time in a long time, I have an actual social security number, a passport, and a driver's licence, though after my trip in the mean machine I'm amazed she's gone for putting me behind the wheel again. I'm sure, of course, that none of this is strictly legal, but I'm also sure that Sephy is smart enough to have tied up any loose ends that could incriminate me.

I sit on the bare mattress, stripped of the bloodstained sheets that were collected as evidence along with the murder weapon, looking around at the destruction. I keep my back to the large bloody stain in the middle of the mattress, which has not yet been washed clean, not wanting to think about the last moments of her traumatic end.

The carpet has been pulled up from the edges of the room, no doubt my demonic attempt to get rid of the second bloody stain by the edge of the bed, where the red had dripped down. The curtain rail and drapes are on the floor, wallpaper has been ripped from the walls, and the marble of her floor has been smashed beneath my fists and feet. The Grecian pillars, which surround the bathtub, have been destroyed too, leaving my knuckles bruised and bloody even still, not that I care.

My bag is on the couch opposite the bed, perhaps the only piece of furniture I've left untouched, packed and ready to go. I stare at it, more lost than I've been in a while.

Go where?

I can't go back to Mortaria, and I have all this money now— I suppose I should probably go travelling, see the world, just as she had wanted, but the thought of seeing so many new places without her sarcastic commentary alongside just makes the grief even less bearable.

Getting to my feet, I walk over to the door and pick up my bag on the way, slinging it over my shoulder, which is clad in my favourite leather jacket. I breathe out, looking over the remnants of the pastel room one final time before I turn my back on what could have been and step out into the hall.

My tread is heavy on the runner, the high rich colours of the walls more isolating now than ever before, and as I reach the landing, I find Jules coming up the staircase, a look of irritation plastered on his face.

"What is it?" I ask him, concerned. He purses his lips, a silver tray held level with his ear.

"Peter continues to run me ragged like some kind of pack mule. I know he's angry, but it's hardly my fault." I look at him with a pitied stare and frown, my lips twisting into a disapproving grimace.

"Want me to kick him out? I mean technically, this is my house now," I remind him, remembering the hell of the last few days.

Lawyers, meetings, and endless paperwork to sign. Who knew so much money came with so many damn forms and dotted lines on which to put my name. I was kind of hoping they'd roll it up in a van full of silver suitcases, like something out of a James Bond movie.

"Going somewhere?" he enquires, ignoring my last comment as my bag comes into his eye line. I shuffle atop the bottle green runner beneath my feet, awkward as I shift the strap of the bag up on my shoulder and meet his gaze with an open demeanour.

"I don't know. I don't know what I'm doing, but I thought maybe I'd take a trip," I express, before adding, "I think I need to get out of this place for a while. I'm having a hard time. Every time I turn a corner I just—"

"Expect to see her sassing you?" Jules finishes my sentence with a sad smirk, and I nod, sighing out as I run my fingers through my hair. The motion reminds me of her fingers doing the same thing, causing my heart to become momentarily heavy as lead.

"Yes," I breathe, grief sneaking up on me like a tidal wave. I thought I was over the spontaneously wanting to go to sleep and never wake up part, but apparently, it's still ongoing and never fails to take me by surprise.

"Do you want me to call the jet?" he enquires.

My eyebrows rise on my forehead.

"Seriously? The jet? We have a jet?!" I exclaim in surprise. He smiles.

"Of course, you have a jet. You're a billionaire now, Xion. Your wish can be made reality. All you have to do is pick up the phone. Do you have your phone with you by the way?" He looks suspicious, and I huff.

"Yes, though I don't like it. Just to be clear. What is this incessant need of being able to harass someone at any hour of the day or night? It's a little creepy if you ask me," I express, and he shrugs.

"You've got me there, but nonetheless, I'd like to be able to contact you, just in case I actually do want to have Peter made suddenly and unapologetically destitute." The look in his eyes is playful but sad and unmistakably exhausted.

I wonder a moment, looking at Jules' broken yet remarkable upright form, whether Peter should be given the right to stay here at all. I know out of us all, he's the only one with actual blood relation to Sephy, and yet he seems to be the one with the least amount of love in his heart for her, which makes no sense to me at all.

"Call the jet." I make the decision in the moment, and Jules nods.

"Right away. Peter will have to wait on his— tea with exactly 415 grains of sugar in it," he rolls his eyes, and I snort, finding the pomposity of Sephy's uncle sickening.

Descending the stairs, my steps echo out into the high ceilings of the open-plan space. Then, I make my way through to the now immaculate sitting area in the lobby.

Where should I go? I wonder, leaning back into the same chair I'd taken to at the wake.

In all the world— I have the choice to pick anywhere, so where?

I ponder this, listing off a myriad of dream vacations in my head, but cannot come up with anywhere that sounds like it would be truly fun alone. I need to get away, but an island vacation, sun, sea, and surf, without Sephy seems lacklustre at best.

Maybe I should go somewhere rainy, somewhere cultured.

England, perhaps?

I know Sephy was brought up there in boarding schools and then made into the person she was at university, so perhaps it would be nice to see some of the places that had been a part of her life.

Thinking this is as good of a plan as any, Jules returns.

"The Jet is waiting for you at the airport. Want me to call you a cab?" he asks me, frowning. "One moment," he steps with agility over the chequered marble, the heels of his polished black shoes ringing out with purpose as he moves over to the window. Staring, I watch him with interest as the audible sound of gravel crackling under the high-speed motion of tyres reaches me.

I get to my feet, moving to stand next to him at the ceiling-high arched pane, the roar of a feral engine sounding moments after.

"Do you know who this is?" Jules asks me, moving the enormous drape aside from the glass, which looks out over the front of the estate. I peer out, and as the sports car gets closer, my eyes narrow and my heart sinks.

The car is a Ferrari of some kind, a new one by the looks of it, and it's been customised in jet black with electric blue flames climbing up the front of the hood and around the wheels.

"I'll handle this," I growl, grabbing my bag from the sofa and heading out of the large front doors. The car stands stationary on the drive, no doors opening, no sign that it's not on autopilot.

Storming across the gravel, the stones crunch beneath the fury of my tread as a tinted black window rolls slowly and dramatically down.

"Xion," Haedes' voice calls out to me.

He's in the driver's seat, a pair of fluffy blue dice hanging down from the rear-view mirror of this modern mean machine. He's wearing sunglasses so I can't see his eyes or guess his mood and a black trilby covers his abnormally coloured hair. His face is pale and lined with worry. I'm surprised at his presence to say the least. I haven't seen him in the mortal world for years because he knows it ages him. I mean, he hadn't even made the time or effort for Sephy's burial.

"Haedes," I reply, not giving anything away. I have no desire to speak to him or have anything to do with him at this point.

"Get in," he commands. I keep my face masked with cool reserve.

"I can't; I have a plane to catch," I state in a dull tone, and he smiles, like a cat licking cream.

"What a coincidence; I'm looking to travel myself. I'm heading out on a little retrieval trip," he informs me.

"What's that got to do with me?" I ask him, nonchalant, and he gives me a deadpan stare.

"Well, if you'd get into the damn car, I'd tell you," he retorts.

My curiosity rears its head.

"Well, I do need a ride to the airport," I express, putting aside my fury and satiating my curiosity instead. The door rises from the vehicle vertically, and I duck beneath it before pulling it closed as I relax into the leather of the seat. Haedes wastes no time in putting the car into gear and taking off at top speed back down the driveway, causing my fingers to dig into my seat as the world begins to move around us in a high-velocity blur.

"So— are you going to enlighten me before I die in a highspeed fiery inferno?" I press him for an explanation, and he snorts.

"I'll have you know I'm an excellent driver," he claims. I roll my eyes as I rub off the sweat on my palms, pushing my hands against the snug roughness of my jeans.

"Cut the crap. I'm not even supposed to be leaving the country while the investigation is underway, so as soon as we hit the tarmac, I'm out of here," I retort. He smirks, only causing my fury to grow.

"Oh, no need to worry about that. I am owed quite a debt by the Chicago chief of police. I've had the case diverted onto a more likely candidate." He says it like it's nothing, and I gawp.

"Like who?" I ask him, and he shrugs.

"The person who's been sending her flowers with no note or card, calling Sephy hundreds of times from an unknown number. I'm having them look at the florist to try and pinpoint who was sending them," he elaborates. I frown. Why hadn't Sephy said anything?

"Someone was sending her flowers?" I ask him.

"Yeah, a lot of them. I came from the police station, looked through the evidence locker, found her cell phone, which they'd neglected to check—" He rolls his eyes at the incompetence of the investigative team, and I feel disappointment settle in. He catches my look of aggravation and glances at me, seemingly kind this time. "Don't worry, Xion. We'll catch this bastard. When we do, he'll wish he was in hell— you mark my words." The threat lingers between us as we screech around a corner and I lurch sideways in my seat. It is from this point we begin to charge down a street lined on either side by large fancy houses and tall equidistant oak trees.

"Okay, so you've taken me out of the hot seat. Great. But that still doesn't explain what you're doing here. You didn't even come to the funeral." I condemn his cowardice, and he turns to me after checking his rear-view mirror and breaking harshly at a set of oncoming traffic lights as they turn red.

"I've been busy," he replies.

The car stills to a halt, and we wait to turn a corner so we're heading towards Chicago and out of Forest Glen. The rumble of the engine coming through the bottom of my seat is making my stomach churn, making me want this little journey over with even faster than I'd originally thought.

"I'm sure whatever it is wasn't more important than your daughter's funeral." I continue to grill him, and he frowns.

"Actually, it is. I've been trying to locate The Book of The Dead," he announces.

I frown, confused.

"What's that?" I press him to reveal more, bored of waiting, and he gives a small smug smile at my lack of knowledge.

"It's an ancient Egyptian book of dark rituals and spells. The magic originated from Ra but was carried out most successfully by Moloch. There are rituals inside that can resurrect the dead." My eyes widen, lips parting slightly as I feel horror begin to bloom in my stomach.

"Haedes. No. We can't. Those things, they used to go wrong all the time. I won't have her as some reanimated corpse puppet!" I exclaim, and he rolls his eyes.

"And you think I would? Of course not. I simply want to find the book and discover what can be done." I gape at him, and he pushes down hard on the accelerator as the lights move from ruby, through amber, to emerald, and we begin moving toward Chicago as the outside world becomes a blur yet again. I feel myself pushed back into the seat as we take another turn and hit the I-90 West towards the airport.

"Look— I—" I begin to protest some more, but Haedes turns to me, taking his eyes off the road for longer than he probably should as traffic begins to merge.

"You were right. With what you said before. If it was Demi— I would have raised hell. I owe Sephy this. We need to find out if she can be brought back. I need to exhaust all the options before accepting she's dead." He tries to plead with his stare, though I can't see his eyes behind his shades, and I wonder if it really can be done.

Can Sephy really be resurrected?

Would she want to be?

I know what I want— but it's selfish.

I want her back. I want her to be here with me. I want a second chance at happiness.

But do I want to risk her coming back messed up for my own selfish reasons?

I can't, can I? I wonder as we continue to gobble miles beneath the tread of the tyres. The engine roars, and Haedes and I fall into silence as the journey continues and the traffic flow moves on without pause.

I look at him, at how he's seemingly in control, more so than I've seen him in a long time.

"What is the likelihood of this going wrong?" I demand and he frowns, pursing his sculpted lips together and exhaling a heavy sigh as he changes into a higher gear. That's certainly not the expression of an optimistic man.

"Honestly? I don't know. I know resurrection has been done successfully in the past, and I'm talking full resurrection, beating heart, ageing, the whole works, not just utilising the flame. But it was performed by Gods of Ancient. I don't know if it can be done now," he admits.

"And you're willing to risk some of your lifespan to find out?" I ask him. He looks sad, his mouth remaining a firm hard line of determination.

"I'm here, aren't I? Though, I'll be keeping my convecting to a minimum, it's bad for my crow's feet." He looks in the rear-view mirror again, examining himself, and I ponder on the predicament I'm in.

On the one hand, we could bring her back.

On the other, we could cause some serious issues for her when she's at peace already.

"Do you know where she is?" I enquire.

"That's the other thing. Hercules has informed me that Zeus is not allowing her to ascend to Titan status. Says she hasn't earned it." His voice is bitter, and I watch the tips of his hair turn orange beneath his hat as his grip tightens on the stitched leather of the steering wheel.

"So— she's just floating around in The Nether?" I ask him, and he nods.

"It would certainly appear that way."

At this response, my heart goes cold in my chest. Moving on at the thought Sephy is free from pain, from being hunted, is one thing, but The Nether Realm is— strange, or so I've heard, and I can't bear the thought of her floating around in limbo and not having the peace she'd been searching for.

The rest of the journey passes in silence. We speed down the freeway, finally reaching O'Hare international airport in a record time of under fifteen minutes.

Driving around the outside of the building to the runway's private entrance, we finally pull onto the tarmac, making our way through the barriers after flashing my newly acquired identification.

The plane is ready and waiting on approach, evidently having just been fuelled as the smell of jet fuel moves through the air conditioning vents and into the car. Haedes pulls up just short of the shiny white aeroplane with people scurrying around the wheels, performing checks, and carrying out other tasks I couldn't name. It's not a branded jet, I'm sure for privacy's sake, but it's definitely sleek and stylish as I've come to expect from the Sinclairs.

"Thanks for the ride." I vocalise my lacklustre appreciation, looking to Haedes for a moment, thoughtful, before pushing the door of the car up and stepping out into the cool air of the afternoon.

As I stand, looking at the plane and then back at the car, I have a terrible thought as the wind whips around my form, stealing all the heat from my body.

What if I could bring her back, and I don't?

Can I live with not knowing?

Can I go forward in this life without her, knowing I had the opportunity to hold her again, kiss her again?

I don't shut the door of the car as I hover in the moment. I take a few seconds before bending down and calling through to Haedes.

"Are you coming then?" I ask him, and his cobalt eyebrows rise on his forehead beneath the brim of his hat. He nods as he takes off his sunglasses, eyes sparkling beneath in victory as if this is what he wanted all along.

Stepping out of the car, his gaze travels to mine across the roof of the low vehicle. I examine him, outlined against the grey backdrop of the cloudy sky overhead as he stands, dressed in a black velvet suit with a red silk shirt underneath and a black cravat to match.

"Thanks," he calls, breaking the long silence between us. I shrug.

"I'm not doing it for you. I'm doing it for her," I remind him, not wanting him to think all is forgiven. I still think he's an utter jackass, after all.

We rush towards the jet, making our way up the stairs and into the plush interior as I duck beneath the white metal of the entranceway. The cabin is padded out in deep mahogany woods and dove grey velvet with large seats. Flutes of champagne next to buckets where more bottles on ice are waiting atop a small trolley sit at the back of the plane, and I look around the multitude of flat-screen televisions, kitchen facilities, and sleeping cocoons held inside this narrow cylindrical tube.

I've been on a plane before, but it was never like this.

"This is nice," I comment, and Haedes gives a nod of agreement. I inhale the spring fresh scent of wood polish and carpet cleaner as I duck, proceeding forward.

"Yes, the Sinclairs have always had great taste," he replies, though I wonder if he'll maintain this opinion once he learns that I've slept with his daughter.

I guess, though, I'll leave that little gem of information for later.

Haedes and I take seats opposing one another and buckle up for take-off. He looks nervous, and I wonder if this is his first time on a plane, though it seems unlikely given his long lifespan.

"So where are we heading?" I ask him, and he smiles.

"First stop, Egypt," he announces.

"You'd better go inform the pilot of that then," I express.

He doesn't reply, simply pressing a call button on his armrest as he takes off his hat before speaking clearly into the microphone.

"Cairo please," he requests a few moments after the captain's feminine voice comes through the speakers.

"We'll be taxiing for take-off shortly. Please ensure you are acquainted with all pre-flight emergency procedures. You can find the safety booklets in the tray under your seats," she informs us.

Haedes and I look at one another and smirk. If this plane did crash, neither one of us would have any intention of following safety procedures, that's for sure.

I sit back, looking out of the window and wondering if I'll ever hold her again. If she'll be the way she was.

Haedes orders some lobster and whiskey from the single flight attendant dressed in a dove grey suit. She has kind eyes, a sweet smile, but she's not Sephy. No one will ever be Sephy ever again.

Not unless—

I continue to wonder about our prospects as the engine of the plane starts up and Haedes relaxes back into his seat, placing a provided gel mask over his eyes as we begin to taxi down the runway. Neither of us has anything to say nor the desire to speak. I look out the window as the world becomes a blur, and when I look down as we begin to soar, I realise how small mortals really are. How fragile.

It isn't until the sun is heading towards the horizon that we reach the full height of our ascent into the air. I cross my legs, staring out of the window as we float above the clouds, leaving the world below us behind.

I don't know what lies ahead, whether it be triumph or devastating defeat. I don't know where we'll end up or if anything Haedes has suggested is possible.

I do know one thing though; this being something that Sephy Sinclair taught me from the moment I met her.

Fortune favours the brave.

EPILOGUE

PANDORA

I AM SITTING, THE scrutiny of the Demon Lords burning into my flesh as they stare daggers at me from around the table. It's been over three weeks since Sephy Sinclair escaped the clutches of the Dark Colosseum, and I've been trying to stay out of their way. However, they've summoned me here, and I can't help but wonder if that is not in fact because they fully intend to kill me.

"I think we can all agree that this has been an utter disaster," Barbas announces with a gaping feline smile. He's wearing indigo today, in silk, and it really isn't his colour, especially because in the red light pouring down from the hole in the roof, it looks sort of neon pink.

"Yes. I think that is obvious," I retort, spiteful in tone as my frustration refuses to diminish beneath my usually cool demeanour. The red sky overhead darkens in only seconds, another spark shower imminent no doubt.

Suddenly, as Abraxis opens his mouth to speak next, their gazes move, surprised, to behind where I am sitting.

I spin in my seat, eyes resting upon a woman who I never expected to see again, let alone here.

"Anubis?" I say her name aloud, the glimmering silver of her gown, which is encrusted with emeralds, causing her to stand out like a sore thumb in the crumbling ruins and squalor.

"Yes. That is my name. Was it not you who summoned me?" she asks, and I shake my head, innocent.

"How did you even get here?" I demand, and she shrugs, the green beads braided into her dark hair clinking against one another as she moves.

"Chariot of course. Bit of a bumpy ride. It wasn't you who sent the Gorgonian escort to clear my path across The Ashen Waste?" she interrogates me, and I shake my head again, eyes revealing my mystification as I twist back to look over my shoulder at the Demon Lords.

"What is the meaning of this?" I ask them, and Gorgon leans forward, smiling a knowing smile.

"I believe Anubis had a rather interesting conversation with Haedes recently, or so my children tell me," he expresses. Anubis scowls.

"No Gorgonians have been inside The Icon. That is ridiculous." She dismisses the claim immediately, flicking her hand and shooing the insinuation away like a bad odour. Gorgon smirks at her arrogance, and I wonder if he has been sending demons into the city without our knowledge.

"How?" I ask him, and he smiles.

"Well, you gave such a wonderful speech about working together, I got some of the Abraxians to pose as guards to let them in." His explanation makes the corners of my mouth upturn, pleased that at least one of the Lords has taken my advice and done some serious thinking about how to best utilise our forces.

"That's very simplistic. Kind of beautiful, don't you think?" I ask Anubis. She folds her arms across her chest, looking warily between us.

"What do you want, Gorgon?" she barks, clearly not in the mood for small talk or games. Gorgon leans back in his seat, propping his feet up on the stone of the table and placing his arms behind his head in a relaxed pose that reeks of his own special brand of arrogance.

"I want what every other Demon Lord at this table wants. I want our hunting grounds back. I want the Gods of Ancient to return and rule like they were supposed to. This place belongs to the children of Uranus. Not Gaia." He licks his bottom lip, his quick, forked tongue flicking in and out of the gap between his teeth in a flash.

"And what does that have to do with me?" I look to Anubis, her eyes flashing a warning as their dark depths, ringed with deep green, shine, though with excitement or threat I cannot tell.

"Well, I'll tell you. You know what we need to free the Gods of Ancient, don't you?" he asks Anubis, and she narrows her eyes.

"Yes. You need a pure-bred god to conduct the ritual. But you won't find one in me. I'm merely a Titan. You'll also have noticed that Zeus has made very sure to have any god or goddess who would even so much as think of undermining his rule killed. I mean, you remember what happened to Prometheus— don't you Pandora?" She looks at me now, with a warning glance, and I frown. I do remember what happened to him. He was sentenced to die a million times over until Zeus was content with his penance, before his soul, ashes, and the flame he had stolen were separated and stored across three different dimensions.

He wasn't just killed, he was massacred.

"Yes. I do recall." I flutter my fingers. Brushing the tale aside as I feel my rage for Zeus growing, the memory bubbling close to the surface.

"So then, again, I ask, what does this have to do with me?" she demands of Gorgon, who smiles.

"Haedes' daughter was murdered, was she not?" he asks.

Anubis gets a sly look.

"At your hand, I have no doubt." This time her gaze falls, hot, to me.

"Actually no; a happy coincidence, but not my doing," I confess, still irritated that some unknown mortal achieved what I could not.

"Regardless, my children tell me Haedes is trying to find that which my Master lost. A little text known as The Book of The Dead." Gorgon unleashes this information, and the Demon Lords around the table mutter amongst themselves, shifting with interest as they listen in closer.

"That is correct. Not that he'll find it. It's been lost to us for aeons. You know that." Anubis says this like Gorgon is stupid, but I know she underestimates him.

"If he should find it, by chance, what would you say to trying to bring back Ra?" he asks. Anubis inhales in a sudden gasp. I watch her with interest as she shifts in her heels, eyes narrowing in on each Demon Lord in turn.

"To what purpose?" she enquires.

Gorgon laughs.

"I thought that would be obvious — to bring your god and our gods back to power." He smiles, and Anubis looks thoughtful, if not a little aggravated by how this plan has been brought to her attention.

"It's a nice plan. A wonderful plan. But I think you're overestimating Haedes. He is merely putting off his grief. He will never find that book. I've been searching for it for years and have come up empty. I told him where to start looking, but I doubt he'll find anything where I could not. I am not even entirely sure that it still exists. Then, even if it does, nobody around here has the kind of dark magic required to perform those rituals anyway." She is certain of his failure and is also making me aware that, as ever, the odds are stacked against us. It causes my anxiety to heighten. We are quickly running out of options.

"Regardless, I assume if you're invested in the idea, you'll keep us informed of his progress?" Gorgon asks her, turning his face sideways slightly so the light catches his sharp cheekbones.

"I may do. If I feel it wise." Anubis looks between us with a wary glance. I take this opportunity to speak up, smoothing the plum silk of my gown beneath nervous fingers.

"I would expect you to think it wise. After all, I might just find myself a little loose-tongued. Wouldn't want Haedes knowing it was you who handed over his daughter on a silver platter now, would we?" Her eyes narrow at me as she takes a few steps back from the table. I get to my feet.

"It wouldn't be wise to threaten a Titan, Pandora," Anubis warns me, turning on her heel and moving to exit the building.

As she goes, I place a hand in my pocket, wrapping my fingers around the edges of my power. The box. It warms at my touch, and I smile as I hear Anubis' steps ring out into the chasmic hallway that leads to the exit.

Nothing is certain, but if everything aligns in our favour, then we may just have a chance to claim back Mortaria yet. Claim it back and bring forth a force so powerful that even Zeus will quake at their presence.

"Bring it on," I call after Anubis, voice echoing out in a loud staccato before turning back to the meeting chamber and the Demon Lords, hopeful, as ever, that fate will be kind.

ALSO BY

Queens of Fantasy Saga Reading Order
(As Suggested by Kristy Nicolle)
PLEASE NOTE:
The Tidal Kiss, Ashen Touch, and Aetherial Embrace can be read as individual 3 book stories, or in order as part of the saga.

QUEENS OF FANTASY SHORTS AND NOVELLAS

TIDAL KISS SHORTS AND NOVELLAS
Beyond The Shallows
Waiting For Gideon
Vexed

ASHEN TOUCH SHORTS AND NOVELLAS
Death Blooms
A Touch Of Smoke And Snow

AETHERIAL EMBRACE SHORTS AND NOVELLAS
Ambrosia Nights

EXTRAS
Infiniflash Fiction Volume One

OTHER GENRES FROM KRISTY NICOLLE

DYSTOPIAN ROMANCE:
Something Blue- A Dystopian Romance Standalone

POETRY:
I Am Arcana- A Tarot Inspired Poetry Collection
Starsong- A Zodiac Inspired Poetry Collection

To keep up to date with the latest release dates, spin offs, and exclusive content, head on over to kristynicolle.com

ACKNOWLEDGEMENTS

It feels like only yesterday that Sephy Sinlair, Haedes, and Mortaria first popped into my head and now the first third of The Ashen Touch trilogy is done! I can hardly believe how fast it all seems to be going, and the next novel in this trilogy marks the half way point in the Queens of Fantasy Saga which is INSANE! A huge thanks, as always, to my wonderful partner Mark who has suffered through my doubt yet again as well as agreeing to put his mugshot forward for my Xion promos. I think that's fair, seeing as Xion is basically you! Thanks to my Nanny, Mum, Dad... that barista at starbucks who spells my name right on my coffee cup, I couldn't have done it without you either! A huge shout out to my fabulous editor Jaimie Cordall, who in spite of moving and finding out she was pregnant, all in the space of about five minutes I might add, still found time to trek through this monster! I also want to say an enormous thank you to Winters Rage, my fantastic Alpha Reader who constantly puts my neurosis to bed, and my fabulous beta readers, Emma Harrison, Dawn Yacovetta and ESPECIALLY Leeah Minick who has gone above and beyond in the amount of time she has spent letting me bounce ideas off of her and searching for plot bunnies! I have such a phenomenal team behind me, and honestly not a single one of my books would be out there floating around if it weren't for them! It takes a village to raise a child, but also to help put a book out, so thank you to my village, it wouldn't be half as much fun without you!

ABOUT THE AUTHOR

30-Year-Old British Author of Award-Winning Indie Fantasy Romance, Kristy Nicolle is escaping the pain of Ehlers Danlos Syndrome by crafting intricate and immersive worlds for her readers. She lives in Norwich, Norfolk, with her long-time life partner Mark, and can often be found writing in her local coffee shop - *Botany and Beans,* with a peppermint mocha, surrounded by beloved witchy paraphernalia and plants she knows only too well she'd kill at home.

FOLLOW KRISTY NICOLLE ON SOCIAL MEDIA OR FIND HER AT KRISTYNICOLLE.COM